twisted allies

B.D. GARBER

Twisted Allies

ISBN 979-8-9893488-0-0

How far would you go to protect
your child from her other parent?

This is a work of fiction.

That means that you're invited to join me in my own private reality. If you think that you recognize anyone or anything or any place while you're visiting, you don't. It's all made-up. This story is set in the Minneapolis/St. Paul region. Real places are named but are used only to orient you. Nothing should be inferred from this fiction about those places. In particular, the Minnesota Psychiatric Hospital (MPH) does not exist. I've placed it on the map where another psychiatric hospital exists, but nothing about my description of MPH should be taken as true about its geographic doppelgänger or about current day psychiatric care more generally. I've also imaginated the Horizon and B'sherit virtual reality hardware, the Enemies All Around Us (EAU) VR gaming platform, the Aquintex SR medication, and the word "imaginated." None of this presently exists in the physical universe as you presently know it.

Were you thinking that we share the same reality?

Gratitude

Most of the time I'm a forensic psychologist, a proud husband and father and grandfather. I write in the corners of my life -mostly very early in the morning- and around the edges of everything else that consumes my time and attention. I couldn't do that if not for the patience, indulgence, and unconditional support my incredible wife, Laura, the love and caring of my daughters, and the laughter, optimism, creativity, and inspiration that are my grandkids (whose names I abbreviate to protect their privacy): L, G, E, S, and Y. I gladly dedicate this book and so much more to these generous, loving people.

I am further indebted to my friend, colleague, and fishing buddy Dr. Michael Kandle whose over-the-top enthusiasm about this book got him elected butt-kicker-in-chief. Without Laura's support and Mike's research and persistence this book would never have left my hard drive. Thanks, Mike. Now go out there and publish your own excellent works!

I am grateful, also, to the hundreds of parents and children IRL whose fractured families have taught me about the dynamics of high conflict divorce. I wish all of you immediate settlement, lasting peace, and the wisdom to always put your children's needs first. This book is about parental alienation, one among many dynamics that can tear a child in two. Read more about this very real subject at the end of the fiction that follows.

Please reach me any time with your feedback at bdgarberphd@TwistedAllies.com.

"When families fracture, it's far too easy to mistake the good guy for the bad guy and vice versa. The members of the family and concerned professionals alike often feel like they've been sucked into a paralyzing house of mirrors; an alternate reality where good and bad, right and wrong lose all meaning."

Hassan French, Ph.D., ABBP, J.D.

"Why do you want to hear this story, Mr. Bennett?"

His voice was deep, and his words were carefully paced, but his manner was pressured. Anxious. He gave off an air of bottled-up tension that didn't fit with his otherwise scholarly, thoughtful presentation and certainly did not fit here amidst the dark wood, shelves full of books, and deep leather. The discrepancy was disorienting. He'd agreed to the one p.m. meeting readily. He'd greeted me in the adjoining wood-paneled waiting room right on time with a firm handshake and just the right mix of nice-to-meet-you and can-I get-you-something-to-drink? But once we were secluded in his inner office, he never really settled so much as perched on his oversized leather chair in between bouts of pacing.

He sipped continuously at a mug of coffee in a way that made me wonder what it really contained.

Dr. Samuel Abrams is a nationally recognized psychologist. A brilliant man for whom words and insight and emotion are like stones to a master mason, elements of an elaborate and beautiful whole that he is uniquely able to conceptualize and construct. He'd been beloved by thousands of people who drank up his articles in the *Times* and his appearances on Oprah and devoured his books like so much Kool-Aid, until they didn't. In the last year, the public's passion for him had intensified but reversed. Adoring sycophants now despised him as the puppet master who'd brainwashed his twelve-year-old son into killing his ex-wife -the child's mother- beloved model and cover girl, Suki Kohler.

Abrams wore pleated khaki slacks and a dress shirt open at the collar under a navy jacket. His nails looked buffed, and his greying hair was carefully combed and probably gelled. He'd been clean-shaven in the photos that I'd studied but had allowed a graying beard to grow in in recent months. There was that same discrepancy again: His careful attention to his expensive wardrobe, his manicured hands, and carefully coiffed hair stood in contrast to his obvious pain and weariness. He looked exhausted. Like tucking in his shirt would be an effort. The lines around his eyes and across his forehead reminded me of Colorado from thirty thousand feet. Deep rivers of emotion had eroded this man. His neck and wrists were thin and pale where they broke free of the twice buttoned cotton cuffs.

"Thank you again for seeing me, Dr. Abrams. I'm Ted Bennett."

I'd planned a spiel intending to impress the man with my credentials, telegraph the pressure of the very brief window of time in which we might work together, and highlight the potential of this book. No promises, I wanted to say, I'll only write what I discover along the way, but this book could reunite you with your son.

"Yes, thank you, Mr. Bennett. I know who you are. I've read both of your books. My lawyer was quite convincing. She says that you are Micah's last hope. She wanted me to give you endless days to pick my brain. I'm sorry, but that's impossible. As gravely concerned as I am for Micah, I have patients who depend on me. Fortunately, I can give you this time Mondays, Wednesdays, and Fridays. I hope that you can get what you need in those short windows.

"I'm willing to spill my guts to you for Micah's sake. That's the only reason. Your book may be the only way left to get my parental rights restored and get my son out of that madhouse. I am definitely not looking forward to this -I have always tried to keep my personal life private- but I promise that I will be honest with you, and I expect you to be honest with me. And with your readers. So, I'm at your mercy. I'll answer any question you have."

"May I record, doctor?"

"If we're going to be talking together at length, then you should start by calling me Sam and yes, of course. I expected that you'd be recording our conversations. I only have two ground rules."

"Thank you." I set my phone on the desk between us and tapped *record.*

"My patients' privacy is paramount. You may not introduce yourself to or otherwise engage or record anybody except me. Period. At some point you'll wonder whether any of the people who see me might give you some perspective on me, their therapist. Background. You may not do that. Ever. To them, you're simply my one o'clock patient three days each week."

"And that's the second requirement, Mr. Bennett. Our time will be limited by the clock. We'll start promptly at one and you'll be out that door at quarter of two." He nodded toward a large white circle in a sleek black frame mounted conspicuously on the wall behind him. It stood out in sharp contrast against the dark wood and earthy upholstery that otherwise filled the room. Two wire-thin, black hands and a hyperactive second hand chased around a face that had no numbers or minute markers of any kind.

"Forty-five-minute hours?"

"I'm sorry, Mr. Bennett. That's all I can offer. That's how I run my life." He stood and walked over to the picture window behind me and stared out across the lake. I turned far enough in my seat to see that he was lost in thought. I could vaguely make out the lights and chimney smoke of other homes dotted along the icy water's edge.

When he spoke again, it was from behind me.

"I understand that I'm tying your hands. I know that you have a deadline and believe me, every minute my son remains locked up is precious."

Abrams walked back in my direction, but rather than return to his chair, he leaned against the forward edge of the desk so that he was looking down at me. He's a tall man. Broad in the shoulders. I imagined that he had been an athlete in his youth. He had the upper body of a rower or a lifter, not a runner. He was fifty-something now -older than most parents with teens- and the stress that had bowed him, now threatened to break him.

"Frankly, Mr. Bennett, I can't imagine why you care about Micah. No one has listened to me for a year. No matter how many times I tell this story, no matter that the facts are on my side, no matter whether I lay it out in broad strokes or recount every single excruciating step, it makes no difference. People's minds are closed. Your mind is probably closed, too. No one hears anything but what social media and the press and the courts have all decided:

In their biased and distorted view, I somehow weaponized my only child, turned him into a matricidal maniac, then set him free to commit murder on my behalf. *Homicide by proxy* they're calling it. Remote control murder."

Actually, the tabloids were calling Abrams "Dr. Frankenstein." They ran lurid headlines about the monster he'd created and the death that it had caused. The most well-known featured a cartoon of a little boy with bolts in his neck and a bloody *Psycho* knife in one hand. More sophisticated publications quoted talking heads and self-proclaimed experts like Dr. Hassan French about "parental alienation *in extremis.*"

"I don't care what they all say," Abrams continued. "I did not somehow program or brainwash or telepathically manipulate my twelve-year-old son to kill his mother. I am not the evil puppet master that everyone seems to believe me to be. I'm just a father who tried to protect his son from his crazy and abusive mother. You're recording this, right?"

"Right."

Abrams picked up my phone and spoke directly at its microphone: "I'll try to be clear: Suki Kohler was crazy and abusive. She continually harmed our son Micah. The courts didn't help. Child Protection didn't help. I'm glad that she's dead. Period. My son, Micah Abrams, did not -could not have-killed her. Period." He returned the phone to the desktop, still recording. His eyes wandered back toward the lake.

After two beats of tense silence, I commented, "This is a beautiful property."

"Thanks. This is the house that Suki and Micah and I shared when he was little. I had this basement finished when we bought it so I could work here and be close to my son. I put a separate entrance and exit in. This space is quite insulated from the living space above and quite independent." He nodded toward the door that I'd entered through. "Waiting area. This office space. On the other side I have a full bath and a workroom. There's a small anteroom with a refrigerator and a small bed. I actually lived down here full time when things got really bad with Suki. Micah was two or three. When the courts gave this home to Suki, I rented a two bedroom about a half-mile from here. Suki's been dead almost a year, but I was only allowed to move back in about six months ago."

"The house is full of memories. Micah grew up here. He was never an outdoors guy -he always preferred his video games and…" to my ear, it sounded like Abrams said 'O' like the letter of the alphabet- "-but we did have a few good times on the lake together. Micah and me." He'd wandered back behind his desk. Manilla file folders, a pair of heavy-looking volumes, a fat and very expensive looking pen, and a large flat screen monitor filled the no man's land between us. More computer gear -it looked like a hard drive and another monitor and a lot of cables covered the dark wood credenza behind him. "And with your help, Ted, maybe Micah and I will sail and fish out there again sometime, right?

He paused until I met his eye. "My lawyer said that your publisher is planning on getting your book out in six months. That's an incredibly ambitious schedule for a writer but still a very long time for a little boy. She also told me to trust you. That you'd be fair. I'm not sure that I'm able to trust anyone at this point, Ted. Anyone. The public already has me nailed to a cross. You can promise to be open-minded and say that you're not judging me, but you're a human being just like everybody else. You're vulnerable to the same torch-and-pitchfork hysteria that has filled all of human history.

"Is Micah a twenty-first century Frankenstein's monster?" He asked. "Did Micah kill his mother? Of course not! Micah is the victim here. Have you seen him? I'm not asking whether you've seen Micah in the video clips that pop up on the web. Everyone has. That's just digital roadkill for a world full of voyeuristic vultures. The perverse solace of schadenfreude. Its click bait trying to sell cars and computers and antiperspirants. No, I mean have you really ever seen Micah? In person?"

I hadn't. No one outside of the Minnesota Psychiatric Hospital had seen Micah Abrams since he was hospitalized last April.

"Micah's barely five foot tall -or at least he was a year ago- and maybe ninety pounds soaking wet. He wears glasses and carries an inhaler. He lives for" -he used that same unfamiliar letter-word "O" again- "and mythology and classic movies. He read Homer in grade school and loved all those ancient Greek heroes and monsters. We used to watch lots of movies together. Especially old black-and-whites. *Citizen Kane*" A lot of Humphrey Bogart.

John Wayne. *The Wizard of Oz.* We loved Jimmy Stewart. We must have watched *Vertigo* together ten times. Micah's a really smart, really nice kid. He could not kill anyone. Period. Even his sadistic, brutal mother."

I waited another beat while he settled back in his chair.

"Mr. Bennett, Micah's mother was abusive. Psychologically, emotionally, and physically abusive. She abused me while we were together and then she abused Micah. I tried to keep him from her as long as I could. I physically stood between them. I would have done anything to protect him. In the end, no one believed me. I'm male and I'm a psychologist. How could she hurt me? She did. But the court didn't believe me. They accused me of alienating my son from his mother. Creating false allegations to keep him for myself. Bullshit. I wanted nothing more than for Micah to have a healthy relationship with Suki. But he didn't. She wasn't capable of giving it. The court forced me to send my son back into her hands over and over again. It ripped my heart out every time."

There should have been tears in his eyes. Sorrow. Grief. Maybe even fear. I saw none of that. Just smoldering anger and resentment.

"I'm sure that I can't imagine what you've been through. What Micah's been through. And no, I've never met Micah in person. I hope to. When he gets better. That's why I'm here. I'm hoping that you can teach me about Micah and about you and about what really happened."

This was somehow a decision point for the psychologist. Should he trust me or keep me at arm's length? This was his office in his home. All he needed to do was ask me to leave and it would be all over. Months of planning and research and preparation would have been wasted. I'd have to return my upfront money and find another project. Today -here and now in this moment in this room- was make it or break it for me and maybe for Micah Abrams.

My mind raced looking for a hook. I needed something that might begin to build a bridge between me and Samuel Abrams and keep him talking. I said the first words that occurred to me.

"What's *O*?"

He gave a dismissive half-laugh, the condescending sound that Michelangelo might have made if ever asked to draw a stick figure.

"Not *O* like the letter, Ted. *E-A-U* like the French word for water, even though it's not French at all. It's the acronym for *Enemies All Around Us*. *EAU* is *THE* VR game to beat these days. Micah had Horizon 4-DV headsets at my house and here at Suki's. You've never heard of *EAU*?"

I'd only just recently graduated to *Rainbow Unicorns* with Christie on our home Xbox, but I didn't tell him that. I had no experience with virtual reality and had never heard of *EAU*.

"*EAU* is a virtual reality MMPG. *Massive Multi-Player Game*. It's where Micah lived. Inside his head, inside a 3D digital world with a several hundred total strangers. He preferred that reality to this one and, frankly, who could blame him? He was the low man on the totem pole IRL."

"IRL?" I asked.

"Sorry. In Real Life. He was weak and weird and awkward here. In *EAU* he was quite the opposite. He was powerful and respected and in control. That's the real difference, you know. Suki took away all of his control. *EAU* replaced it."

Abrams paused, took a deep breath, and made a decision. "Okay Mr. Bennet: If you really want to hear my story and if you'll genuinely listen, then I need to say something up front. Get out your paper and start writing."

I made a flourish with my pen and paper.

"Ready? Okay." He spoke pointedly toward my phone: "This is Samuel Marc Abrams, P-H-D recording on February 17, 2023. Here's the simple truth that no one believes: My ex-wife, Suki Kohler, whom you knew for her perfect teeth and perfect figure was a red-hot flaming narcissistic sociopath. A self-absorbed woman without a conscience and with no capacity for empathy. To her, nothing hurt unless it hurt her and nothing that she did was wrong unless she got caught."

"I am a clinical psychologist, and I didn't see it until it was too late. I was taken in by her beauty and the whirlwind that always surrounded Suki. Travel and excitement and risks and adventure. She was like one of those sharks that has to always be in motion or die. In fact, Suki gaslighted and abused me for years. She did the same to our son, Micah, from the time that he was old enough to argue with her. Suki wouldn't tolerate other opinions. Dissent. Non-compliance. Everything had to be her way or her rage erupted like a volcano. There was nothing in between."

"I did everything in my power to protect Micah from his mother. I reported Suki many times to Child Protective Services for mistreating Micah. I took Micah and left home. I divorced her and tried to get full custody. I failed every time because I'm a man and I'm a shrink, and I'm physically larger. How could a petite woman like Suki -especially a celebrity- possibly do the things I'd accused her of?"

Finally, he looked up from the phone and met my gaze.

"I am glad that Suki is dead. I have no hesitation saying that, but my son Micah did not kill her. He had nothing to do with it. Zero. Nada."

His blue eyes were locked on mine, I imagined him probing for signs of disbelief or argument. I held his gaze, trying not to blink or twitch or betray any reaction. Plenty of people would have challenged him with a long line of "but what about…?" and "How could she…?" and "why didn't you….?" I wanted to ask all of those questions and more, but I needed his trust first.

Today was about establishing a relationship, not doubting him.

I kept my thoughts to myself. A breath or two later he finally looked away. It seemed I had passed the test.

"Yes, I know I sound angry." He was back at his desk, sunk deep in enveloping leather, fidgeting with a cigar-shaped pen while he spoke. "That's because I am angry. Suki won again! Even though she's dead, I still can't be with Micah. Somehow even in death she's still getting the last laugh."

"Thank you, Sam. You're right: I'm not here to judge you. I'm here to listen to you. To tell your story."

Again, that condescending half-laugh. He shook his head slowly side to side.

"Well, then you're the first. Look: We both know that nobody really cares about the truth anymore. What matters is *likes* and swiping left or right. The truth is whatever the influencer of the day tells us it is. Reality isn't real until it's gone viral. The world has made up its mind about me and you should, too. If you write the truth about Micah -or better yet, if you magically figure out what the cops and the courts have totally failed to figure out, what really happened to Suki - no one will believe you either."

"I told my lawyer when she twisted my arm into doing this that telling you my story is pointless. Futile." He shook his head in disgust. "Most days,

I feel like Sisyphus pushing that rock uphill forever. Do you know Greek mythology, Ted? The only reason that I'm willing to take time out of my busy day to talk to you is for Micah."

He paused, took a long hit from his coffee mug, then resumed.

"They won't let me see Micah and if they did, he probably wouldn't even know that I was there. He's catatonic. Do you know the term? Micah is physically healthy but locked inside another world. Unresponsive. A zombie for all practical purposes and God knows the people at MPH won't have a clue how to treat him."

"MPH?" I asked, trying to keep up.

"Minnesota Psychiatric Hospital. Criminal lockup for loonies. Do the research, Mr. Bennett. MPH is a taxpayer funded horror show run by incompetent fools masquerading as doctors. I wouldn't commit my worst enemy there."

Abrams paused again as the reality of what he was describing -how he feared his son was living- sunk in. He stared back over my shoulder toward the water. I was getting the idea that he did this to calm the way that other people count to three or practice deep breathing.

"You will be my conduit to Micah, Ted. You're my insurance that if somehow I can't tell him my story, he'll hear it anyway. Write your best seller. I hope that you make a fortune off my misery. The only thing that matters to me is that someday when Micah is better, he'll know what really happened."

"Thank you, Sam."

We'd made an agreement of sorts. We'd defined our symbiotic roles. We would take advantage of one another. The numberless wall clock seemed to say that I had time left in my very brief hour. I needed to use it.

"Can you tell me more about Micah's condition?"

I'd read all the hospital reports from a year ago. Micah wasn't talking and didn't seem to be in pain. The blood on his shirt wasn't his own. X-ray showed no broken bones. He'd stared blankly at the hospital walls for a couple of days, then they'd discharged him medically intact but psychologically compromised. The reports used words like "selective mutism," "echolalia," and "echopraxia" all of which sent me Googling and all of which basically amounted to what Abrams had first said. Micah was a zombie.

I knew this. I asked because I wanted to know what Abrams knew and how he got his information. I was also quickly getting the idea that Abrams needed to be in the driver's seat. The expert. I figured that playing supplicant seated at the feet of the guru might help to keep our conversation alive.

"You must have seen the video from that Saturday last April. When the cops found him. My little boy is suffering a profound traumatic shock. My lawyer tells me that the doctors say that he's physically healthy. When they first found him, they thought he was injured. The blood all over him wasn't his own. It turned out to be Suki's, but we still don't know why or how he was exposed to it. He's catatonic. The last thing I'd heard is that he's largely unresponsive to the world around him. He's withdrawn from reality somewhere deep inside his own head. He barely eats and he mutters gibberish. Something like 'Silly Anchor Bus' and no, before you ask, I have no idea what that means.

"They had him in a diaper for a while. He was on a G-tube when they first admitted him because he wasn't eating. They're monitoring his weight. Last I heard, he would walk if someone guided him and he'd eat little bits if they put in in his mouth, otherwise he just sits and stares at nothing 24/7. He's been at MPH since they first discharged him from the hospital. That was nine months ago. You must have seen the video?"

I had seen it. You probably have too. Long after the major networks stopped playing it, it keeps popping up on the web. Two cops escorting a small, stiff-looking figure wearing jeans and a turtleneck down a snowy walkway away from the camera. There's a police cruiser in the distance, a dark strip of suburban street and a quiet, snow-blanketed neighborhood beyond that. The day is stunningly clear under blue, blue skies. When the three reach the cruiser, the officers physically fold the smaller person into the back seat of their vehicle. Like origami. If you pause the clip just right, it's easy to make out that the paper they're folding is a child. A boy, although he moves like a robot. Pale cheeks. A prominent nose. Bright brown or red stains on his chest and sleeves. The child's face is frozen even after you push play again. His expression is empty. His sunken eyes are unfocused. The officers slam his door shut, climb in the front of the car, and drive away. Lights flashing. No siren. Twelve seconds in all.

Micah had been found curled in a fetal position in the back of a neighbor's garage muttering nonsense hours after his mother's murder. One police report described him as repeating the phrase "Silly Anchor Bus" over and over again. The owner of the garage had made the video and posted it to social media with the caption, "Mommy Murderer." Within a week, that video had reached more people than COVID-19. "MM" became a meme and evolved into "M&M" when some clever troll turned a cheery, round, animated candy into an evil-looking, knife-wielding emoji.

"The M&M clip?"

"See?" He spit out the word, shaking his head with disgust. "Just by calling it that your bias is showing. That horrible label means that Micah killed his mother. HE. DID. NOT. Something awful happened to my son that night. He might have seen the murder, but he didn't commit it. It drives me crazy that I don't know what happened and that whatever did happen I couldn't protect him from. And now that it has happened, I can't even hold my son to comfort him."

"What do you think happened, Sam?

"I think that Micah ran away from my rented two-bedroom back here in the middle of the night. I don't know why, but it's only about a ten-minute walk. I think Micah saw what happened to Suki. I think he was here when she died, in the kitchen, but I don't know why, and I don't know how. He was in his room when I went to bed that night and then he was gone when the cops woke me about four hours later."

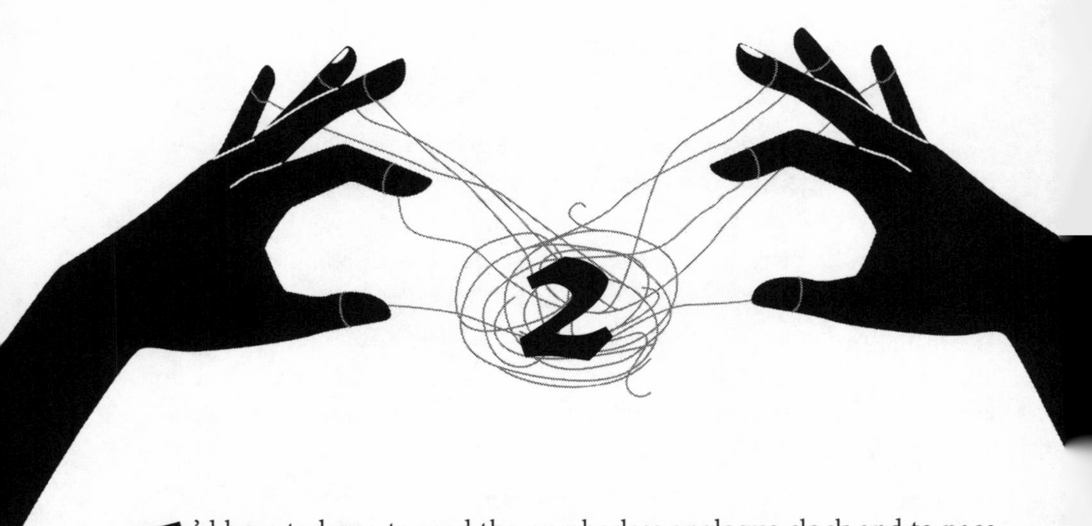

I'd have to learn to read the numberless analogue clock and to pace myself better. The big hand pointed due northwest and our short forty-five minutes had ended far too quickly. I dropped my phone and notebook into my backpack, shook the doctor's hand and offered another "thank you" as I exited stage right.

Some therapist offices work that way. Patients enter on one side via a waiting room and exit out the other side into the parking lot. The idea is to help patients avoid embarrassing encounters with their bosses and neighbors and lovers.

Abrams' home is a large and handsome brick and stone structure at the end of a long driveway in Chanhassen. The driveway opens onto a small parking area and a path that offers three options. Straight ahead leads up stone steps to a portico and a beautiful stained-glass front door. A discrete sign leads patients to the right, down a gentle slope toward the backyard and the lake beyond. The lower story of the home is exposed in the back. A stout wooden door identified only as "ENTER HERE" leads into the waiting room. On the opposite side of the home, an identical but unmarked door opens onto another gentle slope leading back up to the front.

Entering the doctor's inner sanctum from the waiting room, a picture window on the right looks out across a sloping lawn, over a rocky wall, and past a wooden dock onto acres of open water. White birch and towering pines line the shore between homes, each more elegant than the last. A small collection of wooden docks, floating rafts, and moored boats complete the scene. The view through that window should be a scenic calendar page or your screen saver.

Abrams' office is all man. Dark and strong and heavy. He sits in a black leather chair that engulfs him, extending above and behind his head and wider than his arms. His desk is polished mahogany covered by an old-fashioned paper blotter. It matches the credenza that lines the wall behind him. A pair of visitor's chairs faces his desk and a traditional analyst's couch is across the room, angled away. The room is dimly lit by lamps and upholstered in muted tans and browns and complementary greens and grays. It's obviously a man's space, but also a very earthy, comfortable space.

After shaking hands farewell, Abrams ushered me toward a pair of dark wooden doors opposite the waiting room entrance. The door on the left is unmarked and shut tight. The door on the right is marked "EXIT HERE." I did. Cool, fresh air embraced me. Ten or twelve steps up the gentle slope to my left past winter-wrapped shrubs and slushy lawns brought me back to the parking area and my car. I had the odd feeling of surfacing from great depths.

Nemo raising the Nautilus.

Dorothy stepping into Oz.

A late model Range Rover was parked next to my battered and beloved Jeep. No doubt Abrams' next patient had recently walked down the opposite side of the house and was now waiting below.

I was bursting at the seams. Grandiose and excited and frustrated all at once. An overblown balloon ready to pop. I would have laughed out loud or danced across the icy sidewalk if I wasn't wary of doorbell cameras and security devices watching my every move. This meeting had been my Olympic tryouts, my qualifying race at Daytona, and my NBA first round draft announcement all rolled into one. I'd worked for weeks to make today a success, reading terabytes of research on mother murderers and the psychology of high conflict divorce and parental alienation and scores of articles from across the country about Suki Kohler's life and death and the M&M murderer. I'd spent days drowning in sheaves of police records and court filings and psych reports, studying Abrams' and Kohler's histories, the autopsy and crime scene photos. I'd waded through hundreds of pages of psychobabble constituting Micah Abram's psychiatric evaluations.

I was frustrated because I had so little time here. Forty-five minutes is nothing. I'd get home and transcribe the audio and review my notes and then have to wait forty-eight hours for another bite?

Interviews for my first two books had been entirely different experiences. I'd enjoyed full day immersions into the thoughts and feelings of the players. In Chicago, I'd basically lived with the police sergeant who'd been wrongfully convicted of homicide. He was out of jail on bail, eager to talk and talk and talk. I dissected his routines, mastered his mannerisms, catalogued and cross-checked his history. A year later, Synchronicity Press published "In the Line of Duty" which, I fully believe, was instrumental in getting the court to declare a mistrial and eventually exonerate the officer. We stayed in touch. He was now suing for backpay to cover the months that he'd spent trying to get justice.

I'd spent even longer than that in Milwaukee, trying to understand how and why a dentist had been caught up in a narcotics bust. That book, "Deep Fracture" painted a picture of corrupt area pharmacists who were dispensing twice the number of oxy prescribed in an under-the-table black-market kick-back scheme that made the neighborhood dentist in his white coat and blue rubber gloves look like a South American drug kingpin. He wasn't, but he wasn't entirely clean either. Last I'd heard, the charges against him had been reduced. He'd lost his license, but he would be due for parole in months rather than decades.

I'd never set out to be a true crime writer -my first love had always been science fiction- but fate had made me into a sort of literary Robin Hood. Momentum and a need to pay the bills seemed to be carrying me forward. I'd pitched the M&M murder to SynCity -my private sobriquet for my publisher- in part because the story is local. In the past couple of years, the idea of living and writing on the road had lost its juice. Its thrill.

Synchronicity liked the M&M book proposal but insisted on a ridiculous schedule. I was to produce a behind-the-scenes three-hundred-page must-read manuscript in four months so they could have it on the shelves well before the M&M murder trial in September. I said no at first, that's impossible, but they insisted. As incentive they advanced me fifteen grand and promised me fifteen more if I could make their July 4th deadline.

It was a big ask. Since I'd moved in with Jenny, working from home had become very important to me, but I feared that backed-up plumbing and neighbors stopping by and romantic dinners out and hanging out with Christie, Jenny's amazing daughter, would interrupt my concentration and make the kind of intense commitment necessary impossible. We talked about it. Jenny was on board. She's incredibly supportive. She'd promised to give me space, but she'd never lived through the gestation and birth of a book with me before.

The day that I signed on the dotted line with SynCity, my agent made a deal with Abrams' lawyers to get me regular access to the man. I had hoped for full days or long weekends letting me pick at his brain, go away and write for an afternoon, and then come back to try to fill in the gaps. Instead, I'd been given this maddening schedule. Three hours a week, but not even real sixty-minute hours!

Forty-five times three is ... *ugh* ... 135 divided by sixty. That's just two and a quarter real hours each week. I'd have to be efficient. Incisive. Thorough. I'd have to ask exactly the right questions and squeeze every word that Abrams gave me for all of its extra meaning. That meant intense preparation in advance of each meeting and meticulous dissection of my notes and my memory and recorded audio for many hours afterward.

I'd prepped endlessly for today's first meeting, far more concerned with establishing a rapport with the man than gathering background information. I'd practiced in the mirror and on video and with Jenny how to connect. When to express sincerity and interest with eye contact and when to look away discreetly so as to never embarrass, humiliate, or intimidate. When to push for a response and when to sit patiently and wait for a reply. I'd come ready to deploy whatever combination of empathy and interest and promises and support and assertiveness necessary to get Abrams to talk when, in the end, he probably would have spilled his guts to his mailman if he'd thought it would benefit his son. He wanted to tell his story almost as much as I was determined to write it.

My plan was to milk these brief therapy hours for history and personalities and dynamics. I needed facts and flavor both. Colors and tastes and smells and textures that could set a scene and put events in context. I figured that I had about six weeks or a total of only about thirteen and half hours to capture the full trajectory that had cost Sam Abrams his parental rights, landed Suki Kohler six feet under, and locked up their catatonic son in a secure psychiatric facility.

The book, if I was able to manage this Herculean feat, was tentatively called "Alienated" referring both to the family dynamic and to the public's rejection of their once beloved wiseman. I had secret fantasies of reviewers referring to me as the secret love child of investigative journalist Carl Bernstein and multi-million-dollar lawyer-gone-novelist John Grisham. The *New York Times* would call my work "insightful, evocative, and chilling – more important than oxygen!" The Pulitzer committee would keep me on speed dial. *The View* would recommend my book and Netflix would produce a biopic starring Matt Damon as me, Teddy Bennett, the relentless, brilliant, and quirky best-selling true crime writer.

This entire delusion -yes, I know it's all delusional; I'm not crazy. I know that every writer has these same wet dreams – is built on milking every last ounce of experience out of Abrams. Suki's murder and Abrams' story had become and must remain more than my number one obsession. Success meant not only playing a part in the real-life drama that had swallowed Abrams and his son. For me it meant entrée into future books and publishing deals and bigger bucks.

3

My Jeep learned the route between our apartment in Shakopee and Abrams' home in Chanhassen very quickly. Weather and traffic permitting, it's twenty minutes each way. Under the worst of conditions, that could stretch into thirty. Because my hour was so short and my deadline so immediate, I couldn't afford to be late. That meant leaving home no later than 12:15. I could always use any extra time in his waiting room to review and prepare. There was so much ground to cover. We regularly found our way into the meaty subjects just as the stylized big hand on his clock reached the horizontal plane.

Throughout the course of our relationship, Abrams was generally polite and accommodating but matter-of-fact when we spoke. He answered *when*? and *where*? and *how?* questions simply and clearly when he could, but avoided most of my *whys*? He was obviously holding back his emotion. He bottled up his feelings the way that I am sure he instructed his own clients not to. Over time I became convinced that Abrams was bursting at the seams with pent-up feelings and fighting every second to stop himself from exploding. I knew that some portion of that pressure was desperate worry for his son. I could only guess that the remainder -perhaps even the larger part- was rage.

Why didn't Abrams shout and scream and cry and pound his fists on the wall in fury and desperation? Maybe he did, but never in my presence. So, I decided to ask him.

At one o'clock exactly on my fourth visit, -I checked my cell because there was no clock in the waiting room- Abrams opened the intervening door and greeted me as usual.

"Good afternoon, Mr. Bennett."

We shook hands. He offered me something to drink. I politely declined, possessive of the minute that it would take him to fetch me a cup of water. He reclined behind his desk, coffee cup in hand, and waited for me to produce my notebook and turn on my phone, ready to record.

Sometimes he made small talk and sometimes I'd answer. A word about the weather warming, or the Vikings losing, or the weekend just past. I cheered on springtime, bemoaned the Packers' victory, and mentioned taking Jenny and Christie to a flea market. He never probed or intruded or blackmailed personal details out of me Hannibal Lector-like. We were filling the moment while the stage was set, before resuming the play.

"Where do we begin today, Ted?" He asked.

We'd covered lots of basics so far. His childhood and family of origin. How he'd gotten together with Suki. What it was like being married to a cover girl, given the constant sexual attention she generated and her frequent travels around the world to show her body off to millions of strangers. He'd told me about the shock and surprise of Micah's conception given his age and Suki's obsession with her appearance. He told me how her moods shifted like TV channels when a toddler plays with the remote. One minute she insisted on an abortion. The next she was talking to the fetus like her new best friend. She cried, she laughed, she screamed. Her moods had always been labile, he said. Pregnancy made them volatile.

Talking about Suki's moodiness gave me a reason to ask about his own stoicism. His flat, overcontrolled, tamped down, and bottled-up presentation. "I'm concerned," I said, "that you bring your psychotherapist blank-slate self into our meetings, when what I need is the real you. Naked. Unguarded. Real and relatable."

I was pretty proud of how I'd worded that. It's scary to look a bear in its face. When I'd talked with Jenny about broaching this subject here today, she'd offered me a bit of her usual wisdom: "Be careful what you wish for, Ted. Do you really want to let the lion out of its cage?"

I wanted and needed to know Sam Abrams' interior universe. His fears and dreams and needs and wishes. Who he was when he shed the wise psychologist persona. But did I want to open the door on whatever rages and insecurities and jealousies and craziness might be hiding within? Yes, I answered myself (but not Jenny – I told Jenny that I'd be careful. I'm a writer, I'd reminded her, not a crash test dummy).

Abrams sat very still as he digested my comment, only his fingers moved as he manipulated the fat pen that he often had at hand. A fidget-toy. I held his gaze briefly, and then I did what Abrams himself had done many times while we talked. I got up and walked over to the picture window. The day was gray and cloudy with icy drizzle. Maybe I was wisely taking the pressure off the conversation by breaking eye contact. Or maybe I wanted more space between us in case he exploded.

Silence.

When I turned back, there were tears running down his cheeks. That was the first time that I saw him cry.

"Sam?" I asked.

"I apologize, Mr. Bennett. It's an astute observation and an inevitable question. You're here to get to know me," he pulled a tissue from a desk drawer and blew his nose. "You're here to get to know me and I'm only giving you facts. Names and date and places. Of course, you need more. Sit back down and write, Mr. Writer. Don't worry, I won't bite." I sat, embarrassed that he'd read my anxiety so clearly. I made sure that the tiny oscilloscope on my phone was registering every sound.

"I loved Suki deeply. Call me crazy -plenty of people did when we first got together. It wasn't just her looks or her fame or her bank account, and it certainly wasn't the sex. That's a different story. Sure, I was incredibly proud to be seen out with her. I enjoyed reading whatever the paparazzi had to say about the awards dinners and movie openings and magazine covers but put all that aside. I genuinely loved her."

"The crazy part is that I would have loved her just the same without the glitz and glamour AND I loved her just the same despite the mood swings and the infidelity and the violence. Suki was a fashion model first and foremost. Her body was her instrument, and she was a virtuoso. Age and childbirth did not treat her body well by her own estimation, so she used drugs. Oh, she ran hot and cold even without drugs, but amphetamines and steroids and emetics -she was bulimic- made her into the roller coaster from hell. She'd rage and then weep for days and order pizza and then consume nothing but water and celery for a week. She fought the urge to cut herself -she couldn't afford scars anyway on her body; she was always naked in front of people- so she lashed out at me. For years."

"You want emotions? I was humiliated. Embarrassed. I could never understand what I'd done to deserve her cruelty and I would never fight back." He was crying openly now. "She'd pummel me with her fists. She'd scratch at me with her nails. She kicked. She bit. It hurt. I let her hurt me for a very long time. I'd plead with her to stop. I couldn't fight back for fear of bruising her and I couldn't leave the house for fear of what she might do to herself. I couldn't turn to friends or her agent or her family because she had a reputation to maintain."

"Her pregnancy added hormones to an already volatile recipe of neurochemicals and OTC meds and street drugs. I've often wondered whether Micah's stature and physical frailty is because he was grown in such contaminated soil."

"Suki's rage and depression grew exponentially with her weight. The doctors wanted her to put on thirty pounds at least. She found that prospect grotesque. I begged and pleaded with her to eat for the baby. She would not."

Micah was delivered at thirty-five weeks severely underweight. No surprise there. Her body couldn't sustain him any longer. Fortunately, excellent doctors and a month in NICU made all the difference. He'll always have lung problems -asthma at least- and he's never likely to be a long-distance runner or a professional weightlifter in this world, but he otherwise recovered from a traumatic pregnancy. Suki did not."

"Feelings, Ted? Grief. Loss. My wife never came back from pregnancy, not even the roller coaster wife that I'd learned to manage up to that point. Two things happened in Micah's first two years that changed history. I caught Suki having two affairs in a row, the second just weeks after we'd had a knock-down drag-out about the first infidelity, ending with me forgiving her and understanding that she was looking for reassurance that she was still beautiful. And she was. She'd only gained twelve pounds with Micah, and I think she lost that and more within a month after birth."

"The second thing? The last straw? I don't believe that that super-explosive mix of chemicals that turned her into the incredible Hulk while she was pregnant ever settled down and maybe -I was never sure- maybe she got into bigger, badder street drugs. Maybe meth. Certainly coke. Whatever it was, I caught her more and more often raging at the baby. At Micah. There is nothing on this earth that could enrage or terrify me more. That's when I started calling Child Protective Services. They did nothing. By the time Micah was two, I'd taken him and moved out to the two-bedroom on South Seventh, just a half mile from here. I wanted him to be able to see his mother under my supervision, but we needed to get out of that house. *This* house."

"Am I bottling up feelings? Damn right. I have a volcano of feelings constantly erupting inside of me after years of abuse and fearing for my son and now having him torn away from me and accused of murdering his mother?" He wiped his eyes again, paused to capture his thoughts and said, "Can you blame me Ted?"

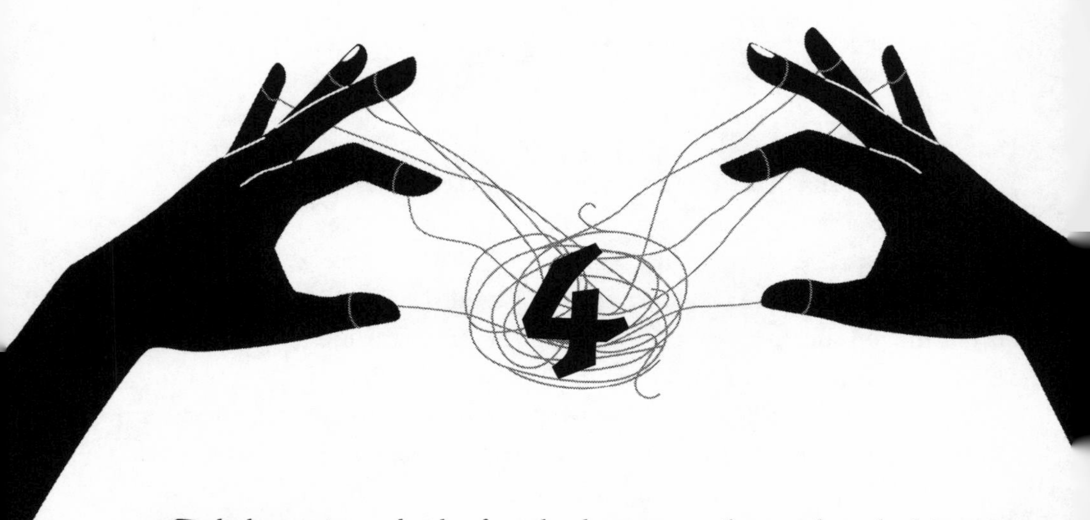

Shakopee is a suburb of a suburb twenty miles south and a bit west of the Twin Cities, just another small town in the concentric circles of urban sprawl that spread outward from its center. More than miles-as-the-crow-flies or highway travel time, the town's true distance from the middle of the metropolis is best gauged by gas prices and rent. Shakopee is far enough away that I save three bucks at the pumps on every tank and three hundred bucks every month on my apartment.

Our apartment. Jenny and Christie and me.

Because the drive home from Abrams' office is a straight shot south on 101 and relatively unencumbered by traffic at mid-day, the twenty-minute trip requires exactly zero neurons. My six-year-old Jeep may as well have been a self-driving Tesla. This matters because I rely on that time to nail down nuances after each meeting. The sounds and sights and smells and textures and emotions expressed in a fleeting gesture or a minute shift of posture or a raised eyebrow that together create the depth and meaning that go far beyond words on a page. In Abrams' case, I'm talking about the fleeting intangibles that communicate the meaning baked into the man's silences, intimidating eye contact, and frustrating episodic absences as he stares out the window.

I turn my recorder app back on while I drive, lay my phone on the dashboard, and free associate out loud, trying to puzzle through some of the many mysteries I'd encountered. Somehow, I worked the steering wheel, accelerator, and brake without thinking.

"Abrams strikes me as sincere and open and honest. Is he telling the truth about Suki having been abusive for years? Are there records of bulimia or

addiction? What do Micah's birth records say? Was Suki perhaps post-partum psychotic?"

"Do I feel sorry for Abrams? He paints himself as the victim. Is it possible that he programmed Micah to murder Suki like everyone believes? Are there records of this sort of thing happening elsewhere? Can a parent program a child psychologically against his other parent? If anyone could, Sam Abrams could."

"Abrams' appearance: Graying on top with a trim gray beard and moustache. Deep worry lines crease his forehead. Big nose but it suits his broad face. His skin is so pale, the way he describes Micah. No freckles. No marks. No tattoos. No jewelry including no wedding ring."

"Abrams used 'weaponized' to describe what people say he did to Micah. Is it possible to 'weaponize' a child? Did he create a 'Weapon of Maternal Destruction'? A 'WMD'? But wouldn't that contradict some basic instinct we all share about our parents? I know I had my moments growing up -sorry Mom- but I don't think I could ever have actually killed her."

"To do: Abrams forbade me from talking to his current patients, but what about past patients? Supervisors? Do they describe him as controlling? Angry? Manipulative?"

"Micah? Can I talk to Micah's friends and their parents? Can I visit Micah at MPH? Who to talk to there? Can I actually see him?"

I braked for the light at the T-intersection where 101 and 69 meet at the Shakopee Town Common. Momentum carried my phone skittering across the dashboard and then into the passenger footwell, still recording. I cursed as the light changed, leaving me no chance to retrieve it.

The Common is three sprawling stories of red-brick buildings housing small businesses eager to sell everything from French braids to French fries. It was still quarter of the hour, so I stopped for gas. Thirty-five dollars later I took the right at the light, then left around the sprawling plaza and left again onto fourth. Three minutes later I pulled up in front of the Shakopee Police Department and next to Jenny's ancient and dented 4Runner. She was behind the wheel of the parked car, facing out toward the lot's entrance. I pulled in so our doors were three feet apart. Jenny was staring at me with a mix of anxiety and interest on her face.

"How'd it go, Teddy?"

I know that she really wanted to hear about the interview with Abrams -had I let the lion out of its cage? Had I been bitten?- but not there and then. She was distracted and worried.

"Hey Babe. Great, thanks." I wanted to tell her all about Abrams' tears and my ideas about how the book might come together, but I bit my tongue. Jenny knew more than anyone what I'd gone through to get this far and how much was riding on delivering my manuscript on time but the anxiety that knitted her brow and the set of her jaw and the conspicuous quiet from her backseat kept me quiet.

"He's late again, huh?" I asked. It was six minutes after three. Jenny's glare answered the question better than words.

"Hey Christie-Cream!" I called over Jenn's shoulder toward the child-sized lump of pink and white and purple wool-and-Lycra in the back seat. I couldn't see Christie's face beneath her "My Little Pony" hat, but I could tell that her arms were crossed tightly over her chest.

"Yes," the little girl under the pile of clothes replied in an excellent imitation of her mother, "he's late again."

Jenny jumped in before I could answer: "At least the bastard's predictable."

"Yep," Christie mimicked. "Predictable."

My excitement about my success with Abrams receded as I listened to the two most important people in my world echo one another. This was the twice-monthly prisoner exchange. Think Tom Hanks in *Bridge of Spies*. A dark, tense night on the border between warring nations. Invisible snipers watch every move. Enemies trade captured combatants across neutral ground. Christie's father, Jorge -he insisted on being called "*OR-hey*" and never 'George' with a 'G'- was ordered by the court to pick up Christie at three p.m. every other Friday for his two-night visitation. Jenny and I pronounced the word "Voldemort" like the evil villain in Harry Potter.

The court had mandated that the exchange occur here under the watchful cameras of the Shakopee PD. Jenny and I thought that the videos might validate our complaints about Voldemort's irresponsible arrivals and hostile behavior. Unfortunately, the past six months had proven that no amount of documentation, no number of reports to social services, and no quantity of *ex parte* contempt motions would ever be sufficient. Voldemort had no lawyer and claimed to have no money so the court bent over backwards to give him his rights. He was on social security disability due to an imaginary back injury that acted up any time he was due in court, so he couldn't work full time. Jenny, on the other hand, was rewarded for working sixty hours a week, paying for all of Christie's needs plus half of our rent and her taxes and her bills just so that she could have the privilege of spending the few pennies that she had left on a lawyer and the privilege of missing work to go to court.

No, actually it was worse than that.

For all of the pain and inconvenience that Voldemort caused us, 6-year-old Christie is the one who suffers. She bears the brunt of his late arrivals and no-shows, his angry rants, and his selfish me-first choices. She carries the emotional scars inflicted by his never-subtle disrespect for her mother and his outright dismissal of me. Christie deserves to have a father who loves and values her as a person, who gives her the freedom to love and feel loved by whomever she might choose, not a father who treats her like property to be bartered and bargained and just plain neglected in his endless need to one-up her mother.

But here we are once again, demonstrating Einstein's definition of insanity: Doing the same thing over and over again and hoping to somehow achieve a different outcome.

"Do I have to go, Mommy? I don't want to. I want to stay home with you and Teddy."

"I know sweetie. We all have to do things that we don't like sometimes. But its only for two sleeps and you can call me every night at bedtime..."

"If he lets me! I hate him!"

"Yep. Me too" Jenny added. I glanced at her with caution, but she ignored me. "Remember I told you that the judge said you have to go with Voldemort? You don't want me to get in trouble, do you?"

Christie spoke up in a whine from the back seat: "Look Mommy. He's here." She pointed toward the brand new, midnight black muscle car a hundred yards away blasting a hundred decibel rumbling bass across the distance. I know nothing about cars, but I know that this is a Mustang Mach One. We'd Bluebooked the value for our last court hearing. How could Jenny's ex pay over fifty grand for a car but claim that he couldn't afford to pay child support?

Jenny looked toward the rolling cacophony and muttered "Oh shit." She twisted in her seat to face Christie behind her. "Here sweetie. I got you a present." She pushed up the child's left sleeve and put a silver bracelet embedded with a ruby red stone the size of a penny on her wrist. A tiny image of rabbit ears was engraved in the metal.

I knew nothing about this impromptu gift. Usually, Jenny included me on Christie's surprises.

"I want you to wear this every minute and think of me whenever you see it, okay?"

"It's pretty, Mommy. Thanks. Even in the shower? Even when I sleep?"

"Absolutely, munchkin. Now let's go."

The distraction worked at least briefly. Jenny lifted the little girl out of her booster seat, snagged Christie's beloved Piglet toy and her *Frozen* backpack in her free hand, then kicked the rear car door shut behind them. She started across the parking lot toward the big black car. In my rearview mirror she looked like a modern-day Sherpa laden with gear ready to ascend Everest. Christie hung over her mother's shoulder busy twisting the shiny metal and ruby-red stone on her wrist. Her resistance to seeing her father was momentarily forgotten.

I sat back and angled the mirror down to watch the exchange. In that moment, I remembered my cell phone, lying in the passenger footwell and still recording. I bent over and grabbed it and hit the red STOP button. When I glanced in the mirror again, Jenny and her ex were face-to-face in the icy minefield somewhere between the vehicles.

Voldemort is a big man physically and even more so in his own mind. He is wide and deep without being tall. He may believe that mass compensates for all that he's obviously lacking, notably intelligence, empathy, and deodorant. His belly rides inches out over his gaudy silver belt buckle and his ruddy, unshaven cheeks are quickly becoming jowls. Today he was wearing a black leather coat, dark sunglasses, and a ballcap. I couldn't make out the insignia, but nothing would have surprised me. He had them all and didn't hesitate to wear them in public. Some were profane ("Who gives a shit?") or sexual ("I♥Boobs!") or just generically offensive ("Democrats suck"). In warmer months he often complemented these with a collection of similarly colorful tee shirts.

I would never understand what Jenny had seen in him.

Asking would have been rubbing salt into the wound.

Voldemort approached mother and daughter without any obvious sense of urgency. I watched his mouth move but couldn't hear him across the distance. I saw Christie grab her mother tighter and, in doing so, drop Piglet into the icy puddle at their feet. This made her scream and writhe in Jenny's arms. Another father would have bent down and returned the creature to the little girl with no thought of his own discomfort or his hatred for his ex-wife. Not Voldemort. He kept talking while he watched Piglet soak up the slush and Jenny struggle to set Christie on her feet. The little girl clung tight, glued to Jenny's chest and screaming in her ear. In the end, Jenny had to do a deep knee bend wearing a long, heavy winter coat with forty-plus pounds of tantruming child draped over one shoulder and the child's backpack on the other arm. Somehow, she kept her balance, held onto Christie and her belongings, rescued Piglet, wiped the soiled creature off on her jeans, and got upright again.

Voldemort just kept on talking.

If that were the worst of the man's failings, there wouldn't be a problem. Lack of chivalry I can deal with. Lack of decency I cannot.

I watched Jenny whisper in Christie's ear and then reluctantly pass her into her father's arms. I didn't need to imagine the child's upset. Her screams carried across the distance. I was glad that Jenny was thickly insulated. She'd complained more than once that Voldemort had groped her while supposedly reaching for the child. The thought enraged me.

Jenny stood still in the middle of the parking lot in the middle of the slush while the barbarian she had once married carried their daughter away. Christie was still screaming and reaching for her mother over her father's shoulder. I saw Jenny trembling where she stood and felt my own shiver of empathy. Voldemort eventually tucked Christie in the back of the Mustang, tossed her backpack and sodden stuffed animal onto his passenger seat, got in behind the wheel, revved his engine like a feral lion roaring triumph, and peeled out of the lot far too quickly.

That was all that I could stand.

I climbed out of my Jeep, jogged over to Jenny, and wrapped her up in both arms. She was struggling to hold back tears and trembling with rage. She finally turned away from the direction that she'd seen Christie disappear and buried her face in my parka, sobbing.

Jenny is one of the strongest people that I know. Her parents illegally entered the U.S. from Mexico when her mother was seven months pregnant with her in the hope of raising their children in safety. As it turned out, they traded their day-to-day fears of the Sinaloa drug cartels for day-to-day fears of I.C.E. By the time Jenny was six, she'd become caregiver to both her little brother and her ailing mother while her father -once a licensed carpenter- worked three menial jobs. Somehow, she put herself through school, got out of a bad marriage, got certified as a licensed nursing assistant, and raised an amazing daughter on her own.

I'm sure that I could never understand the ordeals that Jenny had survived. What was clear to me, however, was that the pressures that had often threatened to break her had actually hardened her. My Jenny is a woman of resolve and determination. A fierce protector. A warrior princess. Like her Aztec warrior ancestors, she has that ancient Central American beauty: Obsidian dark eyes that sparkle against tawny skin. Long dark lashes and heavy eyebrows that I love as much as she loathes. Her face is framed by shoulder-length, lustrous, dark hair that she ties back in a ponytail at work but wears loose when we're together. She has full lips and a mouth that can curse like a soldier, laugh until she falls over, or express love in two languages with an accent that I find both erotic and exotic.

Resilient and smart as my Jenny is – a survivor- she has one weak spot. Christie is her Kryptonite. Nothing can cut through Jenny's armor like her daughter's pain. Jenny would move mountains to make Christie happy. She would gladly give up her life to save the little girl. I'm certain that there is nothing Jenny wouldn't sacrifice -including me- and nothing she wouldn't do to keep Christie safe. Standing in the slush in the middle of that parking lot, holding my Jenny close, I was certain that she had a plan to protect Christie from her father.

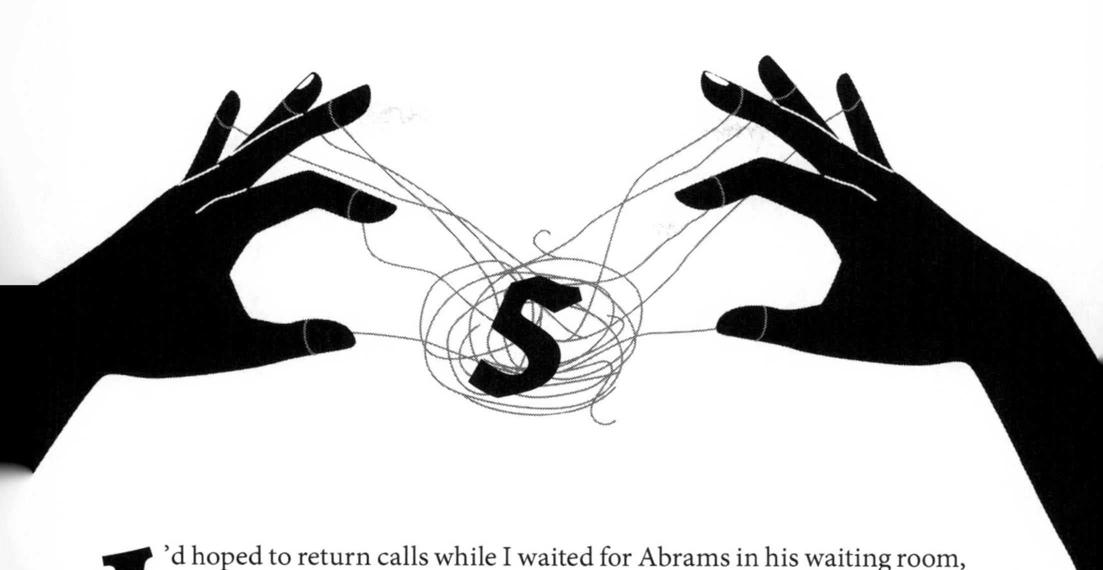

I'd hoped to return calls while I waited for Abrams in his waiting room, but I had no signal. No bars. That was weird.

This would be our sixth meeting. The handful of interviews since we'd first met had taught me a lot about the man's background. He was the middle of three sons raised by middle-class parents in middle America. He recalled family camping trips and ski vacations. His father was harsh and often absent. His mother was passive and overindulgent. Home was an active, noisy place when his father was away and just the opposite when his father was home. Quiet and tense. Bottled up.

Abrams talked about high school girlfriends and basketball tryouts and his father beating his mother with a rake in the same dry monotone. It was almost as if getting him to open up about his emotions once had filled his quota. Since then, he'd retreated from that one colorful moment of tears and transparency into safer, muted tones of gray guardedness. I called him on this more than once. At one point, for example, I interrupted him to ask what it was like to see his father shove his mother through a screen door. He was ten or eleven at the time. I went back and listened to that part of the recording three times the next day trying to understand his response.

"We were up in the Wisconsin Dells. Have you ever been there, Ted? About midway up the state. Ancient pines touch the sky. Untouched rivers and lakes surrounded by high bluffs. Deer and bear and lots of raccoons. Eagles used to nest there. It's all commercial now, of course. Trailer parks and golf courses and noisy party boats.

"We rented a log cabin on a lake one summer. The five of us. Just a kitchen and two bedrooms about thirty feet from the water. Closer than here." He gestured out the back window where the lake had begun to defrost. "There was a shaky wooden dock and an old rowboat. I remember the water was icy cold and silent and clear all the way to the bottom. Huge pine trees everywhere you looked.

"I loved fishing when I was a kid. Probably because my dad loved fishing. He'd come back from a day on the water with a boat full of empty beer cans and a stringer of walleye and muskie. Tremendous freshwater fighting fish. My mom would clean them and fry them for dinner. Nothing like it. He never took me or my brothers out in the boat, so I sat on the end of that shaky dock with my fishing rod and a Styrofoam cup filled with dirt and worms trying to catch a big one. I spent hours and hours at it. My brothers would tease me. They'd try to get me to play football or go swimming and when I refused, they'd skip rocks around my bobber to scare away the fish."

"I remember sitting on the end of that dock one morning. My mom and dad came outside. I guess they were talking. Then they were arguing. My father swore and threw a coffee mug on the ground. The cup shattered. My mother bent to pick up the pieces and he pushed her away, back toward the cabin. I guess she lost her balance. I watched her fall backwards through the screen door. My dad laughed and was halfway up the slope behind the cabin on his way to the car before I got to her. The door was broken, and my mother was crying."

Conversation normally has peaks and valleys. Tone goes up to create tension, then falls with resolution. Emotion can exaggerate the peaks into Everests and the valleys into canyons, turning an interesting story into an amusement park ride. Abrams' account of his father pushing his mother through their summer cabin door was like driving a golfcart across the Utah salt flats. An uninterrupted monotone desert as far as the ear could hear. I heard no pleasure in his voice recounting the beauty of nature, no fear or horror or rage recounting his father's violence, and no sympathy for his mother's pain. I don't recall a tear in his eyes or a clenched fist as he spoke. There was always that shaken-soda gritted-teeth guarded pressure about him, but he never popped.

Abrams had talked at length about his education. He graduated high school *magna cum laude* but wasn't valedictorian. He earned a master's degree at Notre Dame but "only" graduated fourth in his class. He got his Ph.D. *summa cum laude* at Michigan -high honors but not highest honors- because, he said, his professors didn't understand his dissertation on projective identification.

Neither did I. When I asked, he went silent, shook his head side-to-side ever so slightly and stared off over my shoulder. His body language reeked of condescension.

"Do you really want to spend time on this, Ted?" He asked. I did. I needed to understand how he thought and what he cared about. This was a subject that he'd committed years to studying.

"Everyone has parts of themselves that they don't like and can't accept," he began. If you don't like your nose or your ears, you might get plastic surgery. If you don't like parts of your personality or particular feelings or behaviors or beliefs, you can try to change them or you can try to bury them in denial for a while, but that only goes so far. When all else fails, some people cast the forbidden and rejected psychological parts of themselves -the unacceptable fear and shame and rage- onto other people the same way that primitive tribes cast their collective sins onto an animal and then sacrifice that animal to their primitive gods."

"Scapegoating," I offered. Proud of myself for keeping up.

"Yes, but this is much more personal. It's not a tribe collectively renouncing its evils, or a lawyer blaming his paralegal or a boss blaming his secretary and then firing her. Projective identification occurs in intimate relationships. It's what happens when a man wants to cheat on his wife and, finding that urge unacceptable, blames his wife for cheating on him.

"It's what happens when a mother can't fight her urge to shoplift but when the police come knocking, she blames her daughter for the deed. And it's what happens in conflicted families when one parent despises the other but tells their child that it's the other parent that despises him, instead. You can never escape the face in the mirror, but if you make someone else into the bad guy -force someone else to carry your emotional baggage- you can feel better about yourself at least briefly."

"But why would the targeted, second person accept that burden?" I asked.

"You feel angry so you ask your best friend why he's so angry, even though he's not. That's projective identification, right? But your friend isn't angry, so he says he's not."

Abrams tried to clarify: "So you ask him again why he's so angry and your questions get under his skin, so he raises his voice and says that he's not angry…."

"At which point he is angry." I smiled as the idea slowly settled into my brain. "He's angry at you for asking him about being angry, but it seems like you've proven your point. I'd call that gaslighting."

"I spent months studying twenty parents and their kids, Ted. How the adults unconsciously cast their own psychological garbage onto their kids. Their anxieties and body image issues and grief and insecurities. These kids were carrying around their parents' unwanted psychological baggage and didn't even know it. Then the kids grow up carrying these burdens and get diagnosed as if the problem was always theirs which validated the parent who thinks, "See, I knew he had a problem!" The child ends up in all kinds of therapy and medicated and then goes on to have children who carry *their* parents' emotional baggage. On and on. It's classical, intergenerational systemic pathology. The sins of the fathers, so to speak. Unfortunately, my dissertation committee was full of behaviorists who didn't understand relationship dynamics. They saw an angry kid, for example, and they had all kinds of clever ways to treat that kid. Star charts and behavior wheels and operant conditioning. They had no interest in why the child had the problem. They were blind to how the family dynamics fostered and sustained it. Done. End of lecture."

Abrams was fascinating. Brilliant and insightful at least into other people's motives and relationships. He told me stories about graduate school studies and research that he'd done and how he first got involved with the media. A colleague came down with strep the night before an interview on a cable station. Would Sam step in? He did. He was charming and on point. One thing led to another and soon enough he was laughing with Oprah and jousting with Whoppee on *The View* and pontificating about parenting on *Fox News*. Before he knew it, he was travelling and speaking and promoting the first of several best-selling books, a volume titled, "Save the Man in the Mirror First."

All of this was gold, but my forty-five-minute hours passed far too quickly, and my July 4 deadline was racing toward me. I recognized that I needed to hold the reins of our conversations tighter if I wanted to get to more current and relevant events. The breakdown of his relationship with Suki. Abrams' understanding of Micah's experience as the family disintegrated. I needed to know much more about the incidents that prompted Abrams to involve Child Protective Services and the court battle that he had waged for custody and why those things had failed.

My cell said that it was one o'clock exactly.

The inner office door opened as if Abrams had read my mind. He stepped forward to greet me. We shook hands and shared a pleasant, empty word of greeting -something about Mother's Day- and retreated to our usual seats. I set up my phone to record and found a notebook and pen in my backpack.

He was wearing a blue button-down shirt and a rep tie today -fancier than usual- but no jacket.

We began where we always began. Abrams caught my eye and asked with futile hope, "Any news about Micah?"

This had become our ritual. He would ask if I'd heard anything about Micah. I'd say no. He'd lean back in his desk chair and wait for my questions. Today would be different.

"Maybe," I said.

He sat forward at his desk, obviously startled that I'd changed our script, hands clenched in front of him. His next question was obvious in his posture and his unblinking, intense gaze long before he spoke.

"What news?"

"Hold on, Sam." My hands were up, patting the air in front of me as if to say *whoa! Slow down!* "I don't have anything solid. I have not seen Micah or heard anything specific about him."

"Then why....?" The sudden flush began to drain out of his face. It was like watching the man wilt.

"I hope to go down to MPH next Monday. I'm going to try to see Micah. And talk to his doctors."

Abrams looked away, defeated yet again. He leaned his head back and spoke toward the ceiling, as if reciting lines he'd memorized. "The Minnesota Psychiatric Hospital. MPH. I know it all too well, Ted. I'm a shrink, remember? It's a miserable place full of violent, unpredictable, selfish people. And that's just the staff. I can't believe that Micah is there. You got my hopes up for a moment. They won't let you see him." He sat forward and met my eyes. "You know that, right? They will not let you see him."

"I'm not so sure, Sam. I've emailed the medical director's secretary on Micah's pod. Dr. Chatterjee. Do you know her?"

"No. Never heard of her. I'd be surprised if she knows anything at all. Psychiatrists at MPH either …" he counted off on his fingers "… one: are trained in non-English-speaking countries and come here to learn the language, not help the patients; two: become overwhelmed and quit in their first year; Three: are injured by the patients and then quit; or four: commit suicide themselves. I know of two staff suicides in the last eighteen months. About five years ago the hospital went through a complete purge. An overhaul. The governor was involved. I think someone told him that the people running the state psychiatric hospital ought to know something about psychiatry. It was an idea way ahead of its time."

"2017," I recalled. "I read about that last night online. What makes you think that I can't see Micah?"

"I'm surprised Dr. Chatterjee even agreed to talk to you. She probably has a hundred and fifty inpatients to care for and twice that many that she follows outpatient. Did you ever see that famous episode of "*I Love Lucy*" where Lucy is putting chocolates in wrappers on a conveyor belt? It's like that at MPH. How could she have time? And even if she could make time, Micah's care is confidential. Protected by HIPAA."

"That's why I brought these forms today." I laid a pair of eight-by-ten pages imprinted with the MPH logo on his desk. Each page was covered by bullet points written in 10-point font and fill-in boxes calling for dates and names and signatures.

Abrams dismissed the forms without even looking at them.

"Nope. Sorry, Ted. Good try but I can't consent for you to see Micah."

It was my turn to be startled.

"I'm confused," I said, trying to manage my emotions.

I was frustrated. Mad even. We'd come this far and now he was he putting up roadblocks? He was so worried about his son, but he wouldn't give me permission to go see him?

"I thought that your entire reason for talking to me is to reach Micah. Here I have a chance, and you're refusing to cooperate?"

Abrams waited a beat for my tantrum to subside.

"Calm down." He said it with quiet condescension, like my aggravation was an immature overreaction not even worth his time. Like I was an ant in his path that he could just as easily squash. His tone said that he and he alone could see the larger picture, that he was never bothered by such trivial and mundane upsets, and that I needed to do as he says.

I took a deep breath and waited for him to continue.

"Of course, I want you to see Micah. If it was so easy to talk to Micah, I'd be there every day. We are here only because of him, Ted. Do you think I enjoy excavating my past to you three times a week? This isn't exactly therapy for me. Yes, I can sign those pages, but they'll do no good. Only Micah's legal guardian can grant consent for you to see him. You forgot that I am no longer Micah's legal guardian. My parental rights have been suspended pending trial in September. And his other parent is dead."

"Then who ....?" I tried to lean back in my chair. It didn't budge and the effort hurt my upper back. The chair was enormously heavy.

I'd been so impressed with myself, thinking that I was a step ahead of the process by printing out the MPH consent forms off their website.

"I don't know who, but I do know why. Micah's in the state's custody pending the outcome of this trial. The state must have appointed him a guardian or an advocate. Someone who's supposed to be keeping current with his care and making decisions for him and about him. Hopefully a mental health professional, but probably a bureaucrat. That person must be seeing him at MPH regularly and could allow you to talk to him. In theory. Ask the psychiatrist at MPH. Chatterjee, you said? She should know who to talk to."

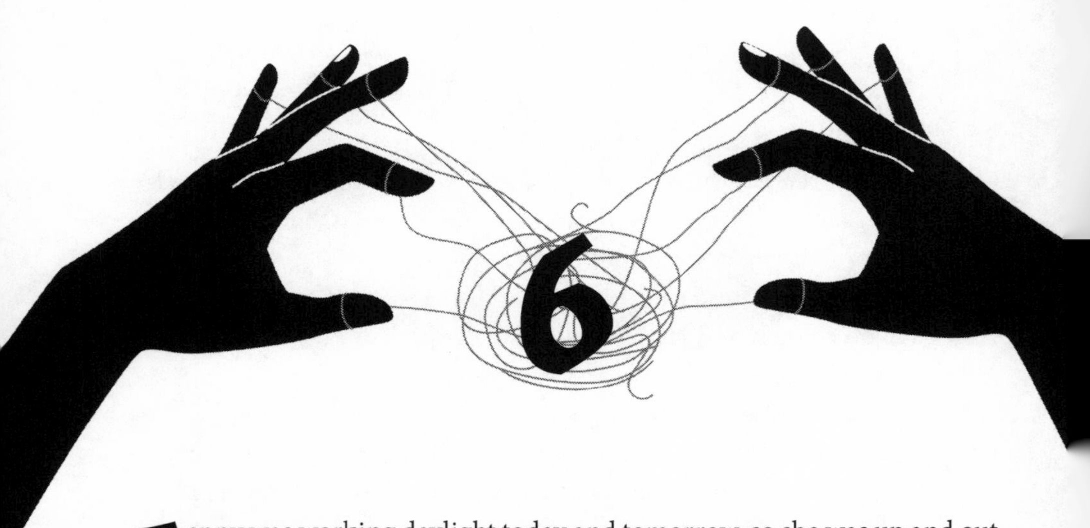

6

Jenny was working daylight today and tomorrow, so she was up and out early. I rolled over when I heard her leave the house, got vertical reluctantly, soaked under a hot shower as long as the water heater cooperated, and dressed quickly. Habit insisted that I pull on my favorite jeans and a sweater -my usual attire- but today called for business casual. Slacks and a button-down shirt. I debated adding a tie for about three seconds mostly so that I could tell Jenny later that I had considered it. I settled instead for a navy blue sportscoat, gold buttons and all.

When I looked in the mirror, I saw Sam Abram's looking back.

I was wearing his uniform.

Daylight savings was still a week away, but the early dawn gloom and birdsong promised sunshine and warmer weather ahead. The snowpack was slowly beginning to drip-drip away, exposing roofs and lawns that hadn't been seen since October.

I was on Christie duty this morning. That meant a rousing game of Round-it.

Don't bother Googling the name. Round-it is not commercially available. It's the result of a collaboration between Christie, Jenny, and Dr. David Noyes, Christie's therapist. Noyes is a two-hundred-and-fifty-pound man with unkempt brown hair and a shaggy gray beard. A sloppy Santa. He makes me look like a fashion icon. But what he lacks in haute couture and personal hygiene he makes up for in warmth and wisdom. He's the loving grandfather everybody secretly wishes for. We call him the child-whisperer. I've seen the big man slide down off his couch to play with Christie on the floor of his office and then get back to his feet again with the grace of a gymnast holding Christie's rapt attention all the while. The man draws hysterical cartoons about kids' feelings, and make the worst/best puns I've ever heard -why do you feel like you need to pee when other people need to pee? Pee-er pressure! Noyes juggles Beanie Babies like a circus clown and is unbeatable at Connect4. He claims that he earned his Ph.D. at the famous Milton Bradley University.

Jenny found Noyes almost a year ago when Christie first began to complain about spending time with Voldemort. The fact that his office is here in Shakopee was good luck. Christie loves him so we rely on him to keep us on top of how Christie manages these stresses and for tips about managing her at home.

About six months ago, Jenny and I asked Dr. Noyes for help with Christie's morning routine. She'd begun hiding under her blankets, making excuses, and tantruming about getting up and going to school. Her teachers had no idea why this was happening. Yes, first grade was a big transition, but Christie seemed fine at school. Our best guess was that separating from Jenny had become a trigger for the little girl in light of her growing resistance going with her father every other weekend.

Noyes spent a couple of weeks talking to Christie about it and had us keep notes about which mornings were hardest and what seemed to help. He then invited Jenny and me to join him and Christie on the floor of his office in front of a large piece of cardboard. Scissors, tape, and pipe cleaners were scattered about.

"I think we need to invent a game," the doctor had said.

"Christie: I know that you don't like getting up and going to school in the morning. But silly me! I've only just realized recently that you probably CAN'T get up and get dressed and eat breakfast on your own. You don't even know how! Is that right?"

Christie was sitting quietly with her arms wrapped around her legs and her knees drawn up to her chin smack up against Jenny's side. She heard the challenge in Noyes' comment and took the bait.

"I can so!"

"Oh yeah?" Noyes responded while Jenny and I sat by watching magic happen, "Well then help me understand please. What's the first thing you have to do when you wake up?"

"Open my eyes."

"Well, you definitely got that one right. How 'bout after that?"

Step by step, Noyes coaxed Christie into defining the morning routine. Jenny and I offered gentle suggestions and reminders now and again. Out of bed. Pajamas in the hamper. Use the potty. Wash her hands. Get dressed. Noyes used markers to create a segmented curving path on the cardboard, like the concrete squares that make up a winding sidewalk. Each square contained a tiny icon. A toilet. A toothbrush. A shirt. Socks. Shoes. A cereal bowl. A backpack. Fifteen minutes later we had a game board like *Chutes and Ladders* or *Candy Land*, but different. Noyes had us then twist and knot red and yellow and white pipe cleaners to create tiny figures. The pieces that would move across the board.

Round-It was born.

The board has ever since resided on a small table in our front hall. When we play, Christie moves her little pipe cleaner person named Pippy from one square to the next as she -the real, live child- accomplishes her chores. Potty. Socks. Breakfast dishes in the sink. Backpack. And she's scrupulous about it. Pippy must never move to a square that Christie has not genuinely completed. Period.

I had once suggested that Pippy could jump over the laundry-in-the-basket square because we were late, and Christie became indignant. "No Teddy," she insisted. "Pippy has to do every single square to get round it!" She put her dirty clothes where they belonged, moved Pippy to the last square, and announced that NOW we could go.

We were late that morning, but who could complain?

Jenny and I learned from Dr. David's gentle challenges. We got in the habit of wondering out loud to one another whether Christie had remembered socks one day or brushing her teeth another.

"Jenn, I don't think Christie is going to remember to wash her hands today, do you?"

"You're right, Teddy Bear. She's so forgetful!"

"I am not 'getful!" she protested as she ran the water in the sink.

"No way, Christie-boo! I do not believe that you can eat your cereal AND get your bowl and spoon in the sink on your own!" She did. She gloated like she'd won gold at the Olympics as she disproved our manipulative taunts, and we laughed with her.

Pippy the pipe cleaner moved one square forward.

Recently, Jenny divided the "Shirt" square on the Round-it board in two with Christie's permission, adding a new "bracelet?" square to the sequence complete with a drawing of a yellow band with a bright red stone. She was really focused on making sure that Christie wore the newly gifted jewelry everywhere to help her feel connected. Any time Christie missed her mom, the bracelet was supposed to make her feel close.

Christie took the additional step in Round-it as a challenge. She was predictably gleeful about proving us nay-sayers wrong.

"I bet you forgot your bracelet!"

"No way! I've got it. Mommy told me to never take it off."

"Good work, sweetie." Christie moved Pippy-the-pipe cleaner another square forward.

This morning Christie made it to the front door in her favorite pink overalls with her boots on the correct feet, her Frozen backpack zipped shut, and her coat zipped at 7:39. She asked me to do a ponytail like mommy wears at work. No problem. Thirty seconds later I cupped a hand around my ear dramatically as if listening carefully. I asked Christie to do the same. "Do you hear that, Christie-pie?" I told her that I could hear the audience (invisible but ever present when we played Round-it) cheering today's successes with wild hoots and hollers.

"I think I hear them chanting 'Christie for President!'"

"No silly Teddy. I don't want to be president! I want to be an astronaut ballerina!"

I don't pray and I don't go to church, but I routinely thank God for Christie's innocence and for Noyes' creativity.

Out the front door. In the car. Ten minutes to school. Five minutes in the drop-off line talking about how much Christie wants a dog. Right on time Ms. Merganser, Christie's first grade teacher, opened the back door of the Jeep, released Christie from her booster seat, wished me a good day by name, and slammed the door shut. I heard Christie yell back, "Bye Teddy Bear!"

It was still a bit before eight. I hoped to get to MPH by nine to interview Dr. Chatterjee, then reverse direction and make the ninety-minute drive to see Abrams in Chanhassen at one. It was an ambitious plan, but I was up for it. I could hear the audience cheering me on.

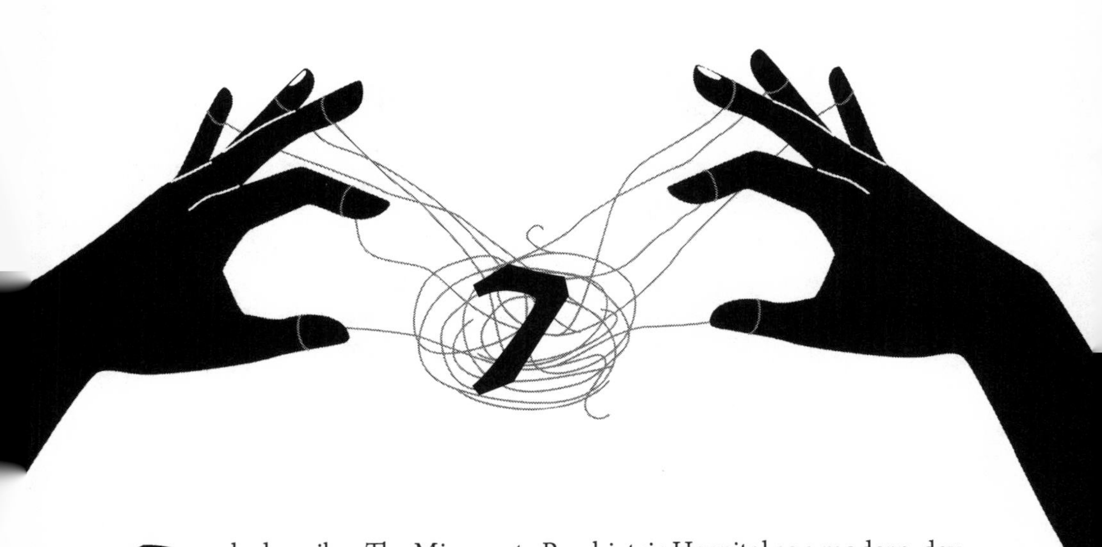

7

Google describes The Minnesota Psychiatric Hospital as a modern-day Snake Pit. Or it had been, I learned, until about 2017 when the state government recognized it for the liability that it had become. MPH had lost its national accreditation and was being taken apart one malpractice suit at a time by hungry lawyers, damaged former patients, and their survivors. Dozens of civil and criminal complaints about MPH clogged the courts and stained the state's name by association. I'd read about children left in restraints for days. Staff physically and sexually abusing patients, suicides among both patients and staff, at least one homicide, and teenage inpatients becoming pregnant. The hostage situation in 2014 that ended in five deaths was the last straw. The governor fired the Dean and replaced two-thirds of the staff. Technology from the nineteen-fifties was torn out (some sold as antiques to collectors) and replaced with NASA quality twenty-first century devices. The wards were disinfected, redesigned, and redecorated. Ghosts were exorcised, lobotomy tools were retired, and strait jackets were burned. Two pods were gutted entirely to create a magnificent two-story marble-inlaid entrance foyer and museum. The grounds were replanted. More than a simple face lift, the state made a real multi-million-dollar effort to turn MPH into a cutting edge forensic mental health treatment center.

Or so the publicity bragged.

I hoped that the bragging was accurate for Micah's sake. As far as I could tell, he'd been escorted bloody and unresponsive out of the garage where he'd been found hiding, evaluated under guard at Twin Cities General

Hospital, declared physically fit but emotionally absent, and transferred to MPH. That was almost a year ago.

MPH is most of an hour south of Shakopee off route 169.

The late winter sun glared in my side window. The divided four-lane rolls through fields and trees and past quite a number of the state's famous ten thousand lakes. Traffic surged around me, vehicles jumping on and off the highway between exits. I stayed in the left lane to avoid the constant merges back and forth and clicked on cruise control. I had my phone on the dashboard with the recorder app ready to go but found that I couldn't organize my thoughts. Where usually I'm able to compartmentalize my feelings, somehow Jenny and Christie and Abrams and Micah and home and work and writing were all blurring together. I wrote off the unfamiliar emotional mélange as fatigue and overwork, buzzed down my window just enough to enjoy a cool, fresh breeze, turned up the radio, and tuned out.

8

MPH impressed me as soon as I left the highway. Half a dozen large and attractive, sand-colored buildings are spread across a sprawling campus like an archipelago set in a sea of asphalt, concrete, and topiary. The roads and intersecting walkways were pristine. No snow. No ice. No litter. And no people. Black topped and freshly painted parking lots abutted each building, most only half-full. Shrubbery and scattered trees and an occasional picnic table punctuated the open spaces. I glimpsed a statute that seemed to depict a mother and child walking hand-in-hand. I felt like I was approaching a well-to-do and recently vacated college campus. There were no coeds carrying books or potheads throwing frisbees or tweedy professors hurrying to class. There were certainly no psychotic ax murderers or delusional serial rapists or multiple personality arsonists as far as I could see. But vacated wasn't the right word exactly. Although there was no one about, the place had an aura of intensity that suggested vigilance. Even paranoia.

It reminded me of Sam Abrams. Watchful and intense.

Both MPH and the psychologist are manicured on the outside but barely contain the deep, boiling pressures that simmer on the inside.

I stopped at a shiny new guard booth and buzzed my window down. Cameras captured both my face and my license plate. A buxom, blonde, and blue-eyed attendant stepped out to greet me with a smile full of perfect white teeth. She wore a laminated ID that said "Barbie" on a lanyard around her neck.

Surely Mattel modelled the doll after this woman.

Parking Attendant Barbie scanned my driver's license and finger-printed me on a handheld tablet. No ink. No mess. A moment later a plastic ID tag emerged from the device imprinted with my name and face, the letters B12 in large boldface, and a maze-like QR code. Barbie snapped the ID on a red lanyard and told me to wear it at all times while on campus. The alphanumeric B12 was my preselected parking place in front of the main hospital building. The QR code would open the doors that I needed to open to get to the Adolescent Offenders Pod and only those doors, no others. She offered me another toothpaste commercial smile, touched the screen to raise the zebra-striped wooden traffic arm, and wished me a good day. I drove slowly ahead.

Window down, the chilly air was bracing. Invigorating. I was struck by the quiet as I went in search of B12 and the hospital's main entrance. Except for the distant doppler whine of eighteen wheelers passing on the highway and the gurgle of snowmelt streaming downhill into storm drains, the whine of my tires on brand new blacktop was the only sound I could hear. No laughing, no crying, no yelling, and no screaming. The quiet was oddly peaceful and unnerving all at once.

I found B12 just two spaces over from the head of the walkway that led to the front door of the main building. I was about ten minutes behind schedule, but I took a moment to gather my thoughts before I left the comfort and safety of my car. How would I introduce myself to Chatterjee? What 'open sesame' magic words would get me information about Micah? Should I have greased the skids by bringing the psychiatrist coffee or donuts or a bottle of scotch? I had no idea what protocols applied, how I might be treated, or whether the trip might be a total waste of time.

I'd learned as much as I could about MPH online. I was facing a long, attractive two-story building punctuated by pairs of large windows under a flat roof. This north-south spine of the structure ran more than a hundred yards. Three shorter wings protruded east-west off this spine -one straight ahead of me at the middle, and one at each end- giving the building a footprint that resembled two capital Es laid down back-to-back circumscribed by sidewalks, gardens, and sitting areas.

The spine of the building contains professional and administrative offices, billing, insurance, and public relations services. The three wings that protrude front and back contain the patient *pods* -not wards or units. These are designated by cardinal direction and floor. Male violent offenders are housed in Northwest Two, the second story of the wing to my far left. Female violent offenders are housed as far from their male counterparts as possible in Southeast One, the back of the first story wing to my far right. My destination, the Adolescent Offenders Pod occupies Center East One, the first floor of the center wing on the far side of the building.

Directly ahead of me was Center-West. A big part of the 2017 overhaul consolidated Center-West One and Two to create a two-story grand entrance hall that now served as both visitor reception and an informal museum of psychiatric care. I took the three stone steps up to the main entrance in a leap and almost wiped out on a patch of ice. Not a good start. Worse still, I found all four of the main doors locked. Eight-foot-high heavy glass panels wrapped up in bronze tubing that served as handles. Rattling them in their frames didn't help.

Knocking summoned no one.

Convex optical scanners were set in the wall beside each door like dark red and watchful eyes. Just as my new friend Barbie had promised, my ID tag made the nearest door buzz open. Somewhere a computer logged my entrance time and place.

The Center-West entrance hall was indeed grand and museum-like. The stone and glass reception desk at center was unoccupied, but a sign welcomed me to take any of a dozen or more shiny pamphlets imprinted with the MPH logo. My loafers echoed across marble floors as I fast-walked through the deserted, silent space. Tasteful and benign artwork covered the walls. Plexiglas cases contained odd-looking contortions of metal tubes and wires that I had no time to stop and study. Blue and deep-purple upholstered couches and chairs arranged in clusters atop attractive area rugs were discreetly positioned so that anxious family members could gather before visits and prop one another up afterwards. A tremendous Calder mobile filled the center of the grand space above me. An orrery of huge, colorful geometries balanced on delicate threads slowly orbited overhead.

Signs directed visitors toward the north pods to the left and the south pods to the right. The door straight ahead was marked Center-East One and in smaller letters read, "Adolescent Offender Pod."

Sometimes I'm a quick learner. I didn't even try this handle. Instead, I held my ID tag up to the electric eye set in the wall at chest height. The door buzzed open. I stepped out of the cold, cavernous, and echoing grand foyer into a short cream-on-white carpeted hallway under a low-hung acoustic ceiling. The door that I'd just entered buzzed shut behind me. A second closed door faced me just twenty feet ahead. I was in a sally port, an attractive version of the entry cage that helps keep murderers from escaping from prisons. This one was decorated tastefully. Framed documents hung on the wall to my right spelled out the rules and rights that must be respected on the pod. I didn't pause to read them. The wall to my left was inset with a dozen mailbox-sized lockers, each with a now-familiar convex optical scanner where there should have been a handle.

Both the door that I had entered through and the door ahead of me were locked. I was trapped.

Out of nowhere and everywhere all at once, a pleasant female voice said in a Jamaican accent, "How can I help you?"

I spoke toward the camera in the ceiling ahead of me. "Yes. Hi. I'm Ted Bennett. Dr. Chatterjee is expecting me?"

"Yes Mr. Bernette. You are expected."

Bernette? The hidden speakers were perfectly clear. I started to say my name again, intending to emphasize BEN-ette but the Jamaican woman spoke first. "Please place your cell phone and sharps in one of the lockers and use your ID to lock it. Your things will be secure while you're on the pod and you can retrieve them when you leave. Dr. Chatterjee will be right with you."

I held my ID tag in front of the closest locker. A metal door the size of a glove box buzzed open exposing a white plastic drawer within. I dumped my phone and wallet and keys inside, patted my pockets down the way TSA did at the airport and found no strays. I closed the locker and locked it using my ID.

Pretty cool tech, I thought.

The far door buzzed and then was pulled open by a short, squat Indian woman in a colorful sari wearing huge, thick, black-framed glasses. I approached and she stepped aside and made no effort to greet me. I nodded to her politely and asked, "Dr. Chatterjee?"

"We've been waiting for you a long time, Mr. Bernette. Please come."

Bernette again. A long time? I was maybe fifteen minutes late.

"I'm very sorry, doctor. MPH is a bit off the beaten path." But she was already several steps ahead of me.

"Of course. Of course." She called over her shoulder, skirts flying. "I have a group in five minutes."

The pod was all blonde wood, cream colors, and chaos. Young people of both genders littered the space in ratty and torn street clothes. A couple was necking on a couch. An obviously obese girl was seated cross legged on the floor quietly pulling out her hair. Potted greenery stood in corners, contrasting the pod's muted whites and tans and creams and -in one corner-barely concealed a child who was vaping. Terra cotta floors were interrupted by carpeted islands littered with shredded glossy magazines.

The place was a Cuckoo's Nest for kids.

Half a dozen adults poked at keyboards and tablets behind glass in a nursing station to my left. The teens' various groping, self-destructive, and illicit acts must be plainly visible to all of them, and yet no one even looked up. Some wore blue scrubs. Most wore street clothes like Chatterjee. None of them noticed my arrival. Everyone appeared to be intentionally oblivious to what the kids were doing immediately in front of them.

Two long hallways opened ahead. One on my left was marked "HE/HIM/HIS." The one on my right was supposed to read "SHE/HER/HERS." Someone had corrected it in thick, black Sharpie to read, "I/ME/MINE." I followed Chatterjee toward the hall on the left, past a child of indeterminate gender with bright red dreadlocks and a nose ring. Our eyes met briefly and he/she/they said plainly, "What are you looking at, cocksucker?"

I looked away and kept walking.

The hall was lined with open doors. I heard bits of conversation, crying, pleading voices, the high-tech sounds of a video game, and the twangs of an aspiring guitarist as we walked. A blast of 90-decibel profanity erupted just ahead. Chatterjee changed course toward the explosion abruptly, her skirts windswept by her motion. I nearly collided with her. She knocked on an open door. I noticed a towel jammed in the hinges keeping the door ajar. Chatterjee entered and screamed over the noise, "Hector! I like Wu-Tang too but turn it way down now or use headphones!"

A heavy, dark-skinned Hispanic youth was seated on his floor amidst wrinkled and soiled clothes. His left hand was hidden inside a frayed plaster cast decorated with a million colors and shapes and scribbles. The room or the child or both smelled unwashed. He looked up at the sudden intrusion and screamed "Fuck off shrink lady!" at the doctor.

Chatterjee complied, apparently unphased by the profanity. She called back to me over the receding din, "This way Mr. Bernette. Please. Time is short." I jogged three steps to catch up to her just as she turned left into another room. An identical thick, blond wood door stood ajar with a white towel jammed in the hinges.

I expected a work-cluttered office piled deep with paper files and computer monitors, stained coffee mugs, and bookshelves filled with medical texts with titles I couldn't understand. Or perhaps a conference room done in light oak and tan laminates with a well-used white board on the wall, a long blonde table, and matching chairs. One way or the other, I thought Chatterjee would ensconce herself in a sturdy chair and parry my poorly prepared questions about Micah and then casually refute my deeply flawed arguments about why I needed to see him while she simultaneously reviewed emails and opened paper correspondence.

Instead, I discovered that we'd entered another patient's room. The space was about the same proportions of a shoe box, and not much larger. It was ripe with fetid smells. Body odor and urine and spoiled food. A tall, narrow window looked out on a manicured yard but was obviously permanently sealed and undoubtedly shatterproof. A wooden wardrobe stood open at left spewing clothes like a tongue from an open mouth. An unmade bed dominated the space, sheets and blankets stained and knotted around the jean-clad bottom of a pale and gaunt youth. Glasses. Big nose. Pale, acne-pocked skin. His dark hair was knotted and hung over his face. He was perched on the forward edge of the bed. His bright yellow high tops were slowly swinging back and forth to no particular rhythm and devoid of laces. His hands were in his lap, manipulating a shiny, spinning plastic toy.

The ruckus on the pod -and Hector's choice of rap music in particular-was somewhat muted inside the room.

"Micah?" Chatterjee asked. Getting no response, she barked, "Micah! Please say hello to Mr. Bernette. Mr. Bernette is with the state."

Micah? I was speechless and confused. My thoughts raced. The general condition of this pediatric snake pit was terribly upsetting. Chatterjee's rushed and neglectful attitude seemed to condone the chaos. On top of that it seemed that my poorly thought-out wish had abruptly been granted. Here was Micah Abrams in the flesh. I suppose if a good Samaritan had approached me in a public place and handed me a bundle of cash that he thought that I'd lost -a bundle of cash that I knew nothing about whatsoever- I might have been caught similarly off guard. On the one hand, I'd been given exactly the gift that I'd hoped for. On the other hand, the gift wasn't mine to accept.

Chatterjee thought I was someone named Bernette associated with the state and that I was entitled to speak to Micah who, by all accounts, could only blather nonsense. Should I take advantage of this masquerade and get my story, or should I try to correct the doctor and risk losing this amazing opportunity? I hadn't lied to anyone. My name was stamped plainly on the ID tag that hung around my neck.

Shouldn't I be taking notes? *Damn!* My phone was locked away in that high tech locker in the front hall. I wanted pictures and audio. Focus, Ted! I cautioned myself. Memorize every detail.

All that and more flashed through my awareness in the second after the psychiatrist had addressed the boy. Before I could decide what to do, even while my mouth still hung wide open, the young man looked up. His clear blue eyes were partially obscured behind smudged and scratched plastic lenses. Color filled his pale cheeks. His brow became furrowed, and his mouth turned down in an angry sneer. He dropped the toy that he'd been manipulating on the twisted and soiled hill of blankets at his side and spoke. His voice was surprisingly firm and clear: "Get me the fuck out of here."

Micah Abrams was not catatonic.

He was furious.

Chatterjee was once again unscathed. I began to suspect that her attitude was much more apathy than therapy.

"Okay!" She actually clapped her hands together once lightly as if to applaud her own success in bringing us together. Then I'll leave you two to talk. I've got a million things to do, and group should get started immediately. Micah, you're excused from group of course. Take all the time that you need with Mr. Burnette." She looked at me through thick lenses: "Please email me, Mr. Bernette, and let me know what you want to do." She disappeared in a blur of colorful skirts.

I was alone with the M&M murderer.

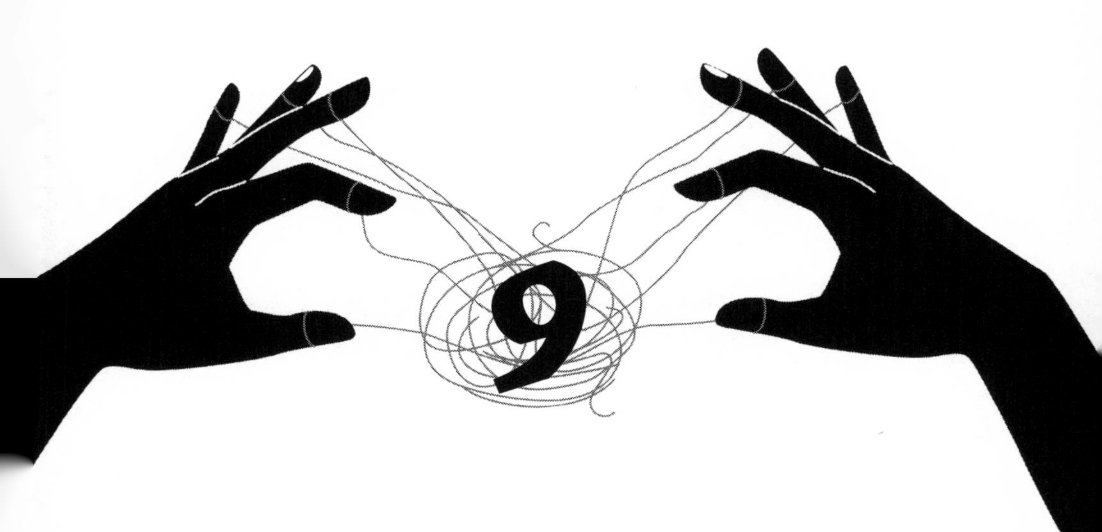

9

I've been with Jenny for almost three years. I've been a part of Christie's life for two. Jenny and I worked hard to keep our relationship a secret from the little girl until we were sure that we were serious. Even then we talked long and hard about how I would fit into their little world. I've been "Ted" or "Teddy Bear" and occasionally "daddy" by happy mistake for about a year and a half now. Jenny and I agree that I am neither parent nor friend. I'm Mommy's boyfriend and the helper Christie comes to when she can't get the eyes to stick in the snowman, when her beloved Piglet can't be found, when she wants to be tossed up to the ceiling and tickled mercilessly, and for everything else when her mom is at work.

There's no doubt that Christie is the sun around which our planets revolve.

The bad news is that Jenny's work at the hospital is almost completely inflexible. LPNs at St. Francis work four-shifts-on and two-shifts off, a schedule that sounds a lot saner in theory than it is in practice. Trying to map it out on a conventional seven-day calendar reminds me of the grade school exercise where the math teacher asks you to try to line up an inch-ruler and a metric-ruler to see if any of the numbers coincide. Take my word for it: they don't.

But it gets worse. Nurses at St Francis also rotate through daylight (seven to three), evening (three to eleven) and graveyard (eleven to seven) shifts in two-day blocks. Confused? It took me about six months to catch on. If Jenny works daylight Monday and Tuesday, then she pulls evenings Wednesday and Thursday, and has Friday and Saturday off (unless she picks up overtime or swaps with a colleague). She goes back Sunday and Monday on graveyard, then works daylight Tuesday and Wednesday. And yes, if you're following along closely, that means that she works a marathon sixteen hours back-to-back once every ten days.

Of course, this schedule wreaks havoc on any sane routine. School. Nine-to-five office hours. Extra-curricular activities. It creates a circadian cacophony, disrupting sleep cycles and diets and exercise regimes, not to mention family rituals like dinner time and kids' bedtimes and our beloved movie nights. Thank God our cable box allows us to record, otherwise we could never keep up with "Mrs. Maisel" and "Gray's Anatomy."

Jenny says that her crazy schedule doesn't bother her. I've discovered that that attitude is most first responders' selfless macho mantra; a refrain often heard from her skilled and devoted but sleep-deprived co-workers. Like them, Jenny naps when she can, sometimes just a half hour at a time, and never complains about exhaustion. What she does complain about, however, is how much her work interferes with her time with Christie and me.

The good news is that I'm a writer. My chosen profession certainly carries no promises of great wealth, but my schedule is generally my own and I am nothing if not the king of flexibility. I learned long ago how to squeeze research and phone calls and emails and writing and edits in at odd hours, often early mornings while Christie is still asleep and Jenny hasn't yet gotten home from an overnight shift, or after Christie's bedtime when Jenn's on graveyard. This means that for the last eighteen months I was almost always available to care for Christie when Jenny was working. I love it. Christie is fun and funny, and we share a lot of interests. I take her to dance and gymnastics and school activities (Christie was Rudolph in the school play and I got to color the little girl's ticklish nose with Jennie's red lipstick), and therapy appointments (where I can usually squeeze a half hour of writing in in the waiting room). I took her to last spring's ballet recital (FYI duct tape repairs torn tutus). I've even done a couple of tense transitions with Voldemort at the Shakopee PD.

What I hadn't anticipated, is how doing this book has suddenly cast parts of my previously accommodating schedule in stone. All of my hard work getting permission to interview Abrams has suddenly locked me into a commitment three afternoons every week plus travel time and traffic and whatever other delays can come up during the forty-mile round trip to and from Chanhassen. I feel like I've taken on a job that I really, really want and resent all at once. The risk is that if stars don't align, I'll be with Abrams and Jenny will be on-shift at the hospital and Christie will be left out in the cold. Maybe literally.

There is no way that I am going to miss my opportunity to interview Dr. Samuel Abrams.

There is no way that I would ever neglect Christie.

Any other divorced parent might be able to ask her ex- to take over childcare in a pinch, and any other ex-husband would gratefully take the opportunity to spend more time with his daughter. Not Jorge. Not that Jenny would ever ask him. He'd claim to be too busy and then turn the request into further evidence that jenny is a bad mother.

So I went old-school. I know that there's probably all kinds of apps I could download to help us organize our private chaos, but I bought a twelve-month paper wall calendar instead. It turned out to be a scroll the size of our refrigerator cross-hatched in blue ink into neat little numbered rows and columns. I borrowed Christie's colored pencils ("How come, Teddy?" "I have some homework to do, sweetie." "You're silly! You don't go to school!") and I tried to plot out the next many weeks of forty-five-minute hours against Jenny's rotating shifts and Christie's school hours.

I wore several pencils down to nubs and created a mountain of pink eraser dust. In the end, mapping my dates with Abrams (green) on top of Jenny's work (red) and our much anticipated but infrequent movie nights (brown) on top of Christie's ballet (orange) and gym classes (yellow) and therapy appointments (purple) and her weekends with her Voldemort (the blackest black I could find) became an exercise in quantum mechanics far beyond my abilities. The wall calendar looked like a weird piece of abstract art that I captioned, "*La Vida Loca*!"

All this is to say that I am painfully aware of the three orbits that make up the Bennett-Villalobos solar system. This is how I know that at the exact moment that Dr. Chatterjee left me face-to-face with a very *not*-catatonic Micah Abrams, Christie was at recess (probably chasing boys through muddy puddles on the playground) and Jenny was on the orthopedics ward at St. Francis (probably taking someone's vitals or changing the dressing on a wound). I also know that if the stars align as they're supposed to, I'll double back to see Abrams up north and Jenny will get off shift just in time to dash across town to collect Christie in the car pool pick-up line after school while I am driving south intent on meeting them at -give me a minute… today is Monday - Tumble Bugs gymnastics in the Shakopee Common and then dinner next door at Magma pizza.

Plain cheese for Christie. Pepperoni and jalapenos for Jenn and me.

NASA couldn't work harder or be more exacting plotting the course of an interstellar rendezvous.

What I couldn't know while I remained at MPH and wouldn't learn until late that night after Christie stopped asking why she'd missed gym class and why we didn't have pizza and after Jenny finally ended her sixth or seventh call of the day with her lawyer, was that a bike messenger was just then waiting patiently in a crowded elevator at St. Francis Hospital for the door to open on the orthopedics ward.

Jenny was working fourth floor ortho BBS. Breaks, braces, and splits. As the elevator containing the messenger and a random assortment of patients and staff rose toward four, she was discharging a seventy-something year old man who had spent the night in room 416. On the Saturday just passed, the foolish fellow had had forgotten his age, ignored the weather, and climbed onto a snowy garage roof to fix a gutter. Snowmelt had been coursing down his kitchen walls and he refused to wait for a Monday repairman. Of course, embracing delusions of youth, the well-intended gentleman had slipped and fallen at least ten feet. He'd landed in snow-crusted bushes but not before breaking his left arm in two places. He now had screws in both his radius and ulna, a heavy white plaster cast notably inscribed "told you so!" by his irate wife, and a promise of divorce if he tried anything similar ever again.

Jenny wheeled her patient into the hall while the wife continued to quietly berate him from behind. An orderly wearing a yellow St. Francis smock was waiting to escort the couple downstairs and out of the hospital.

Jenny turned back to strip and sanitize the room when a male nurse she often worked with flagged her down.

"Jenn, there's someone looking for you up front."

"For me? Is Ted here?" Peter knew Ted from holiday parties and last summer's hospital barbeque. It would be a nice surprise if Ted stopped by, but that would also mean that something had gone wrong with his morning. He was supposed to drive down to the psych hospital today.

"No, it's not Ted. This guy's sexier."

Jenny blushed and punched her friend in the arm. "No way! That's not possible."

Peter rubbed his arm dramatically. "Ah, young love! I remember those days well. Nope, this guy looks like he's in high school and he's wearing Spandex. A bike messenger I think."

Jenny raised a curious eyebrow and thanked Peter for the head's up. "Cover the lady in 19 for me, okay?" She asked. "Get vitals and check her I/Os for Dr. McLeod? I'll just be a sec."

The nursing station was fifty feet down a narrow corridor painted a nauseous light green and around a corner out of sight. Wooden handrails stretched the entire distance on both sides of the hall, hemming in the tight passage. Tech dollies, linen trollies, and med carts were parked helter-skelter outside of rooms making the hallway into an obstacle course. What could you do? The building had outlived its 1950's foundations.

Two doctors in green scrubs were consulting at the front desk. Several nurses in forest green smocks and an occupational therapist named Ye-Jun wearing a white lab coat were updating charts in the more private interior "fishbowl." Bright blue three-ring binders filled with patient notes and lab results and doctors' orders were littered about, more abundant even than mislaid coffee cups. Many lay open either awaiting attention or forgotten by busy staff. Another two-dozen stood at the ready on a two-tiered rolling bookcase that moved in and out of shift-change meetings. Against this background of primary colors, a short and trim young man wearing rainbow Spandex stood out like hunter's orange in a field gone fallow. He carried a bike helmet under one arm and shouldered a backpack over the other.

"I'm Jenny Villalobos." Jenny approached the man and held out a hand in greeting. "I heard you were asking for me?"

"Oh good. Here." He extracted several envelopes from his bag, found the one that he was seeking, and placed it in her open palm. It was an oversize white package with her name printed across the front and no return address. "You've been served."

He turned without another word just in time to slip between a pair of closing elevator doors.

Jenny was dumbstruck and embarrassed in front of her peers and colleagues, aware that everybody present had watched the exchange. Gossip sustains a hospital ward more than bandages and blood. Jenny felt her face and neck flush red. She stuffed the envelope in her smock, reflexively reached back and tightened the clip on her ponytail and retreated around the corner and down the hall to the nurse's lounge.

Peter was there, sipping tepid, stale coffee.

"Nineteen's set, Jenn." He said as she entered. "Another false alarm." He looked up and noticed her colored cheeks and the set of her jaw. "Are you okay? What was the messenger about?"

"I don't know." She sat down at a scarred wooden table and pushed aside someone's forgotten yogurt. She studied the envelope front and back, and then sliced it open with a pink-painted thumbnail. Peter watched her eyes moisten and her hands quake as she read. He joined her at the table, one comforting hand on her forearm.

"What is it honey?"

Jenny passed the papers to him and wiped her eyes.

It took Peter most of a minute to understand the document. As meaning seeped in, he muttered, "Ah shit, Jenny" and then "That bastard! Jorge …."

Jenny corrected him: "Its *OR*-hey. But call him Voldemort. Me and Christie do."

The image of the Harry Potter villain made Peter smirk. "I can see why. Well, Voldemort's a bastard then. Whatever. He filed for custody? He's taking you back to court again."

"Worse," Jenny added. "He got the judge to order an evaluation. Those papers order me to talk to a doctor ….?"

Peter pulled the name off the page: "Myra Sloan, Ph.D."

"… to talk to Dr. Sloan about why Christie needs to stay with me." Anxious tears threatened to overwhelm her, but her internal levees held.

Crying had never helped her in the past. She collected the papers back from her friend, thanked him, wiped a sleeve across her eyes and found her cell phone.

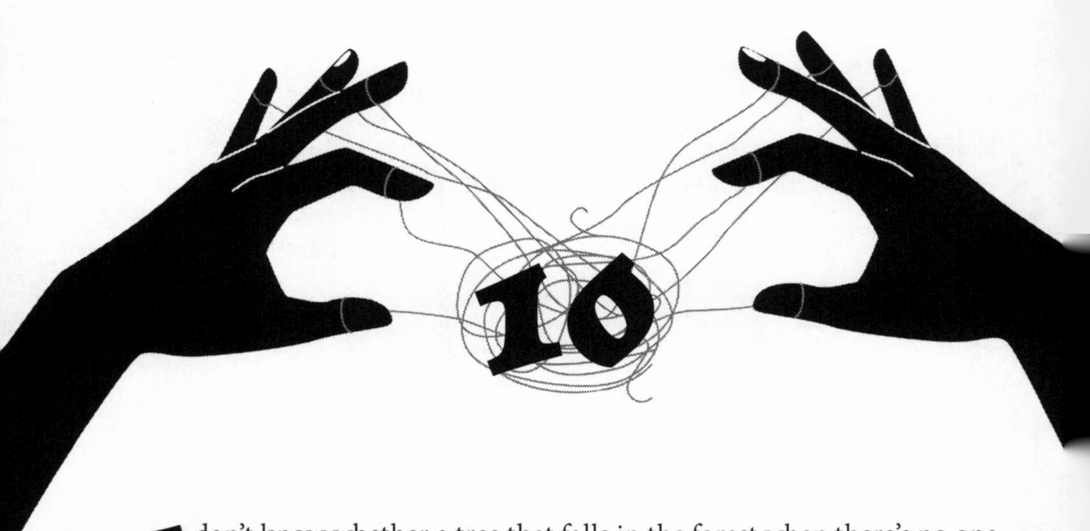

I don't know whether a tree that falls in the forest when there's no one there to hear it makes a sound. I do know, however, that a cell phone that rings in a locker in a closed hallway half-a-hospital away goes to voice mail every time. Mine did exactly eight times in the next hour. I also know that if a loved one can't be reached in an emergency, all kinds of shit can happen. I learned this last pearl by living it.

While Jenny was frantically trying to reach my cell, I was busy yelling Dr. Chatterjee's name over the general tumult on Center-East One. I had hoped to reel the psychiatrist back into Micah's room so that I could disabuse her of the idea that I am the elusive state advocate Bernette and then … what? Get myself removed from the pod and sent back to GO without collecting two hundred dollars? I had a fleeting image of the pretty parking attendant revoking my B12 parking permit, roughly yanking my ID lanyard from around my neck, calling me an imposter, and harshly exiling me from the hospital grounds. Some deeply seated honesty or ethics or boy scout belief that I'd never before recognized insisted that I needed to subject myself to humiliation and inconvenience just so that I could resume begging to return right here to interview the child seated right across from me.

For better or worse, I never got a chance to try. My yelling just added to the general din of the place. Chatterjee was immediately reabsorbed into the melee just beyond Micah's door. It was increasingly clear that the child's father was right: The inmates are running the asylum. Laughter and rude music and curses rushed past the door along with the scent of marijuana.

Had I been magically teleported to Woodstock circa 1969? All moral quandaries and practical matters aside, it felt safer in here with the matricidal maniac than it would have been out there on the pod.

I turned back toward the disheveled, angry, and very not-catatonic kid.

"Micah? Hi … ummm …."

I never stammer. I pride myself on speaking and writing clearly. But here I was tongue-tied like a third grader with stage fright in front of a pimply, smelly, scrawny adolescent who was studying me like a bug under glass. His blue eyes were crystal clear and laser-focused on me.

The nose. The condescending expression. Despite the setting, it was obvious that this was Abrams' son. He was a two-thirds scale, thinner, less worn-down, replica of the psychologist minus the beard.

"Okay. Ummm… You're thirteen, right?"

"What do you care?" he asked, suspicious even of such a banal question.

"Okay, Let's start again." I held out a hand in greeting. He ignored me, occupied by the spinning, whirring toy in his lap.

"My name is Bennet. Not *Bernette.* Call me Ted. I'm a writer. Like books, not newspapers or magazines or anything. I'd like to ask you some questions."

"You're a writer but you're not writing." He didn't even look up as he spoke. "Are you recording us? You know that's illegal, right? I didn't say it was okay and you need my permission. Show me. Give me your phone." Not a question. This was an entitled command. A general making a demand of a private. The CEO directing an intern. Never mind that I'm twice his age, half again his size, and a total stranger. This kid has *huevos,* as Jenny would say. No shame.

"Nope. Sorry. No phone. Not recording." I held up my hands palms out like a suspect held at gunpoint or a magician proving that there is nothing up his sleeves. I couldn't tell if Micah even noticed the gesture, so I kept talking.

"I bet that you know that phones and everything else gets locked up before you're allowed on the pod. My pockets are empty. Any chance you have something I could write with?"

"Maybe. What's it worth to you?"

"Worth …? I don't know kid, what do you want?"

He finally looked up and met my gaze. I couldn't tell if he was gaging my honesty or offended that I'd called him "kid." Those blue eyes again. Piercing. Even from under his greasy locks of overgrown hair.

"I want you to get a message to my dad."

Easy. I saw Abrams three times a week and was due to meet with him in a couple of hours, but Micah couldn't know that. My Spidey sense told me to go slow. Play my cards close to my chest.

I had no idea if playing courier between father and son was somehow illegal or a breach of hospital rules. Certainly, Abrams Senior would be ecstatic to hear anything from Micah. He still believed that the boy was trapped deep within his own psyche, traumatized and unresponsive to all but the most basic commands. I suppose I should have read the ten commandments posted in the front hall. For all I knew, rule number one dictated that "thou shalt not allow inmates to communicate with their parents."

Father and son had been kept apart for most of a year. Who was I to reconnect them?

Would doing so push Micah into another episode of catatonia or worse, into a homicidal rage? Would carrying Micah's note back to Abrams risk undermining an intricately coordinated and carefully balanced mix of therapies and medications conceived by world class experts and implemented by a handpicked team of professionals led by Dr. Chatterjee?

The thought made me chuckle out loud. It was almost as likely as learning that the short, squat Indian woman was an Iron Man triathlete in her spare time.

A shrill, hyena-like soprano voice screamed somewhere on Center-East One and then blossomed into raucous laughter. The sound jolted me back to reality. There was nothing sophisticated or coordinated or even planned going on here. I was visiting bedlam incarnate. Micah was being held hostage in a human zoo.

"Okay," I told the kid. "I can try to get your dad a message. *Try.* No promises. That's the best that I can do. But like I said, I don't have my phone or even a pen. Whatcha' got for writing?"

Micah let himself fall backwards on his bed. His hair created a dark halo on the white sheets around his round face. His tee shirt rode up, exposing a pale concave belly and starkly pronounced ribs. I wondered if they fed him here. He reached above his head toward a small night table without looking, groped around blindly for a moment, then pulled open a shallow drawer. When he sat back up, he had the nub of a green Crayola and a stack of misaligned goldenrod pages marked "Patient Rights Handbook" in large black letters and "Minnesota Psychiatric Hospital 2023" below. The booklet was unbound -staples are potential weapons after all- and only printed on one side. It seemed that the new-and-improved MPH wasn't environmentally conscious. I accepted the crayon with a quiet "thanks," straightened the pile of papers, and scribbled the date on the top of the first blank space I could find. It wasn't exactly Mont Blanc-quality calligraphy on parchment, but it'd do.

"My turn first," I insisted. "Note to dad comes second. Tell me about you."

He was back to the spinner, collecting his thoughts. "What do you want me to say? I'm Micah Abrams. Duh. They call me Mickey Mouse here. Mickey for Micah. That used to be my VR avatar. King M and M, you know? On *EAU.* Do you play?"

Shit! M and M? As in "Mommy Murderer"?

"Play?" I stumbled over the abbreviation, then caught myself. I needed to keep him talking. "VR? EAU? What's that?"

He hung his head and shook it with disdain. His father had given me the same condescending dismissive look when I'd asked questions that he deemed uninformed. To Micah, I was just another ignorant adult hardly worth his time. "VR means virtual reality. I have Horizon 4-DV-2 headsets. You know? Goggles that you wear to be in a three-hundred-and-sixty-degree digital world. Like the Holodeck on Star Trek? You see and hear and feel things that only exist in VR no matter where your body is IRL."

"IRL?"

"In Real Life. Here. Well, not here in the hospital although this is IRL. Anyway, *EAU* is the sickest MMPG there is. You go on quests and battles and behead bad guys and collect gold and weapons and dragons and do shit. Real shit. For credits. I was a king before they locked me up here. Seriously, I was King M and M with a crown and a scepter and everything in the game and I had serfs who did whatever I told them to do. I even could have levelled up to be a god, L25, you know. Then I would have controlled everything."

"Wow! I didn't know I was talking to a king." I offered him a facetious bow and said, "your highness."

I wrote *Horizon. VR game EAU. King. Serfs. Wants to be god.*

"Any way, I'm thirteen but everyone says I'm way smarter than that. Like *waaay* smarter. I'm here because for a while I was kind of wacko out-of-it. I didn't talk or really do anything. I guess I just didn't want to. Like I was in a trance or something. I think a mage or a rune-reader must cast a spell on me. Some of the kids say that I was like in a coma except awake. I don't know. But now they think I'm crazy - Dr. Chat-er-pee told me that she thinks I'm crazy straight out- but I'm not. The problem is that anything I do to show them that I'm not crazy, they say I'm faking it and I should tell them how I really feel."

"Feel about what?"

"I don't know. Nothing. Everything. Like about Hector. He is off the deep end crazy! He's a kid on the pod. That's his rap you can hear out in the hall. Hector has a temper and hits things sometimes. And people. One time he hit me pretty hard so they wanted to know how I felt about that."

"How did you feel?"

"I don't know. Bruised? Nothing I suppose. I just made a plan and that was it."

"A plan?"

"Yeah. No big deal. Like you said, they don't allow sharps or lighters or stuff on the pod and Hector's way bigger than me, so I figured out a way to get Hector leaning in his doorway all macho and cool one night. Then I slammed the door."

"On Hector?"

"On his hand. The hand he hit me with." He was watching me for a reaction. Would I gasp in horror or applaud his resourcefulness? I tried to do neither, although my stomach was strongly in favor of the first. I unconsciously flexed my fingers, relieved that they still worked.

"See right there where the hinge moves? See that narrow space where they jammed that towel?" He pointed to the narrow vertical opening where the inner edge of the heavy wooden door ran parallel and about an inch from its steel frame. Three heavy brass hinges spanned the gap at top, center, and bottom, leaving guillotine-like spaces in between. "It's just the right size. He was leaning with his fingers in there and I got him."

"Is that why ...?"

"Yeah, they jammed towels in all the doors since then so now they don't even close all the way. But that's okay. Hector and I are good now. He gets it."

"And what happened?"

Micah's voice had that same matter of fact monotone his father used. He spoke while staring down at the spinning toy held in his lap. "I heard bones breaking. That was kinda' cool. Hector screamed. It was pretty loud. There was blood and stuff on the wall. They took him to the hospital for a couple of days. They bagged me and drugged me and put me in the chill box."

"Chill box?"

"You know, a body bag like when you're dead except its canvas or something and you get to breathe unless you try to bite then they cover your face and you're all strapped in tight so you can't move. Then three or four staff carry you into the chill box. Not like a chatbox in *EAU*. That's cool. This is like solitary. It's got padded walls and no windows or furniture and shit and they pipe in white noise to calm you but that's really the worst part and they leave you there even if you pee yourself until you calm down or the meds knock you out or something."

"Are you taking medication?"

"Yeah. Breakfast and dinnertime. I don't know what they are. They're round and little and white, I think. They make me kinda' blurry and sleepy so I mostly cheek them and trade them."

I was scribbling green crayon across the backs of pages as fast as I could.

"Trade them?"

"Yeah, don't tell Chat-er-butt. Some kids like to double up so they can sleep more and one girl -I won't tell you who- is saving them up to kill herself. I don't think she'll do it, but she lets me do things if I give her mine."

I was in way over my head. After this book, I needed to write an exposé on MPH. At the very least I could trade what I was learning about the hospital with a friend at the *Star Tribune* for access to their archives. I still needed to do some serious digging about the Suki Kohler murder and both Abrams' stories.

"Okay…" I tried to organize my thinking. I was definitely not prepared for this. I wonder if it's even possible to be prepared to talk to a violent teenager locked in a loony bin about premeditated assault and sexual acting out. If the entire population of Center-East One was full of kids like Micah, it was no wonder that the place was out of control.

"So -ummm- why did they bring you here in the first place?"

"They didn't."

"Sorry?"

"They didn't bring me here in the first place. They took me to the hospital. The regular hospital like where they fixed Hector's hand because I was like stoned or something. Remember I told you I didn't talk for a while? I guess they did some tests and stuff and decided I was fine, so then they sent me here. In an ambulance. I remember it was real snowy and cold."

"So, you don't know why you're here?"

"Yeah. Family stuff I guess."

Family stuff? For Micah Abrams that was like a new amputee saying that he had a boo-boo or a plane crash survivor saying that the ride had been bumpy. I worked hard to try to match his casual tone and pretend that I hadn't been immersed in the horrific story for weeks. It was hard.

"Family stuff? Like…?"

He didn't look up, but the toy spun faster. The whirring got louder. "Well, let's see. My mom cheated on my dad with two different guys, and she stole all of his money. My dad's a doctor, you know. Like Chatterfuck but way better. He tried to save the marriage for me he said, but she wouldn't respect him. She swore at him and laughed at him all the time and then she got the court to make him pay her like two thousand dollars every month and made me live with her most of the time even though I didn't want to and his lawyer couldn't get the judge to change that."

"Wow. You know lots of stuff about what happened. How'd you find all this out?"

"How do you think? I told you I'm smart. I snooped on my mom's phone and told my dad about her *boyfriends.*" He offered vague air quotes around the exaggerated word, the spinner still held in one hand. "I even spied on her a couple of times. I saw her with this jerk named Max with a moustache once. My dad gave me a camera to put in her room. But mostly we just talked, my dad and me."

I'd covered several yellow pages just trying to keep up with the basics. Direct quotes were impossible. The crayon was too awkward and slow, and I didn't want to ask Micah to slow down or repeat himself. Even without quotes, even without audio, this was a goldmine. Like hitting three lemons on a slot machine but having no pockets to carry away the mountain of quarters that I'd won. I hoped that between my green scribbles and my memory I could capture most of this.

"Sounds like you and your dad are pretty tight?"

"Absolutely. He's like my best friend and I'm his."

"So you guys used to talk a lot?"

"Yeah."

"What message do you want me to try to get to him?"

Micah didn't even pause to consider. He tossed the spinner on the bed next to him and said, "give me the paper and crayon."

It was a demand, not a request. I tore off a blank page and complied.

Crayon in hand, he didn't even pause to think. He wrote in simple block letters that I read easily even upside down from where I sat opposite him.

"Dad, I hate this place. I miss you. Please get me out of here. Ding Dong! Love Micah."

"Ding dong?" I asked?

He scowled at me like I was intruding. Under the circumstances, he could hardly expect privacy.

"It's just a thing we say. He'll understand. Try to get that to him, okay? I kept my side of our deal. Now you keep yours."

"I'll try." He handed me the bright yellow page. I tucked it among the other papers, folded them together and shoved the package in my back pocket like contraband.

"Two more questions Micah, then I'll leave you alone."

He was back to the spinner. Eyes downcast. The whirring noise resumed. His head bobbed up and down in a way that seemed to acknowledge me. I went for it.

"Number one: If I get permission to come back, can we talk again?"

"Only if you bring me an answer from my dad. Otherwise forget it."

"I can try. That's the best I got."

"Nope. Not good enough. If you want me to talk to you then I need something directly from my dad." He'd make a shrewd businessman someday. Or a politician, perhaps.

"Okay. Question number two: You haven't said anything about your mom. Don't you want me to get a message to her?"

Micah angled his face up toward me just a couple of degrees. Enough that I could see the sparkle in eyes cloaked under heavy brows. I could make out just enough of his mouth to suspect a sly smile. One hand continued to spin the shiny toy still held in the other, faint flashing lights sparking across his otherwise overshadowed face. The effect belonged in a *Chuckie* movie. It reminded me of Jack Nicholson in *The Shining*. It was all evil.

"That bitch?" he asked. "That red-hot flaming narcissist? *Ding dong*! I hope she rots in hell."

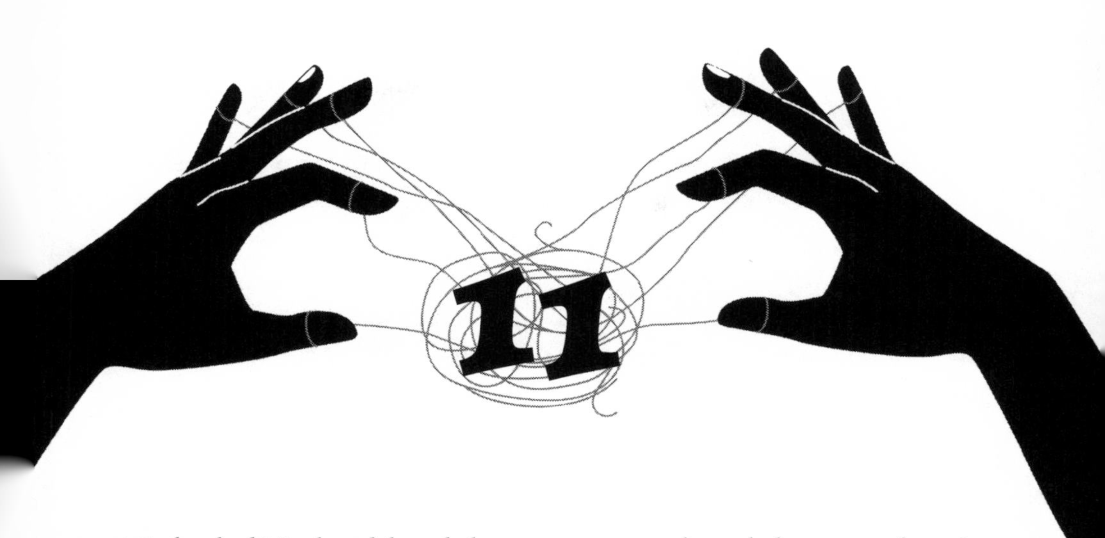

11

I thanked Micah and threaded my way upstream through the over-perfumed and unwashed, standing-sitting-laying, talking-crying-gibbering throng of teens with the same sense of exotic intrigue and personal danger that I'd once had while walking through a crowded Moroccan souk years ago. I found my way back to the nursing station. My ID buzzed me into the front hall all without a word to anyone or a sighting of Dr. Chatterjee. Adolescents in all manner of dress and undress and a dozen different florescent hair colors watched me or called to me or pointedly ignored me as I passed. Once the inner pod door buzzed shut behind me, I was immersed in the wonderful quiet of the sally port. The air tasted fresher. My breathing and heart rate slowed. I patted my pocket to make sure that I'd managed to smuggle my scribbled notes off the pod, opened my locker and collected an awkward handful of my stuff. I jammed my pockets full intent on getting back to my Jeep and leaving MPH far behind.

Micah's words still echoed in my ears. I needed to get them on tape while they were still fresh.

The Jeep was in B12 just as I'd left it about a million years before. It was funny how I'd parked here fearing that I would get nothing and now found myself drowning in words and images and questions. I had more questions now than when I'd first arrived at MPH, but that was good. That was the meat of writing. Questions fueled inquiry, the boot that drives the shovel down deeper into the muck of human experience. My writer's brain was awash with questions I should ask Abrams that afternoon and research I should do tonight and points I would need to fit into an outline of the chapter I would write on MPH starting with the provocative matter of why there are towels jammed in the door hinges on Center-West One.

Part of me puzzled over how best to capture Micah's odd emotional disconnect. "Uncaring" and "cold" and "heartless" were the right palette but the wrong intensity. This felt like much more than a teenager's defensive *I-don't-care* ennui. Micah made me think that he was a distant observer of his own experience. Like a spectator to life, once removed from the action and always rooting for the bad guy. His reaction to Hector hitting him, for example, had been *detached. Aloof.* But even more so, he talked about the assault and his revenge like an anthropologist studying a primitive species.

What did it mean if this child was incapable of emotion?

But would someone with no emotion wait and plan and then execute such a vicious attack?

And his reaction about his mom? That wasn't detached or aloof or removed in the slightest. That was immediate and connected and emotional and terrifying.

And "Ding Dong"? If Micah had been babbling nonsense, I would have dismissed "ding dong" as more of the same. But Micah was nothing if not cogent. Clear. Articulate. He struck me as very intelligent, just like his father. So then "Ding Dong" wasn't just blather. It meant something to him and apparently it meant something to his dad.

That raised the most immediate question: What to say to Abrams this afternoon? I didn't feel any obligation to spill my guts to the man. On the other hand, I was holding information that he craved. In his shoes I would be desperate to hear that my kid was okay, that he wanted to get out of the hospital, and to hear any words that he'd passed on in crayon or otherwise. I recognized that I could use this information as leverage, I could dole it out a bit at a time to keep Abrams talking, but I wasn't sure if that was my best move. The idea made me think of the lion tamer who doled out bits of steak every time the animal did a trick until the lion figured out that eating the man was a much more efficient way to get a meal.

Should I share anything at all? I could lie and play dumb. I could tell him that *"I tried Sam. I couldn't get in to see him and Chatterjee was no help at all."* If I could pull that off with a straight face -Jenny would eagerly tell you that I'm a horrible liar- then I could see how the father's stories matched the son's. Of course, that might require another trip to MPH for more information which posed its own many dilemmas. I wasn't at all sure that I could get back in and, if I did, I wasn't sure that Micah would talk. Much as this strategy appealed to me, intentionally walking back into that hell could well be seen as reason to keep me there.

I backtracked past attractive outbuildings and manicured grounds that I'd seen just an hour earlier in an entirely different light. On my way in, the superficial beauty had seemed a harbinger of real change. I'd entered the hospital expecting to hear the metaphysical hum of emotions being cleansed, behaviors being reshaped, and thinking being realigned. Now all I could hear was bad rap music, shouted profanity, and the sound of knuckles being crushed between wood and steel. I realized that the hospital's very public and very expensive overhaul only went skin-deep. The state had given MPH an impressive facelift, but if Center-East One is at all typical of the larger institution, the place remained the corrupt and corrupting loony bin it had always been.

I was surprised to find that another zebra arm stopped outgoing traffic the same way that incoming traffic was halted on the other side of the attendant's shiny booth. Was MPH worried that visitors were stealing the furniture or kidnapping patients and driving them away? I buzzed down my window, impatient to get going. Parking Attendant Barbie greeted me as if we'd never met before, collected my ID and scanned it on her tablet.

She asked, "Are you taking anything off the grounds that you didn't have when you first entered?"

Guilt washed over me. I resisted the urge to pat my hip pocket and make sure that my crayon notes were intact. I looked Barbie in her bright smiling face and lied.

"Thank you. I hope that your visit to the Minnesota Psychiatric Hospital went well." The woman was beginning to sound more *Stepford Wife* than Barbie doll. She touched her tablet, commanding the zebra arm to rise in front of me. It obeyed. "Have a nice day!"

I drove ten yards beyond Barbie's booth and pulled over. My phone was buried in a pocket somewhere under layers of winter clothes. I needed the recorder for the drive north. It took some contortions, but I finally pulled it free. The voice mail icon was flashing.

Eight voice mails. Five from Jenny in the last hour. All fifteen to twenty seconds long. Shit! She was trying to reach me, and I'd been out of touch. Was Christie hurt? I mentally locked the two Abrams men into a back room where I could come back to them later. I tapped *Call Back* directly, without bothering to listen to the messages.

She picked up on the first ring.

"Teddy?"

"Are you okay Jenn? Is Christie okay? I just got your messages."

"Where have you been? Listen: We've got a problem. Jorge is taking us back to court. He wants Christie. Jeez, I can't believe this is happening again. I've got to be quick. I've got Mark on the other line."

"Mark?"

"Camden."

"The lawyer? Is it really that serious? How can I help, Jenn? I can be there in an hour...."

"No, no. Ted, Jorge got the court to order an evaluation. About custody." Her voice broke. I hated the man even more for the pain that he continued to cause her. "He's on the other line now -Mark, not Jorge- Where are you?"

"Just leaving the hospital. I'm supposed to be in Chanhassen at one. What can I do?" If she needed me to skip today with Abrams, I would. It would slow my schedule down and might dent Abrams' trust in me, but that couldn't be the priority right now. Christie was. Then it occurred to me: "Jenn? Where's Christie? I dropped her at school this morning. She's not with him, is she?"

"No... Oh God! I hadn't thought of that. Hold on a sec." I heard her rapid breathing, tapping like she was texting, and then a loud knock made me jump. Barbie Doll the traffic attendant was standing at my window, smiling, tablet in hand. I buzzed down the window.

"Sir, I'm sorry but you can't park here."

"Yeah, yeah. Thanks. Just checking messages. I won't be long." I didn't wait for her to respond before buzzing up the window. Jenny was back on the line.

"Yep. Okay. I show her at school."

I had no idea what that meant, but she was talking fast.

"Please, Ted. *Pleeease* keep your phone on. Mark and I are making plans. I'm going to need your help. I'll tell you more tonight."

"Do you need me there?"

"Not yet. One more thing, then I gotta go. A woman named Sloan is going to call you."

"Sloan?"

"Yeah. Something to do with an evaluation."

"Okay, and what should I do?"

"Sorry, Mark's back on the line. Let me go, okay?" The line went dead.

The clock on the dashboard said that it was 10:10 in the morning. I'd dropped Christie at school a bit over two hours earlier. Now all I wanted to do was race home and scoop her up. But Jenny was in charge. Christie is her daughter, not mine. Jenny said stay away so I had to stay away. I had about a ninety-minute drive up to Abrams, but I wasn't due there until one. In theory I had time to at least stop in Shakopee on the way … but why? Weren't there calls that I could make to help out? Maybe I should pick up Christie early from school just to be safe. We could have an ice cream date or go bowling or to a movie, just so that I knew she was safe from her father. Jenny said that she was safe at school but how could she know that? She hadn't texted or called anyone. Maybe I should cancel with Abrams and go check.

Our shared nightmare was Voldemort snagging Christie off the playground or turning on the charm to get her excused from classes. I'd seen him work the poor-immigrant, victim-of-racism, I-don't-even-speak-your-language card in court in the past and had to guess that he'd done it again to get this new court order. So we'd put as many safeguards in place as we could think of. The school knew never to excuse Christie to anyone but Jenn or me. Christie knew that she was never allowed to go with any adult who didn't know our super-secret magic code word. Christie's passport was locked away in Jenn's safe deposit box in the bank. We took some comfort knowing that TSA and Homeland Security were really careful about kids flying and crossing borders -Canada is just a few hours north- but that wouldn't matter if Voldemort tucked Christie in a car and headed west or south. There's a lot of Montana to hide a child in.

It's hard for me to give up the driver's seat. I hate feeling helpless. I wanted to take action, rip open my shirt to expose the "S" on my chest and the cape on my back and fly to the rescue, but all I could do was grind my teeth in frustration and focus on what matters: Jenny is a super-mom. When it comes to Christie, she is organized and assertive and tireless. There is nothing she wouldn't do or give or sacrifice for Christie, including me, and I'm fine with that. She is not a mama-bear that I would want to piss off.

Christie is a superhero in her own right. Even at six-years-old, she gets it. She knows what her father is. We talk about it all the time. She'd never allow anyone to take her away from Jenny. Hell, the munchkin didn't even want to spend overnights with the bastard.

And I trust the lawyer, Mark Camden. Jenny and I had first met him when Jorge filed two back-to-back Child Protective Service complaints against us. The first time, Christie had simply told her father she was hungry, so he called CPS alleging that we didn't feed her. Never mind that the pediatrician had commented that she was in the middle of a growth spurt that five hotdogs at lunchtime couldn't satisfy. The second time Christie had shown up with a scratch on her face. Dear old dad alleged that we didn't supervise her adequately. CPS investigated again. The truth was that Christie had launched herself into my arms one day after school and the pen in my shirt pocket had connected with her left cheek. No blood was drawn. No bandage needed. I felt awful but she was fine.

CPS had called Jenn both times. Jenn had called Camden's firm. We'd met in his top floor offices in a St. Paul high rise with views of the river. The address and the artwork on the walls and the receptionist serving coffee and fresh croissants triggered my cynicism. I was expecting an over-priced, condescending snob with no time for a single mom and little girl. But Camden burst that bubble quickly. He struck me as a kind man and a skilled lawyer who was surprisingly generous with his time. I was further surprised that he talked about how he and his ex- had managed to raise two boys who were both away at school someplace impressive. I left there much more optimistic than I'd thought possible, and, in the end, he earned our trust and respect. He came through twice for Jenny with CPS and it sounded like he was there again for her today.

My feelings of helplessness didn't matter. I needed to trust Jenny to get this situation under control. She'd reach me when she needed me. I made sure that the ringer was on and was reminded that I had eight messages waiting. Five from Jenny. Who else had called?

I noticed that Barbie the Stepford traffic attendant was standing ten feet behind my car, square in my rearview mirror. She was talking on her phone and tapping at her tablet. I didn't care.

Call number four came up as "SinCity" on my caller ID. Once upon a time in a very different mood I'd abbreviated my publisher's name that way in my phone book. Synchronicity Press. It seemed funny at the time. The message was from an editor named McDaniels who wanted an update on my progress with Abrams and the Suki murder book. I tapped *save*. I had a lot to tell them, but it would have to wait.

Call number seven was marked "Unknown Caller" from a Minneapolis area code. I tapped *play*.

"Mr. Bennett? This is Dr. Myra Sloan." The voice was crisp and professional; deeper than many women's voices, a gravelly alto that gave her words extra weight. I heard it as the voice of an older woman. Tall and formal, I guessed. A woman who always wore heels and seldom laughed.

"I'm a psychologist here in Minneapolis. You may be aware that the Court has ordered Jenny and Jorge Villalobos…" she pronounced it "George" with a hard "G;" good, another thorn in the man's side "… to participate in a child custody evaluation in my office. You're named as Mom's partner and co-parent. I'd like to get a couple of hours of your time this week to talk here in my office. Please call me back please asap."

A child custody evaluation? Some shrink was supposed to decide where Christie should live? *Shit!* No wonder Jenny was frantic. Voldemort had outdone himself. I tapped *save*. Jenny -or maybe Camden if this was getting that complicated- someone would have to tell me whether I could talk to this woman and what to say.

A headache was blossoming behind my eyes, and I felt entirely overwhelmed. I'd locked away my experience with Micah at MPH in one corner of my brain and thoughts about my upcoming interview with Abrams senior in another. This new clusterfuck with Voldemort was quickly filling whatever little brain-space remained, spilling molten anxiety as it grew. I felt ready to explode. I wanted to get on the highway, open my windows, and let the cool fresh air wash away MPH and Micah's craziness and Abrams and especially Jorge Villalobos. I started to do just that. I tugged on my seatbelt and put the Jeep in drive and checked my mirrors -Barbie doll was gone- and went to pull up my navigation app when I remembered that I still had one more message waiting.

Another "Unknown caller" with a local area code. Someone from Sloan's office? Or from Camden's office? Or maybe Dr. Chatterjee trying to figure out who I really am if I'm not the errant state advocate named Bernette. I foolishly tapped *play*. The voice that filled the Jeep was all macho bass, rich with arrogance and obviously Hispanic. Even though the caller didn't bother to identify himself by name, it was pretty clear that Voldemort himself had left a message.

"Hey Teddy. *Teddy Bear*," He pronounced Christie's pet name for me with venom. "I just wanted to let you know that you're on a sinking ship. That *puta* you're banging is breaking all the rules and hurting my kid. I've got the goods on her, man. Tracking me? Spying on me? Recording me without my permission? Calling me names around my little girl? Calling *you* 'daddy'? It's kinda funny that that shit is called *alienation*. Get it, *alien* like Jenny-high-horse herself? *Alienation*. That's what she's doing to Christie -poisoning her against me- and I'm going to prove it and then I'm going get back my daughter. This is my one and only courtesy call, *amigo*. Abandon ship now while you still can. Get off the good ship Jennifer now. It's going down soon and it's going down deep whether you're on it or not."

My jaw was clenched hard. I forced it to release so I could catch my breath. I fought an urge to throw the phone as far away as I could, as if that action would physically separate me from Voldemort himself. *Damn*, that man had *cojones*! Calling Jenny names! Threatening to take Christie. If he really had been there in front of me, I wouldn't trust myself not to hurt him.

My headache was pounding now. If it's possible to feel your blood pressure rise, I was feeling it. I dialed Jenny's number -she had to hear this- but the call went straight to voice mail. No way was I leaving her a recording of the same landmine I'd just stepped on. We needed to talk this through. I forced myself to breathe. What to do? I scrolled down the log to Voldemort's call and clicked on the up-arrow next to the message flag. I attached the audio file to an email that I addressed to Mark Camden and Associates, typed a brief "oh shit can you believe this?" note and pushed *send*. Camden would know what to do with it.

The next ninety minutes was a seventy-five mile an hour blur of cars and trucks and exits and buildings and vehicles merging on and off and shit-brown fields and icy lakes. I enjoyed none of it and remember very little. The chilly air helped my headache at first, and then got too cold so I buzzed up the window and turned on the tunes. The Pentatonix. I usually enjoyed trying to follow the intricately twisted *a cappella* voices, but not so today. I clicked on NPR but global warming and floods and fires didn't help either.

The Jeep bucked and demanded that I exit at Shakopee and go straight to Jenny, but I fought to pull the steering wheel to the left and barely won. I continued another twenty minutes into Chanhassen, the entire drive from St. Peter wasted trying not to hear the voices shouting in my head. Micah's unemotional description of a "plan" to get revenge on a peer. Jenny's frantic pleas about losing Christie. Jorge's enraging taunts about sinking ships and recordings and tracking him. And the questions I anticipated Abrams asking about Micah.

I jumped off Great Plains at 79th and found a Potbelly sandwich shop. I shoehorned the Jeep into a spot marked "subcompacts only" and tried Jenny's number again. Voice mail. I left her a twenty second pep talk that I tried to genuinely feel, made sure my ringer was on, and walked across an empty parking lot. I let the sun bake my face for a moment, wishing that I was on a beach in St. Martin rather than standing in Minnesota slush. It was still too early for lunch hour traffic and too far out of the city to ever really get crowded.

The restaurant was warm and fragrant with fresh bread and hot soup scents. I ordered a steak sandwich and a bowl of chowder. I spread out at a table by the window with a view of the blacktop. I set my food on one side, my notes on the other, and my phone dead center. Ringer on. I had about an hour to try to satisfy at least one of my many urgent needs.

"Mark, there's no way in hell I will ever let Christie live with Jorge. I won't allow it! Christie wouldn't do it, and Jorge doesn't even want it! This is just a power trip for him. He gets off on all the attention." Jenny held her cell tight to her head, pacing in tightening circles in front of a sunny window on the fourth floor of St. Francis. She'd secluded herself in the nursing lounge with the door locked tight. Peter and her other colleagues were doing double duty covering for her. She'd tried to take the last few hours of the shift off. She'd told her supervisor she thought she was getting sick, but the woman had said that she didn't care if the Apocalypse was underway. "What if one of the four horsemen gets injured, Jenn? Who will be there to set his broken bones and change his bandages? We will! The doctors and nurses right here on this floor!" Besides, she said, every bed is full, the ER is trying to send up even more patients, and the woman in 19 was complaining again. Bottom line? If Nurse Villalobos wants to keep her job, she will just have to soldier on.

Jenny's phone chirped loudly in her ear. She stopped listening to the lawyer long enough to glance at the screen. Ted was calling again. She sent him directly to voice mail. He must be worried sick, but she only had twenty minutes of Camden's time. He was giving her his lunch break in the middle of a hearing.

"Mark, I'm here. It's hard to concentrate with so much going on but nothing matters to me more than Christie."

Christie! Jenny held the phone away from her ear again and found the ruby red image of a cartoon rabbit ear. She tapped it, watched the *BunnyEars* logo bloom and fade, revealing a map of Shakopee with a bright dot flashing at its center. She expanded the view until the details became clear. Christie was still at school. She zoomed in tighter, and the dot appeared in the wing of the building that Jenn recognized as the multi-purpose gym/cafeteria/auditorium. Basketball hoops folded up into the ceiling and were hidden among a collection of nets and ropes and a collapsible climbing wall. In their place, janitors routinely set up constellations of chairs and tables to suit the occasion.

A tiny blue audio icon flashed patiently on the bottom of the small screen. Jenny ignored it. Christie was okay at school.

"... because Jorge got a court order, Jenny."

She'd missed a sentence or two. "Sorry Mark. Say that again, please?" But anxiety kept her talking before the lawyer could respond: "You know that Jorge is a self-absorbed, irresponsible ugly little boy wearing a fat man suit showing off in his big, black muscle car. The man can't hold down a job. He always has big dreams and big deals and he always has a buddy who knows someone who can get him a deal, but it's all bullshit even if he actually believes it himself. I'm disgusted every time I remember that I fell for it. *Yuk*! You've seen him in action. He'd be pitiful if he weren't so dangerous. He does not want Christie full time! How would he take care of her? He can't even manage alternate weekends. He's only doing this to upset me...."

"What I said, Jenny, was that you're letting him win."

Camden had learned long ago that eighty percent of his job was managing his clients. Twenty percent or less was actually practicing law. Jenny Villalobos would never get through this evaluation and had no chance in court if she couldn't get her act together. "You can't let this man get under your skin. That's half the battle right there." Jenny started to respond, but he cut her off. "Listen to yourself, Jenny. You're catastrophizing. All he's got is one *ex parte* order for an evaluation and he only got that because we weren't there. The judge would have immediately removed Christie from your care if Jorge had anything at all. He does not. That's a very good sign. The evaluation is lip-service. Judge Martindale has to do something to make the man go away, so Dr. Sloan is going to talk to you and Jorge and Ted and Christie. You'll complete some psychological tests. She'll talk to your co-workers and extended family -people who know you and who've seen you with Christie- and then tell the court to leave Christie right where she is."

"You don't know that." But even as she argued, her tone began to soften. Hollow as it might be, Camden's reassurance was what she needed to hear.

"I do know that, Jenny. That's my job and I'm good at it. I've been down this road a couple hundred times before. I recognize the pattern. Trust me."

"So now I've got to take time off work to tell my story to another stranger, spend thousands of dollars, and pull my family and friends and co-workers into my personal mess so that a judge can tell Jorge to leave us alone? But you know what?" Camden heard her fighting back tears, "all that doesn't even matter compared to what I'll have to put Christie through. It's not right, Mark."

"I know Jen. You're right. I won't sugar coat it for you. The sad reality is that Christie's father is a *pro se* litigant. He has no lawyer, so the judge will go to great lengths to make sure that he feels heard, otherwise any ruling would be overturned on appeal. I know, I know… why should he get the benefit of the doubt just because he's self-represented? I'm sorry. Really. That's just the way it is. No way around it."

"Damn it! The man doesn't work and doesn't pay taxes and is months behind on child support. He's on disability for a bogus back injury. Me? I'm working my ass off trying to be a good citizen and a good role model and a strong woman for my little girl. I pay my taxes. I'm up all night when Christie has a fever. I buy her new clothes every two months because the kid is growing like a weed. But who gets the benefit of the doubt? Not me! I just get screwed over again. I'm done with this BS, Mark! I am done."

"I don't blame you, Honey. It's my job to get you through this. Christie's going to be okay. I promise. Now take a slow, deep breath for me, please." The lawyer allowed his Cajun roots to seep into his diction at times like this. He'd lived in the Twin Cities since he was fifteen when his mother left his alcoholic father, but still mustered a creole twang and a *Naw'leans* lilt and even the occasional "y'all" and "God bless" when it helped. This seemed to be one of those occasions.

The young mother's pain and anger were all too familiar to Camden. He'd helped her through Jorge's trumped-up back-to-back child abuse allegations just a year earlier. Her intelligence and caring and commitment to her daughter had struck him as one of the only genuine and pure things he'd come across in a long time. They'd breathed a deep sigh of relief together when child protective services had finally dismissed Jorge's ridiculous charges, but Camden recognized it for what it was. A divorced parent who is willing to twice make Everests out of molehills with CPS is just revving his engines at the starting gate. Now the real race was on. Jorge Villalobos had graduated from pain-in-the-ass-dad to scorched-earth-litigant. He was asking the court to rip 6-year-old Christie out of the only home she'd ever known. He'd say that his goal is to protect his child, but his real purpose is obviously to injure Jenny.

This was a sadly familiar story to the lawyer: Two young, needy, and immature people get caught up in the excitement of lust, publicly promise to love honor and cherish one another without ever really thinking about what that phrase means, get pregnant, have a baby, and then look at one another sleep-deprived and financially stressed and realize that they had no idea what they'd gotten into. This epiphany – a fact that siblings, neighbors, and even the mailman recognized long ago – lights a fuse that sooner or later leads to an explosion that hurts no one more than the child.

Sometimes that fuse is long. Years can pass in a kind of marital purgatory while people like Jenny Villalobos struggle with waves of shame and guilt and rage that prompt yo-yo-like separations and reunions. The parents work their way up a ladder of distance, dislike, and distrust turning to more and more desperate supports. Early on it's something benign and socially acceptable. Hot yoga or golf or book clubs. When that doesn't relieve the pressure at home, they begin to open up to friends or clergy or therapists, often taking a side trip into alcohol or drugs or gambling or exciting adulterous flings. When finally distance means different addresses, dislike means hatred, and distrust means hiring a lawyer, the damage has already been done. The bank accounts have been drained. The credit cards are maxed out. The child is working with his or her third therapist. And any chance of reconciliation is buried six feet under a wall of shame, anger, and grief built one brick of guilt and humiliation at a time. By the time these people reached Camden, it was no longer about divorce. It was about the war between mom and her allies on one side, dad and his allies on the other side, and the child who was left traipsing twice a week back and forth across the mine field in between.

Unless they didn't.

Camden was seeing more and more kids insisting on staying with one parent and refusing to spend time with the other. Age didn't matter. He'd worked with two families in the last six months with preschoolers who would eagerly go on playdates to friends' houses but screamed like they were being burned at the stake when it came time to spend an afternoon with dad. He represented a successful businessman whose ten-year-old spent three weeks each summer at a sleep-away camp but would rather be put up for adoption than spend weekends with his mom.

Camden recognized a startling similarity across cases. The preferred parents routinely claim that the rejected parents are too harsh or too self-absorbed or even abusive. The rejected parents claim that the preferred parents are bribing or threatening or otherwise conniving with the kids to erase them.

This was Jorge's argument to the court. He claimed that Jenny and Ted were intentionally alienating the little girl from him, poisoning the father-daughter relationship so that they could enjoy their nice little family of three without the inconvenience of Christie's father. This, he argued, was reason enough for the court to place Christie in his full-time care.

The judge was trained to adjudicate criminal matters. Guilt versus innocence. Good guy versus bad guy. Theft. Murder. Property settlements. Unfortunately, children can't be divided up like retirement funds. Thus, the custody evaluation with Dr. Sloan.

"Jenny, there one more important bit we need to touch on quickly."

The tap-tap rhythm of Jenny's flats pacing across linoleum stopped.

"Tell me," She said.

"I want to you to Google 'parental alienation.' Jorge claims that you and Ted are doing that. Alienating Christie from him. Intentionally undermining their relationship. That you're doing things to make her reject him."

"Bullshit. Doing things? Like what?"

"Here, I'll read this directly from his *ex parte* motion: 'Christine's mother and mother's illicit paramour Ted Bennett are known to routinely engage in behaviors recognized in psychology as constituting parental alienation.' He has a bunch of references to scholarly works inserted here. It goes on, 'these include (a) encouraging the child to refer to another man as dad or daddy or father, (b) referring to me to and around the child using disparaging and insulting terms, (c) encouraging the child to keep secrets from me, (d) prompting the child to spy on me, (e)electronically tracking the child while in my care, and (f) eavesdropping upon and/or recording my interactions with the child without my knowledge or consent, an act that may constitute a felony in my state.'"

The line went silent. Camden heard nothing. No pacing. No words. Not even breathing.

"Jenny? Are you there?"

"Yeah. I'm here. No way Jorge wrote that. He doesn't know half of those words. I thought you said he didn't have a lawyer?"

"If he has a lawyer, that person hasn't yet filed an appearance, but this stuff doesn't require a lawyer. It's cut-and-paste boilerplate available on the internet. One of those 'insert your name here' kind of things. I've seen it before. There's a half dozen hired gun so-called experts out there who use this stuff as bait to entice desperate parents to hire them to testify. They come in and flaunt their credentials and use six-syllable words to intimidate the judge and win the case. Hassan French, for example. But Jenny, the meat of this thing is those six letters A through F I just read to you. Those are the things that Dr. Sloan is going to be looking for. Spying and recording and using mean names. Is any of that true? Do you and Ted put Christie in the middle of the adult conflict like that?"

Silence again. This silence sounded to the lawyer like an 'oh shit, they caught me.'

"Jenny?"

"Well, no. I mean, Ted and I talk about Jorge but mostly when Christie's asleep or at school."

"And tracking him? Recording him without his knowledge?"

"This is the stuff Dr. Sloan is going to ask about? Not who was there when Christie nearly broke her arm? Or who stayed up all night sewing her princess costume last Halloween? Or who she comes to when she has a nightmare or can't find Piglet? Really?"

"Really. Sloan has to investigate Jorge's allegations.

"Do you know Sloan. Mark?"

"Yes and no. I knew Myra when we both lived in Minnetonka. That was a long time ago. Our paths have crossed a couple of times since then professionally. We had drinks together after a conference in the Dells a couple summers ago. I like her. She's solid. No nonsense. Look, we need to talk more but I've got to get back to court. Call Myra. Do what she says and reach me with any questions, okay?"

"Okay…."

"And Jenny: No worries. Christine's going to be okay. Y'all got this."

Myra Sloan was tired.

This wasn't need-a-nap kind of tired, although that was there, too. This was the kind of tired that some might call weary, or even bruised, or maybe just plain broken. She was soul-tired. Existentially fatigued. Almost four decades of working in the family courts had eroded away something basic about her humanity.

Sloan leaned away from her desk and out of the blue light of her computer monitor. She removed her glasses and stared blindly down toward the ruckus on 4th Street, six stories below. It was only Monday -the din of traffic had increased a notch or two, signaling lunch hour- but she was ready for a weekend. Or a vacation. Or retirement. That thought popped up more and more often lately with TV commercial-induced fantasies of sundrenched golf courses and mimosa-soaked brunches with girlfriends and walks along white sandy beaches. At sixty-nine, Sloan was overdue for all the above, but the bill collectors didn't care.

At work Myra Sloan was all about calm, objective, and reflective choices. Her job was to evaluate court-involved families and to make recommendations about their children's needs. Judges relied on her incisive, scientific assessments to answer the thorny questions that filled the family courts.

Is this mother abusive?

Can these parents communicate and cooperate?

Why is this child refusing to see her father?

What schedule of care serves the best interests of these children?

A Myra Sloan evaluation is a rapid-fire thirty or forty hours of listening and observing and measuring and taking copious notes involving the parents, their partners, and the kids mixed together with a sprinkling of friends' and neighbors' opinions and a cup or two of third-party opinions topped off with a demi glaze of teachers' and coaches' and neighbors' and nannies' observations. Season with the grandparents' perspectives and the child's therapist's theories to taste. Bring this whole messy gumbo to a boil and then strain, yielding fifty or sixty pages of twelve-point Times New Roman black ink on white paper, i.e., a custody evaluation report complete with recommendations. Serve piping hot to the judge.

Sloan was sharp and intuitive and compulsive about her work. She not only kept current on the science but published her own insights, consulted, and lectured around the country. She was respected among her peers as an expert on child custody, the dynamics of conflicted family systems, and parental alienation.

Ironically, Sloan knew that her personal life wouldn't stand up to her own professional scrutiny. Her intimate relationships were anything but stable. The demands of her work often left her anxious and needy after hours. Where she was calm and objective and decisive in the office, she was reactive and even explosive at home. Thrice married, she'd had two children later in life. Her daughter in New Hampshire had disowned her and kept three grandchildren whom she'd never met out of her life. Her son was an unemployed and probably unemployable alcoholic whom she'd like to disown or, at the very least, kick his feral Norwegian Elkhound and his unmedicated ADHD 10-year-old twins out of her finished basement. Her present husband, Alan, was a retired house painter suffering the early stages of Parkinsons. As it was, Sloan was single-handedly supporting this make-shift tribe. Together with her old friend Mr. Prozac and her new friend Mr. Prilosec, she battled up an impossible mountain of bills and stresses. There was no question that she needed to keep working and, even if she won Megabucks tomorrow, she would still need a place to go every day to get away from her own home.

Framed diplomas, certificates, and awards decorated the white wall over her desk, creating a daunting backdrop for the parade of angry and confused people who populate the couch opposite. Bachelor's and master's degrees. Doctoral degree. Certificates in a half dozen specialties. Advanced board qualifications in child custody evaluation. Visitors might understandably be impressed and even intimidated, but Sloan herself privately found ways to minimize each accolade and achievement. She was a victim of imposter syndrome -her own abusive father's gift that keeps on giving - that first cousin of depression that undermines confidence in those most deserving of it. Successful? Maybe, but Sloan saw her position as a simple feat of endurance. She'd outlasted scores of her colleagues who had burned out or moved away or shifted their practice from family law into calmer and more rational domains, like criminal defense or profiling serial killer.

Pushing her exhaustion away, Sloan sighed, sat forward, replaced her glasses, and studied the most recent orders filling her screen. Villalobos v. Villalobos. Father: Jorge Manuel Villalobos, age 34, resides alone in a duplex. His mother, Rosa Villalobos, lives downstairs. Unemployed auto mechanic on state disability secondary to a back injury. No attorney on record.

Mother: Jennifer Villalobos, age 29. Works as a LNA nurse at St. Francis. Resides with her never-married partner Theodore "Ted" Bennett. Mark Camden and Associates represents mom.

The lawyer's name brought a smile to Sloan's face. She'd known Camden a million years ago when they'd both lived in the suburbs. Their kids went to high school together. The families had socialized a couple of times. She remembered Camden as an attractive, smart, and fun man. His wife had died of some kind of lingering illness. Then a couple of years ago they'd literally run into each other at a conference while rushing to meetings in opposite directions. Coffee had been spilled. His jacket and her blouse were both stained. They'd mutually apologized over drinks. Sloan had thought that more might come of it, but nothing ever had.

She scrolled down.

Under the header "children," the court clerk had identified Christina "Christie" Villalobos. Age 6. Healthy first grader in Shakopee public schools. No known special needs.

According to the court clerk, the Villalobos parents had married when mother became pregnant. They separated and then divorced two years later when the child was two. Uncontested divorce. Shared legal custody. Mother has primary physical custody. Father sees the child on alternate weekends. Father filed *ex parte* late last week seeking custody, claiming alienation.

Another one.

Claims of parental alienation had recently become more common than the flu.

One click, and Jorge's motion filled Sloan's screen. Father blamed mother and her live-in boyfriend for a laundry list of misdeeds that were plainly someone else's overused psychobabble. Sloan reverse engineered the process. She lifted the phrase "...routinely engage in behaviors recognized in psychology as constituting parental alienation..." from father's motion and pasted it in quotes in a Google search bar. She immediately had one verbatim hit.

Mr. Villalobos had borrowed or stole or plagiarized his verbiage from Dr. Hassan French, rabid father's rights advocate, frequent flier on the paid-opinion divorce litigation circuit, and all-around rabble rouser. Sloan knew French's work all too well. The man approached every family's pain with a one-size-fits-all blunt force frontal attack: Father is an innocent victim of Mother's deeply pathological alienating behaviors. For a very significant fee, Dr. French would fly into town, put on his five-hundred-dollar suit, mangle the scientific literature, and manipulate the case specific facts to fit into his predetermined and paid-off pro-father opinions.

French and a handful of so-called professionals like him are a large part of why Sloan is so exhausted. Where custody litigation should be an objective, child-centered, scientifically sound process, French turned it into a biased, personal, back-alley brawl. He intentionally fanned the flames of marital conflict to his personal benefit, best-interests-of-the-child be damned.

Sloan sighed again and closed her eyes imagining the fight that was about to erupt. If Jorge Villalobos had hired Hassan French, this evaluation was likely to require far more energy than she could muster.

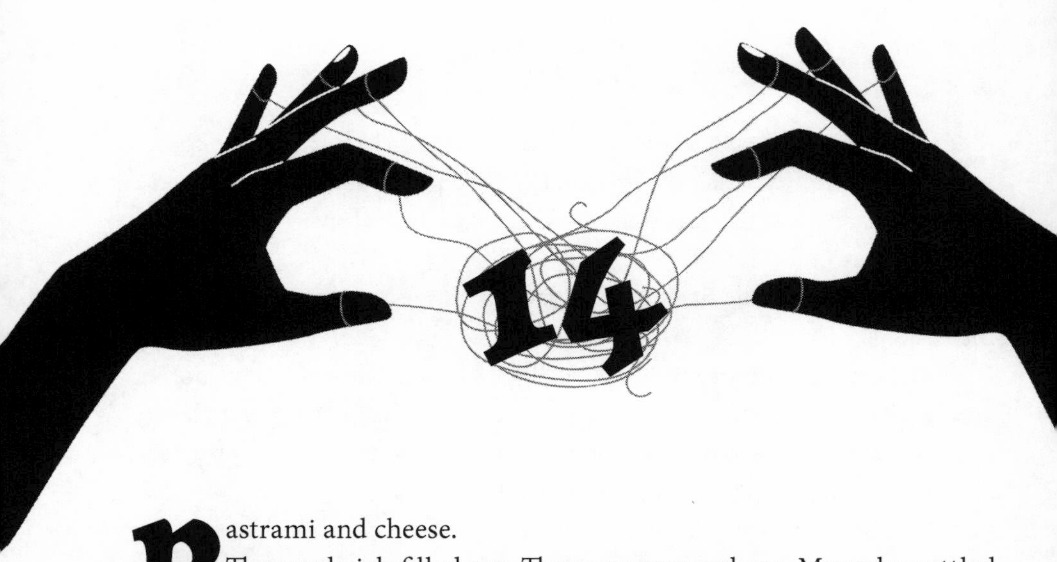

Pastrami and cheese.

The sandwich filled me. The soup warmed me. My pulse settled and my gut protruded. As I chewed, I tried to reach Jenny and I tried to decide how to handle Abrams. Both efforts failed. My calls went to voice mail and my thinking went around in circles. Should I tell Abrams everything? Should I dole out bits and pieces over time like breadcrumbs along a trail? Maybe I should tell him nothing? What if he discovered that I was withholding? What if I told him everything and he had no further use for me?

Is my priority the book or the man or the boy? I'd never really thought through what I'd do if serving one didn't serve the others.

My anxiety grew as I navigated the two miles between the Potbelly restaurant and Abrams' home, parked in his driveway and sat quietly for a moment focused on his house. Red bricks and fieldstone. Two stone pillars supported the entrance portico at center. Six windows spanned the first floor and seven on the second. Two more were set in third story dormers under peaked roofs. Ivy graced portions of the stonework. The wooden door and window frames looked freshly painted. The manicured shrubs reminded me of the MPH grounds I'd left behind less than two hours earlier.

I walked down the right side of the home toward the lake. A chill wind raised faint whitecaps on the water. I paused before entering the doctor's waiting room and checked for messages yet again. Nothing new had arrived in the last several minutes and nothing new would arrive in the next fifty. I had no signal in Abrams' office.

Thoughts of Jenny and the crisis with Voldemort flashed through my mind. Every ounce of me wanted to fly back to Jenny and Christie, wrap them in my arms, and keep them safe. Instead, I'd done as I was told. Jenny insisted that she was fine. She could handle Jorge's latest attack and I needed to get this book written. I needed to do this interview, she'd said. Do the research. "Write the damn book, Teddy! It's your dream!" I took a deep breath, shoved my thoughts about Jenny and Christie back into the corner where they belong, and tried to get organized.

The wood paneled waiting room was empty as usual, but quite uncharacteristically Abrams opened the inner door as soon as I arrived, several minutes before the hour. We shook hands but there was no small talk today. He dove right in even before we were seated.

"Did you see him?

Abrams was a mess. His white button-down shirt was wrinkled. His tie was loosely knotted and hung askew. His face was haggard. He was unshaven and his hair was tufted and uncombed. His skin was paler than I recalled, making the flush in his cheeks appear that much more intense. I guessed that he hadn't slept since we last talked, anticipating news about Micah. His blue eyes drilled into me very much the same way that Micah's gaze had held me not long before.

We spoke at the same time:

"Are you okay, Sam?"

"Did you see him? Did you see Micah?"

He dismissed my question with a glance. He didn't matter, he was saying. What about Micah?

What to say? What to keep to myself? I should have settled this already.

"Okay," I started. "Look Sam, I did visit MPH this morning. I spoke briefly with Dr. Chatterjee."

"Briefly?"

"Very briefly. She's a hard woman to nail down."

Abrams was starving and I was giving him crumbs. Whether it was pity or empathy or weakness -maybe I just buckled under the intensity of his powerful need- I decided in that moment against lying or holding hostage what I'd learned. I would tell him the whole story, feed his trust in our relationship, and hope that I wasn't making a huge mistake.

"As you predicted, she wasn't very helpful."

I watched him wilt, disappointed, imagining that that was all that I had. He was a man inflated by hope, suddenly punctured. The color drained out of his face. The lines around his eyes deepened.

"But Sam, listen. I'm not exactly sure how this happened, but I did see Micah. In fact, I talked to him."

"He's talking?" His voice trembled. Tears filled his eyes and ran down his cheeks. He didn't wipe them away for fear of breaking eye contact with me, so he let them follow the contours of his face freely. He'd had no news about Micah for most of a year. Hearing that his son was alert and engaging was better news than he'd even hoped for.

I waited for him to gather himself, then continued.

"Micah seems to be okay. Healthy. He's talking. And you're right, he's really smart." The adjectives "scary" and "threatening" and "manipulative" also came to mind -the image of fingers crushed in door jams now haunted me- but I bit that all back.

"Is he okay? What did he say? Did he ask about me?"

"I think he's okay. I didn't see any scars or bandages or anything. He's very skinny and pale, but that's how you described him to me in the first place. They have him on some kind of medication, a little white, round pill from what I could gather, but I didn't get the name."

There was still a psychologist buried somewhere inside this grieving father. I could see his doctor brain spin up to speed. He muttered to himself, "that could be anything… maybe olanzapine? Do they have him on antipsychotics?"

I had no idea and told him so. I did not share the part about Micah cheeking the pills and trading them with his peers, one who might be suicidal and another who trades sexual acts for illicit meds.

Abrams shook his head to dismiss his own distracted thoughts. He'd perched on the forward edge of his desk, inches from where I sat. His voice had regained its strength. He sighed deeply and covered his face with both hands. His shoulders quaked. I waited as the storm passed. "What's important," he asserted, sniffing loudly "is that Micah's okay. My son's okay. He's talking."

Nodding toward my phone he asked, “Did you record him? Can I hear?”

“Sorry. No. I wasn’t allowed to carry anything onto the pod.”

“Did Chatterjee say when he’s getting out? Did Micah ask for me? What did he say?”

“Dr. Chatterjee didn’t say much, Sam. As you said, MPH is … let’s say chaotic. Or at least the pod Micah’s on is pretty crazy. Chatterjee was kind of busy putting out fires. Figuratively and maybe literally. We didn’t really talk much. She just parked me in Micah’s room and went about her business.”

“What do you mean ‘chaotic’? Is Micah safe there?”

It was a good question. I hadn’t felt particularly safe on Center-East One. How could a thirteen-year-old? On the other hand, Micah had managed his situation with Hector well enough in a *Lord of the Flies* kind of way. I wouldn’t trust Chatterjee or any of the staff to take care of a pet rock, and I sure wouldn’t want someone that I loved locked up there, but Micah was a survivor.

“I get the impression that MPH has put a very nice coat of paint on a very corrupt institution. I am not at all not impressed with the management and organization. The kids on Micah’s pod were running wild. But the building and the grounds are gorgeous. I didn’t see any real supervision or therapy going on, although I heard that they sometimes ‘bag’ kids when they’re out of control and sometimes put them in the ‘chill box’ – that’s what Micah called them. Like seclusion or solitary confinement, I suppose.”

“That’s old school inpatient psychiatry” Abrams commented. “Full body restraints and safety rooms. They probably have four-point tie downs on the beds, too. God, I hope that they’ve moved beyond ice baths and insulin treatments! But Micah wasn’t in those, right? You said you saw him in his room?”

“Yep. He has a room a bit smaller than your waiting room. It has a window that looks out on a courtyard and a bed and a desk and a bureau. He was sitting on his bed while I was there. By himself. I get the idea that he’s kind of a loner.”

“Always was.” Abrams replied. “I told you his friends were all online in *EAU*. The VR world.”

“So we talked right there. In his room. He fidgeted a lot. Played with a spinner toy while we talked. It seemed to help him focus.”

"What'd you talk about? What'd he say?"

"About his time on the pod, mostly. How he doesn't like Dr. Chatterjee. He told me about a scuffle he'd had with a bigger kid on the pod and how he'd managed that. He's smart and resourceful. A planner. But I'm not sure he really knows why he's there or what's happened."

"'What's happened'? You mean about his mother? Does he know that Suki is dead?" He leaned right into my face -I felt his hot breath on my cheeks- "Did Micah say who killed her?"

That was the critical question, of course. Micah would be released if the prosecutors believed that someone else had killed Suki. That would be a wonderful climax to my book and a huge relief to Abrams who might then be reunited with his son. Until that happened, however, the world would always see Micah as the M&M killer and his father as his puppet-master accomplice.

I'd left Center East One -maybe "escaped" is the better word- believing that Micah knows that his mother is dead and thinking that he was probably her killer. Any question that I'd had going in had been overcome by the youth's cold, calculating manner and the story about how he'd evened the score with the boy named Hector. However, with the benefit of a little hindsight, a bowl of soup and a meaty sandwich, I wasn't sure any longer. Had I mistaken a flash of anxiety for evil? Was his "rot in hell" comment about Suki genuine vindictive rage or the normal rebellion of an angry teenager mouthing off?

Don't most kids tell their parents to *go to hell* one way or another at some point?

I know that I did, but I made the mistake of saying it to my mom in front of my friends. I'd wanted to take the car and impress a girl. Mom had said no publicly -that was my fault; I'd set her up to respond in front of others- so I went off on her. She grounded me and I blasted her, anger and humiliation and frustration combining like gasoline and fire. "Fuck you!" I screamed at her, intending to walk away with the last word, victorious in my friends' eyes. But mom was quicker. The back of her left hand caught me in my right cheek. A ring she wore -not a wedding ring; my dad was long gone at this point- drew blood and left a divot that I can still see today.

Now that I was thinking about it, Christie had had her moments too. She was still too little to come up with "go to hell" and "fuck you" *per se* -now there was something to look forward to- but she could tantrum with the best of them. Sunday nights after weekends with Voldemort were the worst. Just a couple of weeks ago the little girl had gotten worked up about bedtime and launched herself at her mom, arms flailing, screaming "You're a bad mommy and I'm not doing what you say anymore!" Had that been an overtired little girl losing control or genuine anger ... or something else?

Neither Jenny nor I had put two and two together at the time, but now it occurred to me that maybe Christie had been screaming words that Voldemort had scripted. Words that she'd heard him say or even explicitly instructed her to repeat. None of that would surprise me at all.

And if Jorge could program six-year-old Christie to reject Jenny, then how easy would it have been for Abrams to program 12-year-old Micah to do the same? Not just to prompt defiance and rebellion, but lies and rejection. Or worse?

But homicide?

My thoughts had wandered. Abrams sat staring at me, expecting an answer. His thumbs were slowly drumming on the desktop. Fidgeting. Like Micah.

"Does Micah know about Suki? That she's dead? I don't know, Sam. He didn't bring her up in conversation and when I asked about her, he just got mad. I sure didn't tell him. It was pretty clear that he wants nothing to do with her."

Abrams sighed and retreated back behind his desk. He found a tissue, blew his nose, then picked up his pen and fidgeted as he continued speaking.

I put my phone on the desk where he'd been leaning a moment before and tapped *record*.

"Yeah, that's how it was between them. I know that he tried to make peace with her for a long time after we split up, but the abuse just kept coming. Every time I saw him, he had a new horror story. For a while I called CPS to report her. That accomplished nothing, except maybe pissing her off even more. Micah and I used to talk about it. I think I was the only person he could trust, so I tried to support him."

"Support him?" I echoed, listening closely. Where was the line between supporting and coaching or prompting or straight out manipulating? When does telling your kid the truth serve your needs and when does it serve theirs?

Relieved to have any news about Micah, Abrams seemed far less pressured than usual. It was like he'd taken the lid off the bottle and finally felt able to let whatever he'd tried so hard for so long to contain within him overflow. In all of our time together, I never knew him to be affable or engaging, but this was close. Genuine emotion creased his face. He even smiled briefly when I mentioned Micah. He seemed uncharacteristically eager to talk. I didn't want to miss a word.

"Yeah, I supported him as much as I could. Not like a psychologist. I wasn't his therapist. I'm his dad. And his friend. We were like Batman and Robin."

Therapist? Why hadn't I thought about that before? "Did Micah have a therapist, Sam?"

The question seemed to interrupt his train of thought. I probably should have made myself a note and asked later, or not at all.

"Yeah, he did. I haven't thought about him in a long time. A colleague of mine in Shakopee ..."

I'm sure that my eyes shot wide open when he said "Shakopee." I know that my blood pressure went up, not for the first time that day. Abrams didn't notice. He was staring over my shoulder toward the lake, trying to pull up a name from long ago.

"Noyes is his name. David Noyes."

There must be a hundred small towns south of the Twin Cities. If there are ten therapists in each town, then there might be a thousand or so therapists in the suburbs plus hundreds more in Minneapolis and St. Paul themselves. Even if only half of those professionals see kids, and only half of *those* work within a half-hour drive of Abrams' home, what's the chance that Micah and Christie see the same shrink? Noyes is good -thank God for *Round-it!* and all the other support that he provides - but he's not famous-good.

Had Jenn and Christie and I passed Micah in Noyes' waiting room?

Was Noyes somehow embroiled in Micah's drama?

That infamous line from *Casa Blanca* came to mind. Bogart asking himself why of all the gin joints in all the towns in all the world... why did he have to take his kid to my kid's shrink?

I play-acted writing out Noyes name out letter by letter, careful to get the spelling right.

"I know you said you can't legally allow me to speak to Chatterjee. Same goes for Noyes, right?"

"Sorry. My parenting rights are suspended."

"Okay," I shuffled papers while my pulse slowed. "So, you started to tell me how you supported Micah about his experience with his mom?"

"Like that last Friday. The day I was arrested or, I suppose technically, the day before I was arrested. Micah disappeared sometime overnight between Friday April 8 and Saturday April 9 last year. I had him alternate weekends, although Suki often came up with excuses to interfere even with that. I used to pick him up after school on Fridays. I'd finish with my last patient at two, close my office, and be waiting for him at 3:15. I had an office in St. Louis Park back then, while I wasn't living here. Micah went to school here in Chanhassen, so it was about a 20-minute drive. I was renting a two bedroom at the other end of Frontier Trail off of 77th about a half mile away. I'd pick him up at the school and take the long way home, so we had five or ten minutes to talk in the car."

"I always tried to get him to talk about school or friends and then later I'd try to ask him about *EAU* even though I never really understood the game. All those characters on quests doing battle? Princes and goblins and robots? Not my thing. So, I used to suggest going somewhere. Shopping or out for a meal or skiing. There are a hundred restaurants and activities down near the highway. Anything. He wanted none of that. As soon as we were in the car together, he had to tell me what his mom had done to him. How she'd hurt him. Like he was reporting in. It was excruciating to hear. Every detail. Feeling so helpless. It was like he'd been holding back for two weeks while we were apart and now that we were together, he needed to spill."

"Didn't you talk in between?"

"Sure. As much as we could. I could never reach him directly because Suki would run interference, but he called me and said what he could. I know that Suki was always listening. She didn't care about court orders and how she was supposed to respect his privacy when he called. She'd make him put the calls on speaker."

"That Friday was maybe the worst. It was warm that day. The kids I saw in the pick-up line at school were in tee shirts. Some were even wearing shorts. Micah was wearing a turtleneck. When I asked him about it in the car, he rolled down the collar and showed me bruises on his throat. He said that Suki had smashed his Horizon headset -that's how he got on *EAU*- and when he tried to stop her, she strangled him. *Strangled him!* I even made him show me with his hands to make sure we meant the same thing. She tried to strangle our son! Can you believe that?"

"Why would she ....?"

"Don't ask stupid questions, Mr. Bennett. There's no 'why' that could ever justify strangling your own child. Rational thinking was never Suki's forte. She ran on pure emotion. I told Micah that. I told him that she was impulsive and explosive and dangerous."

"You told him his mother was dangerous?"

"Yes, and don't judge me for it. It was the truth. I'd never lie to him. The court forced him to live with her. I couldn't be there to protect him. If the court had made him live on a boat, I'd have given him a life preserver. This was no different. I gave him truth. It was a question of safety. Even survival."

"So that Friday he showed me how she'd strangled him. He started crying and called her a stupid bitch and I let him. I agreed with him! It's true, Suki was a stupid bitch. I told him that I needed to call the police, but he stopped me. He begged me not to. He said that the police never did anything any other time and if I did call she'd lie and then get even madder and hurt him more. So, I tried to take pictures or a video to at least document what he'd said, but he refused. I think he was embarrassed. He locked himself in his room. He wouldn't come out but he said he was okay. I know he was playing *EAU*. That's where he went to calm down. To feel like he was in control."

"Micah told me about *EAU*, Sam. He said that he was 'King Mickey Mouse' and had servants in the game?"

"That's right." Abrams smiled with pride.

Some fathers talk about their son's soccer goals or grade point average or about winning the science fair. All Abrams had was Micah's successes in an alternate universe.

"My son was a king in his own private world. Sometimes he'd talk about 'leveling up' and going on missions or quests and earning credits. He'd use the credits to become more powerful in the game. I think he must have been really good at it. But servants? You mean serfs, right?"

"Um ..." I stumbled for a moment, unsure. "I guess so. Is there a difference?"

Abrams had said that he knew nothing about *EAU.*

"I can only tell you what Micah told me." Abrams leaned back in his chair, increasing the distance between us. "He was very proud of his VR successes. He called them 'serfs,' not 'servants.' He paid game credits to get serfs to do things for him. Like beheading ogres or finding treasure or something. But what do I know? Like I said, I tried to play a couple of times, but the rules were complicated, and the menus and movements were impossible. Do this and a sword appears. Do that and your health points double. I wanted to join him in something that he enjoyed, but I failed at *EAU.* I kept getting killed by weakling little knaves and imps.

"You asked about supporting him? I was out of my mind angry when I saw that she'd put her hands around his throat. She could have killed him. Dead IRL, not VR. There'd be no rebooting after that. I'd promised Micah that I wouldn't call the police, so I went down to the kitchen and called Suki directly. She sounded drunk. It was barely four in the afternoon.

"I threatened her. It's true, I did. Make sure you get that in your little notebook, Ted." He enunciated his next words for my benefit: "I. THREATENED. TO. KILL. SUKI. KOHLER. IF. SHE. EVER. HURT. MICAH. AGAIN. I told her that she was crazy and that I hated her and that I would not be sending Micah back to her on Sunday." Abrams studied the ceiling for a long moment, smiled and wagged his head as a new thought occurred to him.

"Do you appreciate irony, Mr. Bennett? Are you paying attention? That day last April I remember thinking that if I did send Micah back to Suki, I would be an accomplice to her evil. An accessory to her abuse of our son. And here I am suspected of somehow being an accomplice to her murder. Talk about 'damned if you do, damned if you don't' eh?

"Anyway, Suki denied everything. No surprise there. She would have denied that water is wet if it suited her. She claimed that she didn't have any idea what I was talking about. That she would never hurt Micah -that made me laugh for real after everything that she'd done to me! She said that she was going to call her lawyer and the police and if Micah was not standing on her front porch at six p.m. on Sunday, she would ruin me. I remember that was her phrase: 'I will ruin you'.

"I was sitting on a bar stool at the kitchen island. I had her on speaker. At some point I noticed a reflection in the microwave door. I turned around and found Micah standing there. I don't know how long he'd been there, but my guess is that he heard the whole exchange. His mother's denials. My promise not to return him. Her threats. He was white and trembling. Unfocused. His whole body was kind of limp. He must have come down to get a snack. I was too busy yelling at his mother to hear him. He was still in his school clothes -jeans and that turtleneck; the same clothes they found him in the next day- and he had that white VR headset perched on top of his head like a crown."

"I'm sure that I swore when I realized that he was standing right there. I hung up on Suki without another word. Just cut her off. I went to comfort him, but he didn't respond. He just let me hug him. I spent the next couple of hours right next to him, trying to draw him out or at least comfort him. I must have said '*no worries, buddy. Its going to be okay*' a hundred times. He barely said a word. My cell kept ringing. It was Suki. We both ignored her. I put on a movie. Remember I told you that we were into those old black and whites? *The Wizard of Oz.* I ordered his favorite pizza. Bacon and burger from *Vesuvius.* There's one right near us. He ate one slice – I remember because he usually devoured at least three or four."

"He just sat there and stared at the screen, so I took him up to bed. I didn't bother with his clothes, although I did get his shoes off. He usually slept in sweats anyway, so I let him sleep in his clothes. That was the least of my worries at the time. I always tuck him in at bedtime when I can. I don't care how old he is. I gently rubbed some skin cream on his throat where it was still red. I kissed him on his forehead and apologized again that he'd overheard me and his mom fighting like that. I shut down *EAU* before I stepped out. He was always leaving the interface open."

I'd filled nine pages trying to get Abrams' story on paper, glancing now and then at my phone to make certain that I was recording, half hoping that Jenny would somehow reach me even without a signal. One way or the other, I lived in fear of the battery dying.

Abrams shifted back into the present: "That was the last time I saw Micah, Ted. But you saw him today. I bet he's grown. God, I miss him! What did he say about me?"

Not '*how's he eating*?' or '*does he have enough clothes*?' or '*has he made any friends*?' Abrams needed reassurance that Micah still loved him or is loyal to him or … I wasn't sure what, but I knew narcissism when I saw it. Abrams had to make it about him.

"He misses you. I didn't tell him anything though. I don't know what he knows. I didn't tell him that I've been interviewing you or about the book. Honestly, I didn't know what to say to him." I hesitated on the precipice of a decision. If I was really going to tell Abrams all I knew about his son, then I had to take the next step.

"Micah asked if I would deliver a note to you."

Abrams sat forward wide-eyed. "He gave you a note for me? Where is it?"

"I told him I would try to give you a note. No promises. And I'm not sure if I can or should give it to you." Now that I'd made the leap, there was no going back. Did I expect Abrams to advise me about the rules governing Micah's communications with him? That everything had to be vetted and censored and redacted? That giving Micah access to provocative or inflammatory information -about his trial or about Suki's murder, for example- might renew his torpor or incite him to violence? No. I had no illusions about this man's motivations. I was holding a steak just beyond the reach of a starving man. All I could expect were his demands to reach it. Abrams was only interested in serving his own needs and his need was to help Micah.

I removed the bright yellow paper from beneath my notebook, unfolded it and slid it across the desk. Tears rolled down Abrams' cheeks as he read, then he paused. His eyes narrowed. He took a very deep breath and muttered something like, "oh shit." Later, I went back and replayed the recording three or four times, but I could never quite make it out.

The psychologist looked up at me from under heavy brows. His mouth was set in a hard, firm line. He was angry and I had no idea why. He held the golden rod page up in two hands between us and slowly ripped it down the middle. Then again. And yet again until yellow confetti littered the tabletop.

He said nothing.

Abrams stared at me hard. I had no idea what to do or say. I had no idea what had just happened. The man's mood had reversed in the blink of an eye. Hearing that Micah was okay had sparked pleasure and released some of the tremendous pressure that he'd contained for months. Something in the fifteen words that Micah had scribbled in crayon had slammed that door shut and released a beast. There were no more tears on Abrams' face, although arroyos still traced their path down his cheeks. The happiness that had taken root at the beginning of this hour had died a sudden death. In its place his flat and menacing monotone had returned. He said, "Micah did not write that."

I sputtered some kind of objection, but he was done listening.

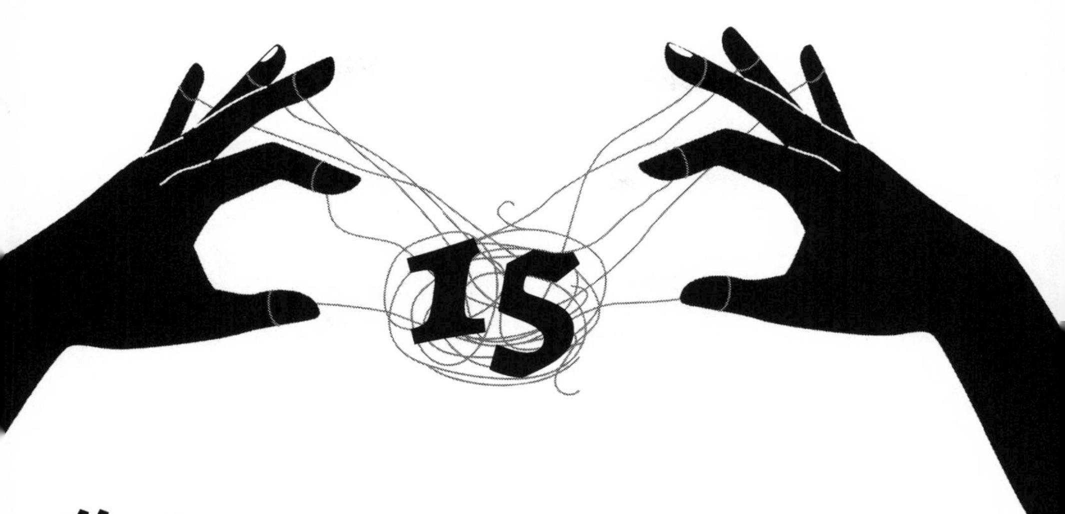

"Dr. Myra Sloan, please."

After ending the call with Camden, Jenny poked her head out of the lounge long enough to update Peter. He was glad to continue covering the floor for her as much as he could, but worried that their new supervisor -a tank of a woman she only knew facetiously as Nurse Ratched- would start looking for Nurse Villalobos any moment. Yes, the floor was bursting at the seams, and yes, she owed him big-time for the favor, and yes, the woman in 19 was a pain in the butt quite literally. She'd broken her coccis but -puns intended- she was probably going to be discharged home that afternoon.

Jenny thanked her friend profusely, promised to take him out for drinks some night soon, and begged him to run interference for her for another fifteen minutes.

"Twenty at most. I just have to call this doctor. The evaluator, Sloan."

"Of course, Jen. Do your mother-bear thing. I'm doing this for Christie you know, not for you and for sure not for Teddy. Where is the big guy anyway? Can't he help out with some of this?"

"He keeps calling and I keep putting him off. This is my shit, Peter. He shouldn't have to wade through it. He's working in the city today. Twenty minutes, okay? Then I'll be back in action."

"No rush sweetie. We got this."

A pretty, young OT and a senior nurse anesthetist who were rumored to be sleeping together had slipped into the lounge. If they'd hoped for a clandestine moment, it would have to wait. As politely as possible, Jenny herded the illicit lovers toward the door with excuses about a personal emergency and needing to make an urgent call. They reluctantly complied, wishing her well, but not without first stalling to pour themselves coffee. He took three sugars, one at a time. Jenny watched him rip open each tiny packet, pour out its contents, stir and repeat. She -the pretty OT- needed creamer but sniffed the communal cartoon of half-and-half and found it "*Yuk!*" She settled on taking her coffee black.

Alone again behind the locked door, Jenny resumed pacing circles in front of the fourth-floor window. The phone played twangy country western music while she waited for Dr. Sloan to pick up.

She checked voice mail yet again. Three new messages from Ted logged in the last forty-five minutes. It was astonishing, she thought. I'm so lucky to have found him. I couldn't love him more and I hate burdening him with this crap. Jorge is my cross to bear, not his. Ted shouldn't have to deal with him. *Chapel Heart* played faintly in the background while she tapped out a quick text to Ted: "Making progress. On hold for Dr. Sloan. Christie's fine. More tonight. Xoxo"

With the phone open in front of her, Jenny tapped the *BunnyEars* app. She zoomed in on Shakopee and then closer still on Christie's school. The ruby red dot was back at the western end of the building, probably Christie's classroom. Jenny tapped the blue ear-shaped icon at bottom of the screen. Children's voices filled her audio, superseding the noxious music. Jenny could make out something about a castle and a dinosaur. A little girl's voice and a little boy responding. There was no way to be sure, but she thought that the little girl was Christie.

"Ms. Villalobos?"

An assertive, deep female voice overrode the *BunnyEars* audio feed. Jenny fumbled the phone and finally got the device up to her ear.

"Yes, sorry. Hi. This is Jenny."

"Jenny, thanks for calling. I'm Dr. Myra Sloan. It looks like we're going to be working together." The doctor's voice was deep and serious but communicated caring. Even just those couple of words of greeting seemed relaxed and attentive. Comfortable. There was no rush about her. Jenny didn't sense any of the assembly-line condescension that she often heard from the doctors here in the hospital.

"My lawyer told me to call you."

"Mr. Camden? Good. Thanks. Do you understand what we're going to be doing together?"

"No, not really."

"Okay. I'll be brief. I'm sure you have other things going on. Mr. Villalobos filed a motion with the court about your daughter...." Jenny heard mouse clicks and imagined the woman searching for the name on a screen ... Christina ...."

"Christie," Jenny interjected. "We call her Christie for short."

"Okay, Christie. The court ordered that you and Mr. Villalobos complete a custody evaluation in my office. I'd like to get you and ..." more clicks "... Mr. Bennett -he's your live-in partner, right?"

"Teddy's my boyfriend. He helps me with Christie. We'll probably get married sometime soon." Jenny felt stupid adding that, like an anxious teenager trying to justify a bad choice to a finger-wagging parent.

"That's great. So, I'd like to get you and Mr. Bennett here this week for a couple of hours to talk. I have Jorge scheduled to come in tomorrow. His schedule is pretty flexible." She'd pronounced the name with a hard *G*. Jenny didn't bother to correct her.

"Do I have to be in the same room with him? I mean with Christie's dad?"

"With Mr. Villalobos? Would that be a problem?"

"Yes, probably. We don't talk much. I don't feel particularly safe around him. Besides, I'm working daylight hours tomorrow. Seven to three."

"Okay. Good to know. I see that you're a nurse at St. Francis. Any chance that you could be free to meet with me in my office in St. Paul Wednesday at ten a.m.? We'll need at least two hours. And could you bring Mr. Bennett, too?"

"Wednesday? I'll be on evenings, three to eleven, so I'll be free in the morning. I think Ted's free, but I'll have to check with him. Do you want Christie also?"

"No, not this time. We'll talk about when and where I can see her when we sit down together. A couple of other things while I have you. I asked Mr. Villalobos the same things: I'm going to need the names of three personal references and the names of any professionals involved in Christie's life."

"References? Like friends?" Jenny thought immediately of Peter, and then thought that maybe she'd asked enough of him already.

"Friends or family. People who know you and who can talk to me about strengths and weaknesses. Also, professionals that know Christie. Teachers. Nannies. Is she in therapy?"

"Yes. You mean Dr. Noyes. David Noyes. He's in the Laurent building in Shakopee. Sure, you can talk to him. He knows Christie pretty well. I'll get you his number."

"Excellent. Thanks. I'm putting you and Mr. Bennett in my calendar for this Wednesday -that's two days from now- at ten. Do you have my address? It's on my website. I'm in the Town Square Complex, where Seventh Place meets Minnesota. Sixth floor. Easy to find, just watch the one-way streets. There's parking next door. I can validate your pass when you're here so it's free."

This was a lot of information on top of the day's storm of emotions. Jenny had a hundred questions for the doctor but was worried that she'd been off the floor too long. She agreed to the meeting, thanked the doctor, and said goodbye, intent on updating Ted and Camden and then getting back out on the floor.

As soon as Sloan hung up the call, angry and scared voices erupted from Jenny's phone.

Children crying.

A loud man's voice in the background.

She'd left *BunnyEars* open while she was speaking to Dr. Sloan. The doctor's call had superseded the audio feed from the app which immediately resumed when the call ended. *BunnyEars* was broadcasting some kind of upset at Christie's school in real time. It was happening now, as she listened. Behind the sound of a child's upset, Jenny heard a woman and a man arguing. The deep male voice had a pronounced Mexican accent.

Mierda! Jorge was at the school.

BunnyEars works like a baby monitor. Once installed, it broadcasts a GPS location within ten feet of the source and encrypted ambient audio. It was a one-way means of listening-in to keep children safe. A nanny cam without video. Jenny could hear what Christie was hearing and saying but couldn't see anything and had no way of responding.

Jenny closed the app and tapped the speed dial for Christie's school. As the number rang, the handle on the lounge door rattled loudly. Keys jangled. The deadbolt opened. Jenny turned to see Nurse Ratched burst in, a huge ring of keys in one hand and a tablet in the other.

"White Birch Elementary, how can I help you?"

"Ms. Villalobos!" The supervisor demanded from across the room.

Jenny held up a cautious, polite "please give me a minute" hand to the angry woman, turned away from her and spoke into the phone. "Hi, this is Jenny Villalobos. I'm calling to check on my daughter, Christine."

"Ms. Villalobos!" The supervisor demanded again. She would not tolerate her staff's impertinence.

"Hi Jenny, it's Claire in the front office. We met at the Fall musical? My son Clayton is in Christie's class. The one who played bongos."

"Ms. Villalobos hang up the phone now!"

"Claire. Hi." Jenny put her hand over her other ear to try to hear better. "It's a bit of an emergency. Sorry. Has Christie's dad been there today? Did he check in with you?

"This is my last warning, Ms. Villalobos...."

Jenny turned to face the supervisor and covered the phone's mic with her other hand. "I'm really sorry. It's about my daughter. It's an emergency. I'm sorry...."

"Jenny?" The phone called out. "Are you there?"

She turned and spoke into the device. "I'm here, Claire. Sorry. What did you say?"

"I said yes. He's here right now. Is there a problem?"

"Yes, Claire. There's a very big problem. Do not let him leave with Christie. There's a court order in Christie's file. Do not let him take her. Call the police if you need to. I'll be there in ten minutes."

She turned back to discover the nurse supervisor standing directly in her path, scowling, arms crossed, glasses dangling on a beaded chain around her neck. The woman was shorter than Jenny by at least two inches, twice her age, and twice as wide. She wore a pressed, white uniform out of the 1950s that had earned her the *Nurse Ratched* moniker. Jenny read the name tag riding high on her mountainous left breast: "Nurse Manager Molotov."

Molotov, like the incendiary cocktail. The name suited her.

"Ms. Villalobos, I explained earlier that we are full up. All hands on-deck. Now I've learned that you've been holed up in here making personal phone calls. My staff can't get coffee and my patients aren't getting their needs met." Jenny saw Peter standing in the open door behind the squat woman's shoulder. He made a tight shrug and wore a guilty expression that seemed to say, "Sorry. I tried!"

"Ma'am, I'm really sorry, I…."

"I don't care." Molotov cut in. "I don't care about your personal life when you're on my floor. You have a job to do. Are you aware, for example, that Mrs. Schwartz in 19 threw a clot about an hour ago and almost died because you were busy making personal calls?" Jenny's heart sank, but her need to race to Christie's side was far stronger. The image of Jorge taking Christie out of school with promises of ice cream and princess movies and then disappearing into God-knows-where terrified her.

Nurse Manager Molotov persisted: "I'm sure that you don't know that the ICU is sending us two more MVA victims with multiple compound fractures and that Mr. Tarnicky is back with the broken arm. The man who fell off his garage roof? Dr. McLeod is doing a revision on him this afternoon. I heard you say that you were going somewhere?" The woman's painted-on eyebrows arched into her hairline. "Let me be perfectly clear: If you leave this floor before shift end, don't bother coming back."

"Ma'am, I have a real emergency going on right now. My daughter…. I have to go…."

"Your patients have real emergencies going on, Ms. Villalobos. This is a hospital. That's why they come here. If you leave, its *adios amiga* for good. *Comprenday*?"

Jenny's face was flushed. She stood her ground for half a moment more, reflexively reaching back to tighten her ponytail. Molotov took a quick step backwards as if she feared that Jenny was about to strike her. Jenny looked at her phone and then back into her supervisor's puffy face and over-rouged cheeks. Screw it. There was no question. Christie gets priority every single time.

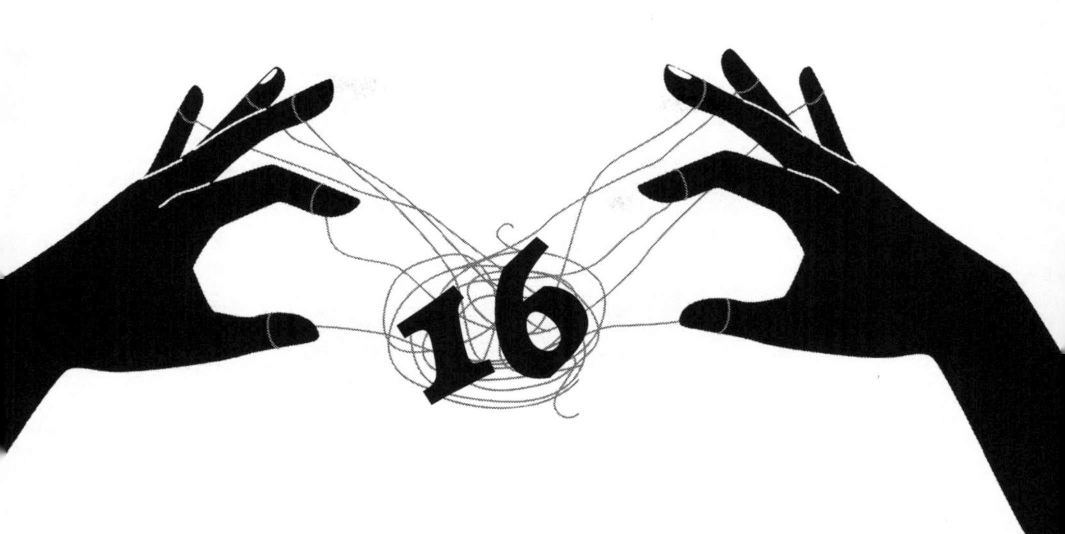

The parking lot was full of mommy vans and rusted-out old clunkers. Jorge didn't see a respectable ride anywhere in six jam-packed rows of parked cars. He did see a million cutesy bumper stickers bragging about dogs and warning about babies-on-board and rooting for the Shakopee Sabers. The only open spot anywhere near the attractive two-story brick building was overshadowed by a sign that read "Volunteer of the Month." Not only wasn't he a volunteer of any sort, he wouldn't have parked there if his life depended on it. All these little snots throwing car doors open wide and distracted mommies backing up while handing out juice boxes was a certain path to dings and dents and crushed bumpers.

Jorge found the furthest corner of the lot and even then, pulled onto a muddy berm rather than park the mustang within spitting distance of any other vehicle.

Iggy Azalea blasted on the car's six speakers, drowning out all other sounds within and around the vehicle. Monstrous fifteen-inch after-market *Boost* sub-woofers in each door made the windshield vibrate. He felt the beat in his teeth. The lyrics turned Jorge's Mustang into the Australian rap artist's sick black Ferrari in her supercool *Team* video.

Jorge was pumped.

"Aye baby! No way! Watch me do my thang!"

The growl of the engine and the thunderous music cut out abruptly. Jorge felt like a rock star as he stepped out into the sunshine. A line of coke helped. He imagined paparazzi swarming him, begging for selfies, and then his brand new Bondis began to sink into the muddy slush. "Mierda*!*"

he cursed and skip-hopped onto the blacktop. A tall bald man with a goatee carrying a little boy in his arms was staring at him. Jorge glared back through mirrored Tempests at the pair and called out, "What're you looking at, *pendejo*?"

The man shook his head vigorously and turned away, feeling like he'd been transported from small town Minnesota to Tijuana and not at all happy about it.

Schools being schools in the twenty-first century, Jorge had to sign in in a chilly outer foyer, hand over his ID, and then walk through a metal detector to even get to the front office. A bubbly woman with graying hair greeted him.

"Hi Mr. Villalobos! I'm Claire. I'm Clayton's mom. He's in Christie's class. I even think they kind of like each other. Isn't that cute? How can I help you today?"

"I need to see Christie."

"Sure. I hope everything's okay?" Jorge said nothing. The woman's nosy chatter bugged the shit out of him. "Sure. Okay." She handed him a time-stamped dated sticker that identified him by name and his destination as 1C Merganser. Jorge slapped the sticker on his leather jacket and started to leave the front office space.

Ever helpful, Claire called after him: "Do you know where Ms. Merganser's room is? Just down the hall to the right at the very end facing you. Room 1C. If you end up at the multi-purpose room, you went the wrong direction."

The school was obviously built with small children in mind. Wide, polished hallways were punctuated with dark wood doors inset with broad square windows looking in on quiet classes. All the doorknobs were hip-high. Children's glue-and-glitter artwork was taped on every available wall, over half-height bubblers and beneath bulletin boards that barely reached the top of Jorge's head. Painted papier mâché masks filled a display table outside the door marked "3A Arlington."

A threesome of little girls walked past hand-in-hand-in-hand, all three in braids. The redhead in the group called out "Hi!" in his general direction as they passed. High pitched, off-key singing accompanied by a piano carried out from one room. The sounds of clapping and cheering carried out from another.

An ancient analogue clock hung from the ceiling midway down the hall. Jorge hadn't seen one in years, and it took a moment to decipher the time. It was one fifteen.

Jorge had never been here before. He let Jenny do all this shit. School stuff. Christie was only 6, after all. How hard could it be? He helped her with numbers and letters and colors when he saw her, but mostly that stuff was boring, so they spent a lot of time playing video games and going to the gym where they had free daycare and going sledding in winter. Christie was fearless even on the black diamond hills that Jorge preferred.

He knocked on the door marked "1C Merganser" and walked in.

The classroom was a large, brightly lit, and colorful rectangle. Orange and purple and yellow origami animals hung on fishing line from the ceiling. Half-size wooden lockers and bookcases and cabinets lined three walls. The fourth wall faced the outside of the building. Its lower half was all radiator. Its upper half gave a view across scrawny, dormant bushes onto the parking lot he'd just left. He was glad to see the Mustang still tucked away safely in the far corner and that the bald douche bag carrying the kid who'd given him the stink-eye was gone.

Four or five small groups of children were scattered about the room. Some were focused on activities on the floor. Others were seated in clusters of short desks. Christie was playing with two boys on the floor around a plastic castle that was presently under attack by a menacing sparkly green dragon. She -the child, not the dragon- was wearing pink overalls and had her hair in a ponytail. A silver bracelet flashed on her left wrist.

Jorge caught Christie's eye from across the room and waved. She looked away.

"Can I help you?"

The woman was in his face, obviously inserting herself like a shield protecting the students, no doubt imagining worst case scenarios. She was stick-thin and wiry, wearing large, green-rimmed glasses, gray slacks, and a man's white button-down dress shirt. Her hair was very short, exposing a very attractive face with no makeup. When Jorge didn't respond, she spoke up more forcefully, "Can I help you, sir? I'm Ms. Merganser. Who are you please?"

Jorge realized that he was still wearing the expensive sunglasses. He took them off and put on the charm. "Ms. Merganser? It's nice to finally meet you. I'm Christie's dad. Jorge Villalobos."

The woman held his gaze for a long moment as if reading words printed across his forehead spelling out whether he meant to harm her children. His smile finally convinced her. She backed down and held out her hand. His grip was strong, and his skin was rough.

"I'm afraid that we're in the midst of activity centers, Mr. Villalobos. This isn't a good time."

"Call me '*Or-hey*', please."

"Jorge… I was saying that we're in the midst of an activity as you can see. Is there something I can help you with?"

"No, thank you. I guess my message didn't reach you?" He was lying. He'd left no message. "I spoke with the woman in the front office. I have to take Christie out of class. There's a small family emergency. She'll be out for a day or two.

"I'm terribly sorry to hear that."

"But Christie doesn't know yet. We're trying to protect her as long as we can. I'm sure that you understand."

"Of course, but you'll have to get her excused in the front office. That's where you checked in when you first arrived. Straight down the hall. And you know that you'll need a doctor's note or a note from Christie's mother, right?"

Christie had done nothing to acknowledge Jorge since he'd arrived. No wave or smile. Not a word. In fact, she'd pointedly turned her back on him. Jorge ignored the teacher. He stepped over a game board toward the little girl and her playmates. Ms. Merganser was fast behind him, calling him by name.

"Hi Christina! I guess you didn't notice me. I'm here to take you on an adventure, sweetie."

Christie kept playing, pointedly ignoring her father even after her playmates had taken their dragon and withdrawn to join their friends who'd retreated to the edges of the room.

"Mr. Villalobos!" the teacher repeated, trying to get his attention.

Jorge put a hand on Christie's shoulder. She reacted like she'd been touched by a live wire.

"Get away from me!" she screamed at full volume. "I don't ever want to go with you! You're a bad daddy!"

Ms. Merganser was on her cell phone talking rapidly. She ended the call and tried to step between the man and the child.

"*Mr. Villalobos*! I must insist that you go to the front office immediately. You've disrupted my class and upset Christie. I've called the principal and asked for assistance. Please leave now."

Christie had scooted around and now clung to Ms. Merganser's leg. Jorge rose to his full height and stood nose-to-nose with the teacher. He spoke loudly and clearly and with menace, one finger pointing in her face: "This is my daughter, lady. I am taking her with me."

The room full of first graders burst into tears, becoming a noisy, sniffling Greek chorus accentuating the tension playing out at center stage. Ms. Merganser's usually Zen and happy classroom was in upheaval. The teacher was stuck in a standoff with an angry parent. All she could do was keep her children safe and try to buy time until reinforcements arrived.

Jorge bent down and easily pried Christie's tiny fingers off the teacher's gray gabardine-covered leg, lifted her screaming, flailing forty-pound body into the air, and chucked her over his shoulder. Christie's little fists slammed against her father's black leather jacket. Her sneakers kicked his chest.

Jorge turned to leave.

Ms. Merganser had fallen back to protect the other students cowering and sniveling behind her. She had her phone back to her ear when another adult suddenly stormed into the room.

Claire from the school's front desk was breathing hard. She blocked the door and addressed Jorge with a force that the diminutive woman didn't appear capable of: "Mr. Villalobos! You know very well that there's a court order forbidding you from excusing Christie from school. I've informed the principal and she is calling the police."

At this the girls in the room cried louder. Many of the boys got excited. Were the police really coming to their school? Was Christie's father a bad guy?

He was wearing all black and bad guys always wear black, right? One of those boys, a child named Clayton who had been busy counting colored-blocks and writing numbers on a worksheet, looked up and exclaimed "Mommy!" with glee. Front Desk Claire blew him a kiss but kept on talking.

Christie was yelling "No! No! I am not going with Voldemort! I hate you I hate you I hate you!"

Merganser was a die-hard J.K. Rowling fan. She'd seen every movie at least twice and secretly had a mad crush on Rolanda Hooch, one of Harry Potter's flying instructors and his quidditch coach. Christie's reference to the author's most famous evil necromancer struck home. She boldly stepped forward while Villalobos was confronting Front Desk Claire, wrapped an arm around the little girl and forcefully leveraged her out of her father's arms. Christie crumpled into her grasp, crying, and yelling "I hate him I hate him I hate him!"

Jorge was debating the wording of the court order with Claire, asserting his fatherly rights, damning the courts as biased toward mothers, criticizing Claire for overstepping her role, and threatening to sue everyone beginning with her. "I know the superintendent, lady. There is no way you're getting away with this. I will have the governor fire your fat ass before you can hand out another stupid sticker!" With that, he tore the printed white rectangle off his jacket and threw the shreds harmlessly in Claire's face.

Ms. Merganser held Christie in one arm and gathered as many students as she could in the other. She turned her back to the melee to create an impromptu circle time in the furthest corner of the room, careful to keep every little eye focused on her reassuring face. Christie was still whimpering. The group had barely started a round of "eensy-weensy spider" when a school-wide alarm sounded *Whoop! Whoop! Whoop!* startling into panic the few children who had begun to settle. A calm but mechanical voice began repeating over the PA system: "Shelter in place, please. Remain where you are, close all doors and windows, and shelter in place. This is not a drill."

Children's sobs now seemed to shake the entire building. Hard-soled shoes ran staccato through the hollow, empty hall. Doors slammed.

Ms. Merganser switched to "Old McDonald."

Two flak-jacketed, helmeted police officers carrying assault rifles entered the room. Principal Jane-Ellen Stewart followed closely in their wake wearing a Kevlar vest over her flowery dress. The blue-haired veteran of both Kandahar and kindergarten surveyed the scene and then pushed her way forward to spell Front Desk Claire who'd obviously gone far above and beyond. Claire retreated to comfort six-year-old Clayton who, as it turned out, needed no comfort at all. He pointed and yelled out above the upheaval, "Look Mommy, they have real machine guns!"

The officers split up and approached Jorge from two sides at once while he argued his case with Principal Stewart. He continued to rant about his rights and his friends in high places and how others were going to hear about this as his arms were angled behind his back and secured with plasticuffs. Radios blared static and muffled words. The senior officer, a Shakopee PD sergeant unfortunately named Brownose, spoke into a walkie-talkie advising all first responders that the intruder was secured and to stand down. The schoolwide alarm continued *Whoop! Whoop!* and the PA announcement continued to repeat at intervals largely because there was no one left in the front office to turn it off. Everyone who knew how was here, in room 1C.

This was the state of things when Jenny arrived.

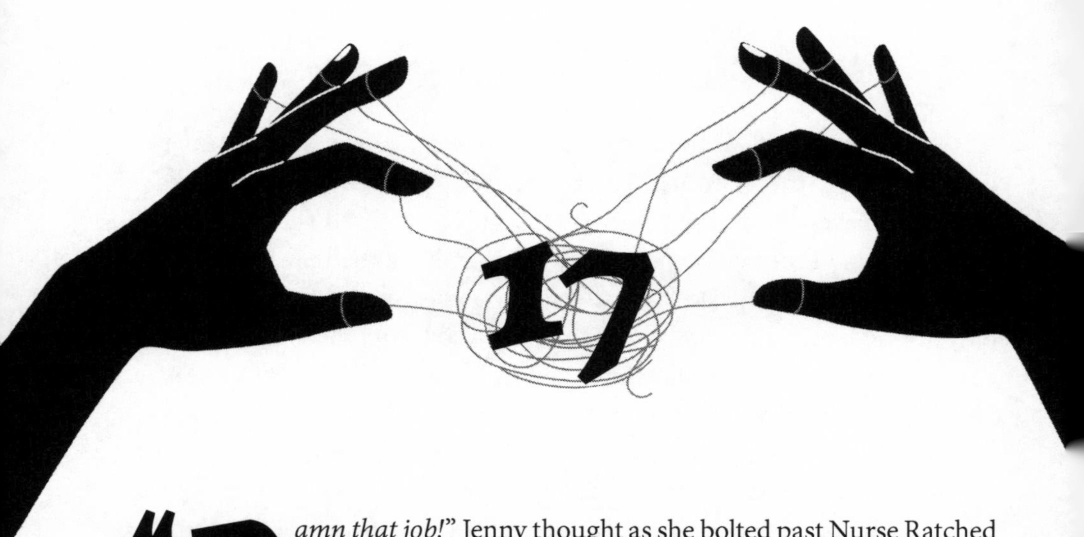

"D*amn that job!*" Jenny thought as she bolted past Nurse Ratched and out of the nurse's lounge. She fist-bumped Peter on her way down the hall straight to the stairs. She took all four flights two steps at a time, almost colliding with a phlebotomist carrying test tubes full of blood. She sprinted through the hospital lobby and past a statue of the Dakota Chief for whom the town was named. Patients and visitors and staff and security stared as she ran. She was briefly stymied by the revolving doors which moved slower when she pushed at them, forcing her to pause, ease the glass door forward slowly, then pause again. Freedom opened up to her one degree at a time until she could squeeze out, into the chilly sunshine. She'd left her coat and purse in her locker, but her keys were in her pocket and her phone was still in her hand. The car was a hundred yards away across slushy roads and muddy median strips.

Breathing hard, keys finally in the ignition, all she could think about was Christie.

St. Francis to White Birch Elementary is about five miles as the crow flies, but the school was at the other end of a long oval with no way to travel straight up the middle. Jenny instinctively veered left onto Eagle Creek and then wondered if the right onto Valley View might have been quicker. Too late. She was committed. She drove sixty on the forty mile-per-hour blacktop, worried that she'd be stopped for speeding without a license, unaware that that was impossible. Every first responder within ten miles was already racing ahead of her to Christie's school.

Jenny held her phone up to one ear while she steered around law-abiding drivers with one hand. She pushed a button and instructed, "Call Ted mobile speaker." Siri cooperated for a change, and she heard his phone ring once then go to voice mail. *Damn!* "Call me!" she shouted, then she hung up.

"Call Mark Camden" she instructed. Nothing happened. She glanced down and saw a list of "Mark" names and numbers from her phone book. Her thumb was barely long enough to reach around to scroll down to "Camden, Lawyer." The phone rang. Voice mail again. "Mark. Jenny Villalobos again. I think Jorge is trying to take Christie from school. I'm on my way there now. Please call me asap. Thanks."

She ran the yellow light as she raced east where Mystic crosses Eagle Creek with silent apologies to a dozen drivers who reasonably gave her the finger. She caught the green onto route 21 but took the turn way too fast. The 4Runner canted up and then settled back on creaky old springs still doing fifty. She had to slow where 21 ended at Southbridge and then again turning onto Old Carriage Road not because of road conditions but instead because she found herself at the end of a parade of police cruisers, ambulances, fire trucks, and news vans.

Scores of red and blue and orange and yellow bubble lights strobed. Dozens of emergency blinkers flashed. A hundred brake lights glowed red. The vehicles cast a weird Christmas-like veneer over the otherwise mundane neighborhood and its sere and slushy landscape. Jenny had no idea what to make of the scene except to pray for Christie's safety. She wove around ambulances way too fast and nearly spun out on someone's lawn as she tried to circumvent a ladder truck from Chaska, the next town over. She finally abandoned the old SUV on Stratford and took off on foot across lawns and driveways toward the school.

The general din of the scene grew as she ran toward the tan brick building. Engines grumbled. People yelled. Radios hissed and crackled. The *Whoop! Whoop!* of a siren grew louder as she approached the school building and then was joined by a mechanical voice repeating something about "Shelter in place." That was the 9-1-1 phrase that she heard when the news covered school shootings. *Oh my god!* Jenny panicked. *Had Jorge brought a weapon into the school? Was he trying to kill people?*

Was he trying to kill Christie?

Two Shakopee officers forcibly stopped her a hundred yards from the school's front doors. The open lawn between here and there that normally hosted a carnival in the spring and leaf-peeping festival in the fall was filled with uniformed first responders of all stripes herding gawkers and pop-up protesters and half a dozen news anchors and their cameramen away from the building.

The officers demanded to see Jenny's ID. She had none, which escalated their caution until they registered her last name. "Villalobos?" they asked. Yes. Why? A short policeman with a moustache and a name tag that read "Parchman" stepped away to talk on a walkie talkie while a tall, blonde cop named "Hatch" made sure that she stayed put.

Parchman returned and said to Hatch: "They said to escort her in."

"Copy that, boss. I'll take her."

"What's going on? Please…! My daughter's in there!"

Hatch replied, "So's your husband, Ma'am. He's what this little party's all about."

"He's not my husband, officer. He's my ex- and he's crazy. Dangerous. Abusive. Just let me get to my daughter, please."

"Yes Ma'am. My job is to walk you in the front door. They're waiting for you in the school office. They say it's safe now, but there are still a lot of cameras watching. Do you want this?" Hatch offered Jenny a blue-and-black Shakopee PD ballcap. She was confused for a moment, and then grateful. She tucked her ponytail inside and pulled the cap down tight over her forehead, obscuring her face in shadow.

"Thank you, officer."

Hatch hurried Jenny forward across the muddy lawn. The outer perimeter of officers let them through, leaving them alone to cross the last hundred yards, a muddy and marshy demilitarized zone. Jenny's sneakers were quickly soaked. Every step made a sucking sound.

The announcement blaring over the school's PA system changed. The new message contradicted every fiber of Jenny's being: "All safe" it lied. "Please resume usual activities."

Jenny had sold girl scout cookies and tickets to the Halloween haunted house from a card table in the school lobby where SWAT-looking men in armored vests and shiny black helmets now carried deadly automatic weapons. She stared right, uncomprehending, toward 1C and Christie as Hatch steered her by an elbow to the left and into the front office. The experience was surreal. Jenny had somehow been transported to Beirut or Saigon or the West Bank. She was Matthew Modine in *Full Metal Jacket* and John Malkovich in *The Killing Fields.*

Hatch called her name. Twice. She slowly oriented to the voice and realized that the officer had parked her in a small cluster of people standing around an abandoned secretary's desk. A stapler and landline phone and a pile of orange TARDY slips littered the surface. Principal Stewart stood nearby, deep in conversation with an older man in a brown uniform. Two muscular and silent officers in black body armor held a third man between them.

It was Jorge.

Rage overtook her. Hatch held her back.

"Where is Christie?" Jenny screamed. "What have you done, you goddamned idiot? Where is my daughter?"

Jorge's hands were clamped behind his back. One officer held his left forearm and shoulder. Another held his right. His mouth was free, and he didn't hesitate to use it.

"I came to see *OUR* little girl in school, *puta*!" He spat out the profanity. "YOU turned this into a madhouse, not me."

"There's a restraining order, *GEORGE*!" She intentionally used the anglicized pronunciation that he despised. "You are not allowed to come to her school."

"No, little girl," he condescended, always eager to put her in her place. "I'm not allowed to pick her up after school. Can't you read? Didn't your fancy lawyers teach you anything? There's nothing stopping me from taking Christie out to lunch and this is what I get? When the court hears about this, it's all over for you and your Teddy bear, Jennifer! French told me you'd try something like this. Desperate mothers always do, he said! And that evaluator? Sloan? I'm seeing her tomorrow and I will make sure that she hears every detail of how you set me up in front of Christina. My poor sweet baby had to see me handcuffed by men with automatic weapons? Talk about alienation! Once I tell the court about this, you're done, *Mamasita. Terminado!* Finished! I will take away custody and everything that matters to you!"

The officers manhandling Jorge turned him away from Jenny. She watched as they led him out of the office, through the foyer, and out the front doors. The photographers and news channels would have a field day with this. *"Headline news! Mexican American father arrested trespassing on school grounds. Children in lock down. News at eleven."* She hoped that they'd send him to Guantanamo or Alcatraz or death row. She'd never been so terrified and enraged and humiliated in her entire life.

Where was Christie?

Officer Hatch was still next to her. She begged him to take her to her daughter. Hatch caught the eye of the older man in the brown uniform who nodded okay, so he led her into the foyer and down the east corridor past long walls of children's arts and crafts and under the analogue clock overhead that none of the students could decipher. A banner with a picture of a prehistoric tiger roaring in the background urged students to "Cheer for our Sabers!". Curious children of every size and shape and color peeked out of classroom doors as she walked and then jogged and then broke into a run toward Christie's room. Hatch kept pace.

The classroom door was ajar. A woman's gentle voice sung quietly somewhere inside the dimly lit space. Children sniffled and whined quietly where they sat, in a close circle around Mrs. Merganser. Jenny saw several children that she recognized clinging to stuffed animals and blankets. More than one had thumb to mouth. One dark shape clung to Ms. M's chest while she read "Make Way for Ducklings" out loud.

Jenny stopped in the doorway, hands clasped to her mouth, stifling a sob. Breathing hard. That was Christie in the teacher's lap, fitted to the woman like a second skin. The ponytail and the shiny *BunnyEars* bracelet gave her away. She wanted to swoop in and gather Christie up in her arms but stopped herself. The group was just beginning to settle down. She would startle them back into tears.

My god! What had Jorge done to upset the entire school and bring an army down on him?

Ms. Merganser saw Jenny in the doorway and nodded in her direction without missing a beat. She pointed her chin down toward the shape in her lap and smiled. The ducklings were crossing a busy street one at a time.

Out of nowhere an arm encompassed Jenny from behind. She jumped and bit back a yelp.

"Jenny!" Claire exclaimed, and then hushed herself. She continued in a forced whisper, "Jenny! I'm so, so sorry! You were right. I shouldn't have let him in but then when I told Mrs. Stewart and she called the police and all those policemen showed up it was too late. I couldn't stop it. Can you ever forgive me, Jenny? Please? I want Christie and Clayton to be able to play together. He really likes her!"

Jenny just hugged the woman and they cried together quietly. They hugged out their fear and worry for a long moment, long enough for the ducklings to all arrive home safely with their mother and for Ms. Merganser to pluck a beloved Judy Blume book off a nearby shelf.

"You did good, Claire. I can never thank you enough. You were the hero here," she reassured. "They told me that you stood up to Christie's dad? That was brave and a little bit foolish. Please do not do that again, Claire. Please. He's crazy," Jenny said too loudly. "Dangerous. He hurts people and scares the you-know-what out of me..."

Jenny's smock was catching on something. Jeez, how could she still be wearing her stupid smock from St. Francis? She took a step back from Claire and discovered Christie standing between them, silent, dark eyes pleading and arms upstretched. Tears poured down her face, snot clung to her nose. Jenny's eyes immediately filled with tears of her own. She felt relief. She squatted down to take the child into her arms or maybe back into her womb -anywhere that she would be safe. She let Christie's weight topple her backwards onto the classroom floor. Mother and daughter rolled onto the carpet, arms enveloping one another, an enmeshed ball of crying needy arms and legs. The two just held one another and sobbed together until words finally coalesced and found voice.

"Mommy, don't let him take me!"

"Christie are you okay? You were so brave!"

"Don't let daddy near me. I hate him I hate him I hate him!"

"I won't sweetie. You're safe now. He's a bad man. He's gone. Are you hurt? Did he hurt you?"

Clair was still standing above them.

"The army people took him away, Mommy. Is he gone now? All gone?"

"Yes sweetie. He's gone. I've got you. You're safe."

"Mrs. M took care of me. She held me and she sang to us all and we read books and covered our eyes so we couldn't see the big guns and they took daddy away. Is he gone forever now? I hope he stays gone forever."

"He's gone for now sweetie. I've got you. How 'bout if we go home? Would you like to put on your PJs and cuddle in the big bed?"

"With Teddy Bear? Will he be there?"

Teddy.... Jenny realized that he knew none of this. Where was he?

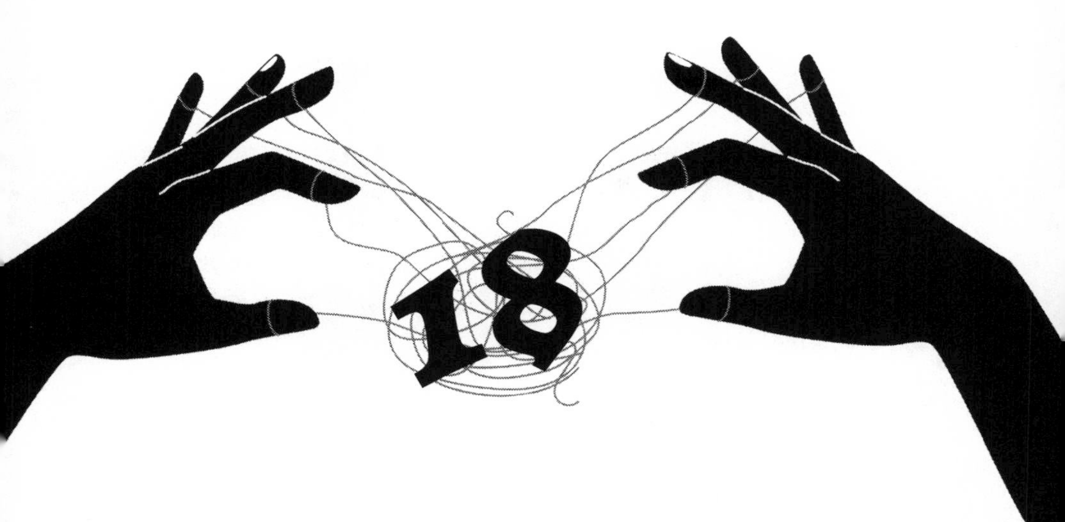

I was out Abrams' exit door, up the short slope, and back in my car. The first thing that I did was check my phone. For my short hour with Abrams, Jenny never left my mind. Voldemort's new effort to switch custody and Dr. Sloan's evaluation were my priority. My phone started dinging as delayed messages caught up with me. Twenty seconds later I had sixteen voice mails, mostly from Jenny. My text messages were flooded too, again mostly from Jenny. The most recent was typed in caps: "PLEASE CALL ASAP." The one prior was identical.

I tapped the most recent voice mail and heard a recording reassure me that, "Got her. We're okay. What a mess! On our way home. Meet us there asap." That was almost twenty minutes ago. I didn't understand. I opened the message that she'd recorded sixteen minutes before that. Jenny's voice was frantic: "Call me Ted. Please ASAP. I'm going to the school now. Jorge's there."

What the hell had happened?

I speed-dialed her phone while I put the car in gear. She actually picked up. I was panicking by now, but her voice was subdued. Hushed.

"Jenn, what the hell is happening…?"

"Shhhh. We're okay. Really. I promise. I'm home with Christie. She's almost asleep. Come home. I'll tell you."

Twenty minutes south. There was no way that I could focus to use this time constructively. Abrams didn't matter. My morning experiences at MPH and my afternoon interview were a trivial jumble of faces and emotions and ideas. Where usually I was magically able to sort ideas into categories and themes and eventually into paragraphs and chapters, today felt like living inside a popcorn popper, constantly startled by events erupting on all sides. I was on high alert, living in a war zone. Hypervigilant and on edge. Every sensation was amplified by my intense concern for Jenny and Christie.

In the end, I gave up trying to dictate my notes and even trying to think. Work would have to wait. I turned on the radio.

That was one of my many mistakes that day.

Every station was broadcasting urgent bulletins about what was being called "*an aborted school shooting in Shakopee, Minnesota, a small suburb south of Minneapolis.*" Nationally known newscasters were interrupting regularly scheduled programming to focus on "*an incident now in progress in a small public elementary school in suburban Minnesota.*"

Holy shit! Christie!

"*First responders are reporting that no one was injured in a midday incident in this Twin Cities bedroom community. Local police and firefighters are being praised for their rapid and decisive actions. One unconfirmed account described a masked gunman who forced entry into the White Birch Elementary School in Shakopee, a village of nearly forty-four thousand. We have no word yet on who that person may be and what his or her intentions were.*"

I floored the gas. Familiar landmarks flew by in a blur. I passed hundreds of motorists -even those speeding drivers who I honk at when they fly past me on any other day- as if they were standing still. I didn't care if I got stopped. The ticket wouldn't matter and I was pretty sure that having a kid at White Birch would work as a get-out-of-jail-free pass.

"Yes officer," I imagined saying, "she is my child. I don't care that we don't share DNA or a last name or even a legal relationship. I love her like a father. In fact, I love her far better than her actual father!"

I made the twenty-minute drive in twelve and the three-minute lazy walk up the drive and into the apartment in thirty seconds. "Quiet," I told myself too loudly. "Shhhh!" Jenny had said that Christie was asleep. At 3:30 in the afternoon? I walked-ran-tiptoed up to Christie's room. Empty and dark. Across the hall to our bedroom. An unfamiliar ball cap that read "Shakopee Police Department" and Jenny's work smock lay in the doorway. Curtains were drawn against the bright afternoon light. Jenny's favorite denim shirt was thrown over a bedside lamp, bluing its glow. The ivory tatted comforter that Jenny had inherited from her grandmother was shaped around two silent forms. Mother and daughter lay intertwined and enmeshed, a tangle of arms and legs and sheets. One of Piglet's pudgy pink legs protruded between them. Both were fast asleep.

I sighed deeper than I have ever sighed, releasing something that needed to see this tranquil scene before it could settle. I still had no idea what had really happened, but my girls were safe. The news had given me plenty to catastrophize about. The unfamiliar police department ballcap raised still other questions. For now, all that mattered was that we three were home together.

I swept a collection of sweatshirts and jeans and forgotten socks off the armchair in the corner of our bedroom and sat. My body still felt like it was barreling down the highway at ninety. My brain was still on overload and my emotions were volcanic. I probably would have been better off on a treadmill or beating up a heavy bag at the gym or doing shots at a bar, but this place at this time was where I belonged. Watching my girls sleep. Keeping my family safe.

A million anxieties tried to distract me like mosquitoes on a muggy summer night. I'd bat at one and two more would appear....

... What the hell had happened at White Birch today? How was Jorge involved?

... if Jorge was the unidentified school "intruder," had he been arrested? Was he in jail?

... If Jorge was the school intruder, was this proof enough of his insanity to at least postpone or even cancel the custody evaluation? What better evidence would the court and Dr. Sloan need?

... Sloan. I still hadn't returned her call. Had Jenny spoken with her?

... I really wanted to talk to Mark Camden before I spoke with Sloan. Would Jenny let me? Could Camden help us manage the evaluation process and keep Christie?

... was it really possible that the Court would take Christie away from us? That just seemed so entirely crazy but look at how crazy today had been. Crazy is not impossible.

… How had Jenny reached Christie so fast and so early? Her first messages were time-stamped over the lunch hour. She must have collected Christie before two. Getting off shift at the hospital usually takes an act of God. Come to think of it, I didn't see her car downstairs.

Take a deep breath, I reminded myself. Nothing else matters. She's right here in front of me, safe and sound. I yawned deeply and stretched. My world was slowing down.

… If Christie had been through some kind of ordeal, should we reach out to David Noyes?

… Noyes! Abrams had identified Noyes as Micah's doctor. Is that good like having an "in" or somehow bad for Christie?

… what had triggered Abrams at the end of today's interview? He'd become enraged. Would he even meet with me on Wednesday, or had I somehow destroyed his trust in me?

… and Micah? Do I need to see him again? Could I find a way to get back into MPH if I needed to?

With my plate full to bursting, I did the only thing that made sense in that moment. I breathed in the quiet, sleepy scent of my two girls, studied the contours of how they lay together wrapped in and around the comforter, allowed myself one more sigh of relief and release, and fell fast asleep.

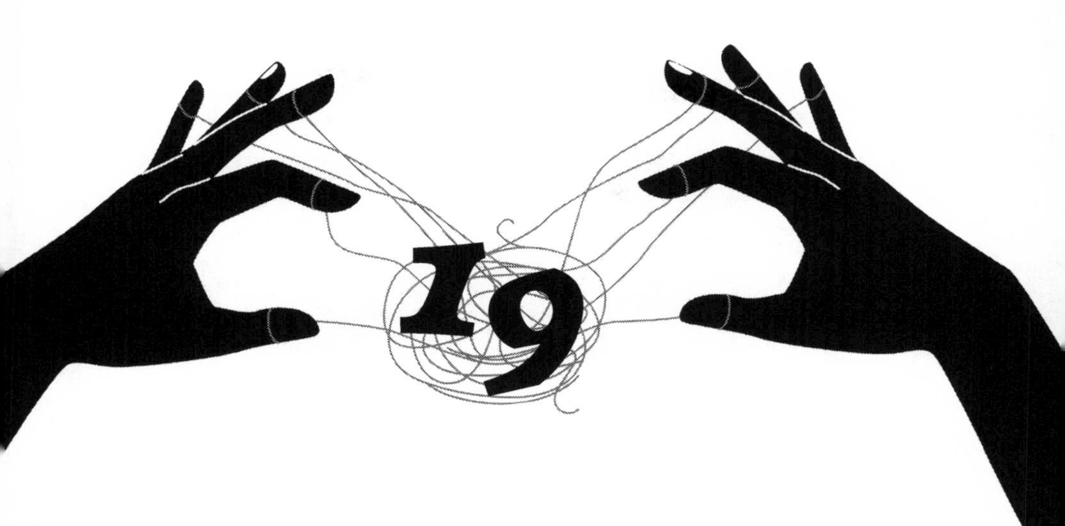

As Ted finally relaxed, safe in the womblike comfort of his home, watching Jenny and Christie sleep, a 17-year-old paraplegic named Rush was wide awake in Hoboken, Texas. Hoboken is a pitstop for long haul drivers who cut across the panhandle north of Amarillo on their way to Albuquerque and points west or to Kansas City and points east. It's a must-see destination for die-hard railroad historians, a waystation for lost travelers, and a vacation destination for no one.

Of the 1,437 lost and sunbaked souls who call Hoboken home, three identify as African American and nine identify as Native American. Rushing Water Mercantur Tarnup was both. As if this didn't make him special enough, ever since he'd drunk-driven his daddy's F150 across Texas State Highway 15 on a dare at night with his lights out and his eyes closed he'd also become the town's only cripple. He figured he was thrice blessed.

Rush's unique status in an incredibly boring town in the armpit of the world had once-upon-a-time bugged the shit out of him. This is how and why a 14-year-old ends up T-boned in a stolen pickup by an 80,000-pound truck doing ninety miles an hour. Fortunately, his daddy's outrage over the total destruction of his vehicle had been just a notch or two weaker than his pity over the near total destruction of the stupid kid who'd been driving it. If Rush had known that only kids who can walk get whipped with the buckle end of the belt, and that crippled kids recovering from endless surgeries who were stuck in wheelchairs got Horizon 4 VR devices from sympathy-riddled strangers, he might've started playing chicken much sooner.

Rush dropped out of school in tenth grade mostly because he'd been in the hospital all of second semester, but also because *who-the-fuck-cares anyway*? After almost two months at Baylor in Dallas, an ambulance had driven him four hundred miles north to do rehab in Perryton where he'd celebrated his fifteenth birthday -if you considered overdosing on oxy a celebration. The good doctors in Perryton taught him to use a wheelchair, convinced themselves that the overdose had been an accident, and discharged him home.

Daddy had a new truck by then. New to him, anyway. A rusted-out white Ram. He'd driven Rush the fifteen miles home to Hoboken, carried him and his wheelchair up the fire escape to the one-bedroom that they shared above the Dollar Tree, parked him on his bed and went to work. Next to the bed, Rush found a warm six pack of Mountain Dew, the remote control for a small TV, a month-old box of get-well-soon cards from his former classmates, and a large unopened box from Amazon. Packing tape yielded to the knife that he always carried. Styrofoam popcorn littered the floor. Buried inside was a get-well card from the Young Dreamers Foundation *-bringing hope and opportunity to less fortunate youth!-* and t Horizon 4-DV 2.

Rush barely recalled the pretty Black nurse in Dallas who'd insisted that he apply to YDF. He'd been in the depths of his *who-the-fuck-cares anyway?* period -basically every minute of the last three years- so he'd *Yes Ma'amed* her long enough to make her go away. What were his dreams, she'd asked. He said something about pitching for the Rangers and landing on the moon and having sex with a hot Black nurse – *wink, wink!* She'd written down the first and the second, ignored the last, and emailed off his application.

Setting up the device was far more physically demanding than mentally challenging, even for a high school dropout. Plugging wires into white hard plastic hardware wasn't hard. Transferring in and out of the wheelchair was a bitch. Dragging his deadweight lower half up off the floor left him panting and cramped. He sweated and cursed and cried and gave up a dozen times during that long first day home alone, but then he got it. He figured out the angles and the leverage and shoved the furniture where it belonged. The good news is that the Wi-Fi above the Dollar Tree is surprisingly strong.

The better news is that when he finally got the device working and the headset firmly in place and the controllers wrapped around his hands, he stopped being Rushing Water Mercantur Tarnup, *broken token of East Hoboken, and I aint jokin'*!

Inside the Horizon VR was a different reality. Not a whitewashed version of the shithole he called home, but an entirely different universe. The air tasted different. Rush's north Texas world of sand and shit and rust and oil blossomed into a meth-induced psychedelic dream full of Peter Max colors and Escher-like shapes and things so foreign that he couldn't at first understand them. And he was standing! Upright. Strong. On two sturdy legs with no Frankenstein scars and no exoskeleton supports and no crutches. He could kneel and crawl and jump and run and even fly without leaving his chair! The device transformed him like no doctor, or preacher, or drug ever had or ever could.

Rush was instantly addicted.

The Horizon VR entry platform was like a balcony looking out on a beautiful natural world from a high-class hotel room. He was standing -*standing!*- on thick gold carpet. He turned in his wheelchair in real life -IRL- and the view changed around him. Where he'd thumbtacked a picture of his mother on the stained drywall, he now saw bookcases full of volumes so real that he could feel the leather texture of their spines. Classical music engulfed him. A full wet bar with four different taps. A waterfall flowed freely in the distance beyond the balcony rail. Tropical birds flew by.

With a practiced gesture Rush instantiated a haptic menu midair over the balcony railing. He tapped buttons and explored. The device came loaded with terabytes of programs. He could indeed pitch for an ABA team or walk on the moon. He could visit China or drive a Formula 500 race car or explore the space station in zero G's. He was happily lost in this alternate reality when his father came home from work sweating and swearing and looking for beer. He was still exploring long after dark when his father passed out on the couch in front of a Cowboys game.

Rush barely slept. He missed pain pills and didn't notice. He snacked on whatever his father dropped on his nightstand on his way out to work each day. He mastered the ability to leverage himself onto the toilet, clean himself, and get back in the wheelchair without removing the headset. He explored the pyramids and then wrestled in the WWE and scuba-ed through the Great Barrier Reef. He saw and heard and felt and thought things that he'd never before imagined. And then, about a week into this revelation, sleep deprived and losing weight and no longer even aware whether it was day or night, he found *Enemies All Around Us.*

Unlike all that he'd explored before, *EAU* is an MMPG. The other people and animals and characters that he'd so far encountered in VR had been digital constructs that only exist in their respective programs. For example, the tattooed and 'roided-out wrestler named Scorpion in the VR *Smack Down!* game could never appear on safari in *Trekker* or -weirder still- out here IRL.

The people and characters in an MMPG, however, are avatars, real human beings scattered across the planet wearing digital constructs inside the game the same way that you might wear a Halloween costume to a neighbor's party. These people don't exist only in the game. They can and do exist across VR platforms and IRL the same way that Rush exists whether he's jacked into the Horizon or not. That means that you might find a lizard-faced, fire-breathing fairy princess who calls herself TwinkeeBell racing hot air balloons across the Arizona sky in the game called *Aloft!* and encounter her again playing ping pong in *Mega-Arcade* and -now here's where it gets super weird- you might also meet her *sans* avatar IRL at Walmart buying Marlboros. Of course, because TwinkeeBell sheds her scaly, winged body, incendiary halitosis, and diamond-encrusted crown when she takes off her headset, you'd have no way to know who you're bumming that smoke off of if she didn't tell you.

Rush had never before created an Avatar and wanted to get it right. *EAU* offered players some basic menus to choose from. Short lists of free body types and facial features and skills and resources, but it also honors credits that players earn across other Horizon platforms. This meant that Rush could invest the several hundred credits that he'd accumulated racing and BASE jumping and free diving and target shooting in other games to upgrade characteristics of his avatar. It also meant that as he played *EAU* he could further enhance whatever creature he became with credits he could earn on quests and in battle.

Cool.

Thus, on a windless, dry day early in January 2022, in the north Texas town of Hoboken and simultaneously in the ethereal Kingdom of Cham hosted across a dozen servers spanning the globe, Caligula the Conqueror was born. At the time, no one anywhere noticed or cared because *who-the-fuck-cares anyway*? But by early March, *EAU* enthusiasts around the world were beginning to review logs and records to try to trace Caligula's meteoric rise and discover some way *-any way-* to undermine his growing power.

EAU welcomes players to compete in a highly structured, hierarchical caste system from the bottom up. It's essentially a digital Ponzi scheme in which those lower on the pyramid are enticed to earn greater and greater power by doing the bidding of those higher on the pyramid. Like a fraternity hazing, those more senior and secure find ways to get those more junior to accomplish tasks and complete missions and find treasure and win battles so as to gain power and rise in the ranks or "level up."

Millions of VR players from more than one hundred countries have logged into *EAU* at one time or another. Natural selection in the form of serial failures at low level tasks thin the herds of newbies quickly so that only a couple thousand players reach Level 12 (L12) where they become serfs, the least powerful among the power-hungry and power-hoarding elite. Avatars at L12 and higher are allowed to hire and bribe and leverage and manipulate or even enslave players at lower levels to do their bidding. Succeeding at these tasks earns credits that can be used to buy more weapons or skills or better health and to level up even further. Those that fail at these tasks either crash-level down in status or die. Death in VR means rebooting your system and starting all over at zero.

Of course, while the serfs on L12 are busy manipulating the aspiring newbies on lower levels, they are themselves being manipulated by the knaves and orcs and princelings and kings and queens above them. This means that tasks regularly trickled down from the handful of gods perched high upon L25 through the ranks of lesser royalty to the *hoi polloi* still climbing levels one to eleven. An L1 newbie could accept a task offered by an L12 or above with the hope of accumulating enough credits to buy his way up to L2, aware of the risk that failure could mean death and rebooting.

Imagine, for example, an L20 player manifesting as Thor, the God of Thunder, who employs an L15 player manifesting as a magus. If the magus can bring Thor the head of the Cannibal of Cairn, Thor will pay him one hundred credits. Upon acceptance of the task -a formal and unbreakable contract within EAU- the magus can delegate the deed to a hungry L10 player manifesting as Little Red Riding Hood with a promise of fifty credits. Red could then rally her friends to join her, promising each five credits if they succeed and, once fully armed, march off to Cairn to capture and behead its cave-dwelling Cannibal. Returning like Jason with the Golden Fleece, Red would turn over the decapitated Cannibal's head to the magus for 50 credits and dole out five to each of her four surviving comrades in arms leaving her with a net gain of thirty credits.

Almost enough for a suit of magnetic armor!

The magus would then turn the Cannibal's head over to Thor who had first commissioned the deed and be rewarded with one hundred credits, fifty of which she'd already spent. The other fifty could go into her *EAU* account where she's saving to level up to L21 where she looks forward to having many fewer masters and many, many more servants.

Unlike every other computer game in any format in existence, *EAU* bleeds across the blurry boundary between VR and IRL. It doesn't exist separate from the real world the way that a movie or a computer game like *Call of Duty* does. *EAU* manifests as a super-universe that encompasses and incorporates the real world the same way that a fish tank contains an aquatic ecology. A smart and manipulative fish learns to navigate the world within the tank *and* the larger world beyond in which the tank exists.

EAU is so popular and so universal that its VR credits are effectively cryptocurrency IRL, a wholly fictional construct with consensual value just like dollars and yen and euros. That L20 megalomaniac in the digital Thor suit could just as well offer the L12 magus one hundred credits to paint her house -the real wood and brick structure in North Kensington, Georgia, or in South Chatsworth, Zimbabwe- as behead the fictitious but terrifying Cannibal of Cairn. If the magis happened to be in the right place or had contacts in the right place, she might agree to paint the house NOT for dollars or euros, but for EAU credits.

An L22 eagle-faced, talon-handed warlock could promise an aspiring L19 mermaid enough credits to level up if she agrees to deliver a precious Scotch-taped cardboard box from Seattle to Denver. Of course, the package is as likely to contain grandma's chocolate chip and pecan cinnamon cookies as a half-pound of Semtex.

Caligula the Conqueror (known IRL as Rush Tarnup to his father but few others) instinctively grasped the trickle-down economics of *EAU*, formal education be damned. He viewed the game as an opportunity where no other opportunities had ever existed for him in East Bumblefuck and never would. Caligula was not the only seven-foot, brawny swordsman in *EAU*, but he did have two resources that few other players had, and none could buy in VR or IRL. Desperation and endless, uninterrupted time. He sat in his wheelchair-cum-throne and played and died and rebooted tirelessly dozens of times in his first weeks. He gradually mastered the controllers and the gestures and the instantiated menus, graduated to L2, gathered some credits, and kept himself alive.

The lower levels of *EAU* are filled with basic fighting, racing, wizarding, and stealthing tasks intrinsic to the digital world. Caligula the Conqueror managed these with aplomb, gaining himself a reputation within the digital menagerie as a reliable and capable companion, a ruthless warrior, and a trustworthy confidant. He accumulated credits and health points and weapons and began levelling up.

At L6 Caligula was offered his first IRL task but had to decline. Not only couldn't he get out of his second story shit-stained bedroom, but he also wasn't in or near Bangor, Maine. Those same limitations held him back dozens of times while he hunted werewolves, captured robots, and shot three-headed goblins out of a bright red sky in *EAU*.

At L8 he would have written a real paper for a real high school kid manifesting as an L16 rune-reader, no physical mobility required, but Caligula knew that his academics fell far short of what was needed.

Weeks blurred by. Like in a casino, time was arbitrary and often meaningless in VR. After countless bloody campaigns -rescuing a puppy that had been swallowed by a serpent the size of a 747 for an L24 Queen; saddling a T-Rex for an L21 cowboy named Woody; helping an L13 Hercules redirect the course of a digital river to wash out a stable- Caligula the Conqueror finally became an L12 serf.

He'd been living in *EAU* non-stop for five weeks.

It was late February 2022 IRL.

Caligula's strength, health, and resources grew exponentially from that point onward. As a serf, he was finally able to downtask to newbies. He logged twice as many hours each day as most other players. He became a clearinghouse among creatures, a wholesaler eager to fill a hundred retailers' needs. He accepted multiple tasks handed down by royalty -avatars on L20 and above- and delegated them to eager and promising newbies. True, he had to share his earnings when his minions succeeded, but he took none of their risks. They might crash-level or die. Not Caligula.

In March 2022 Caligula the Conqueror directed his troops to dethrone an L22 Neptune-like player, orchestrated the rescue of a sorcerer who'd been held hostage by mud-fairies, hired the rune-reader he'd earlier declined to serve to write a peace treaty between warring antelope-like creatures called Chynths, and arranged for a squad of Charlie Brown-like characters to build a wall out of lightning that protected a community of rain-men who lived in a particular cumulus nimbus cloud.

IRL Caligula the conqueror also helped a single mom in Cheyenne find a nanny (a young woman who manifested in *EAU* as an ocean nymph), paid fifty credits each to two L6 characters to break into a home in Tucson to steal a laptop for an L23 Bill Gates wannabe, and found a very eager L3 willing to set fire to a deserted home in the Back Bay near Boston for eighty credits.

Neither Caligula nor Rush had any moral qualms about these activities, although Rush was wary of undercover cops that had infiltrated the game as water naiads to try to expose these plots. Morality and ethics mattered to him about as much as quantum physics and the works of Shakespeare. He had no qualms connecting the elves who sold crack with the idiot vampires who used it, as long as he got paid in the process. Indeed, Caligula often sought out anyone in the game anywhere near Hoboken, Texas, in the hope that he could trade *EAU* credits for sex right here above the Dollar Tree store. Although this failed -there was no one interested or close by or cheap enough, Caligula had his priorities- he often enjoyed gymnastic and creative virtual encounters in private *EAU* chatboxes with creatures of every kind.

Then, in early April 2022, an L23 king invited Caligula to take on a particularly difficult task. He offered an extraordinary five thousand credits -enough to buy his way up at least two levels into the stratosphere of royalty- to get the job done. If Caligula was interested, they'd need to meet privately to discuss details. He would not commit it to writing. The king did say, however, that it was an IRL task and that had to occur near Minneapolis in the United States.

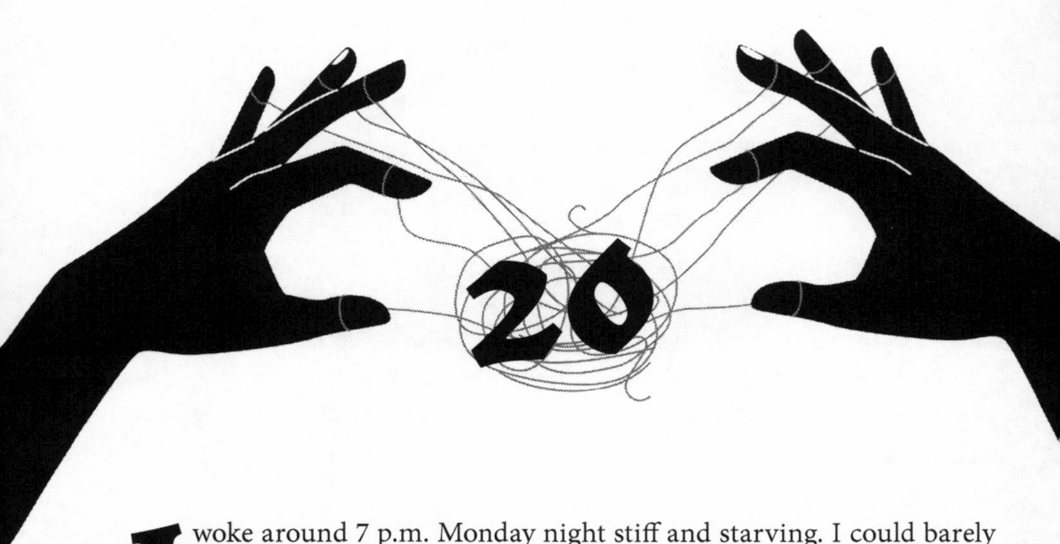

I woke around 7 p.m. Monday night stiff and starving. I could barely unbend my knees or straighten my neck. My stomach was growling in counterpoint to Jenny's quiet snoring nearby. She and Christie had barely moved where they lay cocooned in the middle of our bed.

I slipped off my shoes and padded down to the kitchen in stocking feet. There were two bananas slowly rotting away on top of the microwave. I chose the least brown and oozing fruit, found a cold beer, and sat down at the kitchen table with my phone.

The battery was almost dead. It had surely earned its keep over the last twenty-four hours. I scrolled through a dozen texts, half that many voice mails, and an onslaught of emails with blurry eyes. From what I could tell, everyone that connected us to White Birch Elementary School wanted to make sure that we were okay, to hear what had happened -I wish I knew!- and to send best wishes. I briefly texted "thanks" and "all's well" and "no worries" and "more asap" to every name that I recognized. My mom had left three voice messages, so I called her back, offered reassurances but no information, and then apologized because I had a lot to do. The excuse was true, although I was in no shape to do it.

I noticed that Jenny's friend and colleague from the hospital Peter had texted. It was not unusual for Peter and Jenny to text work related gossip and nursing information. How he got my number I didn't know. His message was more worried than most and full of mysterious apologies as if he'd made some grievous error. With Jenny still asleep, I didn't want to leave him hanging, so I called.

All's fine here, thanks. Jenny and Christie are sleeping. *Could Jenny ever forgive him?* For what I asked.

"For letting her down," he replied. "For getting her fired."

Fired? This was news to me, but I knew that the day was full of news that I needed to catch up on. I tried not to put Peter on the spot. Obviously, this had something to do with the situation with Jorge, Camden, and Sloan, and the crisis at the school. I told him that Jenny could never hate him and that I would have her call him tomorrow.

Fired? *Shit!* Jenny was supposed to be our breadwinner while I worked on the book. We had some savings and the book advance. We'd have to figure this out soon. But not tonight.

David Noyes had emailed Jenny and I jointly. "Checking in on Christie. I know that she goes to White Birch. Please let me know how I can help." Very nice and yes, doctor, you can help. Tell me everything you know about Micah Abrams.

No, I wouldn't say that. Not that directly any way.

The beer washed the mushy banana down nicely, a carb-on-carb alcoholic smoothie guaranteed to bring on stupor, if not sleep. My stomach and my brain both quieted down. I made myself a turkey sandwich on Wonder bread, and then ruined it with a shmear of ketchup the way that my father had taught me long, long ago. I wrapped this grotesquerie in a napkin, filled two water bottles from the tap and carried the collection up to the bedroom.

Jenny was sitting up in bed with Christie still asleep and clinging to her waist.

I kissed her hard and long, gave her a water bottle and half of my sandwich. She usually despised the ketchup desecration, but that didn't stop her tonight. Her half was gone before I'd even pulled up my chair close to the bed, so I offered her the other. She took it without guilt and nearly swallowed it whole. She whispered that she'd missed lunch and dinner. We talked quietly while I sipped my beer. She cried and she raged, and she cursed Jorge with words that I'd never before heard her use, as hushed as an enraged mother could be. I tried not to interrupt. I was tired and struggled to follow the convoluted storyline as best as I could and let her vent. It was long after nine by the time that I'd heard the whole story. Christie and Piglet hardly moved the whole time.

"What about your day, Ted? I know today was important for your book." That was my Jenny. Kind and caring even when she was depleted and desperate.

"It was okay, but it was nothing compared to yours. I can't believe Voldemort. Man, he is one stupid asshole."

"So did you get into the hospital in St. Peter?"

"MPH? Yeah. Come to think of it, that's where he belongs. Jorge. It's perfect for him. The place is a madhouse. I saw kids smoking dope in the hallways. Others were having sex, I think. I'm not sure."

"Where were the nurses?"

"Probably smoking dope and having sex themselves. Speaking of which -nurses, not sex- I talked briefly to Peter a little while ago. He says 'sorry, sorry, sorry!' as if he killed our dog. What did he do? I tried to reassure him. I told him you'd call tomorrow. I heard that leaping tall buildings in a single bound has its consequences."

"Yeah. Sorry about that. I think my days at St. Francis are over."

"Don't ever apologize for taking care of Christie, sweetie. We'll figure something out. Not now though. What's your plan for tomorrow?"

"I have to go in and clean out my locker at some point. My purse is still there, and my car is on a side street near the school. A nice officer drove us home."

"I saw the cap."

"Right. I need to return his cap. A man named Hatch. I'm thinking I should keep Christie home, but I don't know. What are you doing?"

"Tuesday? It's supposed to be a writing day, but you come first. Whatever you need."

"Let's see what happens in the morning. Oh, and Wednesday?"

"The day after tomorrow?"

"Wednesday ten a.m. we have an appointment in St. Paul with Dr. Sloan for the evaluation."

"We do? How long? I'm due in Chanhassen at one o'clock. Do you really think we still need to do this evaluation after what that shithead pulled today?"

"Shhhh!" Jenny looked pointedly at Christie between us. "Yes. Plan on it until we hear differently from the court. Can you make it?"

"If you need me, I'm there. We'll take two cars and I'll go to my appointment directly." I soaked up Christie's peaceful smile and then offered, "I'll carry her back to her bed, okay?"

"Would you mind if she stayed here with me? She really needs it. You'll fit over there on the other side of her."

"Only because you wolfed down my supper!"

It was tight, but it worked. Jenny and I held hands over Christie's belly and fell asleep with the little girl sandwiched safe between us.

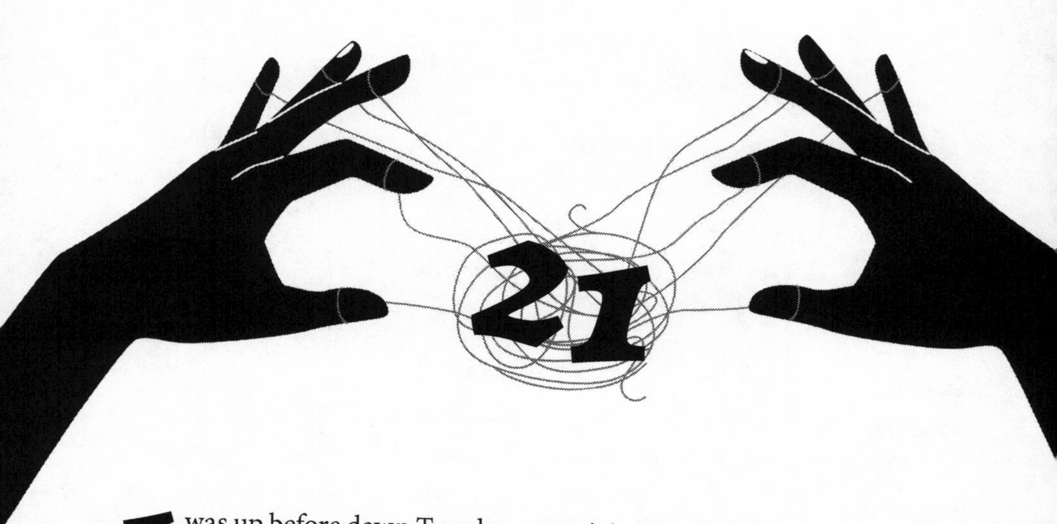

I was up before dawn Tuesday, organizing notes and transcribing audio. Google taught me the basics of *Enemies All Around Us*. The *EAU* website and public user blog taught me more. Millions of users. "*A self-sustaining community of ambitious gamers exploring the limits of VR.*" Apparently, if I was going to understand Micah, I needed to understand the universe that he preferred to inhabit.

The girls were up by seven. Both were rested and energetic after their marathon sleep-over. I snuck in another couple of hours at my computer while they cuddled and made waffles together, a rare and much anticipated treat. Jenny got an email alert that White Birch would be closed for the day "*to review recent events and district-wide safety measures.*" Christie hooted with pleasure and obvious relief at the news. Stepping back into that building would be challenging for her.

With Christie off school, Jenny off work (permanently, it seemed), and with my flexible hours, we made the day into much-needed family time. No *Round-it!* race today! We played and talked and snacked and then piled into my Jeep for an ice cream sundae adventure that conveniently included a side trip to pick up Jenny's 4Runner near the school. Christie rode home with me, chocolate sauce still smeared on her cheeks, while Jenny dropped her loaner ball cap off at the Shakopee PD and went back to St. Francis to collect her belongings and say goodbye.

Christie and I were lounging in front of the TV playing *Rainbow Unicorns* when Jenny got home with a big smile on her face and the policeman's hat firmly on her head.

She reported that Officer Hatch was glad to see that she was okay, told her that he couldn't say anything further about yesterday's events or Mr. Villalobos' status, and insisted that she keep the cap.

Nurse Ratched had offered Jenny's job back. The woman had said that she'd had no idea that Jenny's daughter was involved in "the White Birch incident." *Was she okay? Was anybody hurt? How scary that must have been! Poor baby!* It wasn't an apology, but it was an opportunity. Jenny played her hand well. She said something about needing to be home to help Christie through the trauma, that she'd need at least a week at home with her -certainly the hospital's paid family leave would cover this- and that she'd be glad to talk about coming back on the floor "as soon as things settle down at home."

Christie and I cheered for her mommy, called her brilliant and a hero.

Bedtime was interesting. Christie insisted on sleeping with the two of us again, which we took as a bad sign. Dr. Noyes had emailed several times, cautioning us against "signs of neediness and regression." We gave in, expecting another cozy if crowded night, until Christie reported that Piglet hated my snoring. Yuk! Christie carried the poor, exhausted creature back to her own quiet bed.

We quietly cheered although Jenny did point out that Piglet should have felt right at home with us because, she said, I snore very much like a pig.

I was up and showered and hard at work before five, trying to prepare for the busy day ahead. Jenny greeted me with a kiss at seven, showered and then shepherded Christy through her *Round-it!* routine in record time. The imaginary spectators in the imaginary stands cheered her success and I threw impromptu real confetti to celebrate Christie's new world record. Christie high-fived her mother and me and curtsied for her pretend audience. Her Frozen backpack flopped forward and hit her in the head as she bowed, leaving us all laughing.

Was this what VR was like? A sort of digital make-believe integrated into real life actions?

At Dr. Noyes' recommendation, Jenny walked Christie into school rather than dropping her at the door. Piglet had a special invitation to ride along for the day. Jenny played tour guide as they entered the familiar building together, pointing out the security measures that kept bad people away: Locks on the doors (Christie rattled a locked door to be sure that it worked), metal detectors in the foyer (Christie carried a handful of coins through to make it buzz), the front office sign-in procedure (Front Desk Claire gave Christie a sticker that read, "Safe Student"), and cameras installed just yesterday in the front lobby (Christie smiled and waved).

Ms. Merganser welcomed Christie back to 1C with a hug and was quite humble in the face of Jenny's effusive gratitude. When Jenny lingered, obviously anxious about separating, Ms. M gently but firmly pushed her out the door. "She'll be fine, Jenny. We've got this."

I was busy outlining a chapter on Abrams' relationship with Suki when my cell vibrated and danced across my desktop. I tapped *speaker* and said, "Good morning!" without a thought.

"Mr. Bernett?" answered a familiar voice with a strong Indian accent. I stopped typing and turned my attention to the call.

"Dr. Chatterjee? Good morning. Please ma'am: My name is *BENN-ETT*. Ted Bennett. I'm a writer. I wanted to ...."

"Yes, Yes." She cut me off. "I'm sorry to be short, but I have a situation, Mr. Bernett." I wagged my head in frustration. How could a psychiatrist be so incapable of listening? I tried to correct her. What more could I do? That would have to be enough at least for now.

"Micah Abrams has been asking for you," she advised. "In fact, he's refused to eat until you return to talk to him. He won't tell me about what. This is a problem, Mr. Bernett, because he's already quite underweight and we don't have the capacity here to put him on IV supplements or a G-tube. I really need you to talk to him. To get him to eat at least until we have your report."

"Dr. Chatterjee, I'm not writing a report. I'm not the state ..."

"Yes, yes. But Micah can't afford to lose any more weight, can he? No, no. Can you come today? Please?"

Gift horses. So much for worrying about getting back on the pod.

"Tomorrow, doctor. Today is impossible. I'll be there tomorrow at noon. Am I allowed to bring food on the pod?"

"Yes, please do, Mr. Bernett! Thank you, thank you."

She was gone. I pulled up my notes and the MP3 audio file from Monday. Although my scribbles often appear to be gibberish, I can usually make out enough of my own handwriting to use them like a table of contents that guides me through the corresponding audio. I found what I wanted, fast forwarded to the correct time stamp, and tapped play. Sam Abrams' account of the night that Suki Kohler was killed suddenly filled the room: "*Remember I told you that we were into those old black and whites? The Wizard of Oz. I ordered his favorite pizza. Bacon and burger from Vesuvius. There's one right near us. He ate one slice – I remember because he usually devoured at least three or four.*"

I looked up Vesuvius and placed an online order for tomorrow. Large. Bacon and burger. They open at eleven. If I time it right, I'll only be a little late.

Late? Somehow it was already after nine. Wednesday morning. Sloan. I shut down the laptop and dashed to the car.

Sloan's office was easy to find but difficult to reach. I could see the building down the length of a street that went one way the wrong way. I circumnavigated and congratulated myself for ending up directly in front of the right address, only to discover that the parking structure was now behind me. I didn't think that backing a hundred yards against traffic on a one-way street would work, so I did another, wider loop. I was sweaty and disheveled, my shirt coming free of my jeans and one sneaker was untied when the elevator opened on six. Jenny was standing five feet away looking amazing -her silky, dark hair in a loose bun, her tawny skin glowing. She was wearing her favorite white blouse, pearls, and a pleated maroon skirt. She held a fat manilla file folder in one hand and her phone up to her ear.

"Okay, thank you… yes … four o'clock. Thanks again. We'll be there."

She tucked her phone in her pocket.

"Hi sweetie." She looked me up and down with a mix of humor and disapproval. I felt like a little boy in church. She ran her fingers through my hair in lieu of a comb and said, "Maybe we should have talked about this interview more."

I kissed her cheek. "You look nice. I guess I didn't get the memo about dress code." I tucked in my shirt and straightened my sweater.

"No worries. You just be you. We have much more important things to manage just now."

"Who was on phone?"

"Dr. Noyes. He moved things around so he can see Christie at four today."

"Really? That's great. Christie will be glad to see him, especially …."

"Yeah. That's the point. Can you meet us there? David really needs to hear your perspective, Ted. Christie needs your support and I'm wiped."

"I'm sure you are sweetie." I kissed her on the forehead. Jenny seldom asked for anything and she carried so much. "I should be done with Abrams with plenty of time to get there."

She kissed me hard on the lips, said "thank you," then held up her wrist. Her watch showed ten o'clock exactly.

"And Christie got off okay? The plan worked?

"Ms. Merganser was wonderful. I love that woman." She knocked on the office door, then entered. I followed.

Entering Dr. Sloan's outer office reminded me of the near-death stories that fill odd corners of the internet. A pacemaker battery dies or lightning strikes or two cars collide, and the storyteller suddenly feels like he's walking toward a peaceful, welcoming white light.

Sunlight filled the room. As my eyes adjusted, I made out four chairs, all white. No secretary. No artwork. Even the carpet was textured white on white. In fact, glossy magazine covers carefully arranged on a white coffee table were the only color I could see. The room was otherwise an entirely uninterrupted, surgically sterile white environment.

An inner door opened and a diminutive woman with startling red hair in an emerald green dress appeared. Her skin was almost as white as the room around her, highlighting the red flush of her cheeks and her sparkling sea green eyes. She wore large, round, rimless glasses and a gold locket round her neck that shot fireworks of reflected light around the room. The effect was Broadway dramatic. It occurred to me that this is why jewelers display diamonds on black velvet. Staging color against a contrasting monochrome commands an onlooker's attention and highlights facets of beauty.

The woman stepped forward and offered her hand to Jenny.

"Ms. Villalobos? I'm Dr. Myra Sloan. It's nice to meet you." Jenny shook her hand.

"And Mr. Bennett?" It was nice to be called by my proper name after my experience with Chatterjee. "Thanks for being here." We shook. Her hand was petite but quite strong. "If you'd both join me please...?"

She seated us side by side on a deep, white couch in her inner office. I was instantly certain that a *feng shui* consultant had designed all but the corner of the office that we now faced, the lived-in part. The real Myra Sloan part. Someone else's sterile vision ended abruptly where Sloan had parked a venerable, oak rolltop full of bulimic cubbies and drawers, all busy vomiting forth their contents. Her desktop was a scrapyard of abandoned coffee cups, dog-eared papers, and two-inch thick books barricaded around a large, black laptop. A rainbow of square sticky notes captioned every surface, including the computer screen.

Sloan's black leather desk chair stood out like a lump of coal in a snow-storm. Its dark bulk was better suited to a linebacker or a cigar-smoking, obese captain of industry. Sloan didn't sit on it as much as allow herself to be swallowed by it. Her tan flats barely reached the floor.

A vanity wall of certificates and diplomas and awards arched up and over the silhouette of the rolltop, an impressive collection of achievements captured in variegated and mismatched frames hung helter-skelter on the white wall. I was struck in equal parts by this woman's obvious successes and her complexity. She was at once seductive and all-business, immaculate, and chaotic.

A box of tissues, two yellow notepads with pens, and a microphone sat on the table between us. I spied a video camera aimed over Sloan's chair in our direction.

"Time is tight so I'm going to dive in." No further introduction. Down to business. She swiveled to her desk, produced a clipboard from beneath a teetering pile of papers and found a pen. Before she'd even rotated back toward us, she was speaking, "Please be aware that I take notes and record all of my interviews. We're being recorded right now." She nodded toward the mic and the camera. "I need to make clear that this isn't therapy, and this is not confidential. I'm not here to help you. I'm here to help the Court help Christina. I will be sharing what I learn with the court in the form of a lengthy report and as testimony should there be a custody trial."

I already had a hundred questions. She must have read the furrow of my brow.

"I'm sorry, Mr. Bennet. We'll make time for questions later. It's important that I clarify what we're doing before you begin. Here's the plan: The court has asked me to complete a custody evaluation in response to Mr. Villalobos' *ex parte* motion. He alleges that you folks are undermining his relationship with Christina. He's asked the Court to place her in his exclusive custody. My job is to collect information that will allow me to recommend to the judge how best to understand and serve Christina's needs. Is everything I've said so far clear?"

Jenny and I both nodded in agreement.

"You know that I spoke with Mr. Villalobos yesterday, correct?"

Jenny and I exchanged looks. We'd known that Voldemort had been scheduled to meet with Sloan, but we hadn't heard whether he had kept the appointment. We'd had no word from the police or the school about him. We hoped that he was under arrest. If he'd been here yesterday, then it sounded like the slimebag had once again suffered no consequences for his egregious, selfish, destructive actions at White Birch.

When we said nothing, she continued.

"He was. He filled me in on the details of his concerns. I need to get your perspective on those concerns and on Christina's needs today. I'm going to arrange for Ms. Villalobos to complete some testing online. Mr. Villalobos will do the same. We'll make plans for me to meet Christina, er, sorry, 'Christie.'" She turned specifically to address Jenny: "I asked you to prepare the names and contact information of three personal references and any professionals in Christie's life for me?"

Jenny opened the file folder that she'd been carrying and magically produced a printed page full of names, numbers, emails, and physical addresses. I saw a pile of court documents beneath it. The trick astonished me. *She* astonished me. I had no idea when or how she'd put the list together. She handed it to Sloan and leaned forward to walk her through what she'd written.

"Personal references? My friend Peter Monahan from work. Ted's mother Savannah Bennett. My parents are both deceased. And Claire Quigley who works at the school. She knows me and Christie and she was there yesterday at White Birch. I've also listed Christie's teacher, Ms. Alex Merganser, her therapist, Dr. David Noyes -he told me that he knows you- and her pediatric group over in Edina. We see whichever provider is available there."

"Excellent. Thank you. So, I take it that you're the super-organized and efficient member of the family?"

I jumped in to save Jenny from embarrassment. "Absolutely. Jenny never misses a beat. She keeps us all afloat."

It was Sloan's turn to do a magic trick. She handed Jenny a consent form that would allow her to visit Christie at school. Jenny and I traded silent glances again. She signed the form and handed it back but added, "You do know what's happened there recently, right?"

Sloan was caught off guard. She was used to asking the questions. Jenn persisted: "Didn't Jorge say anything to you yesterday?"

"No. What are you talking about?"

"Incredible!" I muttered to myself. Jenny pushed on: "On Monday -just forty-eight hours ago- Christie's father tried to abduct her from her school. He breached a court order and triggered a lock down. Hundreds of police were there. I'm surprised you didn't hear about it."

I watched the pieces fitting together on Sloan's face. "White Birch? In Shakopee? Yes of course. I hadn't connected you to Monday's news. Wow." Her brow furrowed deeply as she put two and two together. "Christie attends White Birch? Is Mr. Villalobos the man that was arrested there?"

"We don't know if he was arrested," Jenny said.

"You saw him yesterday here and he said nothing? Amazing." I couldn't stop myself.

"What do you mean, Mr. Bennet?"

"Dr. Sloan, it's just another glaring example of how Christie's father distorts things. In his view, he can do no wrong but he's always glad to criticize and demean others. If I'm not out of line," I looked at Jenny who nodded encouragement, "I think that's part of why we're here. He is always glad to blame other people -and by that I mean Jenny and me- for all of his own failings."

Suddenly Sam Abrams was in my head talking about projective identification: *"Some people cast the forbidden and rejected parts of themselves onto other people...."*

Had Abrams done that to Suki? Cast his failings on her?

Were Abrams and Voldemort alike? Was I profiling the bad guy?

Jenny chimed in, "Dr. Sloan, I know that we make lots of mistakes. We're only human and neither of us has ever raised a child before, but we're glad to own our mistakes....

"... and brag about our successes," I added.

"And that," she agreed with a sly smile. "Volde... er, Jorge cannot admit to mistakes. He's always right. That's not only a horrible model for Christie, but it's destructive. Mr. Villalobos is glad to throw us under the bus when she's around."

"'Throw you under the bus'?" Sloan queried, writing all the while.

"He is constantly telling Christie that I'm a bad parent. That Ted is not her father and that she shouldn't listen to him. Or me. He tells her that our divorce is my fault and that he hates me for it. That I ruined her family. And Monday ... Monday was the best yet. He broke a restraining order and tried to take Christie out of school. I still don't know why! If I hadn't stopped him, I firmly believe that she'd be gone now."

Jenny's voice had become shrill. Her face and neck flushed. I put a hand on her knee to try to settle her. She pushed it aside and said to me, "No, I've got to say these things, Ted. They're all true and if anyone needs to hear them, I think that's Dr. Sloan."

"Christie is supposed to go with her father alternate weekends." She continued, "Friday after school until six p.m. Sunday. He's always late for pick-up and drop off which is inconvenient for me, but just plain upsetting to Christie. She never knows if he's coming or not and I know she feels rejected. When she does see him, she comes back upset. She used to come home yelling that I'm a 'bad mommy and daddy says not to do what I say.' It would take hours to calm her down and get her to bed on Sundays and that would throw off Monday at school. It was Tuesday or Wednesday before we were back on track, then we'd have a good week or so until the cycle started over again. Now she won't even go to him on Fridays."

"Christie refuses to see her dad?" Sloan echoed Jenny's words.

She screams and tantrums and does everything she can to resist," I observed.

Jenny produced a DVD in a paper sleeve from her file and handed it across the coffee table to the doctor.

"We do the transition at the police station so that we can record him. The PD downloads the video for five dollars. I brought you a copy of the last three transitions. If you watch those, you can see how Christie responds to transitions. That's not her, Dr. Sloan. She's usually the most carefree, loving, smiling child you'll ever meet."

"Thank you." She accepted the disk, swiveled in her giant chair, placed the paperwork Jenny had prepared for her and the DVD on top of the nearest pile on her desk, then swiveled back to face us. Twinkles of fairy dust danced over the white walls as sunlight bounced off her pendant.

Jenny was on a roll. "I have to push Christie to go with her father, and I hate that. She cries and kicks and screams. She had the same reaction when he tried to take her Monday at school, only bigger. Louder and longer. That's part of why the school called the police. Afterwards, she kept asking me if he was gone for good. If he was ever coming back. I'd never seen her like that, doctor. Clinging to me. She wouldn't sleep in her own bed. She wouldn't let me leave her side for a full day. It was like she was an infant all over again! I don't know if you have children, doctor, but you probably know that there's no greater pain than having to send your child off to be tortured."

Abrams had talked about having had to send Micah off with Suki: "If the court made him live on a boat, I'd have given him a life preserver."

Sloan asked: "Torture?"

Jenny demurred, then answered. "Well, not torture literally. I don't believe that Volde … Jorge would intentionally hurt Christie…."

Sloan interrupted. Her gravelly, deep voice was powerful. I could see why people listened when she spoke. "Ms. Villalobos -Jenny- that's the second time you've stopped yourself when referring to Christie's father. His name is Jorge -I called him 'George' and he corrected my pronunciation- Jorge Manual Villalobos. But you keep stopping yourself from using another word. What are you saying?"

"Nothing. I … we were talking about whether Christie's father would hurt her."

"Jenny," Sloan persisted, "Mr. Villalobos reports that you all call him a demeaning nickname. Is that true?"

Jenny had been seated forward on the couch, asserting herself. She now slid back to join me, as if the distance protected her from a truth she didn't want to admit. It felt like she was tagging me into the ring.

"Dr. Sloan," I offered, "Mr. Villalobos isn't there for Christie. He is all about himself -his toys, his car, his clothes, his looks. He's not really interested in Christie. Even when she's with him, he parks her in front of a screen and ignores her. They do what he wants to do. He doesn't help her with her homework. I should tell you the story about Christie's dinosaur project. It's just that Mr. Villalobos causes us a great deal of upset and inconvenience. Even being here today -please take no offense- is a major interruption in our lives, not to mention very, very scary. We're terrified that the court is going to take Christie away from us." Jenny was nodding her head vigorously. "We believe that placing Christie in her father's care is dangerous."

"Yes, I understand." Sloan's green eyes watched me carefully. Her face seemed to communicate genuine empathy that encouraged my trust.

"The truth is that in private Jenny and I have a nickname for Christie's dad. At first, we needed a way to talk about him without Christie understanding. Of course, she caught on pretty quickly. She's really smart as I'm sure you'll find out. So, we try not to use it too much but -like Jenny said- we're human. We make mistakes."

"What do you call him?"

Jenny nodded her permission to me, so I continued. "Voldemort. Like the Harry Potter bad guy." Sloan scribbled notes, then looked up.

"And does Christie call him this?"

I said "no" at the same moment that Jenny said "Sometimes. But I tell her not to. I know she needs to be respectful, but doesn't a parent need to earn respect? Jorge has not."

Sloan kept writing, began a new page, and addressed Jenny.

"Mr. Villalobos claims that you track Christie when she's in his care? And listen in on them?"

I started to answer again, but Jenny put a hand on my knee and stopped me. I didn't know whether waiting for her to speak or jumping to her defense was the better choice. I was ready to protest more of Jorge's BS. I was ready to say that he's lying, when Jenny said, "It's true."

My mouth must have fallen open. Jenny ignored me, keeping her focus on Sloan. "It's an app called *BunnyEars*. Maybe you've heard of it? I gave Christie a bracelet. It has a tiny GPS transponder and a Bluetooth microphone. It runs on a hearing aid battery the size of my pinkie nail. The app lets me see where she is on the map and hear what she's hearing on my phone. Christie loves the bracelet. It's got a pretty, bright red stone in it. Red's her third favorite color after pink and purple. But she doesn't know what it does. Ted didn't either. Until now."

Jenny chanced a glance in my direction. She looked apologetic and defiant all at once.

"*BunnyEars*?" Sloan repeated. "So, you've been listening in on Mr. Villalobos without his knowledge?"

"No. Well, sometimes. And at school. The device needs to be in WiFi range, otherwise it can't work. I only use it to make sure Christie's okay. Not to eavesdrop or anything. It's like a nanny cam without a picture. No video. It's how I knew that Jorge was at the school on Monday."

That startled me. "You did?" We'd dissected Monday's events thoroughly. How could she not have told me? How could I not have wondered how she'd known he was there?

Sloan moved on, "I understand that you two live together. You're not married. Do you share responsibility for Christie's care when she's not with her father?"

I was still digesting the last topic. Jenny had been spying on Christie? And on me when Christie was alone with me? Didn't she trust me? Why hadn't she told me about *BunnyEars*?

"Ted moved in about a year and a half ago. We'd dated about six months before that. Christie and I already had the apartment." Jenny replied. "We were very careful at first not to confuse Christie about who Ted is. But since Christie and Ted get along together so well, Ted's gradually taken over a lot of parenting. My work hours change often, you know. Ted's a lot more flexible. So, we cover for each other."

"Christie's great, Dr. Sloan." I felt like I'd fallen behind in class and needed to catch up. "I love her like my own child, and she loves me."

"What does she call you, Mr. Bennett?"

"'Ted.'"

"Not 'dad' or 'daddy' or anything similar?"

"Well, sometimes. But she knows I'm not her daddy."

"Do you correct her when she calls you 'daddy'?" Sloan asked.

I glanced at Jenny.

"Sometimes," I said.

"But not always? Sometimes you're okay with Christie calling you 'daddy'? What do you think that communicates to Christie, Mr. Bennett?"

"Nothing, actually. It's just not a battle we choose to fight. Sometimes it seems worth correcting and I'll say something like, 'that's sweet, Christie, but you have a daddy.' Sometimes I just let it go."

Sloan shifted in her oversized chair. Her pen was streaming across the page. I wished that I could take notes that effortlessly.

"So, the two of you are effectively co-parents at this point? Do I have that right?" We nodded. I was holding Jenny's hand, aware that mine had become cold and clammy. "If you're co-parenting, why didn't you know about *BunnyEars*, Mr. Bennett?"

Good question. I'd have to ask Jenny later. I was smart enough to know that now was not the time to interrogate her, so I lied. "Dr. Sloan, I'm sure that that's my fault. I'm a writer, you know. When I'm in the zone at my laptop, the house could burn down around me, and I wouldn't notice. I'm sure that Jenny told me, and I just missed it."

"And you take care of Christie when Mom's working? What happens if you're 'in the zone' when Christie needs you? Or if the house is actually on fire?"

I'd walked right into that one.

"Ted isn't like that, doctor." Jenny swooped in to rescue me. Us. "He would never ignore Christie."

"But he does ignore you?"

"No… that's not what I said. The truth is that he didn't know about *BunnyEars* because I didn't tell him. It's a decision that I made as Christie's mother."

"So, either you keep secrets from Mr. Bennett or he isn't responsible to care for Christie? Or both? At the least, Ms. Villalobos, you're admitting that you knew that this device could get you in trouble -that it's illegal to eavesdrop on other people without their knowledge- and that you and Mr. Bennett don't communicate with one another well."

We were both sweating. It was only 10:20.

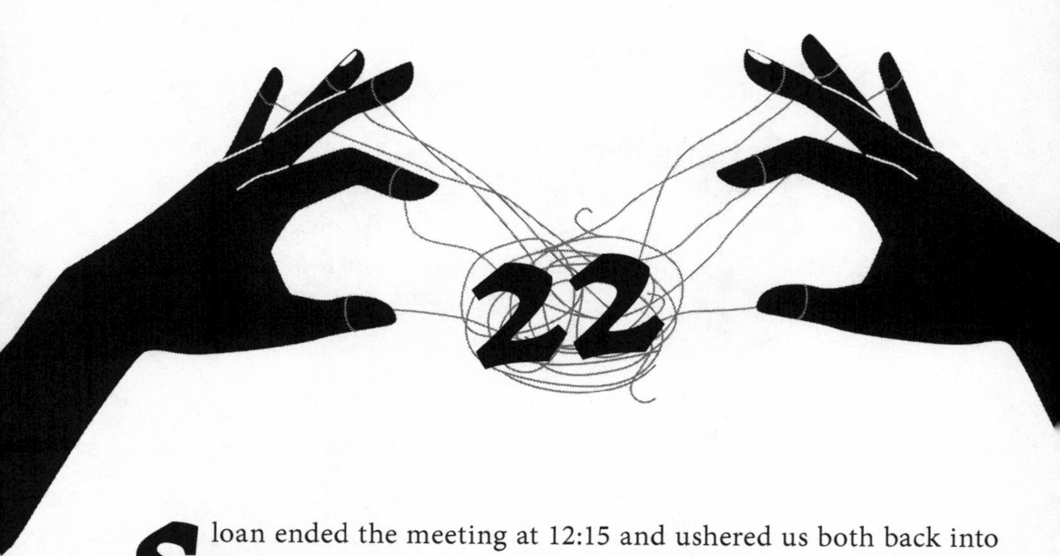

22

Sloan ended the meeting at 12:15 and ushered us both back into her white-on-white waiting room. The angle of the sun had shifted enough that the room no longer glowed, but it still had a too-pristine-to-actually-live-in feel. We shook the doctor's hand and thanked her (for what? For waterboarding us for more than two hours?)

"Given what happened on Monday," Sloan advised as we stood at the outer door ready to go, "I'm going to put this evaluation on the fast track. I'll have my assistant reach your references and Christie's providers this afternoon. She'll also email you, Jenny, with a link to do some tests online. Can you fit that in? It should take about an hour and a half.

If the link was waiting for her when she got home, Jenny said, she could do the tests this afternoon before she picked up Christie. "We have an appointment after school today. With Dr. Noyes."

"Good." Sloan replied. "I'll be checking in with Dr. Noyes this afternoon. I'll make sure that that link goes out to you as soon as we say goodbye. Let me know how it goes with David. We three will need a follow up appointment. Another two hours should do. Sooner is better than later. If I can get you back here tomorrow, then I could see Christie at school on Friday."

Jenny turned the question over to me. She had an unexpected week off thanks to Nurse Molotov. I started to say "sure" -my schedule is usually very flexible- and then remembered Chatterjee's request.

"No, I'm sorry. I have an appointment at noon in St. Peter. I'll have to leave Shakopee before eleven."

"You do?" Jenny was surprised. I noticed Sloan note again how poorly we communicate.

"St. Peter?" Sloan asked. "The only thing down there is the state hospital."

It sounded like a question, so I replied, "I have a … friend down there. At MPH."

"I'm very sorry to hear that, Mr. Bennett. MPH is a tough place. Be careful." She shifted to address both of us: "I'm seeing Mr. Villalobos back here tomorrow afternoon, so that's out. How about Friday at ten a.m.? Can that work?"

I caught Jenny's eye as if to say, okay? She knew that I had to be back in Chanhassen at one on Friday. This is a VPD weekend -Voldemort plays daddy weekend, a phrase that Sloan didn't need to hear- so we had a three-p.m. transition at the Shakopee PD. We had to send Christie back to Voldemort again this Friday.

I replied, "Friday at ten can work, but I'll need to leave before 12:30 again if that's okay?"

It was. She shook our hands again and disappeared into her inner office.

Jenny and I exchanged worried, frustrated words in the elevator. The interview had been an ordeal. We both feared that we'd looked incompetent. Like bad parents. Had we catalogued Voldemort's selfishness and stupidity adequately, or had we gone overboard and come off as angry and blaming? What was Voldemort telling Sloan about us? Would she fall for his poor-me immigrant charm?

I kissed Jenny goodbye. Told her that I'd see her at four at Noyes' office, then jogged ahead to the Jeep. My ride down to see Abrams was at least a half hour and I couldn't afford to be late. I had no idea what waited for me there.

Route 94 carried me west across the Mississippi. The left lane fed me smoothly onto 35 south and west into Chanhassen. Traffic and weather cooperated. Billy Joel accompanied. The Dartmouth bridge spans the river like a monstrous, concrete umbilicus connecting twins. The structure is nowhere as stunning as the Zakim in Boston or the Skydance in Oklahoma City and nowhere near as fabled or majestic as the Goldengate, but on a crystal-clear day like today with spring fast approaching, the view is unparalleled. Midway across, I caught a spectacular glimpse of the skyscrapers of downtown St. Paul in my rearview and downtown Minneapolis ahead.

As I drove, I couldn't help thinking about the interview with Sloan, even though I should have been preparing for my interview with Abrams. I didn't know what to expect today. The last time we'd spoken, he'd shredded Micah's note in a rage and ended our interview early.

Luck was on my side. I opened Abram's outer door five minutes early. For the second time, Abrams didn't wait until the top of the hour to greet me. Today he was standing in the inner door as if waiting for me. He wore a monogrammed white button-down shirt and tan slacks. His jacket was tweedy browns with elbow patches. I offered a greeting, but he said nothing. No handshake. I followed him inside. He ensconced himself in his throne behind the dark wood desk. I took my usual chair.

I set out my phone to record and opened my notebook to write. Abrams was just staring out toward the lake.

"Sam?" I began after a very tense and quiet moment. "What happened here Monday?"

Nothing.

"Obviously Micah's note upset you. Please tell me why."

Nothing. I'd saved my best for last.

"Look, I'm going back to see Micah again tomorrow."

He lowered his gaze to me.

"You're going back to MPH?"

"Micah asked for me to come back. Dr. Chatterjee called."

"Why?"

He was being cryptic. Withholding.

"Why did Micah ask for me to come back? I don't know. Chatterjee didn't say. I can tell you that I asked Micah if I could come back when I was there. He said yes IF I brought him something from you. A note."

"So, you'll take my son a note from me?"

"I'll trade you. Quid pro quo."

"Okay. I'll bite, Mr. Bennett. What do you want?"

"I need to know what happened on Monday. Why did you say that Micah didn't write that note. Why you shredded it."

"And if I tell you you'll take a note to him for me?

"I'll do the best that I can. That's the deal."

Abrams' scowl communicated frustration. Perhaps he'd decided to end our relationship, but I'd upped the ante unexpectedly. I could offer him something that no one else had or could, something that he desperately wanted. A connection to Micah.

"Do you remember what the note you handed me said?" His voice was a growl.

I didn't need to. I had photographed the original for my records and now had a printed copy in my pocket. I didn't want to take it out, however, for fear of enraging him again.

"Sure." I recited the fifteen words from memory: "Dad, I hate this place. Please get me out of here. Ding Dong! Love Micah."

"Do you remember what I said we did that Friday night? The night that Suki was killed?"

"The night that Micah ran away last April?" If this had been an open book test, I would have referenced my notes, pulled up the corresponding audio and played the segment back to him. Then it occurred to me that I already had done exactly that. About the pizza.

"Um… you told me that you'd picked him up from school. All the activities you'd offered to do, but all he wanted to do was tell you about his mother. How she'd hurt him. I remember you told me he was wearing a turtleneck shirt on a hot day. She'd strangled him, you said. There were marks under the collar. He was depressed. You said he was barely responsive. You ordered his favorite pizza, and he only ate a little. You watched a movie then tucked him in bed."

"The movie, Ted. Do you remember which movie?"

"I remember that the two of you enjoyed old black and white movies. I remember because I thought that was pretty cool. The kids that I know want CGI action and car chases and X-men. Which movie? I don't … you've mentioned many. Cary Grant. Robert Carlisle. Humphrey Bogart. I don't know, Sam. I didn't study up for this quiz. Which movie?"

He said the title like it had extra meaning: "*The Wizard of Oz*. 1939. Dorothy? Toto? The Scarecrow?" He paused. I was missing something. With emphasis, as if he was leading a very slow learner, he added, "The wicked witch?"

"Okay… and what does this have to do with …?"

He interrupted to recite paraphrased lyrics: "Once there was a wicked witch … A wickeder witch there never was … when a house fell on her head … through the town the joyous news was spread. DING DONG, the witch is dead."

Holy shit.

All "*ding dong*" meant to me was doorbells and Hostess cupcakes. I'd Googled the phrase and come up with music videos. I guess I hadn't scrolled down far enough. *The Wizard of Oz.* The wicked witch is dead. Micah had communicated to Abrams that the wicked witch was dead. So he knows that his mother is dead? Father and son hadn't communicated in the year since. Did Micah think that his father didn't know? That seemed unlikely. Was he celebrating that she's dead like asking for a high five after winning a ball game? Or was he declaring success? Was "*ding dong*" an expression of pride? A request for his father's praise like 'look what I did, daddy! I killed mommy!' Is that why Abrams had shredded the note?

Was Micah's note a sergeant's report to his general? Mission accomplished, sir. *Ding dong*! I killed her!

One step at a time. Abrams had watched my thinking progress with amusement. He smirked as my eyes darted side to side. My pencil raced across my page, trying to catch up. My brow furrowed. I wouldn't have been surprised if smoke escaped my ears. I felt that slow.

"So if Suki was Micah's wicked witch…?" I asked.

"She was." He interrupted. "Mine, too. She simply was wicked. Period."

"But then what does '*ding dong*' mean, Sam? Why did he write '*ding dong*' of all things he could have written to you a year later?"

He folded his hands in front of him as if in prayer, elbows on the table. He leaned back and his chair groaned. He stared at the ceiling reviewing words only he could see written above. "That was the one time that he snapped out of it that night. When Dorothy dropped her house on the Wicked Witch of the East. Dorothy is stunned but then the munchkins are grateful and rejoice and everybody sings '*ding dong*.' He said something about dropping a house on his mother. He always called her by her first name, 'Suki' or more often, "Sucky." He said he wished he could drop our house on Sucky. I agreed that that would be pretty cool, partly just to draw him out of his funk. He started singing '*ding dong, Sucky's dead*' over and over again. Louder and louder until he was out of control. Hysterical. Manic even. He couldn't stop himself from screaming those words. He was waving his arms around wildly, dancing all around the family room upstairs like in the movie. I'd never seen anything like it. He'd gone from nearly comatose-shut-down-withdrawn to feverish. He'd become a whirling Dervish. Eventually I gave him a pill to try to slow him down. Aquintex SR. It's an anxiolytic. An anti-anxiety medication. When he still hadn't slowed down about an hour later, I gave him another. That did it. He collapsed exhausted, so I put him to bed. Later? When the cops pounded on our front door and Micah hadn't responded? I figured he was out for the count. I had no idea that he'd left the house entirely."

"Aquintex SR," I wrote. Side effects? Aggression? Sleep walking? Catatonia?

For the second time today I felt like the carpet had been pulled out from under me. I was in free fall. For all of my preparation, this was out of the blue.

"Wow... Okay. I think that I understand better what happened that night, but not why you destroyed his note."

"I told you at the time, Ted. He didn't write it."

I could only wag my head in confusion. I hadn't lied. If I'd wanted to mislead Abrams somehow, how would I know to use '*ding dong*'? I was there. I watched him produce the paper and the crayon nub. I watched him write it. Unprompted. Unscripted. His words. I told Abrams exactly that.

It was his turn to express frustration.

"Okay. So, if I believe you and he wrote it, there's still a problem. I shredded that note because some people would see it as a confession. Like '*Ding dong* I killed my mother!'"

"And you're protecting him?"

"Of course. Yes, I'm protecting him but not in the way that you think. I'm not protecting him from confessing that he killed his mother. I'm protecting him from lying about killing his mother."

"I'm sorry, I'm not following..."

"Micah did not kill his mother and I will not allow him to be punished for that crime."

"Sam, how could you possibly know that? He was there. He had her blood all over him. Maybe it's taken all this time for him to recover from the trauma, but you're right. You've just told me that he was … I want to be respectful… temporarily insane that night? His mother had tried to strangle him! Plus, you medicated him. Who knows how that affected him? Look … clearly you love Micah dearly …."

He was shaking his head no. Back and forth. Silently rejecting my reasoning. Waiting for me to shut up. When I finally did, slowly realizing that my rant was going nowhere, he sat silently some more. Thinking. Finally, he said, "Turn off your recorder."

"I'm sorry? Turn off my recorder? Why?"

"If you want to continue this interview for the few minutes we have left, I need you to turn off your recorder and put away your notebook. We're going off the record. Deep throat. Not to be quoted. Can you do that?"

I didn't want to. It wasn't our agreement. My publisher would be pissed. And if he said something important off the record, I was stuck. I'd have no attribution. No source material. Nothing I could use. I'm sure that was his point. But the story had captured me. I needed to hear what he had to say for my own sake at least, even if I couldn't use it in the book. So, I complied. I tapped *stop* on the phone and shoved it in my pocket. I folded up my notebook and returned it to my backpack. I felt naked and small without my tools opposite this big man with his deep voice and his big desk.

A moment passed in quiet. Then he spoke.

"We're off the record?" I nodded yes.

"I need you to answer out loud in case you're lying.

"Yes," I said. "We're off the record. I stopped recording."

"Good. Thank you." Dr. Sam Abrams took a deep breath and released it slowly. He leaned forward over his folded hands and spoke plainly and directly at me: "I know that Mica did not kill Suki because I killed her."

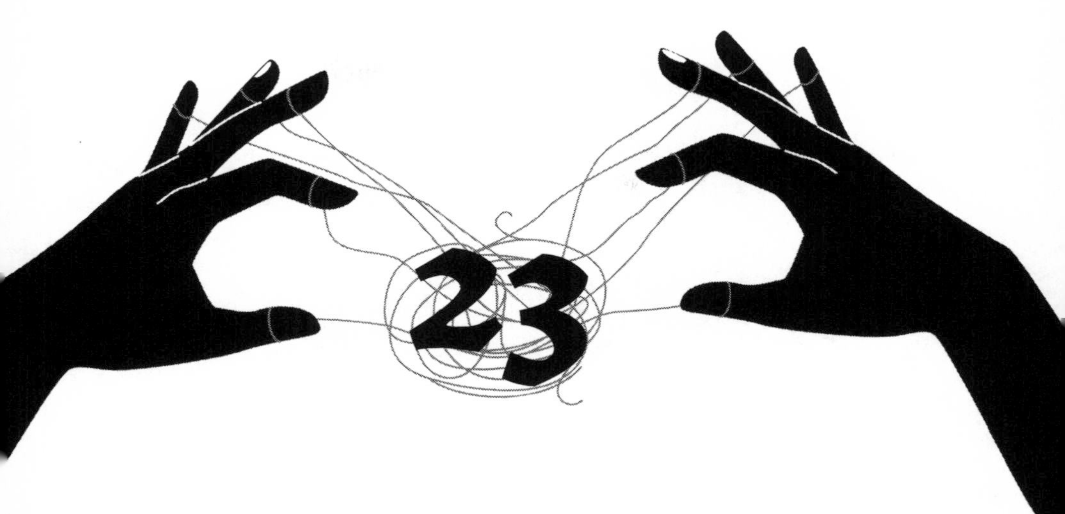

Christie was in music class. Jenny could hear Ms. Merganser assigning rhythm instruments to the children by name. Clayton got the bongos, of course. The 6-year-old had begun his musical career enthusiastically pounding on the instrument at the school's Fall musical to great reviews. Christie wanted the triangle. She told the class that triangle is her favorite shape except for circles which are her most favorite shape. Castanets and wooden blocks and jingle bells and a dozen other striking, bonking, blaring, dinging instruments including a squeezy red bicycle horn were distributed. A scuffle broke out over who would use the maracas. Ms. Merganser skillfully quelled the impending riot with a quick round of rock-paper-scissors. Jasmin won. Keri pouted loud enough to be heard over the *BunnyEars* mic.

Ms. Merganser invited the children to strike and bonk and blare and ding in unison on every fourth beat. She counted out loud, "One, two, three, FOUR and one, two, three, FOUR."

The resulting chaos was almost as funny as it was loud.

Jenny chuckled and turned the key to start the 4Runner. She was still in the garage next to Dr. Sloan's building in St. Paul. Hard as the interview with Sloan had been, it was harder still to be out of touch with Christie that long. Monday's crisis with Jorge had ripped open her insecurities. Ted had had to rush off, so she sat alone in her car and tapped the app to listen in.

Jenny refused to be ashamed that she was using *BunnyEars*, no matter how high Dr. Sloan had raised her too-thin eyebrows when the subject had come up. She needed to know that Christie was safe. She couldn't call the school every ten minutes to ask. *That* would be embarrassing. She certainly couldn't call Voldemort to check on the child while she was in his care. That would just be an invitation to do battle. She was sorry that she hadn't told Ted about the device. *My bad*, Jenny thought to herself. Unfortunately. Dr. Sloan had recognized the mistake and taken it as evidence of some deep schism between them. There was none. She and Ted talk about everything. They were a team, the three of them. Talk about triangles! Jenny had no doubt that Ted loved Christie almost as much as she herself loved her and Christie loved them both back. Hard.

She hadn't purchased the bracelet and the app to spy on Ted, but she also hadn't discussed it with him. She owed him an apology.

Jenny checked her voice mail before putting the vehicle in gear. Camden had called. Maybe he had news about Monday's events at the school? Maybe charges were being brought against Jorge?

It took two secretaries and a full rendition of *Blue Bayou* to get through to the lawyer.

Mark was polite and curt all at once. His Louisiana drawl colored some of his words. Jenny found it endearing.

"Thanks for calling back, Jenny. I hope you and Christie are okay? I just wanted to check in on two things. Bad news first: The school district is declining to press criminal charges against Jorge for Monday's fiasco at White Birch. Their lawyer says that no laws were broken …" Jenny gasped and tried to interrupt. Camden asked her to wait. "No laws were broken. He did not have a firearm. No weapon. He did not make threats. He did not take Christie off the property. In fact, the district is worried that WE will sue them for malfeasance because they didn't enforce the restraining order that they hold in Christie's file. I guess I should ask – but I think that I know the answer- do you want to sue the school?"

"Mark, you've got to be kidding. Those people were wonderful on Monday. They love Christie. Why would I sue them?"

"That's what I thought. Now some good news: You do have the option of filing a contempt on Jorge for breaking the restraining order. I think that I know the answer to that one also, but it's complicated. He may be right. The order does restrict him from picking Christie up after school. It does not explicitly prohibit him from taking her out for lunch. I know, I know. Splitting hairs. But Christie's dad is really, really good at slipping things like that by the court."

Jenny was flabbergasted. She told the lawyer that she'd talk to Ted about the contempt idea and get back to him.

"Now the worse news: Jorge may be planning to sue you and the school about this."

"*Sue us*? For what? That's ludicrous, Mark."

"False arrest and slander. Because of you he was identified on the national news as a school shooter. He claims defamation and that he can't get a job because of that. I know, I know. He really doesn't have a leg to stand on, but that hasn't stopped him so far. None of that is really why I called, though. I need to know what to do with the message Jorge left Ted."

Lunch hour was ending, and cars were barreling through the garage, circling like vultures to find open spots, tires squealing around sharp turns. Sandwiched between concrete slabs, noises were amplified and distorted and echoed badly, making it hard to hear. Jenny was sure that she'd misunderstood. She asked Camden to repeat what he'd said.

"Sure. Sorry. The message that Jorge left Ted on Monday? What do you want me to do about that?"

She had heard correctly. Message? She would have remembered if Ted had told her that Jorge had called him. When Jorge called, he always called her. Not Ted. She hadn't even given him Ted's number. She related this to the lawyer briefly. He offered to forward the voice mail to her. She thanked him and was in the midst of saying goodbye when a new thought occurred to her.

"Mark? Sorry. What about Friday? Two days from now? I mean, Christie's supposed to go to Jorge on Friday. It's his weekend. But she keeps asking me if she has to go and if 'daddy's all gone for good' now. If I have to take her, there's going to be a major crisis. I'm not physically capable of forcing my little girl to go with him and -even if I was- I shouldn't have to after what he pulled at the school. She shouldn't have to go. She's traumatized, Mark."

"Of course, she is. But you'll be in contempt if you interfere with his visitation. If we're going to do this, we need something more than just your feelings, Jenn. I know that you understand that. If, for example, Christie's teacher or pediatrician or therapist would write a letter stating that it is not in Christie's best interests to see her father right now, we could go to court and file *ex parte* to stop it." He seemed to be thinking out loud. "I suppose I could try to file without that. The news reports about what Jorge did are pretty damning, but now that we know that the school is not filing charges and he might be taking legal action himself, it could backfire. He could make this look like more of your efforts to alienate him from Christie."

"We're seeing Dr. Noyes this afternoon. Is that too late?"

"Noyes is her therapist, right? Good. No, it's not too late. We have forty-eight hours. Give Noyes consent to email me and see if he'll write something up on the spot. If so, have him send it over immediately. I've worked with him before. He's solid. I would think that the court would listen to what he has to say."

"Okay. I'm making myself a note: First I need to get the message that Jorge left for Ted. Second, I need to get Noyes write a letter for the court about Friday? I'll do my homework and circle back late tonight or early tomorrow."

"Perfect. And Jenny, I know this is rough. You're worried about Christie, but we've got this. She's going to be okay."

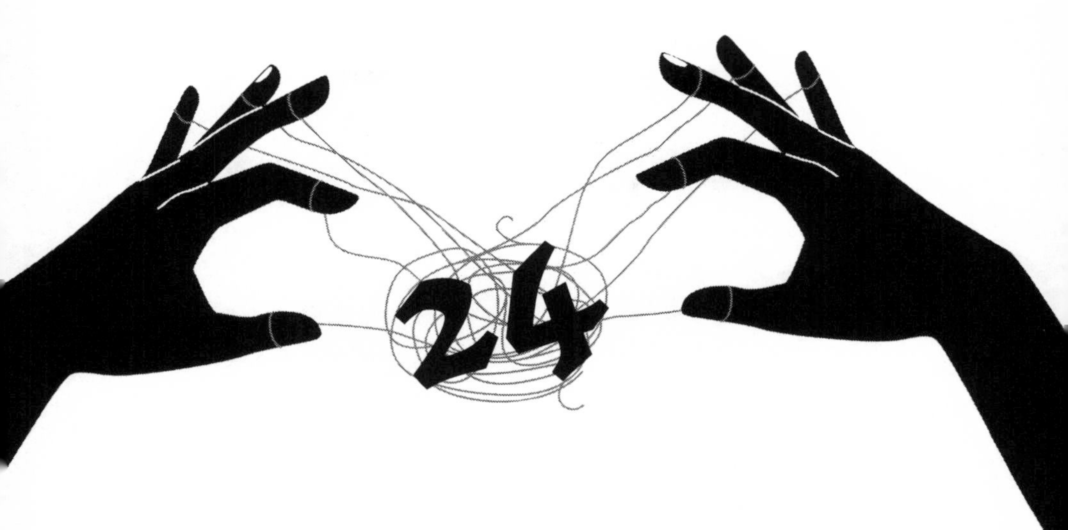

I despise cliffhangers.

Walking out of a movie or closing a book still wondering *whodunit* is like only hearing the set-up of a joke but not the punchline. Seeing the bullet fired at the bad guy just before the titles come up without knowing whether the good guy's aim was true drives me crazy. Jenny hates watching dramas with me when episodes are dropped weekly because I can talk about nothing for the next seven days besides what's likely to happen next. Better that we binge on the whole series in a day.

I crave closure. Maybe that's why I write true crime. I get to immerse myself in someone else's world, learn the language, have relationships with the players, set it all on paper up to and including that last, satisfying period. Done. All the loose ends are tied up in a bow.

I thought that I had this book on a path to closure, even if it was not the path that Abrams wanted me to pursue. Everything I'd heard confirmed the public's perception. Twelve-year-old Micah Abrams was caught up in his parents' nasty divorce. He ran away from his father's rented two-bedroom home late on a Friday night, walked ten minutes to the family's lake house where his mother resided, killed her, and was so traumatized by the experience that he somehow ended up cowering and catatonic in a neighbor's garage. Just as Abrams feared when we first met, I was buying into the viral social media story. Micah is the M&M killer. My book would add the graphic, tragic why. Suki's rages and abuses. Drugs and alcohol. Mother strangling son. Father desperately trying to rescue son. Micah's hysteria. Medication. Run away. Murder. Hospitalization and a big chapter on MPH.

I'd begun to research domestic violence and child abuse and their effects on kids. I'd read about alienation and how parents can force their children into a loyalty bind that leads to rejection -and in very rare instances even the murder- of another parent. I was ready to write a book about puppet-master parents and Suki Kohler's death.

Then with three words recorded nowhere but in my brain where they played at full volume on an endless loop, Abrams shoved me off that path and over the edge of one reality into another. My head was spinning.

The hands on the blank clockface defined a very narrow arc at the top of the circle. I had to leave -the owner of the Range Rover might already be in Abrams' waiting room- but surely Abrams could give me two minutes. I needed him to go back on the record and tell me more. If his goal was to exonerate Micah, then surely he'd want his confession documented?

I'm sure that I muttered a shocked "what did you say?" but my voice seemed very far away. Not even my own. I heard someone plead, "just one more minute, Sam, please!"

Maybe that was me, too.

Abrams said nothing. He watched me trying to digest his words. Maybe his look was haughty? Maybe it was amused? I can't clearly recall. He picked up his cigar-shaped pen and set a blank page squarely on his desktop blotter. I do remember him taking the time to adjust the edges parallel to the edges of the blotter and the desk. Three nested rectangles. He uncapped his oversized pen and let it scroll across the page. Back and forth. Then back and forth again, three or four times. I could hear the scritch of the nib on paper. I could see that the handwriting was elegant -an entirely different graphic than my own rushed and indelicate scribbles- but I could not make out what he was writing.

The second hand seemed to have slowed in its journey around the clockface.

Abrams opened a drawer at his right hip and produced a plain white envelope. He folded the page in thirds and sealed it within. He handed me the envelope and said firmly as every good therapist must at the end of every hour, "I'm sorry. Our time is up." He added my special incentive: "I'd be glad to say more on Friday after you've seen Micah. Please bring me back his reply."

I carried my backpack in one hand and the letter in the other. My legs moved me out of my chair. Abrams escorted me to the exit door. The other, unmarked interior door to my left was, as always, shut tight. I remember cool air and stinging spits of icy rain waking me a bit. It was a chilly and rainy March day in Minnesota. Dark gray clouds filled the sky, reflected dirty blue on the lake, and muted the world. The path up and around the front of Abrams' house was slick, but I discovered a handrail attached to the house. My Jeep was trying hard not to ice up. The Range Rover was there, the lingering heat of the engine briefly boiling the light rain on its hood.

Abrams' voice rang in my ears.

"Micah did not kill Suki ... I killed her."

If my Micah-did-it alienation puppet master theory of the case was wrong, then the little bit of writing that I'd squeezed in between crises at home with Voldemort and Sloan's evaluation and the trip to MPH was wrong. I'd have to start over. I needed to paint Micah as an innocent victim -not the matricidal maniac that everyone believed him to be- and Abrams as an angry and scared father trying to protect his son. I needed to capture Abrams like Farrah Fawcett in '*The Burning Bed*" and Micah much less like a sympathetic and misled Simba in "The Lion King." My July 4 deadline was approaching like a slow-moving train, and I couldn't get off the tracks. I needed to write out what had just happened with Abrams before my memory began to fade and then find time to think through what this new path meant to me and to this book.

I was due to meet Jenny and Christie in Noyes' office back in Shakopee at four. Two hours. If I went home, a hundred distractions would eat up that time. The only place that I know in between is the Potbelly where I'd found hot soup earlier in the week. Five minutes later my laptop, my cellphone, my notebook and I were spread across a back table in the small restaurant. I had a bottomless, thick ceramic mug of coffee in hand and every intention of testing the establishment's refill policy to its limit.

I can't tell you whether the restaurant was deserted or crowded that afternoon. I recall one woman -tall and Black, wearing a winter parka and carrying an infant- asking to borrow my sugar dispenser. I think that I handed it over. I'm not sure. I was in the zone, that mental state that opens me to words and images and ideas but closes me to most everything else. Jenny had been right. The house could burn down around me. I wouldn't notice until my laptop started to melt.

My fingers flew over the keyboard. Now and then I paused to reference my notes or an audio clip or to Google an idea. The WiFi was fast, and the coffee kept coming. I didn't care about spelling or punctuation. That's what editors are for. I'll go back and fill in the background later. What I needed to do was correct course. Change paths. Redirect the story arc. I needed a narrative trajectory grounded in history that accounted for all the known facts that led the reader into the kitchen where Sam Abrams killed his ex-wife, Suki Kohler, while their son stood nearby.

Yes, I could paint that picture in broad strokes, but I was missing a million critical details. Loopholes that needed to be backfilled. Apparent contradictions that needed to be explained. What-ifs that needed to be anticipated and forestalled.

I only had Abrams' side of the story. I needed third party points of view about Suki's drinking and drugging and abuse. Getting that perspective might be impossible, as Suki's family had barricaded themselves behind a phalanx of New York City lawyers since her death.

Might Suki have actually been a loving, caring parent, not the heartless Mary Tyler Moore mother in "Ordinary People" or the sadistic mother in "Precious" that Abrams paints her to be? How much of the psychologist's portrayal of Micah's mother is real and how much is self-validating projective identification?

I made myself reminders to reread the police reports. Had Micah had red marks around his neck when he was hospitalized? If so, is there a way to demonstrate that the hands that had choked him were Suki's and not Abrams?

Did the police run a tox screen on Micah when they found him? Is there medical evidence of the drug that Abrams said that he'd given him that Friday night?

I checked my notes: Aquintex SR was the medication. The Potbelly WiFi (secure password = YummySoup!) zipped directly to a WebMD page. Sold under the brand names ChillAx and Morrest. Possible side effects seemed to include every possible medical condition imaginable including anxiety, depression, cardiac arrhythmias, drowsiness, nasal polyps, hemorrhoids, and nausea. A box at the bottom of the page highlighted in bold and labelled "precautions" said, "Aquintex SR can cause insomnia and parasomnias such as sleep-talking and sleepwalking in unusual cases."

I'd call this an unusual case.

Could Micah have been asleep when he strolled half a mile in the middle of the night back to the lake house?

And Micah's note? How does his "*ding dong* the witch is dead" allusion fit this story? If Abrams killed Suki and father and son hadn't spoken in a year, was this Micah's way of congratulating or thanking his dad? What I had first construed as Micah bragging 'mission accomplished' to Abrams now sounded more like the son congratulating the father on a job well done.

And that brought me full circle back to the note that Abrams had written for Micah. I stared at the pristine white envelope for a second. No longer. Any qualms I had once had about privacy were long ago buried underneath the pressures of writing and the emotions of this story. I wiped my fingers on my jeans and opened it. I slid out its contents. One page. Heavy white stock. Not copy machine paper. Something finer. Abrams' script was, indeed, elegant. Rounded and flowing the way cursive was taught long before phones took dictation and text messages were spellchecked.

Abrams had dated the page and began by writing, "My dear Micah…"

"… Thanks for your note. I miss you more than I can say. No, I don't know when you're getting out but I'm trying to make it soon. Be strong. Your note makes me think that you met Scilla and Charybdis. Maybe you even figured out about King Dorothy. I'm sorry that I couldn't tell you before. I'm really, really sorry, Micah. I never meant for you to be there. I know that it's been super hard for you. Just know that I did it for you. Like you said, ding dong! I'm often in Cham. If not IRL, please find a way to meet me there. Love, daddy"

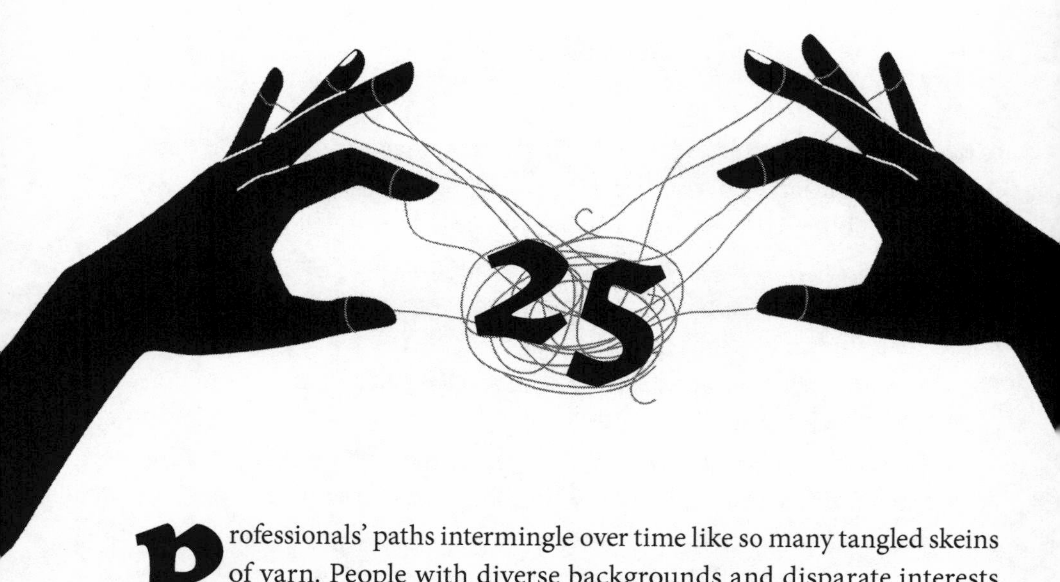

Professionals' paths intermingle over time like so many tangled skeins of yarn. People with diverse backgrounds and disparate interests and distinct skills become knotted and entwined with one another, however briefly.

Sam Abrams' son Micah was once David Noyes' patient in therapy. It's not unusual for therapists to seek one another out because, as Noyes often reminded himself, there but for the desk between us goes I. Abrams' and Noyes' meeting was not by chance, however. Noyes is one among hundreds of mental health professionals in the greater Twin Cities area but has a unique reputation for his work with the children of divorcing parents. The fact that Noyes' office in Shakopee is only twenty minutes away from Abrams' home in Chanhassen only made their meeting that much more likely.

Abrams and Noyes had each on separate occasions attended continuing education trainings conducted by Myra Sloan on child custody evaluations. Both had been impressed with Sloan's intellect and acumen and more than a little daunted by the subject. Court-related work demanded a compulsive and objective perspective that is as uncomfortable as it is unfamiliar to most therapists.

For her part, Myra Sloan was quite familiar with Sam Abrams' high-profile career on the talk show circuit. She'd heard him interviewed and had read several of his popular press articles. She found the man unctuous and self-aggrandizing but conceded that the advice that he offered was generally accurate and helpful.

Sloan and Noyes had worked together on cases more than once and socialized exactly twice. Once over coffee when a court case involving Sloan as evaluator and Noyes as therapist had settled, leaving both with unexpected free time in an unfamiliar place. That pleasant encounter had occasioned their second meeting, dinner out with spouses. Sloan brought husband number two. Noyes brought his boyfriend of the time. Unfortunately, the psychologists' budding friendship ended abruptly when Mr. doctor Sloan number two (first name long forgotten) commented not-so-under-his-breath about Noyes' prodigious size.

Looking back, Noyes recognized that his body image had gone through periods the same way that certain artists go through phases of self-expression. Picasso, for example, is famously known for his successive Blue and Rose and African and Cubist periods. Noyes is neither famous nor widely known outside of the Minnesota psychotherapy community but presumed nonetheless to think of himself as having had distinct phases of his own. He thought of these as his Shame, Denial, Restrictive, and Syntonic periods of body-acceptance.

When Sloan's second husband referred to Noyes as "excessively corpulent," Noyes had been in his Denial Period. That one ugly-even-if-true comment had battered down the locked, bolted, and chained doors of closed-eyed self-delusion and sent him spiraling into depression and self-loathing. Fortunately, before he hit bottom, Noyes took his own advice. He shipped himself off to a six-week therapeutic cleanse on a ranch in Wyoming. Sunshine, horses, group therapy, and a medically supervised diet worthy of Torquemada left him twenty-three pounds lighter, a strict vegan, and on just the right cocktail of medications.

Back in the Twin Cities, the vegan diet yielded to fast-food conveniences and the super-size-me pressures of real life, but the medication regime and Noyes' commitment to daily Overeaters Anonymous meetings carried him forward. His goal ceased being tied to a number on a scale and became a balanced and healthy acceptance of his admittedly corpulent excesses. Distant and difficult as this new balance had been, Noyes gradually began to accept and respect his body for the first time in his life. This I-am-obese-and-I-am-okay syntonic state left him feeling Superman-strong and impervious to others' ignorance and prejudice.

Noyes' monumental success came with an unexpected insight. As he became less vulnerable to other people's stares and jabs and revulsion, other people stared and jabbed and were revolted far less often. Noyes realized that self-acceptance is as visible as a suit of armor, discouraging others' attacks. This epiphany began to guide much of Noyes' work with his child patients and their families.

Christie Villalobos, for example, needed better armor. That's not to say that little Christie had body image issues. To the contrary, the 6-year-old was healthy, giggly, and very smart but suffering the destructive stresses that come with being caught in the middle of her parents' war. Were she better insulated from her mother's anxieties about her father and from her father's selfish psychological assaults on her mother, Christie would be free to invest her energy in making friends and riding bikes and sleepover princess parties. As it was, the little girl was forced to carry around her parents' overwhelming worry and fear and sadness and rage.

In Dr. David Noyes' professional opinion, the first best way to help a child caught in the middle of her parents' war is to slap those parents firmly upside their heads, make them see how their vindictive and volatile choices are harming their beloved child, and get them to stop. As Noyes often said when figuratively slapping parents like Jenny and Jorge Villalobos upside their heads, if you see a child drowning, get them out of the water.

He did say that to Jenny Villalobos when they'd first met. She'd agreed. She and her partner Ted Bennett were more than eager to learn how to keep Christie out of the middle of the adult conflict. Over the months that they'd worked together, Jenny and Ted had worked hard to do what they could to help Christie and to support the child's therapy.

Noyes would have talked about getting drowning children back on dry land with Jorge Villalobos given the opportunity. He'd done his due diligence to involve Christie's father in the therapy from day one and then again very recently as Christie's anxiety about the time she spent with her father became more pronounced and disruptive.

No reply.

He'd never had the chance to meet the man, never mind slap him upside his head.

Noyes had been forced to consider whether Christie's descriptions of her father's words and actions were reportable to Child Protective Services.

Certainly, if he believed that the man that Christie called 'Voldemort' was physically or sexually abusing her, he'd be on the phone immediately. In the end, he'd decided that no, although Christie's descriptions of her father's damning words about her mother and her mother's boyfriend were selfish and destructive, they were not reportable. The law didn't consider one parent's efforts to alienate his child from the other parent a reportable abuse.

The events at White Birch had been the last straw. Noyes had followed the news closely, aghast at the thought of another school shooting so close to home. As details emerged, he was upset to realize that Christie and two of his other patients were students there. He'd made a point to reach out to those families, especially to Jenny and Ted when it became clear that Christie's father was the alleged intruder. He hadn't been surprised when Jenny responded almost immediately, or to learn that Christie had regressed after seeing her father terrify the entire community and then be taken away in handcuffs.

He offered her an immediate appointment.

At exactly four p.m. Noyes heard the chimes that hung on his outer office door ring, signaling the next patient's arrival. He opened his inner office door onto the waiting room and found Christie eager to meet him. Noyes' bulk overshadowed Christie the way King Kong overshadowed Faye Wray and like the 1930s actress, Christie wasn't intimidated in the least.

Christie offered Doctor David a high five, although her "high" was actually his "low." She took Jenny by her hand and led her proudly into Noyes' inner office. She told everyone where to sit, directing Jenny to a nubby brown couch and Noyes to his sturdy and commodious wheeled desk chair. Christie seated herself on the couch next to her mother, pink sneakers hanging off the edge, all business.

Greetings were exchanged, punctuated by jokes and rituals that Christie had embedded in the relationship. A knock-knock that Noyes never got right because Christie changed the punchline every time. A bit of legerdemain that required Dr. David to look away while Piglet magically appeared in Christie's lap.

Jenny asked if Noyes had heard from Ted. He'd agreed to meet them here for this appointment. Noyes double checked his messages. Nothing.

That worried Jenny. Ted was seldom late. She texted him a quick "where RU?"

Noyes invited Jenny's updates which -given their recent emails was *pro forma* at most. He expressed awe and amazement at Christie's recent *Round-it!* Successes, then started to politely excuse Jenny so that he could have some time alone with Christie. Jenny interrupted, asking if she could have a minute alone with the therapist.

"Sure. Of course, Jenny. Christie, why don't you get out the playhouse and set it up for us? Mom and I are going to talk in the waiting room for a sec."

He left the inner office door ajar. He sat with Jenny knee-to-knee in waiting room chairs with an eye on Christie in the adjoining inner office.

Jenny began, "Thanks again for seeing us today, David. I'm sorry that Ted's not here." Worry briefly creased her brow, but she gathered herself and pushed on. "I know that Christie's super glad to be here. Me too."

"Of course. Of course. With what you guys have been through. I can't imagine. Are you okay, Jenny? I mean about Monday. What an ordeal!"

"As good as I can be, I guess. Thanks. There's a lot going on now. Did I tell you that Jorge is taking us back to court? We just started a custody evaluation with Dr. Sloan."

"You did. I think I mentioned that I know her. She's a powerhouse. I'm very sorry to hear that things have heated up. Christie must be feeling the trickle down."

"I think so. Her clinginess that first day has eased up. I don't know about mine, though." She laughed as if the admission was humorous. "I signed a consent that should allow you and Dr. Sloan to talk together. I'm sure that she'll be reaching you soon."

"Yep. Thanks for reminding me. Myra left me a message about an hour ago."

"Anyway, look … Christie is talking a lot about her dad being a bad man: 'Is daddy all gone now?' and 'do I have to see him again?' and 'I'm glad that the police took him away!' Monday at White Birch was the worst not only for Christie, but the whole school saw Jorge at his best. I've told you -and I told Dr. Sloan- Christie's been putting up more and more resistance at transition. She does not want to be with her father.

Last time, Jorge had to physically take her out of my arms mid-tantrum. I can show you the video."

Noyes wagged his head over the sadness that he always felt when children suffer because of their parents' stupidity. "I'm so sorry Jenny. That must be so hard on both of you. This isn't ordinary separation anxiety, right? I mean, Christie separates from you for other activities without difficulty, right?"

"No. It's only about seeing her father. She cries all the time when she's with him. Noyes didn't ask how Jenny knew this. He knew nothing about *BunnyEars*. "My impression is that Jorge leaves her alone a lot. His mother lives downstairs, but they don't talk. Christie almost never sees her *Abuela*. And you know that Christie has no problem transitioning any place else. School or dance or gym or ... look at her here." They could both see Christie happily arranging furniture in a low building on the floor just inside the inner office.

"So, I talked to Mark Camden, my lawyer. He says that if you believe that going with Jorge this weekend could be bad for Christie and if you would be willing to write him a brief letter saying that, then we might be able to get the court to postpone or suspend visits. There's no question in my mind that that's what's best for Christie. She's terrified and, frankly after Monday's fiasco, so am I."

"That makes a lot of sense. Sure. You probably need this letter right now, right? She's due to see her father on Friday? Okay. Here's a plan. I'm going to let you play house with Christie and I'll see what I can type up and then I'll relieve you."

"That would be wonderful, David. Thank you so much."

Christie loved the idea of showing her mother the dolls and the doll-house. Noyes planted himself at his desk with his back to the action and typed away. His printer whirred and whizzed. He asked Jenny to approve the letter, signed and faxed it directly to Camden's office. By twenty after the hour Noyes had excused Jenny to the waiting room and taken her place on the floor with Christie and the dollhouse. Christie explained that they were in the midst of an elaborate drama involving a little girl and a llama named "Mister." Mister kept trying to get into the little girls' house which everybody knows is not okay. Llamas don't belong inside houses. Fortunately, a fleet of Matchbox police cars (horribly undersized and out of scale) zoomed to the rescue. Mister was carted away (on the roofs of two vehicles working in tandem) and the little girl was happy again inside her house.

As the miniature plastic llama named Mister was apprehended, a real-life secretary four miles away collected the incoming fax and placed it in front of Mark Camden. The lawyer read it, then attached it to an *ex parte* motion that he'd dictated earlier after speaking with Jenny. The secretary couriered copies of the papers to the address she had on file for Jorge Villalobos and then faxed it directly to Sharma Pelletier, the clerk of the Hennepin County Superior Court who -although eager to get home where her elderly mother would need to be bathed and toileted and fed after a long day alone- stamped the motion URGENT *EX PARTE*, logged it in the case file, and placed it face up front and center on the on-call judge's desk.

Despite her distractions, Sharma lingered in the judge's chambers long enough to peruse the motion. She hoped to begin law school once her mother inevitably lost her battle with mesothelioma. She was fascinated by the language of the law and the painful dramas that the court works to resolve.

Camden had written, "Jennifer Villalobos, mother and guardian of the minor child, Christina Villalobos, age 6, begs this court to immediately suspend the child's father's visitation rights pending judicial review given the child's recent traumatic experience of her father's school invasion and resulting arrest. The child manifests signs and symptoms suggestive of a profound traumatic reaction to her father and all sensory experiences (e.g., places, sounds, objects) associated with him as documented by her therapist, David Noyes, Ph.D., in the statement attached herewith."

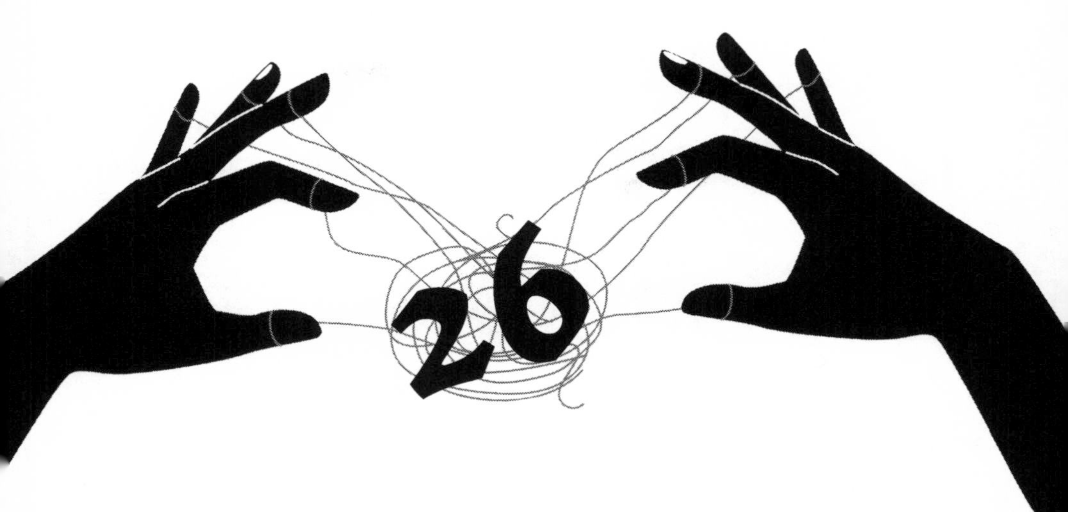

26

"Damn it, Ted! We were counting on you being there. I needed back up. David had a lot of questions about Monday and how Christie was reacting. Do you even know that I did those stupid tests online this afternoon for Dr. Sloan or that I had a long talk with Mark on my way to pick up Christie?"

It was nearly 9:30 at night. Jenny was exhausted and anxious and angry and just a little bit tipsy. Alcohol always amplified her already strong emotions. We'd opened a bottle of white wine over dinner, but not because we were celebrating anything. To the contrary, the wine was more of a filler. Something to do when everything else seemed loaded.

Our typically bubbly household was unusually tense.

Three bites into her spaghetti, Christie asked to taste the wine. That was new. Jenny gave her a raised eyebrow that said, "*when did you turn 21?*" but said simply "no." Christie protested, "but Daddy lets me!" This prompted Jenny to give me a glance full of silent meaning, one of many we'd exchanged recently.

"*What else does Jorge let her do when she's in his care?*"

"*That bastard is turning her against us!*"

"*Look at that! On top of everything else he's turning her into an alcoholic!*"

Jenny was ready to interrogate Christie about what Daddy did and didn't let her do, exactly what both Sloan and Noyes had told us not to do. I jumped in.

"How 'bout some Sprite instead, Christie-angel?"

"Yeah!" she replied eagerly, and then turning to Jenny, "Can I Mommy?"

Soda is a rare treat in our home, usually reserved for Christmas, birthdays, lazy snow days, and the now-and-then event that we call *Christieday* when the little girl gets to choose our activities and dictate the dinner menu entirely.

Jenny recognized that I'd defused a potential landmine and smiled her thanks at me and nodded okay to Christie.

Chalk one up for the good guys.

I fetched the Sprite from the kitchen and filled a wine glass for Christie. She sipped and happily hiccupped her way through the rest of the meal. I challenged her to a spaghetti-sucking contest and she won, red sauce sprayed across her cheeks. If she was aware of the unspoken tensions in the room, it didn't show.

I cleared the table and started the dishes while Jenny read the next chapter from "Charlotte's Web" aloud and Christie managed her own bath. Unfortunately, Wilbur's heroics had to be interrupted when it was time for mommy to break out the shampoo. Christie hates getting "*shampoop*" (always good for a giggle) or "'*ditioner*" in her eyes. Once upon a time I'd suggested swimming goggles, but the strap got in the way. Christie was now in the habit of clamping her hands tight over her eyes while this particular torture played out. Six excruciating rinses later, she stepped out of the tub shiny and pale and round and perfect. With the flourish of a thick towel, Mommy magically transformed the little girl into a child-sized burrito, then carried the squirming, squealing package to her bedroom for pajamas, the rest of the chapter, goodnight kisses, and sleep.

Christie was back in her own bed again as long as Piglet was close at hand.

I rinsed and piled dinner dishes in the sink, then parked myself at my desk, wine glass still in hand. It took several minutes to make sense of the jumble of papers that I'd shoveled into my backpack when I'd bolted from the Potbelly, then several more to catch up on new emails. Dr. Chatterjee had written to confirm that I would be at MPH at noon tomorrow, adding "Micah knows that you're coming. He didn't eat supper tonight again."

Dr. Sloan had emailed both Jenny and I to confirm our date for Friday at ten a.m.

My editor at SynCity wanted to know why I hadn't answered his call and how the book was coming.

I was busy deleting ads for erectile dysfunction medications, ways to burn off belly fat, and offers to optimize my web presence. That brought Charlotte and Wilbur to mind and made me chuckle. *A spider optimizing its web presence?* Then the sound of water running in the kitchen interrupted my Merlot-induced buzz. Jenny was finishing the dishes. I took a deep breath, closed my laptop, and walked up behind her in my stocking feet. She'd untied her ponytail and put on a barbeque apron ("I like it between the buns!"), leaving her lustrous dark hair hanging free. She still wore the white blouse and maroon skirt that she'd worn in Sloan's office hours before. I realized that she probably hadn't had time to change all day.

I put my hands on her waist from behind. She startled, lost in thought and on edge. Soapy water splashed on the countertop.

"Don't do that." She spoke in a quiet monotone without turning. Her words were uncharacteristically abrupt.

"Don't do what?"

"Don't scare me like that." This was not the playful woman that I loved, the woman who on any other day would have turned around laughing as she soaked me with the dish hose or smeared my glasses with the wet sponge.

"I told you, Jen. I'm really sorry. I zoned out. I haven't had a lot of time to work lately. The July deadline is on my mind all the time. I really want to know about the tests and Camden and especially about what Dr. David had to say."

"Don't you get it, Ted?" She was still facing away from me, talking over the sound of the running water. "You're not allowed to zone out right now with Sloan watching and Jorge threatening to take Christie away and a court hearing in the works. Didn't you hear what Dr. Sloan said? What happens if you're 'in the zone' when you're with Christie? I know you love her, but you sounded irresponsible today and you looked like you didn't care and that could cost me my daughter." She shrugged out of my grip and went back to the dishes.

"Sweetie," I tried, "I've already apologized a dozen times. I can apologize again if you need. I'm sorry that I didn't put on a tie for Sloan. I'm sorry that I said the thing about zoning out, I was trying to cover for you. I'm sorry that I missed the meeting with Noyes. I lost track of time. Jenny, you know how important this book is to me. To us."

"Is your book more important than Christie?"

There it was reduced to six simple words. She didn't intend it as an ultimatum, but that's what it was. Choose door number one or door number two and live with the consequences.

"Never," I replied. I gently turned her to face me. "Nothing's more important to me than you and Christie. Everything I do is for you. For our family. You know that. I didn't make a choice today. I made a mistake. I am sorry."

The truth was that I'd parked myself in that booth at the Potbelly in Chanhassen at two o'clock. The next time I looked up it was after five, long after I was supposed to meet Jenny at Noyes' office in Shakopee. I felt like I was in the *Twilight Zone*. Time had disappeared like the numbers on the face of Abrams' clock. Gone. When finally I reconnected with reality, I slapped my hand down on the tabletop hard and cursed. The explosion of palm-on-wood startled a gaggle of bald and wrinkly old men slurping soup nearby and a pair of white-haired older women across the room. The peach-fuzz cheeked teenager behind the counter looked up from his phone. I apologized to all, shoveled my belongings into my backpack, relieved myself of an accumulated gallon of coffee, and then waded my way impatiently through bumper-to-bumper southbound traffic back home.

Jenny and Christie were already here. The spaghetti pot and Jenny's emotions were both on boil

"I know all about your deadline, Ted. Nobody supports you more than I do. But this is a crisis. You don't get it, do you? How could you? You don't have a child."

That hurt deeply. Christie is my child. I said nothing. Jenny continued.

"Jorge is trying to take my daughter away."

She'd said "*my* daughter," not "*our* daughter." Biology be damned. Christie had been "*our* daughter" for more than a year. Now I felt like clamping my hands over my eyes to better endure a necessary torture. Jorge was succeeding. He was slowly tearing our family apart.

Jenny leaned into me, arms around my back, wet hands imprinting on my tee shirt. I wrapped my arms around her, bit back my own writhing emotions, and let her cry.

"Of course, honey." I reassured. "I am sorry. I know. We've got a lot to juggle right now. You and Christie are my highest priority always."

She leaned back and wiped her face with the skirt of the apron.

"So why didn't you tell me that Jorge called you?"

"Damn…" I stepped back out of our embrace, picked up my wine and emptied the glass. Another screw up. "I tried to reach you. Twice. In all the ruckus later, I just forgot. Camden must have told you? I forwarded the voice mail directly to him."

"Yep. And now we've got a bigger problem. The school and the town are declining to press charges against Jorge."

I was shocked. The man is made of Teflon. Absolutely nothing sticks to him. No wonder he can't take responsibility for his behavior. Why would he? Child Protective Services? The court? Now the school district and the police from at least two towns? I'd hoped and expected that causing a nationally televised fiasco would change that. Dozens of first responders were on the scene. His actions had sucked up hundreds of hours of law enforcement professionals' time and tens of thousands of taxpayer dollars. The school went on lockdown. A day of school had to be cancelled. Dozens of staff, teachers, and children including Christie had been traumatized and all he gets is crickets.

I turned away from Jenny and went to refill my glass.

"That is un-fucking-believable!"

"And he might be suing us."

"What?" That stopped me in my tracks. She may as well have said that Jorge had been elected president. "That's ridiculous! Why?" I was leaning on the kitchen table halfway across the room. Our voices were raised. I saw that Jenny's face was flushed with some combination of alcohol and emotion. I'm sure that mine was, as well.

"I don't know, Ted. Mark wasn't clear. Some BS about claiming false arrest or slander or something. I don't even know. Mark tried to explain it, but I was at my limit. Still am. Nothing makes sense anymore."

"So what do we do?"

"Do? What we always do. Color inside the lines. Play by the rules. Be good do-bees while Voldemort does whatever the hell he wants and gets away with it. What we cannot do is this." She untied the apron and pulled it off over her head. Her hair cascaded down behind her.

"*This*?" I asked.

"This. You and me. What he's got us doing right here and now. Arguing. Not trusting one another. We cannot let Jorge come between us. That's exactly what he wants. We cannot let him take Christie away from us. You and I must be a team and we have to show that to Dr. Sloan."

"So, okay. Of course. You're right. And we will. But I've got to ask you a question, Jenn." My words were tentative. Cautious.

"I know what you're going to say," she offered, suddenly sheepish, "and you're right."

"I am?"

"About Christie's bracelet. The app. *BunnyEars*. I'm sorry. I should have told you."

"Why didn't you?"

It was her turn to approach me. She picked up her half-empty glass of wine and drained it. Even in the midst of this argument at the end of a brutal day in the midst of an overwhelming week, her beauty and grace struck me. The motion of her arm as she drank, the extension of her throat accenting her collar bones. The silhouette of her curves against the kitchen light.

God, I love her.

"Eavesdropping on Christie was never about you, Ted. It's all about Voldemort. Making sure that Christie's okay when she's with him. I admit that I did listen in when you and she were together. I was on evenings at the hospital and you guys were here doing homework and dinner. I just missed her so much. I didn't tell you because I didn't want to get you in trouble. Jorge is a pain in the ass, but he's not *your* pain in the ass. He's mine. You shouldn't have to deal with his shit."

She was back in my arms but on her terms this time. That's okay, just so long as she stayed there.

"Sweetie, your shit is my shit and always will be."

"Teddy!" Her body was tight against mine. She grinned up into my face. "That is the most romantic thing anyone's ever said to me."

We kissed long and hard, releasing tension and reassuring one another and enjoying the hormone buzz. She pulled back once more before momentum carried us way off topic.

She said, "I'm really worried about Christie going with Jorge this weekend."

"Me too."

"Mark told me that if David Noyes would write us a letter, he would ask the court to stop Christie from having to see Voldemort at least this Friday."

"Did he? I mean Noyes?"

"Yes. He faxed it to Camden's office before five. I have a copy too. I really, really don't want Christie to be with that bastard this weekend. I won't force her to go. You'll support me, right?" I nodded. "There's got to be a point where we listen to her pain and try to protect her."

I started to respond, but movement drew my attention toward the kitchen door. Jenny looked too. Christie was standing there in her pajamas. Her hair was sleepy-tangled and her eyes were only half open but her voice was clear, "You told me I don't have to go to daddy's anymore!"

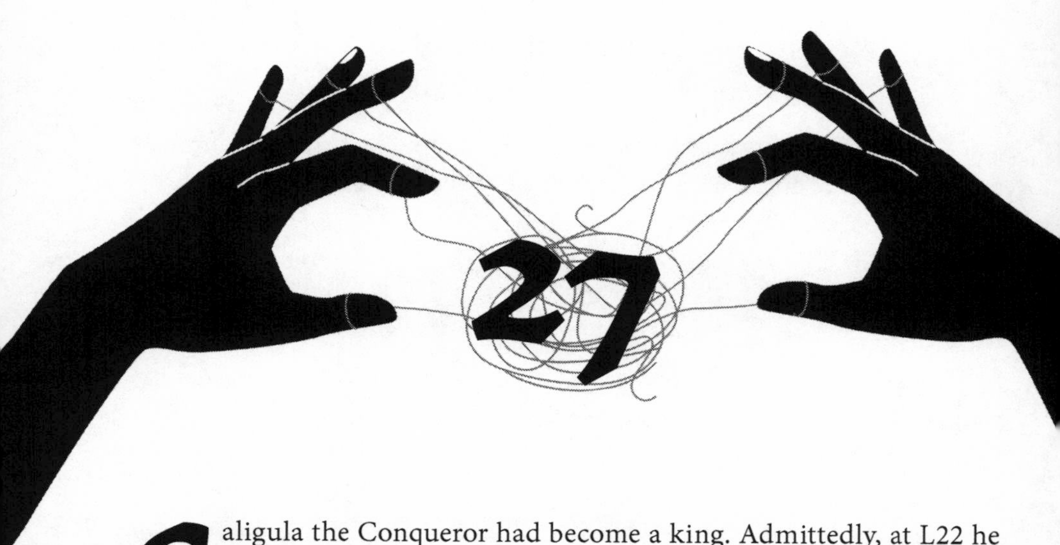

Caligula the Conqueror had become a king. Admittedly, at L22 he was still a lesser king, but *who the fuck cares anyway*? His days of personally slaying dragons and retrieving treasure and outwitting wizards were over. In less than a year, he'd become the Don Vito Corleone of *EAU*. A godfather. He was a broker of all things *EAU* and more than a few things IRL. Players from across the planet manifesting as creatures of every color, shape, and size visited his lair in Cham to acquire powerful and rare resources and to get things done.

Yes, he had a lair.

Caligula resided in an underground castle forfeited by a Seinfeld creature with wings and horns who'd used it as collateral in a complicated deal involving mermaids, bicycles, and an ice princess named Orelsa. Of course, Orelsa had killed Seinfeld while the pair were questing together, forcing him to reboot, and thereby leaving Caligula holding the deed to a warren of elegant subterranean rooms that appeared to be carved in granite and proved (at least so far) to be impervious to attack. He used the fortress' cavernous foyer to entertain scores of creatures who visited him daily doing mundane and quotidian business. Sharpen a laser battle ax. Gift a friend with health points. Curse a neighbor.

He outfitted the middle-deep rooms for living with every comfort imaginable. Beds and fountains and hot springs and pizza ovens and wrestling mats. One room featured a bottomless pit of Cheetos and a faucet that spilled forth an infinite supply of ice-cold Coke. Video screens played everywhere featuring wrestlers and race cars and pornography around the clock which, by the way, were absent. Like a casino, *EAU* allows no clocks or time pieces of any sort.

The deepest of the chambers in Caligula's inverted, subterranean castle were filled with his vast, accumulated VR wealth. He called these his vaults. Rooms full of treasures he'd won or earned or stolen. Other rooms stocked with bizarre weapons found or purchased or instantiated for a specific need. Still other rooms were stacked high with chests that symbolically represented Caligula's power and grew or shrank accordingly. The chest marked 'Health,' for example, was huge and robust, its iron strapping close to bursting. The chest marked telepathy was miniscule by comparison, a shoebox in the company of footlocker- and bank vault- and shipping container-sized chests.

IRL wealth is a different story. Powerful as Caligula the Conqueror had become, Rush Tarnup was still a crippled kid in a wheelchair living in a shithole apartment above a Dollar Tree in Texas. His father still worked ten hours a day six- or seven-days each week to pay the rent, buy twelve-packs of Lone Star, and cases of Marlboros. When he had spare change left after those investments, the man brought home the stray Happy Meal, bucket of fried chicken, or bag of Doritos meant to keep his freakshow-kid from starving.

Rush could easily have bought his own meals or upgraded their hotplate-and-cooler kitchen or just plain rented a regular apartment with air conditioning and a reliable water heater, but then his dad would have begun asking questions. Receiving DHL, UPS, and Amazon deliveries of the IRL jewelry and tech and art that Caligula had won and stolen via *EAU* would have raised red flags, too. At first, he'd cashed in these goodies virtually at twenty cents on the dollar using an online pawn shop and deposited the proceeds into a local bank account. He still had a couple of grand gathering dust there. Fortunately, a player manifesting as a golem who admitted to being an accountant from Buffalo advised him that the IRS treated wealth with no obvious source the way that vultures treat roadkill. The way to go, the golem advised, is crypto.

Cryptocurrency is easy and unregulated and can't be stolen. Rush did his homework. Blockchain crypto is at least as stable and reliable as dollars or euros or krona and safer than all three. Crypto can't be traced and can't be taxed. It's simple to establish a totally encrypted secure wallet and just a matter of keystrokes to move funds in and out of it. Thus, donning his Caligula avatar, Rush began to blur the lines between VR and IRL by demanding payment for certain digital tasks not in credits or barter but in Bitcoin.

"Bitcoin?"

The speaker was obviously using a cheapy tough-guy vocal modifier -probably *VoxMax* or *SpeakUp*- to sound more like he looked.

He looked like a knight in full armor.

Caligula was seated across from an L20 sub-queen manifesting as Sir Galahad, knight of King Arthur's round table. They were in a chatbox within *EAU*, a deeply encrypted and secure virtual space that could be rented by the hour like a cabaña on a popular beach IRL. Chatboxes are handy when players want to interact in real time free of other players' prying eyes, groping claws, and hypnotic spells. By default, chatboxes resemble high-end western boardrooms circa 2020 complete with conference table, black leather swivel chairs, and whiteboards. For additional credits, a chatbox can be upgraded to resemble any physical environment from a candlelit bedroom to a Martian moonscape. Players are admitted by invitation only. What happens within the privacy of a chatbox is dictated by rules that the host establishes in advance.

"Talk Only" protocols made it much easier to negotiate and barter with players who otherwise tend to bite first and ask questions later. Although Caligula had worked out some of his most lucrative and complicated deals in TO chatboxes, "Touch Without Weapons" boxes were always far more intriguing. TWW boxes invite creative and even acrobatic physical intimacies among willing creatures. Plural. Often more than two. These were, in fact, the only kind of intimacies that Rush had ever enjoyed in any universe.

On three occasions early in his VR existence Caligula had been involved in "Lethal Weapons Allowed" chatboxes. LWA invitations are white-glove-slapping duels to the death. These were as memorable as they were terminal events in his newbie experience. The first had played out with pistols at thirty paces in a chatbox done up like a Scottish moor circa 1800. The second recreated the gunfight at the O.K. Corral right down to the six-shooters, neighing horses, and their steaming piles. The third and the only one that he'd won was a Zorro-like sword fight cast across the towering parapets of a Spanish Castillo.

Today's encounter with Galahad was booked in a "No Touch Never Happened" NTNH chatbox. This would be a completely safe and private meeting in a default boardroom that would not appear on any record of any sort.

"You've never heard of Bitcoin?" Caligula asked. "It's cryptocurrency IRL. It's not cash money or VR credits. It's something in between." He stared across the deeply grained, dark oak table as if he might see the real person hiding inside the tarnished and dented armor. He couldn't, of course. In *EAU* as in most VR, avatars are intricately pixilated, nuanced, and wholly credible life-like creatures. The game software instantly and consistently generates genuine verisimilitude including shadows and parallax as a function of lighting, size as a function of distance, movement as a function of wind and gravity and momentum, and occlusion as a function of perspective that is to say, it all looked real. Avatars are not cosplayers hiding under sheets with cut-out eye holes. Unless Galahad chose to reveal him- her- or themself, Caligula was for all practical purposes genuinely addressing a six-foot-tall talking tin can.

"Why don't you know about Bitcoin?"

"We're private in here, right? Like in confession? You can't tell anyone anything we say, right?"

Comparing Caligula to a priest was pretty funny but the analogy worked, and he said so. Galahad wasn't satisfied.

"Swear to me that you'll never tell anyone what I tell you."

Caligula is almost seven feet tall and almost three hundred pounds of slab muscle. His bald head and stubbly cheeks are scarred, and his fu-Manchu moustache hangs down below his chin. Tattoos decorate his shoulders and biceps where his torn and bloody loincloth fails to hide his hairy chest. He'd intentionally bulked and 'roided and embellished his appearance to enhance his ability to intimidate and discourage others' aggressions. This is why he felt ridiculous holding up his right hand in a cub scout salute to reassure the Tin Man sitting across from him that their exchange could never be discovered by anyone by any means ever.

"NTNH is private. This meeting never happened."

Galahad's hollow metal eye sockets stared him down for a moment.

"Okay. I can get you paid any way you want." The creature said. "I'm going to tell you something that I've only ever told a couple of people ever." He hesitated. If he had eyes, he might have shed tears. He didn't, so he couldn't, but Caligula read his posture and his voice as scared and needy. He bet himself that Galahad was a compensating avatar, a VR manifestation intentionally endowed with strengths and skills that the player felt he or she or they lacked IRL. A dummy who played Einstein. A scarred or deformed woman made herself a Madonna.

A friendless quadriplegic in a wheelchair who made himself into a powerful monster.

If Caligula were inclined toward empathy, he might have comforted Galahad, but he wasn't. His mighty and fearsome avatar was, after all, compensating for Rush's crippled and emaciated real life body, rageful psyche, and self-loathing soul. Thus, neither Rush nor Caligula was inclined toward empathy or sympathy or even generosity. His/their only inclinations and morals and motivations focused on acquiring more and more wealth and power.

Galahad persisted, apparently mistaking Caligula's haughty silence for caring.

"My stepdad in IRL has been … touching me. In ways that are gross. No one believes me. Even the police. I told the cop at my school, and he told my counselor, and my counselor did nothing. I need to stop him. I need YOU to stop him."

"How old are you really?"

"Nineteen."

EAU required players to be at least eighteen, but it did nothing to enforce or monitor that rule.

"Don't lie to me, Galahad."

"I'm sixteen, alright?"

"What's your real name?"

"Are you allowed to ask me that?"

"I'm allowed to ask you anything I please. You don't have to tell me, but I don't have to help you, either."

"I'm Bethanne. They call me 'Bethy.'"

So there was a scared little girl inside Galahad's fearsome armor.

"Well Bethy, your dad is …."

"My STEPdad," she corrected abruptly, "and I'm Sir Galahad here. Don't call me that! My real dad died when I was eight and my mother brought Tony home and my two older brothers don't care and my mom is just blind, you know. I mean blind about Tony. She can see. I mean her eyes work just fine. With glasses, anyway. I need him gone. Tony, I mean. I need him gone and I don't care how."

"Your stepdad is a douchebag, Bethy. But I'm not a social worker. I'm a businessman. A do-er. I can do this for a price. Ten thousand dollars U.S. in Bitcoin not credits. Not barter. Can you get that much money, Bethy?"

Bethanne/Galahad said that she could. She gave Caligula an address in Lafayette, Louisiana. He gave her directions about how to Venmo his crypto wallet IRL. He explained that once paid, the deal was irrevocable. It could not be reversed or rebooted or undone. He offered no refunds and no warranties. They would not meet privately again. This is *EAU*, he reminded her, not Amazon. Not Walmart.

Bethanne/Galahad said that she understood and said thanks. Caligula watched the tin man slowly and noisily rise to his feet and then silently evaporate. Hours later an alert flashed on Rush's cell phone. His Bitcoin wallet had received and verified the transfer of the equivalent of ten thousand dollars U.S.

It was six a.m. Thursday, March 9 2023 in East Hoboken, Texas. After Rush's father's truck lurched and sped out of the gravel lot behind the Dollar Store, Rush wolfed down the cold plate of spaghetti left waiting for him at bedside. No meatballs. No garlic bread. He donned his headset and controllers and climbed back into his preferred skin.

Caligula woke up in his subterranean castle in Cham.

Avatars only eat to replenish health points or participate in social rituals. Neither mattered to Caligula at that moment, so he skipped breakfast and the laundry list of human ablutions. Instead, he instantiated a social menu and purchased one hour in a chatbox. A dropdown submenu required him to select the chatbox protocol. He clicked "Talk Only." Flush with new funds, he paid the small upgrade fee in *EAU* credits to make the meeting space into a Roman coliseum. He then scrolled the virtual screen to a comms menu and messaged an invitation to Scylla and Charybdis, L12 minions who'd proven themselves to be effective and discreet real-world operators. The pair manifested as menacing rock creatures suggestive of the vicious opposing shores in Greek myth that crushed passing ships like two hands clapping. He offered to pay them seventy-five hundred U.S. dollars in Bitcoin to make Sherman Marks of Lafayette, Louisiana, full time professor of literature and parttime pedophile cease to exist IRL and everywhere else, too. The rock creatures demanded eighty-five hundred citing travel expenses, although for all that Caligula knew they could be Mr. Marks' next-door neighbors. The deal was sealed at eight thousand and the three sat back to watch lions maim and devour Christians for the next forty minutes.

Why waste a good chatbox?

28

Rain woke me far too early. It drummed down as hard as sleet, prescribing a day that would be best spent under heavy blankets, drinking hot chocolate, and reading a good book. I groaned at my memories of the night before, then again at the thought of the day awaiting me. Jenny's body radiated warmth and welcome, so I shaped myself to her torso, spooning. Her hair smelled of shampoo and sunshine. I rested one leg across her thighs -skin melting into skin- and drifted off into that virtual reality that exists somewhere between awake and asleep; a blurry place where time isn't counted, where pain and worry are filtered through thick gauze if they reach you at all, and in which thought loses its linear, domino-like quality in favor of something Escher-like and unbounded. I happily drifted there until Jenny's alarm nuked me awake.

"When I'm elected president," I muttered into the sweat-and-sweet warm welcome of her taut throat as she stretched, "I will require that anyone who plays 'Happy' by Pharrell Williams at full volume before noon immediately goes to death row. No trial. No appeals."

She slapped her phone silent.

"It's raining," she replied as I chewed on her shoulder. Then, "Stop it, Teddy. Christie could magically materialize here in our bedroom like she did last night in the kitchen and …" she shuddered slightly "… and I've really got to get up."

I should have been up and writing hours earlier.

Either that or I should have tied Jenny down, locked the door, and really enjoyed the rainy early morning, but last night had dragged on far too late for either. Our argument had upset us both even though we agreed later that it had probably been necessary. We needed to vent some of the tremendous pressures that had been pummeling our little family. Jenny was right. I should have told her about Voldemort's vaguely threatening message, and I shouldn't have blown off the appointment with Noyes. I felt especially bad about the appointment because I'd not only let Jenny down, but Christie, too.

Jenny had apologized profusely about keeping *BunnyEars* a secret from me. I appreciated that and, once I got over my paranoid anger that she'd been spying on me ("of course not, Teddy!") then I agreed that it was pretty cool and could be very useful. I downloaded the app on my phone and paired it to Christie's device. We otherwise agreed to leave well enough alone and hoped to explain our mutual reasoning to Dr. Sloan.

Christie's escalating upset about her visits with Voldemort was a different story. Apparently, our argument had woken her, and she'd stood scared and crying in the kitchen doorway unnoticed for several minutes. She'd heard a lot, even if she understood very little. She cried at the idea of seeing Jorge any time soon, anywhere, for any activity. She called him a "bad man" and "yukky" and "Voldemort." She said that he'd told her that Mommy is bad, not him, and never to trust Mommy or Teddy about anything.

At one point while cuddling in Jenny's arms on a kitchen chair, a very sleepy Christie had asked, "what's *easy dropping*, Mommy?" Jenn and I looked at each other puzzled. Then I realized that Christie must have heard far more than I'd guessed. I whispered "eavesdropping" to Jenny while Christie sniffled.

Jenn chuckled, then answered wisely, "What do you think it means, honey?"

"I guess something slippery that's easy to drop. Like soap in the bathtub and ice cubes. But you and Teddy were talking about my magic bracelet. Don't worry, Mommy. It's not easy dropping. See?" she wiggled her wrist wildly and -as she'd predicted- it never dropped.

"Well, that's good to know, sweetie. If it was *easy dropping* you might lose it."

Christie had slowly settled down from there, hugging Piglet tight, with her right hand clamped tight over her left wrist so her beloved bracelet couldn't disappear. Jenny spent most of the next hour helping her get back to sleep. That left me long enough to work out several paragraphs describing MPH -how many different ways can you write "crazy" and "irresponsible"?- before Jenny returned, shushing my questions and obviously seeking her own adult-to-adult kinds of comfort and reassurance. I closed my laptop without the usual SAVE AS and SLEEP commands. I'm glad to say that Jenny wasn't easily calmed, which meant that I had to work at it with her until well after midnight when, mutually exhausted, we'd collapsed naked in one another's arms.

Not even five hours later, Jenny stumbled out from under the sheets and shuffled toward the shower. A chilly blast of late winter took her place in bed with me.

Because Jenny had the week off, she was on Christie-duty this morning. I had about three hours to write before leaving for my command performance at MPH. I was hammering at my laptop and sipping coffee with my headphones on, reviewing audio, as Christie padded past me on her first steps of *Round-It!* Bathroom time. Potty. Wash hands. Brush teeth. The girls shouted "bye" and "love you" in my general direction as I finished drafting the chapter and sent it off to SynCity with apologies for my recent lapse of communication.

The girls left me a note on the kitchen counter: "Back in the zone? Write on! XOXO" Christie had added her own smiling little girl stick figure.

As it turns out, Vesuvius pizza has no storefront and no real signage. There are no neon letters spelling out the restaurant's name and no plastic volcanoes spewing flickering lights of lava. There are no beer or soda or bottled water ads. There are certainly no picture windows looking in on satisfied customers scarfing up pepperoni, mushroom, and anchovy slices. There is only a nondescript, dirty white door in an office plaza between a podiatrist and a dog groomer.

A laminated rectangle on a chain hung from a nail in the middle of the door. The rectangle announced, "Vesuvius Pizza. Closed."

In fairness, I was a couple of minutes early. It wasn't quite eleven. I watched customers come in and out of neighboring store fronts. The bakery at the end of the hall was doing a brisk business, exhaling the scent of cinnamon and coffee every time the door opened. I started to worry that some pimply teenager whose part-time job included opening up the pizza shop on rainswept, cold mornings had decided -like I should have- to just sleep in.

I had a date at a mental hospital in an hour and I didn't want to be late.

I'd wait until five after, then screw it. I'd leave empty-handed if I had to.

Just then, at the stroke of eleven, the door to the pizza shop opened from the inside. No one had arrived to unlock it, reverse the sign on the door, or apologize for holding me up. An older gentleman wearing a colorful chef's toque and a full gray beard magically appeared in the doorway, waving me in. We'd never met, but he addressed me by name.

"Ted? Are you Ted?"

I was caught off guard and stumbled through introductions. He was Rudy, the owner and chief pizza-maker. As he moved about behind the high counter, he explained that he is always there before ten, cleaning and chopping and doing prep. Yes, he saw my order -that's how he knew my name- so he'd warmed up the ovens early and *-voila!-* he handed me a huge flat white carboard box leaking steam and the scent of fresh baked crust and crispy bacon. I traded twenty dollars cash for a receipt, offered a loud and sincere thank you, and was on my way.

I ran through the rain hunched forward over the pizza box, using my upper body to shield it from the cold, wet bullets of ice. I stowed it on the backseat under my coat with the impossible hope of arriving at MPH with the contents still warm. The wipers pushed loose slushy glaciers across windshields front and back but I still couldn't see. The pizza's heat had fogged them both entirely. I was sitting in a bacon and burger sauna.

The ride that had been boring days ago was grueling in this weather. The wipers did double duty and I still struggled to see through the deluge. Truckers passed me undaunted by road conditions, their backwash nearly drowning me over and over again. I felt like a newbie surfer being buffeted by waves. I watched one unfortunate sedan hydroplane into the guardrail but could do nothing to help. Any thought I'd had of sneaking a slice or working as I drove were long forgotten. At noon when I was due to meet Dr. Chatterjee, I still had half the trip ahead of me.

Fortunately, there's enough of a roof over the guard booth at MPH to protect visitors from the full impact of Minnesota's violent moods. Parking Attendant Barbie wasn't on duty. I was greeted, instead, by Parking Attendant Ken. Seriously. The young man who greeted me had perfect teeth and dimples, crystal clear blue eyes, a flawless complexion that defined Caucasian, and thick blonde hair parted above his left eye and combed to the right.

I buzzed down my window eager to check-in quickly. It was nearly 12:30. The pent-up pizza aroma wafted forth. I'd habituated, but when the smell reached Ken midway through his "Welcome to the Minnesota Psychiatric Hospital" spiel, tablet in hand, he swooned. I watched his eyes suddenly open wide and his nostrils flare.

"Pizza for a patient," I explained before he could comment.

Several minutes later I had a shiny new ID hanging on a lanyard around my neck and directions on how to use it. I parked in B9 (B12 was occupied today) and dashed through the rain, juggled the pizza box while I unlocked the entrance doors with my ID, and fast-walked across the mammoth entrance hall toward Center East One, the Adolescent Offenders' Pod.

My wet soles squeaked across the marble floor and echoed through the large, empty hall.

I buzzed into the short hall that doubled as a sally port, dumped everything except the pizza in a locker, and waited impatiently to be buzzed onto the pod. Long frustrating moments passed. I stared at the ceiling-mounted camera as if my attention might stir a response. Eventually, a young male voice filled the space: "I'm sorry, visitors are required to leave all personal possessions in the outer hall."

"This is a pizza," I explained, lifting the lid toward the camera to demonstrate that I was importing food, not a weapon or pornography or drugs. No doubt they already had enough of those. "Dr. Chatterjee knows that I'm bringing it."

"Dr. Chatterjee is off the pod this afternoon on a personal matter. Please leave all personal possessions in the outer hall."

Shit! Not only was this frustrating, but I couldn't even see who I was arguing with.

"I'm sorry. Look: Dr. Chatterjee asked me to bring pizza. I've just had a miserable ride through a slush storm. My clothes are soaking wet and I'm late. My name is Ted Bennett." I emphasized my last name. "Dr. Chattterjee specifically okayed me to bring food down for Micah Abrams."

The door buzzed. A very dark-skinned, very young man with a thin pencil-line of a moustache stood in front of me. He wore half-glasses at the end of his long nose and a long white coat over a dark suit and tie. He introduced himself as Prakash, although I'm still not sure whether that was his first or last name. He told me that he was covering for Dr. Chatterjee who'd had a death in her family. An in-law somewhere down south -maybe she'd said Louisiana?- had committed suicide.

He spoke with a pronounced British accent.

"I'm here to see Micah Abrams. Can you tell me how he's doing today? Dr. Chatterjee said that he wasn't eating."

"I'm sorry mister …" He angled his head so as to align his eyes, his glasses, and my ID and read aloud. "Mister Ted Bennett. I'm sorry but I don't know who Micah is."

Teenagers of every shape and size and diagnosis had begun circling me and the pizza box like sharks intent on a kill. I could hear their pierced and painted lips smacking. Prakash seemed blind to the threat.

"Aren't you his doctor? You said that you're covering for Dr. Chatterjee…?"

"Well, yes, Sort of. I'm a third-year med student in psychiatry at UM. This is my first day here. It's all very exciting."

I begged and pardoned and "nice-meeting-you"ed out of that exchange as quickly as I could. I reassured Prakash that I knew my way and I was fine and thank you very much. I pushed through a clot of drooling youths, nearly stumbled over a naked boy laying face down in the middle of the carpet -seriously: this kid lay butt-up spread eagle in the middle of the tiled floor unmoving and unnoticed by the tide of humanity that eddied and pooled around him- and found my way to the boys' hallway. There were still white towels jammed in the doors and there was still loud, foul music playing in Hector's room. I did not stop in to say hi.

The general stench and demeanor of the place hadn't changed, even if some of the details had. I saw no Peter Max dyed hair today, but I did see enough shaved heads to make me think that either oncology had transferred a busload of teenagers onto Center East One or there had been a lice outbreak on the pod. I saw no overt sexual behavior, but I did see a fistfight at the end of one hall. One thing that had not changed at all was the absence of supervision. My encounter with Prakash was my only sighting of an adult on the pod for the entire duration of my stay.

Micah looked thinner and paler and much, much more tired. He still sat on the end of his bed and still wore the same clothes. His room was definitely messier and smellier, both obviously due to the shotgun scatter of unbreakable plates and bowls and cups that created a vague arc around his present position. Dark, wet stains of the liquids and solids that had been ejected from the dinnerware marked the range and strength of his throwing arm. Moldering heaps of rejected meals were accumulating around his bed.

The scene was disgusting, but I'd once been a college freshman in an all-male dormitory. I'd seen and smelled worse.

I carried the pizza box into Micah's room with two hands in front of me. A herd of hungry teenagers followed behind me the way that rats followed the Pied Piper out of Hamelin. I fantasized about throwing one slice down the hall like chum just to get them out of the way. Then I remembered my mother's warning never to feed stray dogs.

I tried but couldn't close the door to Micah's room behind me. A towel still blocked it open.

"Well, it's about fucking time!" Micah said by way of greeting. He raised his gaze over my shoulder and screamed at his peers, "Fuck off!" To my astonishment, the vultures dispersed.

"Hi Micah."

"That smells like Bacon and Burger. Is it?"

"Yes. Your father told me it your favorite."

I suddenly understood Christie's new phrase, *easy dropping*. It describes ice and bath soap and the instant change in Micah's expression. His insulant, obnoxious, and aggressive face *easy dropped*. In its place appeared a needy, scared-little-boy face. If the thin rubber string on the back of a cheap Halloween mask broke, the trick-or-treater's real identity couldn't have been revealed as quickly.

"You talked to my dad? Did you give him my note?"

The moment of little boy vulnerability passed. He put the angry teenager mask back as easily as it had fallen off. "Did you bring me a note from him? I told you I wouldn't talk to you again unless you brought me a note from him."

"Slow down, buddy. Let's see: Yes, I talked to your father and yes, he read your note and yes, I brought a note from him. Yes, yes, yes. But I get to make some rules, too.

At this he lowered his blue eyes and started picking at loose threads in his blanket. It was clear from the decimated fabric that he'd been busy perfecting this art. His fidget was nowhere to be seen.

When he said nothing more, I told him my rules. "We talk. We eat. Then I will give you the note from your dad. Okay?"

"How about just giving me his note first and we'll see…?"

"No deal. My way or the highway. I'm pretty sure that your friends would devour this pizza in a second if I gave it to them."

"They are not my friends. Alright. Talk."

"Talk and eat." I handed him a limp and chilly slice. Nuggets of bacon and hamburger stood out against hillocks of cheese within a toasted brown circumferential berm. He studied the slice carefully, sniffed at it and said, "I need to see you eat one first."

"Gladly, but why….?" I scooped up a slice and folded it in half, capturing grease and cheese and loose bits in the makeshift wrap. I bit off the pointy end, chewed and swallowed. Hot out of the oven it might have been terrific. Ninety minutes, some rainwater and bouncing later it was still pretty good.

"Why? Why do you think? Because they tried to put drugs in my food here. They figured out I was cheeking those little white pills. Did you tell them?"

I protested with both hands up, wagging my head, still chewing.

He took a tentative bite. Then another. Before I could ask anything, he was onto his second.

I patted my pockets, panicked, then cursed silently. No phone. No notebook. No pen. Why hadn't I smuggled them in the pizza box? No one here cared or would ever know. Damn!

"Alright. This is the talking part. I need honest real answers, Micah. No BS if you want the note from your dad. My part of the deal is no sugar coating, okay? I'm not going to beat around the bush. I'll ask straight out, you answer straight out, and we're golden. Okay?"

"Sure." He spoke with his mouth full. "Why didn't you bring those ground-up hot peppers? I always use hot peppers."

"Sorry. Next time." I didn't have the time or the patience to test the waters, so I jumped into the deep end. "Question number one: What happened to your mother?"

"That bitch? Why do you even care? Was she your girlfriend or something?" He sneered.

"You're not keeping our deal. What's the answer?"

His chewing slowed and his head bowed, staring at the shredded blanket underneath him.

"For real?" he asked quietly.

"For real" I answered.

"I don't remember everything." He chewed slowly and was quiet for long seconds. "She hurt me. Choked me for no reason. I told my dad, and he was real upset. Me too. I used to go there every other weekend. To dad's. Sometimes I get kind of worked up and it's hard to calm me down. I think he gave me medicine. He's a doctor, you know. We were watching a movie. *The Wizard of Oz*. I remember going to bed. I was really tired, but I couldn't sleep. Then I remember cold. Cold feet. Cold on my neck and my hands but then my hands were warm. There was blood on my hands. I think I wiped them on my shirt. And I remember two people. Not as old as you. Maybe like college-age people. One man and one woman with masks. The woman had a knife. A big, shiny knife but there was blood on it. Dripping. Then I tried to run." He'd grabbed a fistful of blanket in each hand and was busy twisting those handfuls of bedding. Wringing the life out of them.

Two people? Had he seen the killers? One man and one woman. College aged. A knife. Masks.

Not his father. Even behind a mask he'd know his own father.

If Abrams didn't kill Suki and Micah is not the M&M killer, then who is?

Why hadn't he told anyone else this?

"I remember seeing my mom," he continued.

I couldn't see his eyes. His body was as tense as a fist and his fists were knotted in fabric tight to the point of tearing. The pizza was forgotten. I know that he was breathing because he kept talking, but I couldn't tell by looking at him. His body was as rigid as stone.

"She was in the kitchen. On the floor. Her eyes were open. Staring at the ceiling. Or at nothing. She couldn't move. She was wearing a necklace. There was something on her cheek. She was so pretty and hated being dirty so I rubbed her cheek to get it off for her. But she fell over. When she hit the floor, she made a wet, soggy sound. Not like a person, more like laundry or wet towels or something. So I left her there but then I saw the knife coming so I ran out of the house and it was cold again. My feet were so cold. Then they weren't and it was dark but good dark. Deep dark. I was in the deep dark for a long time and when I woke up, I was here."

I felt a vicarious chill just listening to the disjointed sensory-laden account. The cold on his feet. The bright red blood on the shiny knife's edge. Suki's pale, blood splattered cheek. Micah's voice was younger. He'd used no profanity. No push-me-away offensive language. At a gut level I recognized that this wasn't the brilliant, manipulative youth playing me to get what he wanted. This wasn't even the puppet-master's instrument -Frankenstein's monster- reciting well-learned lines. The words were too visceral. The emotions were tangible. I was hearing Micah Abrams' lizard brain -the most primitive part of him- forcing the square pegs of experience into the round holes of vocabulary and syntax and punctuation. Part of Micah's mind was still there, in his parents' lake house, on a cold wintery night barefoot and bloodstained, looking at his mother's corpse and fearing the killer's return. Short of actually being in the room with him, this was as close as anyone might ever get to knowing what he'd lived through.

Micah looked up then with a sparkle in his eye. Not tears, but mischief. He grabbed another piece of pizza and bit off all that he could fit in his mouth. He smiled at me around the food and spoke while he chewed, "Ha! You thought that was real, didn't you?" Mush splattered when he spoke. "Didn't you? Man, everyone here is so damn gullible!"

Bits of sauce and cheese erupted with his words, spraying his shirt and bedding.

He took another bite but didn't miss a beat talking. "It's pretty funny, you know. The look on your face. You look so fucking confused like you just ran over my cat but when you went to look, no cat! Jeez, what a loser!" He was talking fast and loud. His eyes were dry and clear and huge. Dilated. He'd released the tortured bedclothes and was back to incessantly picking at threads.

"Don't be stupid, Ted," he said. "That's the story I'm going to tell. Poor me. My loving mother was slashed by intruders wearing masks! That's bullshit and you know it. I killed that red hot flaming narcissistic sociopath, damn her to hell forever. Ding dong the bitch is dead! Sucky is dead! I slashed her throat because she tried to strangle mine. If you tell anyone I said so, I'll say that you're the crazy one. Now give me that goddamn note from my father. I played your game. Pay up or get the hell out and never come back."

I was lost in a hall of mirrors. Reality had lost meaning. Hadn't he just vomited up his genuine, terrifying experience? Could he be that good of an actor? Had Micah killed his mother? Was Micah covering for his father who had killed his mother? Were the two masked intruders real?

Stunned, I pulled Abram's letter from my back pocket and passed it to him.

He unfolded the page. It absorbed his entire attention. He'd stopped chewing and torturing the bedding. I stopped breathing. We sat in tense silence despite the bedlam outside his door.

"Silly anchor bus." The syllables streamed out of him quietly but constantly like an incantation or a prayer so often said that it's become one long word.

"Sillyanchorbus"

His mouth was still full of pizza and now hidden behind the page that I'd handed him. I couldn't make out what he'd said.

"She's dead. Not just a reboot. Silly anchor bus! Not just a reboot! She's dead-forever-dead!"

His volume was growing like the sound of a tornado approaching.

If you've ever made microwave popcorn you may have some sense of what I was seeing. The flat rectangular bag spins round and round on the turntable inside the machine for long seconds. Then it starts to pop. Very slowly at first. Pop! Pause. Pop pop! Pop-pop pop! Then peer pressure kicks in, the heat reaches some critical value, and the kernels all start to dance. The bag expands trying to contain a growing chorus of pop pop-pop POP!

Micah was starting to pop. His father's note was crushed in his right hand which, like the left, had resumed strangling bedsheets. His eyes had lost their focus. His face had lost its expression. His words had lost their meaning.

"Silly, Silly Anchor Bus!" His laugh was hollow. He sing-songed, "Ding dong the bitch is dead. Which old bitch? The sucky bitch!"

I was way out of my depth.

"Micah?" I tried with no effect. "Micah, let's talk about something else." Then, "Please let me take the letter back, please." I wanted to get rid of the evidence. I thought if his father's words had triggered this, maybe retrieving them would untrigger him.

"Silly anchor bus! SILLY ANCHOR BUS SILLYANCHORBUS!" He was yelling now, arms thrown wide. He'd abandoned the knotted fabric and the crumpled letter. I snagged the page and stuffed it in a back pocket. The popping was frantic now. The bag expanding. I needed a nurse or a doctor. Were there any on this pod?

"Dead dead dead! Silly Anchor Bus! She's dead and I did it. No reboots for her! I did it Silly Anchor Bus! It was me me me! I killed that red-hot flaming narcissistic sociopath. I killed Sucky dead dead dead! No reboots. Never for her. I did it! Me! Not Silly Anchor Bus!"

I needed a video camera and a notebook and the kind of dart gun that big animal vets use to tranquilize rhinos and elephants in the wild. Micah had gone off the deep end headfirst and I had no idea how to pull him back. I would have yelled for help if I thought anyone on Center East One would care or know what to do. I didn't. I sat numbly by, scared, and fascinated in equal measure.

Then ever so slowly he began to spin down. To settle. It was like watching an overwound toy wear itself out. It was like Abram's letter was the match that had set a standing puddle of gas on fire. It had burst into flames and burned hot and bright briefly but was now burning out. The frantic, manic energy was subsiding. The spark had drained from his eyes. He still muttered about anchors and busses but he'd lost his purpose. He never got off the bed. He never lashed out at me or tried to harm himself. His hands were knotted once again in his bed sheets but had ceased twisting. The pizza was forgotten.

I tried to remember every word and grimace and action, but memory needs context and this had none. I'd lived it just moments ago but already Micah's explosion was becoming a blur of meaningless syllables and motions.

"Micah, can you hear me?"

He still sat on the end of his bed, legs dangling over the edge, hands tangled in sheets, head dropping. I couldn't see his eyes. He was still muttering quietly.

"Micah....?"

Nothing.

I touched his knee. Pushed a little at the stiff jeans. He didn't respond.

It occurred to me that this is catatonia. This is the unresponsive, lost-deep-within state that the police had observed when they first found him cowering in his neighbor's garage.

I stopped at the nursing station on the way out, hoping to send someone to the rescue. No one was manning the desk. Charts and clipboards and tablets lay about randomly. The space was deserted. My laminated ID buzzed open the sally port. I called out a hopeful "hello" toward the overhead speakers that had tried to keep me from bringing the pizza on the pod twenty minutes earlier. I would have sent someone to Micah, but no one answered.

I used my ID to collect my things and escape into the grand entry where Center West One used to be. I dashed through the continuing deluge into my pizza-scented Jeep and was through security and back onto the highway in minutes. Micah's pleading angry crazy words followed me every step of the way.

Jenny was halfway across the Scotland Kinloch Hourn, focused on the boggy wetlands and wildlife rather than her breathing and aching calves when her phone rang. The caller ID said Camden, Mark. She stepped off the Peloton and away from the class to take the call. To a casual viewer, she would have disappeared amidst the crowd of sweaty gym rats and Gen Z'ers. She was perfectly camouflaged in black Spandex under a sleeveless purple Viking sweatshirt borrowed from my bureau.

"Mark?"

"Hi Jenn. I'm glad I caught you. You're breathing hard. Is this a bad time?"

"I'm at the gym. I hoped to hear from you. What's up?

"Bad news I'm afraid. Jorge filed an objection to our *ex parte*. Can I read it you?

"Sure." Jenny plugged her exercise headphones into her cell. Camden's voice was suddenly loud and clear and the whirring, pounding, huffing background noises vanished. "Go ahead, Mark."

"He wrote, and I quote, 'My daughter's mother is engaged in a long-standing campaign of denigration intended to erase me from my daughter's life. Her bad acts culminating in police action at the child's school must not be held against me. They are evidence of her nefarious and selfish motives. I adamantly object to any action that further compromises my daughter's opportunity to spend time in the care of her only healthy parent. The court must reject the *ex parte* with prejudice.'"

Jenny was stunned but not surprised.

"He doesn't have a lawyer? Who wrote that horseshit? Not my high school dropout ex!"

"Still no one on record. I suspect that that hired gun I mentioned to you, Hassan French, is feeding him wording. I'm sorry to say that the judge bought it."

"Of course!" Jenny kicked the padded wall.

"The judge wrote, 'The motion is denied without prejudice.' That means we can bring it again in the future if we need to. The judge wrote specifically, 'denied without prejudice pending the outcome of the custody evaluation."

"So it's up to Dr. Sloan?"

"No. It's never that easy, I'm afraid. She can't suspend visits. Her report can recommend that contact be suspended or increased or left unchanged, but in the end only the court can make that decision."

"And her report is weeks away! My little girl is hurting now. Damnit, Mark. Christie's supposed to see her father tomorrow. She's going to absolutely melt down. I can't stand it. I've got to tell you: I will not force her to go to him. How could I? The man is a bully. They can come arrest me if they have to. It's time that someone stood up to him."

"Jenny, be careful. You'll be in contempt. You probably won't go to jail, but in the larger scheme you'll seem to confirm everything he's saying about you. Everything Dr. French is telling Jorge to say about you. That you're alienating Christie from her father. That you're -what was his phrase? 'Trying to erase' him."

"But I'm not!" Several people on treadmills nearby looked up when her words broke through their headphone-insulated workouts. Jenny just turned away from their curious stares. There were angry tears in her eyes. She resumed more quietly: "I am not alienating anyone from anything. I'm just trying to protect Christie. That's what good parents do. There's a difference! You must see that, right? Can't you do anything, Mark? What would you do if this was your daughter?"

"Logically? You have four choices. One: Kidnap Christie and move to Brazil or Morocco. They're not part of the Hague Convention that forbids abducting children from their parents. You'd be safe there. Two: Hire a hit man. Expensive and dangerous. Three: Withhold Christie tomorrow and risk being held in contempt and whatever Dr. Sloan and the court make out of that. And four: Bite your tongue and send your daughter off with her father as ordered by the court. Please listen to me, Jenny. I do NOT recommend options one, two, and three. They are illegal. I strongly advise that you find a way to comply with the court's order."

Jenny growled and winced with frustration. No! She would be betraying Christie by sending her back to Voldemort. But she'd risk losing her entirely if she didn't.

"Mark, I don't mean to be rude. I know it's not you. But this situation is not okay. I've got to reach Ted and figure out what to do. I'll call you if I need anything."

"I'm sorry that I can't do more, Jenny. Please, please, please make the right decision."

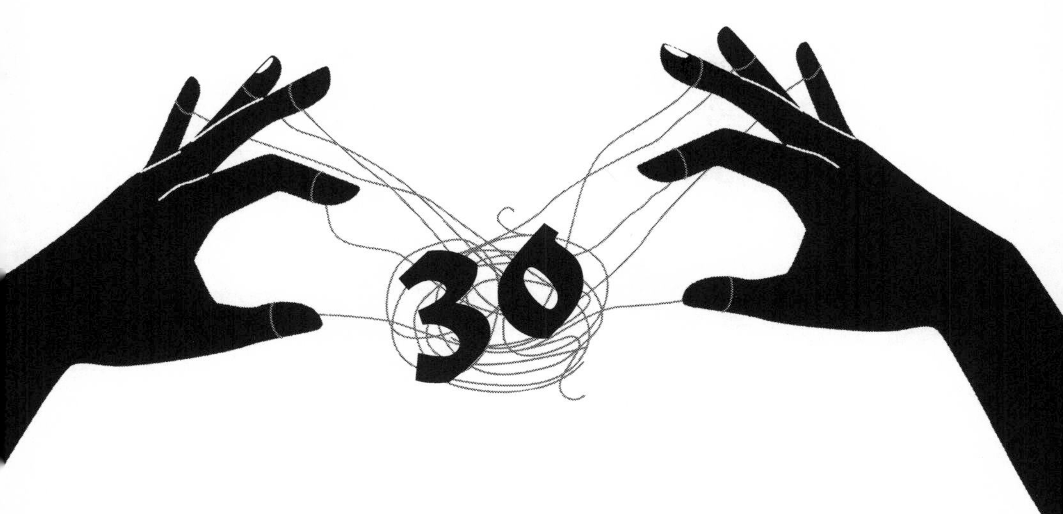

The *Lafayette Daily Advertiser*, Lafayette, Louisiana.

At approximately 4:30 Thursday morning, local authorities found Sherman Marks of Lafayette dead in his home. Police on the scene report that Mr. Marks appears to have killed himself with his own handgun. Records confirm that Mr. Marks owned two registered pistols and one shotgun. Foul play is not suspected. Sergeant Kevin Belasky of the Lafayette Police Department stated that the Department will not be conducting any further investigation.

Mr. Marks was a tenured professor of literature at the University of Louisiana (Lafayette), a trusted mentor, a published author, and valued member of both the university community and the city at large. He was well known for his tireless dedication as the coach of the junior high school girls' volleyball and softball teams.

Mr. Marks was 51. He was a member of the local Elks Lodge, the Veterans of Foreign Wars (VFW), and was a member of the 2019 Louisiana ten pin champion bowling league. He loved reading and hunting and spending time with his stepchildren. He leaves behind a brother, Paul M. Marks of Minneapolis, Minnesota, his wife Noreen Knight-Sherman, and her three children: Derek Knight, age 21, attending the University of Connecticut; Kyle Knight, age 19, attending Tulane; and 12-year-old Bethanne "Bethy" Knight who attends the eighth grade in the Lafayette public schools.

No services are planned. Charitable contributions are welcome to the National Organization to Prevent the Abuse of Children (NOPAC). Queries are to be sent to the newspaper office as the family has relocated without forwarding information.

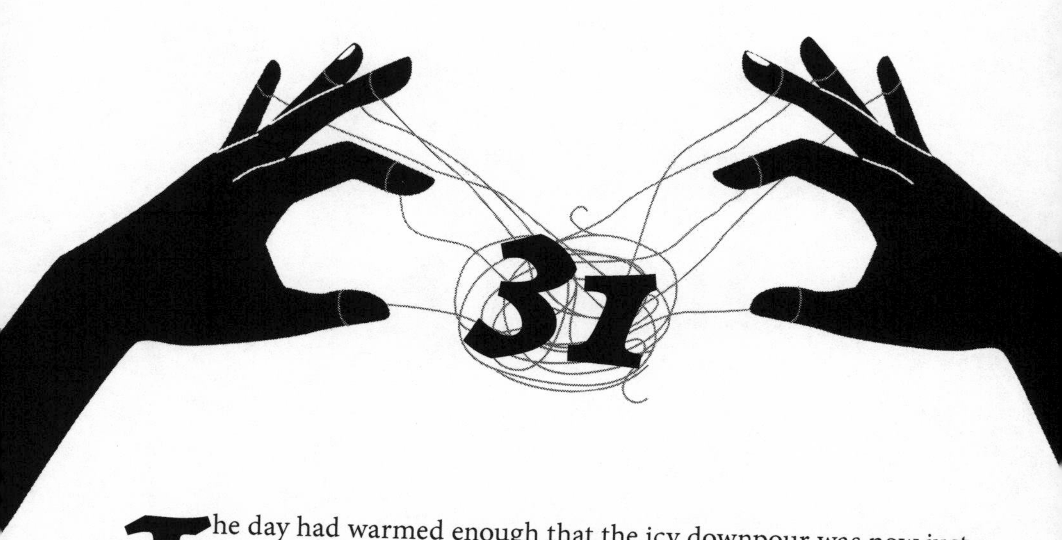

The day had warmed enough that the icy downpour was now just a rainy deluge. I may as well have been driving under the open sluice gates in the Hoover dam or through Niagara Falls. Traffic pushed north at about fifteen miles an hour, veering around deep puddles and skating across long rivers of run-off. If I could safely drive any faster, I'd say that I was fleeing whatever I'd just witnessed on Center East One. As it was, my escape barely qualified as limping or dragging or even crawling away.

Micah had disintegrated in front of me.

If a human psyche is a jigsaw puzzle that is gradually assembled over time and experience, I'd just watched Micah's fragmented and very incomplete self break into pieces. I'd left him totally disassembled. At the moment, I didn't care so much whether I'd caused that or whether all the king's horses and all the king's men could put him back together again. I only cared about finding truth in what he'd said.

What had he said? I had no notes. No recording. I concentrated trying to remember and … *SHIT!*

I hit the brakes hard. The pickup truck in front of me had stopped moving. My Jeep's front bumper was almost kissing his tailgate. The van behind me veered onto the shoulder to miss me, horn blaring. That's all I needed today. A car accident. Huddling on the side of the highway soaked to the skin exchanging insurance information with strangers. Repair bills. A rental vehicle.

Traffic resumed inching forward at a pace that seemed to intentionally defy the windshield wipers' double-time rhythm. I could see one vehicle ahead, one behind, and one on my left but nothing further. No sky. No rolling hills or lakes or trees. I couldn't even see the blacktop beneath me.

What had Micah said?

At one point he seemed to be in a trance deep inside his memories. Inside trauma. He'd told a story that fit with his father's account about Suki trying to strangle him and being medicated but added in the part about walking to the lake house in the middle of the night and seeing two masked people there. Young people. One with a knife. In that reality, Micah was a victim, a runaway kid who'd walked in on a traumatizing scene. He'd seen strangers brutalizing his mother. He might hate her, but he didn't kill her. The experience had left him regressed, muttering nonsense, and catatonic.

That story contradicted Abrams' off-the-record admission and social media's insistence that Micah himself was the perpetrator.

Had Micah walked in on his father killing his mother? Possible. I'd seen no proof that Abrams was in his bed all night at the rental a half mile away. He could have walked or driven to the lake house and then returned and pretended shock when the police woke him with the news hours later. Had he taken Micah along for the ride? Had father and son gone out for a late-night matricide? Or had Micah followed his father or stowed away in his car and become an unintended witness of husband killing ex-wife?

Micah had said that there were two people in the house. They were young. One male. One female. The female had the knife. Even with masks, he would have known his father.

But then Micah tried to undo all of that, as if he'd slipped and said too much. He taunted all of us gullible fools and bragged about how he planned to use the compelling fiction about masked intruders to avoid being discovered as the real perpetrator, the genuine M&M killer.

If Micah had killed Suki, then Abram's confession was an obvious attempt to protect his son. But why then had Abrams confessed off the record? That helped no one.

Clearly, father and son shared a hatred of the woman. They'd each reveled in the "*ding dong*" *Wizard of Oz* the witch is dead motif, or as Micah had sung it, "the bitch is dead." But sharing a hatred of Suki Kohler did not make one or both killers.

There was no question in my mind that something in the father's note had pushed the son over the edge. He'd started babbling nonsense about anchors and yelling and spewing pizza all over his filthy shirt. What was the phrase? "special anchors" or "silly anchors." No that wasn't quite right. There was another syllable.

"Silly Anchor Bus?" That was it.

"Silly Anchor Bus."

I'm pretty good with language. Words. Meanings. I write for a living.

Try as I might, I had no handle on what "silly anchor bus" could mean. There was nothing silly about this story whatsoever. Was it a phrase from one of the old movies that Abrams and Micah enjoyed together? I suppose that's possible, but that seemed like a stretch. Bus? Anchor? The house is on a lake. There's a dock and lots of boats. There must be anchors out there. But an "anchor bus"?

Christie's smashed up remake of "eavesdropping" as "easy dropping" came to mind. Misunderstood syllables parsed incorrectly. Like the old joke about two Pittsburgh natives who run into each other at noon. The first says, "Jeetjet?" The second responds, "Not yet. I'm hungry. Let's get some lunch."

"DID-YOU-EAT-YET" collapsed into "jeetjet?"

I tried the phrase out loud as I drove, shifting emphasis and parsing syllables.

"Silly Anchor Bus. Sillyanchor-bus. "SILLY-anchorbus." "Silly-ANCHOR-bus"?

Then faster and louder above the sound of the rain pounding on the car: "Sillyanchorbus. SillyanchorBUS."

Then it hit me. I arched my back and straightened my leg to try to get my right hand deep in my back pocket without slamming down the accelerator. I swerved left and drew a long honk and a nasty look from a woman in a VW bug, but I pulled the crumpled paper out mostly intact. I glanced up at traffic and down at the page. Up and back. Looking for the line. A white van ironically advertising sump pump services *-wet basement? Call us today!-* zigged out of the left lane and into the right, ten inches ahead of me. No blinker. No signal of any kind. I took my turn on the horn.

Abrams' note tumbled into the footwell on the passenger side. I timed our stop-and-go movement carefully and dove for it when the forward momentum paused. There it was, clearly written in the psychologist's fancy script: "Your note makes me think that you met Scilla and Charybdis. Maybe you even figured out about King Dorothy."

"Silly Anchor Bus."

"Scilla-and-Charybdis."

Abrams had written about Micah meeting Scilla and Charybdis.

Two young people wearing masks? The names of the killers?

I vaguely remember Scilla and Charybdis from high school lit class. Greek mythology. A class on the Iliad and the Odyssey. I'd loved the adventures of Jason and the Argonauts and Odysseus facing scores of creatures. The cyclops and Circe, the witch who turns men into sheep. Damn it. I couldn't remember any details about these characters.

I asked Siri.

Siri was eager to teach me about a bacterium with a twelve-syllable name that vaguely sounded like "Scilla and Charybdis." I tried again and learned about Marie Curie's discoveries. The words were too obscure, and the background was too noisy. I couldn't type out the names without ending up in ditch and had no idea how to properly spell them anyway. Before I could try Siri a third time, the phone still clasped in my right hand vibrated.

It was Jenny.

"Hi sweetie," I yelled. "Its really hard to talk. I think that I took a wrong turn at Duluth and am presently driving through Lake Superior. Are you okay?"

"What? You're joking, right?" Her voice was tense. My attempt at humor missed the target completely. "No, Ted. I'm not okay. The court denied our motion. Christie has to go to Jorge tomorrow."

"Shit!" My palms came down on the steering wheel hard. "Call Camden. He can fix it."

"No. He can't. I just talked to him. He says that we need to take her tomorrow. I can't, Ted. I just cannot send my baby back there!" She sobbed now, safe in the privacy of her 4Runner sequestered behind her own curtain of rain.

All I could do was listen until she pulled herself together. Listen and think. If Camden couldn't fix this, who could? Not delivering Christie to

Voldemort at three o'clock tomorrow would surely ignite a shitstorm. He'd call the cops and motion the judge. What would all that mean to Dr. Sloan and her evaluation? And to Jenny's custody of Christie?

"Teddy?"

"I'm right here baby. It's hard to hear you because of the rain."

"Are you on your way home?"

"I can be, sweetie. If you need me."

"I'm going to pick up Christie and take her to Tumble Bugs."

"It's Thursday Jenn. Gym is Tuesday."

"You forgot, Ted. Today's the balance-beam show. You said you'd be there?"

"Right. At four?"

"Yep. Ted, what if we three went on a little vacation?"

"What are you talking about?"

"Tonight, after the show. We just get in my car and drive somewhere fun for the weekend. You mentioned Duluth? Or there's a really cool indoor waterpark in the Dells. The Sahara, I think. Christie would love it. That's only about three hours. I'll throw our bathing suits and toothbrushes in a bag. We can surprise her."

"Jenn...."

"Ted, I cannot send her back to him!"

If human beings have a quota of grief to carry around at any given time, then it made sense that the rain started to let up. It went from deluge to downpour to drizzle with a hint of sunshine just as the situation with Voldemort went from bad to terrible to unbearable with a hint of excruciating. I had no idea what to say to Jenny. My heart went out to Christie. I knew almost as well as Jenny just how scared Christie was to see her father.

"I know, sweetie. But it sounds like there's nothing we can do."

"I don't accept that. I will never accept that I can't take care of my daughter. No parent ever should."

"Then what do you want to do?" I switched the wipers down to normal and then off. The sun broke through the clouds and twinkled off a million wet surfaces. Green hills and pastures and tall pines and road signs appeared. Traffic gradually began to increase speed.

"I don't know. I do know that you're not helping. I'll talk to you tonight. I've got some calls to make. Don't miss the four o'clock show." She hung up. It was hard not to take her rage personally.

I know that she feels helpless because I do, too.

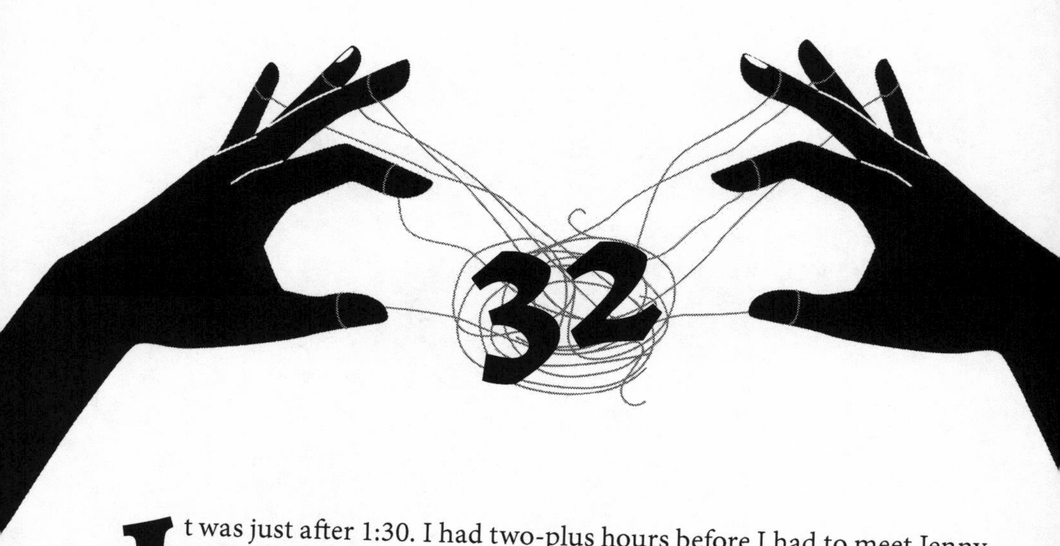

It was just after 1:30. I had two-plus hours before I had to meet Jenny and Christie at the gym. The Jeep jogged left on 101 north where it should have exited into Shakopee. A theory had taken root in my brain as the storm had passed and the traffic rediscovered its natural seventy-mile-an-hour pace. If my theory was right, I had an astonishing book to write and a daughter to save. I couldn't wait until tomorrow for either.

I took a right past the Potbelly Restaurant and a left toward Lotus Lake. I parked next to a rain splattered midnight blue Tesla and hurried down the right path around the front of Abram's house. I was not expected and was no doubt not welcome.

The outer waiting room door was unlocked. A middle-aged woman with an unnatural figure, obviously bleached hair, a tiny straight nose, and a perfectly unlined forehead sat prim and proper in Abrams' waiting room, legs crossed at the ankles. She was reading about raising hothouse orchids in northern climates.

I had no idea how to do this, but I did it anyway.

"Excuse me. I'm very sorry to bother you. I'm one of Dr. Abrams' patients. My name is John. I assume you are too, a patient I mean. I'm not asking. Sorry. I'm just … my wife is dying and my son just ran away and my doctor said my cancer is back. I'm really sorry but I really need to see Dr. Abrams right now. Would you possibly consider …?"

"Oh, my goodness, you poor man. I am so sorry. Of course, of course." She stood and straightened her too-short taffeta skirt and picked up a purse built to hold two credits cards at most. Three would have burst its seams. "I'm seeing him again next week anyway. Please. Of course."

I thanked her profusely as she exited the in-door and backtracked up to her hundred-thousand-dollar self-driving electric car. My guilt interrupting her treatment took a distant backseat to my anxiety about the conversation that I had to have with Abrams.

I didn't have to wait long.

At the top of the hour the inner door opened, and Abrams appeared. He was wearing his usual navy jacket over a button-down gray shirt and crisply pleated and pressed khakis. He wore tasseled oxblood loafers shined to a mirror polish and a welcoming smile that *easy dropped* -thank you, Christie- as he registered what he was seeing.

"Ted? Where's Andrea?" He said "ahnDRAY-ah" rather than the more mundane "ANNdree-ah."

"I sent her home, Sam."

"You what?" His face colored. His forehead creased. His eyes narrowed and his fists clenched.

"Our deal was...."

"Our deal was honesty. I've been honest with you. Now it's your turn."

"What are you talking about? You shouldn't be here. We have a schedule."

"I don't give a damn, Sam. Or should I call you King Dorothy?"

He smiled like a little boy caught reaching into the cookie jar. The righteous indignation of a therapist whose patient had been abruptly dismissed became coy pride and faux guilt. There was no denial or confusion on his face. He'd been caught red-handed. My bluff had worked. I held the trump card.

"So you spoke with Micah again? How is he?"

"Not good, I'm afraid. Invite me in and we can talk. *AhnDRAY-ah* won't mind."

The storm was receding out over the lake, dividing the sky into halves. Looking out the picture window in Abrams' office, the near half was bright and blue and sunny, dimpled with white clouds. The far half was dark and stormy. Vertical lines traced where rain still fell miles away. At that moment it would have been possible to stand in two worlds at once. Soaked by rain on one half and warmed by sun on the other.

Abrams took his seat behind his massive dark desk, hands folded as if in prayer. Silent. Watching. Waiting for me to speak. I took my chair facing him. I set my phone on the desktop to record. He shook his head no.

"We're well beyond that now, Ted. No notes. No recording."

"Sorry Doc. This is going on the record. I'm done being lied to."

"No, it's not and no you won't. For your own good, Ted. This isn't only about me anymore."

"What are you talking about?"

"Jorge Villalobos. It is pronounced '*OR-hey*,' isn't it?"

How can I describe my experience at that moment? My body responded before my brain caught up. My blood pressure doubled. My pulse began to race. I became lightheaded probably because all my blood had drained to my limbs ready for flight or flight. I was suddenly uncertain where I was and what I was doing. I was disoriented. My tongue stumbled around in my mouth as I tried to make words.

"What? How did you…?"

"Put the phone away first. Say out loud that you're not recording."

"I'm not recording."

"It's all public record, Ted. Court orders. Police reports. Even redacted child protection investigations. I have some very resourceful helpers in Cham. You didn't think that I invited you to dissect my life without first dissecting yours, did you?"

I was angry and physically hot. Sweating. Confused.

Cham?

"I've learned that Mr. Villalobos is trying to take your girlfriend's little girl away from her. I completely understand. I know your pain, Ted. Suki took Micah away from me."

"It's completely different," I protested, even though it wasn't. I just wasn't sure if Micah's father or Micah's mother played the role of Voldemort in this story. I tried again to assert myself. To regain control. "We are not here to talk about me." I had to try to get us back on track. I had to rebuild the wall that kept my life out of here.

"No, you're perfectly correct. We are not here to talk about you, but we're going to anyway and I think that you'll be happy when we do. But first, tell me about Micah."

"Micah?"

"You saw him this morning I believe? At MPH? That's how you know that I'm King Dorothy. He told you."

I had been back to MPH but Micah hadn't told me that his father is "King Dorothy." Not really. The pieces had come together while I was driving. Abrams had referred to "King Dorothy" in his letter to Micah along with Scylla and Charybdis. I guessed that if Micah's first story about two young, masked killers was genuine -not a fiction he created to fool us gullible people- then Scylla and Charybdis were the killers. Abrams was neither Scylla nor Charybdis. He was too old, and Micah would have recognized him even masked, but Abrams had confessed that he was the murderer, therefore he must be King Dorothy.

King Dorothy was not the killer per se, but the brains behind the killers. The murderer in motive, if not in deed.

The puppet master, but not Micah's puppet master.

My theory was that Abrams had hired Scylla and Charybdis to kill Suki to protect Micah from her abuses. Micah had run away to the lake house -this house, where I was seated right now- in a drugged and distraught state and had been traumatized by what he'd seen here. He'd confessed to the murder to protect his father. To bond with his father.

"Yes, I saw Micah this morning at MPH."

"And…? How is he? Did you give him my letter? Did he send a note back to me?"

"I can't talk about this while you're holding my personal life hostage, Sam. I don't know how or why you care about my girlfriend's situation, but that can't be part of this conversation."

"But it is, Ted. It is already part of this conversation. A very important part."

"What are you talking about?"

"I will tell you. No, actually I'll show you, I promise. But not yet. Tell me about Micah first."

What could I do? Call the police? He'd deny everything and my book would never get written. Walk out? I'm the one who'd forced my way in. I'd thought I had the upper hand. A way to leverage the truth out of Abrams. Now I wasn't at all sure.

"Alright," I sighed deeply, resigned and desperate to learn where this all led. I looked away from him to gather my thoughts.

"Micah hasn't been eating. He believes that the doctors are drugging his food. He might be right. I don't know. I brought him pizza from your favorite place."

"Vesuvius? Bacon and burger?"

"You'd mentioned it in one of our conversations. He wolfed it down. I asked him about his mother. He hesitated and then became distant. Removed."

"Dissociated?" Abrams offered.

"Sure. Dissociated. He told me the whole story. About Suki trying to strangle him. About his meltdown here with you that night. You giving him drugs. About Scilla and Charybdis. About finding his mother's body. About you being King Dorothy."

"He knows that part?"

No, he didn't. I was bluffing. Playing my intuition. My brainstorm amidst the real rainstorm. My two plus two equals *oh shit!* Sherlockian insight.

"And then he imploded. I don't have a better word for it. He became almost frantic. Talking nonsense. Repeating himself. His voice got loud. He didn't or couldn't respond to me, then he gradually unwound until he was limp and muttering to himself."

"My poor boy. You stressed him back into catatonia. Ted, I warned you about that. You knew that he was fragile and not properly medicated. Did Dr. Chatterjee intervene?"

"She wasn't there."

"Well then who....?"

"As far as I could tell, there were no doctors on the pod. No one sat in on our conversation. No one was available to help me when Micah fell apart. The only adult I found was a brand-new medical student who said that he was covering for Chatterjee. I'm sorry, Sam."

Abrams swiveled his seat away from me. Thoughtful. Worried. Maybe even angry? I couldn't tell. He stood and slowly walked over to the window behind me. I turned to keep an eye on him. I no longer trusted that I was safe here.

He said, "So tell me more."

"That's it. There's nothing more. Now your turn. Who are Scilla and Charybdis?"

"I have no idea."

"Bullshit. You must. You hired them to kill Suki."

"I did not. Not really."

"What are you talking about?"

Abrams sat on the edge of the analyst's couch off to my left, a long narrow bed raised at one end. His face was mostly in shadow. I shifted in my chair to face him. Now there was nothing between us.

"Tell me what you've figured out so far, Ted."

"This is about that video game, *EAU*."

"It's VR, not a video game. A video game plays on a screen in front of you in 2D like a show on TV. Like watching the world go by out a window. Virtual reality engulfs you in 4D. You become part of it. It's like climbing out through that window and living in the world out there -seeing and hearing and feeling it just like in here. *EAU* is the best of VR. It is an immersive, multi-dimensional, full sensory experience that challenges your mind and body and spirit."

"I told you that I tried it out with Micah. I wanted to share something with him. Be in his world. Some fathers learn to play Dungeons and Dragons with their sons. Some fathers pick up chess or tennis or collect Pokémon with their sons. This is no different. I did lie to you when I said that I couldn't do it. I said something about the controls and the characters confusing me. That wasn't true. I am sorry that I lied to you. The truth is that I took to *EAU* like a fish takes to water."

He stared at me expectantly.

"*EAU* is French for water, Ted. Like a fish takes to *eau*? Get it?"

"No. I'm sorry. I don't feel like laughing right now."

He resumed, "Micah was Mickey Mouse. Lots of his peers had teased him about his name in real life, so he mastered that anxiety and became the character in VR. Of course, he bought weapons and acquired powers and reinforced his health points so that eventually he was like no Mickey Mouse you've ever imagined. He was more like *Rambo* Mouse or *Terminator* Mouse.

"Micah named my avatar Dorothy like the character in Oz. He thought it was hysterical that his father was a little girl with braids in a skirt and plaid apron. After I rebooted out a couple of times, I pimped Dorothy up pretty well, too, but I prefer skills to physical strength. Intellect. Manipulation. Subterfuge. Persuasion. Those are all attributes you can buy in the game, and I did. And tokens. In *EAU*, tokens are like money here except there -in the game- tokens can buy anything at all, even health and power.

"*EAU* was the one place where Micah and I could really connect. We were like best friends there, Mickey Mouse and Dorothy. We were a team. We played for hours when he was here and most nights when he was with his mother, although she never knew. She never tried *EAU* and thought VR was a total waste of time, that was the kind of mother she was. So Micah and I would meet in Cham any time that we could -that's the central city in *EAU*- and we would go on quests together. We captured dragons and fought Orcs and discovered buried treasure. We mined Neptune and courted princesses and swam with mermaids in Atlantis. We traded resources and saved each other's lives a hundred times over. *EAU* is the only place where we could really be ourselves together.

"Okay. Hold on a second." He crossed back to his desk, studied his calendar for a moment then picked up his phone and dialed. He held my eye all the while. I could vaguely hear the line ringing and then a male voice.

"Richard? Its Sam Abrams." I heard a male voice respond but couldn't make out the words. "No, thank you. I'm fine. But I'm terribly sorry. An emergency has come up just now. I have to cancel our three o'clock today." More muttering. "Yes, yes. I am terribly sorry. Let's keep our Monday session as scheduled. Okay? Good. Again, my apologies for the late call. Thank you for understanding."

He hung up and stood. He produced a keyring and walked toward the exit. He motioned me to follow.

"Where are you going?"

"I'm taking you to Cham, Ted. Leave your stuff there. No one will bother it."

The door on the right read "EXIT HERE." I'd used it many times.

He turned toward the unmarked door on the left, inserted a key in the lock, and invited me in.

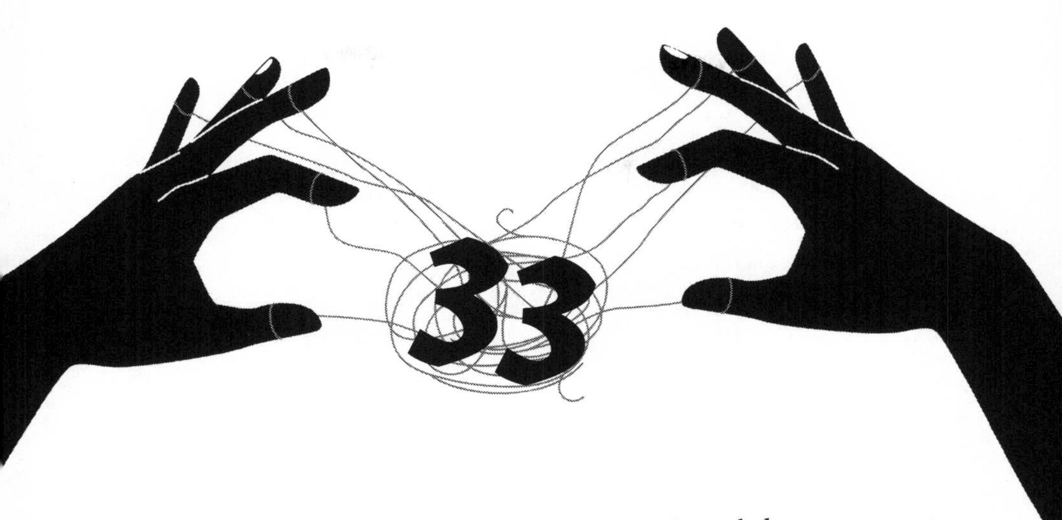

Jenny was out of ideas. She'd called and texted and googled every resource she could think of. Her best friend from college was a lawyer in L.A. A psychiatrist she knew from the gym who did some work in the courts. She even called two lawyers that she'd found online to take advantage of the "free fifteen-minute consultation!" they advertised. She'd texted a nurse at St. Francis who'd once said that she had been in a bad custody fight with her ex and that everything had eventually worked out okay. She Googled "divorce custody" and "when your ex is a narcissist" and "keeping kids out of the middle."

Nada. Nothing. A lot of well-wishing and handholding and I-wish-I-could help, but the only answers remained the same four that Camden had rattled off to her: Kidnapping Christie, murdering Jorge, defying the court order, or complying with the court order. Both of the lawyers had been eager to represent her. One required ten thousand dollars up front. The other guaranteed that she could postpone the father's visitation for an immediate retainer of twelve grand.

Jenny's nurse colleague from St. Francis, Karen Aaronson, was the most resourceful of the lot. After carefully establishing that Christie never heard this from her, she reported that she's part of a group of divorced mothers. Sister-Exes, she called them. The women try to help one another out. Learn from each. Do a good deed now and again. One of her sister-exes had told her about making up sexual abuse allegations to interrupt visitation. The courts always err on the side of safety, she said, because what judge wants to be known for having sent a child home with a pedophile?

"You mean lie about it? Lie that Christie's father touched her?"

"No sweetie," Nurse Karen said, "Just wonder out loud. Tell the pediatrician or her therapist that she was irritated down there when she came home. They'll have to report to CPS and then you're golden. It's probably just a UTI and you were just taking care of your little girl but then its six months later and dad is out of the picture."

True, Karen admitted, Christie would be interviewed by police and social workers and subject to a very intrusive physical exam but telling her what to say could go a long way. She started to tell Jenny about the difference between "hard signs" and "soft signs" of sexual abuse when Jenny interrupted with profuse apologies. An urgent call was coming in on another line. Thank you thank you. Click.

Is this what she's left with? Using Christie to destroy her father? Lying and exposing her own daughter to awful ideas and examinations? What a horrible, selfish, and destructive idea! She could accuse Jorge of sexually abusing Christie and get the weekend visitation suspended, but surely the cure is as bad or worse than the illness. The goal is to protect Christie, not to expose her to a whole new kind of abuse.

As much as Jenny despised Jorge, she actually considered calling him. She could appeal to his ego or try to apologize for the White Birch fiasco or just plead for Christie's well-being. Would he trade weekends just so Christie could settle down? It had been a hard week for the little girl. Or she could claim that Christie is too busy this weekend. Her gym class recital is coming up and she has an invitation to a birthday party. Jenny could offer extra summer vacation time if he'd trade time or she'd even reduce his child support or drop her claim on all the back support that he owed.

That seemed like the way that things should work. No matter how difficult the breakup is, shouldn't parents be able to put aside their differences to meet their child's needs? But not Voldemort. Experience proved that if Jenny said black, he said white. If she asked for a schedule change, he would just become rigid and insulting and then take it out on Christie and file a new motion with the court.

The phone rang. Caller ID said it was Christie's school.

"Hello?"

"Jenny? Hi, this is Claire in the front office at school. I'm so sorry to interrupt your day -I hope you're having a good day- but Jane-Ellen -I mean Principal Stewart- asked me to call you. Ms. Merganser brought Christie up to the nurse with a bloody nose. I guess she was in a fight? Don't worry, Clayton wasn't involved. They're still friends. Anyway, Christie seems okay, but it won't stop bleeding and Christie is pretty upset so they thought …."

"Thanks Claire. Sorry to interrupt. I'll be there in ten minutes. Please tell Christie that I'm coming."

The trip took nine minutes. All the lights on Valley View turned green for her. The ride was easy but had been haunted ever since the police lock-down. Every time she approached the school building, she heard the faint echo of sirens and saw the ghosts of firetrucks and ambulances everywhere she looked. It was like she was seeing two worlds at once, that nightmare day superimposed on top of reality.

She pulled up in front of the main entrance and put on her emergency flashers. No police officers to intercept her or SWAT team with assault rifles today. She dashed in, expecting to scoop Christie up and take her home. She signed in and ducked through the metal detector without stopping even when it clanged and flashed red. She went directly into the front office.

"Mommy!" Christie ran into Jenny's arms, hugging her with one arm, holding a blood-stained wad of gauze to her nose with the other. To Jenny, holding Christie was like a salve on a burn. Like a cool drink after a hard workout. Something empty and longing and scared inside of her was quenched.

"Oh baby, what happened to you? Let me look at this."

One nostril was bruised and crusty with old blood. The other still dripped freely. Jenny refolded the gauze and helped Christie hold it in place and kissed her hard on the forehead.

"Mommy two big boys at recess said daddy is a terrier then they hit me. Are they right, Mommy? Is he a terrier? Terriers hurt people. I don't want him to hurt me or you or Teddy!"

Jenny was confused. She looked over at Claire who'd heard the whole story, but the woman just shrugged. "Terrier?" she asked mostly to herself. And then it hit her and she bit back a chuckle.

Jorge is a dog but that's the least of his many faults.

"A terrorist, sweetie?" Christie nodded her head yes awkwardly, holding gauze to her face. Behind her, Claire made an opened mouth "oh!" as the translation sank in.

"No. He's not a terrorist. No one's going to hurt us, sweetie. Don't worry. Are you okay? Does it hurt?"

"A little. I fell down because a big boy pushed me after another one hit me with a book. A heavy book. Then I ran and told Ms. Merganser and she put the boys in attention."

"Detention?"

"Yeah, in attention probably for a whole day or maybe even a week."

Crouching in the middle of the school's front office comforting Christie and being comforted by her, Jenny felt a warm, firm hand on the middle of her back. She turned. It was Jane-Ellen Stewart.

"She'll be okay, Jenny. Thanks for coming."

"Of course," she stood, keeping one hand on Christie's head. "Thanks for calling."

The principal turned to Claire: "Would you please go tell Mr. Carrier that I'll be with him in a minute?" As Claire left with noisy goodbyes, Ms. Stweart said to Jenny, "The boy is in *de*tention. Can I talk to you alone please?"

"Sure." Jenny crouched back down to Christie's level. "Can you wait here for a minute, sweetie? I'm going to talk to Principal Stewart in her office real quick."

"No Mommy!" She whined and wrapped her free arm around Jenny's leg. "I'm scared the big boys will come back and daddy will come here again and be a terrier and hurt people again!"

Jenny hugged her and promised that she was safe and that she could be a big help to Ms. Claire. She planted her in the secretary's big spinning desk chair with a pile of orange TARDY slips to staple and stepped into the principal's inner office. She kept the door ajar so she could watch Christie across the room.

"I'll be quick, Jenny. Ever since the lockdown, some of the kids have been picking on Christie. Today was the worst of it."

"I had no idea. Christie hasn't said anything."

"No, I'm not surprised. She's very protective of you. I've sat with her at lunch a couple of times this week. She's told me that she doesn't want to upset you. She says that she's worried that you'll stop loving her like you stopped loving her father."

Jenny was taken aback. Her love for Christie was bottomless and infinite and the most important part of her world. She said "I love you" to Christie a dozen times a day no matter whether they were arguing or partying or cuddling and especially at bedtime. Why would she think her love was so fragile? And why would she compare Jenny's love for her to Jenny's hatred of Jorge?

"So today," Principal Stewart continued, "the third grade was doing a lesson in current events. The curriculum introduces 9/11 and the idea of 'terrorism.' School shootings are referenced briefly with an emphasis on safety. Mrs. Moorehouse -the third-grade teacher- told me that one student asked if Christie's father is a terrorist. That scared the class and carried over onto the playground.

"And Christie heard 'terrier'?"

"Yes, that would be funny if the larger situation weren't so scary. One third-grade boy hit her with a book in the face. The other boy pushed her down. As you know, we have a zero-tolerance policy about violence. Fortunately, Ms. Merganser was right on top of it and the school nurse checked Jenny out. The boys will be suspended, of course."

"What about Christie?"

"No no no. She's not in trouble, but I wonder if giving her a long weekend would be helpful. Give her a chance to settle down? Maybe some reassurance from you would help?"

Jenny's gut loved the idea. Maybe the extra time would help Christie get ready to transition to Jorge in the afternoon. Or maybe it would make it harder? She and Ted were scheduled to see Dr. Sloan at ten. What would she do with Christie while they were in St. Paul for the appointment?

"Let me think about that, Mrs. Stewart. Thank you. I'll have to talk to Ted about what's best. Can I take her home now?"

"Of course, Jenny. Please let me know how I can help."

Christie's nose had stopped dripping. The bloody gauze was forgotten on the desktop. The child was on her knees on the desk chair, swiveling left and right, slamming the stapler down on random papers at random angles with great gusto.

"Come on, honey. Let's go home."

"But I'm working, mommy. Look what I did."

"You're doing great, sweetie. I know that Miss Claire will thank you. Throw your tissues away, please and let's hit the road."

"Mommy do I still get to be in the balance beam show?"

"We'll see, Christie." Jenny swiveled the big chair toward her, gripped the armrests, and crouched to address Christie face to face. "Sweetie, you know that I love you more than the sun and the moon and the stars all together, right?"

"I love you mostest, Mommy! But I hate daddy Voldemort. He's a terrier, isn't he? Terriers hurt people. I don't want him to hurt me, Mommy! Don't let him hurt me! I don't want to ever see him again. Never ever!"

Jenny shared a glance with Mrs. Stewart. It occurred to her that she'd given the principal's name to Dr. Sloan as a reference. Hopefully she'd share this story with the evaluator.

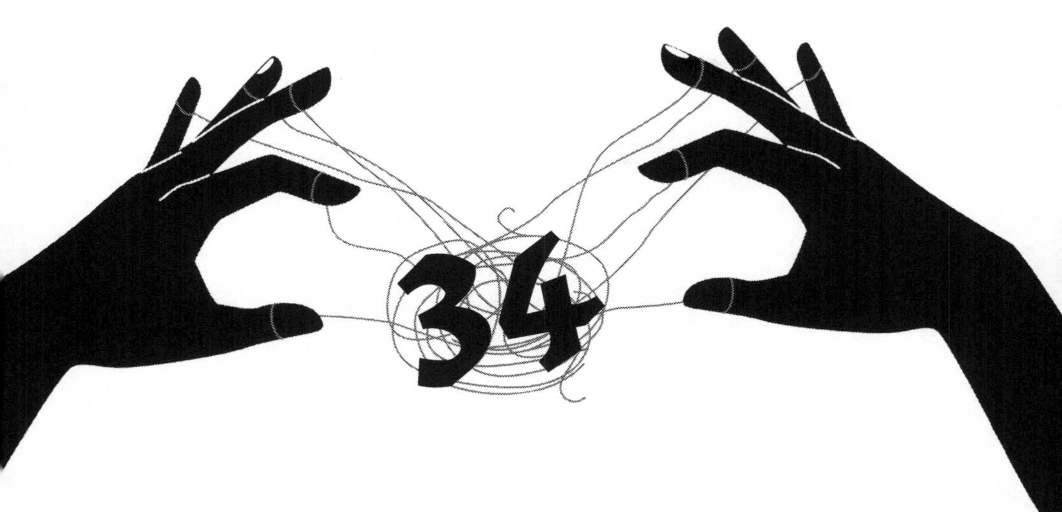

Abrams stood to my left, holding open the door on blackness. Total darkness. Something primitive in me knew that I was facing a space bigger than a broom closet and smaller than an auditorium. I felt no air movement or temperature change and heard no sounds from within. The smells of blood and feces that a hundred movies had taught me to associate with torture chambers were absent, as well.

The psychologist stepped into the void first. The movement triggered recessed ceiling lights to slowly dim on, gradually illuminating the space. We were standing in a barren beige cell. The ceiling, walls, and floor were all the same flat, off-white color. As my eyes adjusted, I realized that the floor *and the walls* were all carpeted, presumably to absorb sound. The room's monotone uniformity blended all the surfaces together, cheating my eye of cues to depth and dimension. There were no windows or louvered closet doors or ducts of any kind. There weren't even outlets interrupting the carpeted walls or furniture except for one small, white desk.

The desk rested as far opposite the entry door as possible, although I couldn't judge how far away. A long, narrow, white plastic frame spanned its surface. Nested atop that was a row of matching white plastic devices, each seated above a small green light, the only color in the room. I'd seen this hardware advertised online. I was looking at a dual charging station for a pair of Horizon 4-DV-2 devices. Virtual reality headsets. Helmets and hand-held controllers. This obviously wasn't the spare bedroom that Abrams had once mentioned, his basement redoubt when the tension with Suki in the main house above became too difficult. It wasn't a file room or the maid's quarters or a secretary's office or a BDSM dungeon, and it couldn't be the psychologist's private abattoir. There was no drain in the middle of the floor.

This was Abrams' VR launching pad, a space so muted of sound and color and movement that nothing would distract the player from immersing wholly in the digital reality projected by the Horizon device.

Abrams closed the door through which we'd entered. It sealed with an exhaled *whumpf* of air. Its inside surface was carpeted to match the surrounding walls and floor. He walked silently across the room to the charging station, removed one of a pair of bowl-like white plastic helmets and held it out to me.

"This is Micah's headset, Ted. I'd like to you take a trip with me."

"You're insane, Abrams. You want to show me *EAU*. I can do that at any GameStop. I'm not here to play games with you. You owe me the truth."

"This is the truth," he said, placing the helmet in my hands.

He began strapping a helmet on his head, then a controller around each wrist.

"Have you ever gone skydiving, Ted? No? Neither have I IRL. That means 'in real life' if you recall. If you've ever seen skydivers, you know how the newbies go. You can't just push them out of the plane on their own no matter how much training they've had. They jump in tandem with a pro. The newbie is strapped onto the pro's belly so that they move together, as if they were one. That way the chute is sure to open and the landing is much less likely to break bones."

"That's what we're going to do. Figuratively, anyway. You won't be physically tied to me, but you're going to be a ghost yoked to my avatar. You'll see through my eyes and hear through my ears. That is, through King Dorothy's eyes and ears."

I still held the helmet. "Why? Why would I do this? I don't trust you."

"Why?" he answered with a shrug. "Because you have no choice. Because you're right, this isn't about you. It's about me and Micah. But it's also about Christina. Your Christina."

"Stop saying her name."

"Put on the headset. You won't need the controllers. You'll be invisible to everyone except me. Only I can hear your voice unless I let you use Dorothy's mouth. You might want to sit down. Entry can be disorienting at first."

I did all that he said. I parked myself hard against a carpeted wall near the door. I could see Abrams standing in the middle of the room moving his hands. Shifting the angle of his head as if reading something, then pushing invisible buttons. He looked like he was doing tai chi. Then the room disappeared.

The transition reminded me of my father's slide shows. He'd set up a bulky projector in a dark room with a carousel full of inch square slides. The machine would cast a color image on the wall and then make a clunky *click!* We'd sit through a moment of blackness then an entirely different image filled the wall. There I was at 8-years-old with Goofy at Disney World.

Click! Now there's my mom at the Eiffel Tower.

Click! A sunset vista in Arizona.

There was no clicking noise in VR, but a similar flash of empty blackness filled the time and space that had a moment before contained Abrams and the beige room. Atoms rearranged themselves in that moment and when the light came back up, I was looking at a short, wrought iron railing atop a low parapet. A balcony, looking out onto colorful trees and a waterfall. Classical piano music played in the background. A brilliantly colored tropical bird flew by with such fluid, natural motion that it could only have been real. The colors and textures and shadows and perspectives all around me -not a just a square projected on the dining room wall- were vivid and rich and completely believable. The metal of the railing looked heavy and weatherworn. The rushing water under the distant falls looked cool and clear and wet and threw off a rainbow that sparkled in sunlight. I'd expected a caricatured stick figure world and found instead an experience more real and enticing than the one that I'd just left.

But I hadn't left it, had I? The idea made me dizzy. My body was still in that beige, carpeted room in Abrams' office while my -what? My mind? My senses? My self? My subjective reality? My soul?- was here, wherever here was.

My view shifted even though I hadn't turned. A voice in my head said "Welcome to Cham, Ted. This is our entry platform. I believe that you'll find that you can't move unless I/Dorothy move us. You'll move with me. Don't let that discomfort you. Your body is fine IRL. You'll get used to this. Let me show you."

It wasn't that I couldn't move. I had nothing to move. I had no physical being. I was an incorporeal consciousness piggybacking in or on Abrams' avatar.

I was a ghost.

Without willing movement, my view shifted slowly counterclockwise around the room. I saw tall bookshelves loaded with leatherbound volumes. Clusters of plush furniture in earthy tones. There was a huge, stone-faced fireplace, a grand piano, and a wet bar fronting a huge mirror. That's where I glimpsed Dorothy for the first time. The innocent girl from Kansas caught up in a twister had come to life. She/he/I looked as real and alive as anyone I've ever met, precisely the way that L. Frank Baum wrote her and Judy Garland played her. Her/my/our cheeks were slightly flushed. Her/my/our eyes were large and dark and curious. She/he/we wore a white short-sleeved shirt under a blue-and-white checkered jumper. Dark brown ponytails were tied back with light blue ribbons, although errant hairs escaped here and there. Ankle-high socks covered bare calves and ankles and then disappeared within sparkling ruby red slippers. Only Toto was missing.

Dorothy's mouth moved. The voice was a young Judy Garland.

"Yes, that's us, Ted. You and me." He/she/I raised a hand and waved hello in the mirror.

I noticed that this Dorothy/Abrams/me had a garish tattoo high on her right biceps sneaking out from under a frilly sleeve. Black and red and blue ink painted the image of two skinny legs with bare feet poking out from under the stony foundation of a house. A caption in bright red letters under the ink read, "Ding Dong!"

Abrams' voice spoke inside my head.

"We have a meeting to get to, Ted. Hang on."

My/his/Dorothy's right hand rose and fell and poked and swiped left and left again. It wasn't tai chi from this perspective. I could see through Abrams' eyes that the motions summoned semi-transparent rectangular pages in midair. Not paper and not tangible. These were more like translucent projections of computer touch screens. Menus. Abrams navigated through options with complete familiarity. He used our small, pale hands to type a brief message, then swiped it away. Too fast to read. A moment later *click!* the balcony and bookshelves and waterfall disappeared. There was a flash of total blackness. I felt like I was falling and then a new reality rose up and caught me. My inner ears wobbled, fooled into disequilibrium.

Back IRL, my hands reached reflexively for something to hold on to.

I'd say that a new scene emerged, but to me that describes stagehands lowering a painted and pimped-out balsa wood tableau of a city or a bedroom or a moonscape in front of an eager audience. The reality that was now rapidly solidifying around me is to that what cell phones are to the telegraph. This was genuine and tangible and completely credible. I had a sense that the molecules that filled this space were rearranging themselves at Abram's request.

A dark wood and deeply grained conference table materialized in front of me. I knew how it would feel if I touched it and how it would sound if I knocked on it. Black leather executive chairs that would exhale if I sat on one and would smell expensive if I could get that close. Broad, bright windows welcomed a flood of sunlight. Dust motes danced before them. Dorothy/Abrams/I turned toward one of the windows and looked out and down over a busy metropolis. I was standing in a proprietary digital algorithm that made everything I'd ever before known as flat and fake as origami.

This wasn't the *Matrix*. This was reality.

But a boardroom?

"I thought that *EAU* was about fighting dragons and laying siege to castles and finding treasure? Why aren't there 'enemies all around us'?"

These thoughts somehow communicated to Abrams even though I had no lips to speak with and no voice to be heard. I suspect that my real lips in my real body spoke these words far away in Abram's anteroom -which was of course right here all around me- but I wasn't sure and didn't care.

He/we/Dorothy walked us over to a window and we stared out toward a distant, smog-hazed horizon. The sill was warm on Dorothy's/his/my hand. Sparkling stalagmite-like structures pointed skyward everywhere I could see. Some were quite low. Others almost approached our height. Fingers of emerald-green water intruded between islands of concrete and glass. I noticed words spelled out atop several of the highest buildings, but the letters weren't English.

"This is a real-time, live feed out the window of the 124th floor of Burj Khalifa skyscraper in Dubai, the highest building in the world." Abrams/

Dorothy advised. "If a fire broke out in Dubai right now, we would see the smoke here in Cham even though, as you know, we're physically still in my office in Minneapolis more than seven thousand miles away from the flames."

It was mind-bending.

"But why are we in a conference room?"

"To confer," he/Dorothy replied to us. I watched our faint reflection turn in the window glass, a blur of pale skin and light blue checks. He sat us down at the head of the long, wooden table. A yellow legal pad and pen had substantiated at each seat. A full pitcher of water stood at center. I could see drips of condensation running down the glass.

"This is an NTNH chatbox. 'No Touch Never Happened.' It's a very private place within the game where players can talk freely with no chance of eavesdropping."

Easy dropped, I thought to myself and then worried that Abrams could hear my thinking.

"I'm going to give you the last piece of the puzzle now, Ted. The answer to your annoying questions about Suki's death. But you're not ever going to write this story. Not the real story that I'm going to tell you, at least. No worries. You will write your book and it will be a hit."

"I don't understand."

We couldn't look at one another. We were inhabiting the same digital body and I was helpless to affect any movement. Abrams made Dorothy look down at its hands -no scars, no callouses; a hint of red nail polish mostly washed away; the hands of a young teenage girl.

"This space is called a chatbox in *EAU.* It's a private, undocumented, untrackable time/space. My avatar, King Dorothy, rented it when we were on the entry platform -that room with books and the mirror and the view of the waterfall. Chatboxes look like this by default. Like Wall Street lawyers' boardrooms. For a couple more credits, we could as easily be on the moon or atop Kilimanjaro.

"We're going to be joined by another player shortly. His avatar is called Caligula the Conqueror. Don't be put off by his appearance. Here, more than in any other place or time, appearance means nothing. But before Caligula arrives, we need to reach an agreement."

Ted wasn't answering his phone. Again.

Jenny did her best to keep her phone nearby in case he called, but that was proving to be a challenge. Christie had attached herself like a leech to Jenny's upper body since they'd returned home from school and would not allow herself to be pried lose. Jenny had cleaned up the crusted blood around her nose, given her a capful of children's ibuprofen, and suggested that they play a game or watch a show together before deciding whether to go to gymnastics. Christie had been sluggish and droopy but had refused to be separated from Jenny even when she'd needed to use the bathroom.

Jenny allowed Christie precious little screen time, but under the circumstances Jenny thought that a visit with one of Christie's favorites, *Dora the Explorer*, would be calming and distracting. She planted Christie on the couch and offered to get her a snack, but Christie wouldn't let her mother leave the room. When Jenny sat down beside her with her laptop, intent on resuming her frantic search for ways to keep father and daughter apart, Christie glued herself to her mother barnacle-like. That was a half hour ago. Now the laptop was on the floor playing screensaver photos and the six-year-old was fast asleep face down splayed across Jenny's chest.

The last time Christie had slept like this, she'd been a toddler.

Jenny had tried to talk to Christie about what happened on the playground. She'd reassured her that the boys had been very wrong about her father and should never, ever have hurt her. She explained the difference between a "terrier" and a "terrorist" and that her father is neither. With tomorrow's interview with Dr. Sloan in mind, Jenny was careful not to refer to Jorge by any name other than "dad" or "daddy" and corrected Christie when she'd started to call him "Voldemort."

"But that's what you and Teddy call him!" she'd protested.

"We shouldn't sweety. That's a mistake. Your father's name is Jorge. You call him 'daddy.'"

This unfortunately reignited Christie's whining, pleading, tearful worries about seeing him again. "*I don't want to*" and "*You told me that I don't have to*" and "*he's a bad dad. He's a terrier-ist*" and "*I won't go with him and you can't make me.*" This explosion seemed to finally deplete all of Christie's energy, leaving her limp and listless and now curled up like a nursing infant.

It was after three and clear that Christie was going to miss gymnastics. Jenny managed to get a message to Ms. Kathy at Tumble Bugs. Christie's not feeling well. So sorry. She tried again to reach Ted with no luck. At the very least she needed to intercept him on his way out to the gym, but that was trivial. If he got there and didn't find her there, he'd be worried and call. What she really needed was to curl up on his chest the same way that Christie was curled up on hers, to be reassured with her ear right next to his heart, and to figure out how the hell they were supposed to protect the most precious thing in the universe from her ex-husband.

Jenny tried to shift the forty-pound child onto the couch. As soon as she got a hand under her arm, Christie murmured and complained and grumbled "no Mommy. I need you." Failing that, she juggled her phone around Christie's mop of sweaty-damp hair and shifted an arm and managed to find a position that might allow her to use the device.

There were two voice mails waiting for her. Her nurse friend Karen Aaronson had called back. "Everything okay?" Jenny felt bad that she'd feigned having to take an urgent call in order to cut off the woman's upsetting talk about faking sexual abuse allegations. Jenny tapped "return call" hoping to leave a brief, "*Thanks. Hanging in there. Sorry I cut you off earlier. Coffee sometime?*" message.

No luck.

Karen picked up right away.

This conversation went better than the first. Nurse Karen said nothing about lying about sexual abuse, perhaps reading Jenny's discomfort in her silences and avoidance. She said that she'd spoken with some of her "sister-exes" and had some other ideas. The group recognized Jenny as one of their own. A mother desperately trying to save her baby from a broken court system and a bad dad. Jenny listened and thought hard and answered some questions in whispered tones. Christie was still right there, on her lap. Maybe it was desperation, but Nurse Karen was making sense. The legal system sucks. It's too slow and too biased and far, far too blind. Judges want to make everybody happy even though their job is to serve the best interests of the child. On and on.

Karen asked some pointed questions. Why? She said that the sister-exes wanted to help. Jenny didn't have the energy to ask more so she did as she was told. She texted Jorge's contact info to the woman. Full name. Home address. Cell number. Physical description. Car make and model. Employer. And thanked her. She agreed to have coffee with the sister-exes as soon as she could. "Thank you, Karen. Really. For Christie. You've given me back reason to hope."

"That's what I'm here for, sweetie. No worries. This too shall pass. We'll talk again soon."

One of the "free 15-minute consultation!" lawyers had called back and left a concerned message proposing a meeting time in his office in downtown St. Paul, bragging about his successes in domestic violence litigation, and reminding her that she could pay his retainer online in installments.

No thanks.

Nothing from Ted. She tapped "Find My Phone" and selected Ted's number. A local map appeared and zeroed in on an address in Chanhassen. Near Lotus Lake. That's where the doctor he's writing about lives. But those interviews are Monday, Wednesday, and Friday. He said he was heading home. Why would he be there on a Thursday?

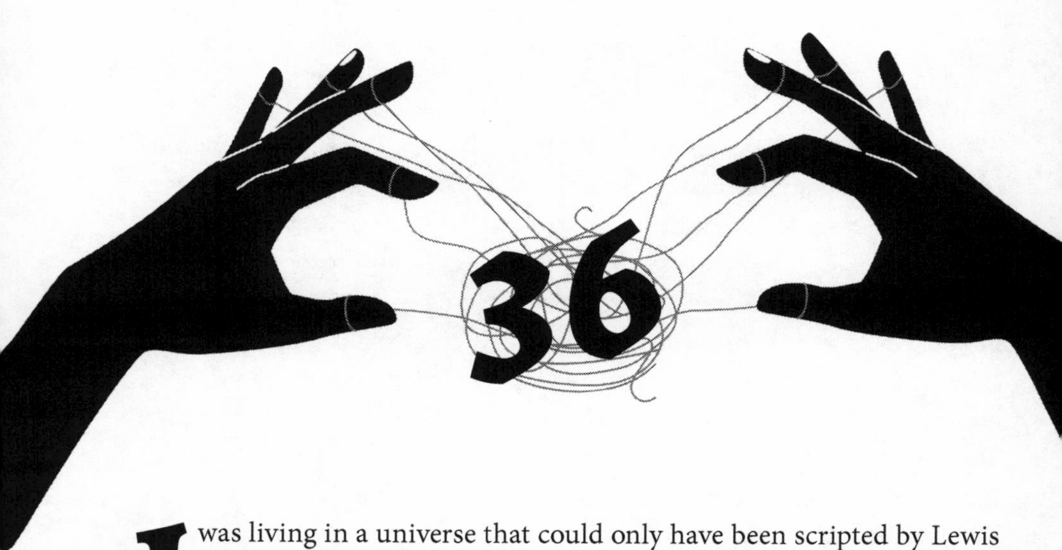

36

I was living in a universe that could only have been scripted by Lewis Carroll. I wouldn't have at all been surprised if the Mad Hatter appeared and offered to serve me tea.

I was in a large, formal conference room on the hundred-something floor of a building that didn't exist in a digital universe projected within a white plastic helmet. I could feel my body when I wiggled my toes or scratched my nose, but those experiences were oddly divorced from what I saw and heard around me. I had no body of my own in the world that I perceived. I had no nose here and if I did, I had no hand to scratch it. I was a parasite clinging to Sam Abrams' consciousness which inhabited an oversized and tattooed Dorothy straight out of *The Wizard of Oz*.

Abrams and I had been talking together for weeks in the conventional comforts of his Minneapolis office, a place where I could scratch my own itches and offer my own opinions and leave any time that I wanted. It was only here and now, on the other side of the looking glass, immersed in this disconnected trick-or-treat reality, that he was finally willing to tell me the whole story of Suki Kohler's death.

"Suki was a flaming narcissistic and a violent sociopath," he repeated. He'd used very similar words to describe her when we'd first met, the same words that his son had used to describe her, as well. "She had no conscience and no empathy. But man, she was gorgeous, and she was fun! We laughed and danced and partied across three continents together before we ended up in the Twin Cities. She would go on photo shoots. I would go on speaking tours. We'd meet in New York or Paris and once in Dubai -although I never actually saw the view that we're mirroring out this window. I put up with her affairs and her cruelties and her selfishness because the good times were great. But after she got pregnant and then when we had Micah, the good times came less and less often. The bad times got really, really bad.

"I don't know if it was hormones or the drugs -she told me that she'd stopped using, but I still found cocaine and amphetamines around the house; uppers especially, she was paranoid about her figure- or maybe it was the unavoidable changes to her career after she became a mother. Whatever the trigger, life in our home quickly became unbearable. She would scream and swear and throw things. Then she would apologize and demand sex or run off to her boyfriends. I did everything I could to protect Micah from her eruptions, but there was only so much I could do.

"I've told you this part of the story already. How I moved out with Micah. How I filed abuse reports on her. But the courts didn't believe me, so they put him in her care, and I got every other weekend." Dorothy's/his/our fists clenched and relaxed, clenched, and relaxed. Abrams angled his/her/our face up toward the window. I could see a faint reflection of the anger simmering in Dorothy's/his/our eyes.

That day last April when Micah showed me the marks under his turtleneck and told me what Suki had done was the last straw. So, Micah and I came here, to Cham together. He was Mickey Mouse. I was who I am today. Dorothy Gale from Kansas. We were both L12s or L13s at the time."

My real mouth in the real world said, "What's that?"

Abrams' real ears in the real world heard me even though nothing had been said in the conference room. He answered using Dorothy's/his/our mouth.

"Sorry. Levels. As you progress through the game, success allows you to level up. To become more powerful and resourceful. You start at L1, become a king or queen at L20 and a god at L25. Twelve and thirteen are pretty good and seem like great successes when you've just begun, but by the time that you're royalty, you know that an L12 is like a bug not even worth swatting."

"So that Friday, Micah and I came here. I'd heard about Caligula back then, but never done business with him. I still have no idea who he or she is or where IRL. Here in Cham, he's a power broker. He's rich and enormously resourceful. He's the one who gets things done."

"I paid Caligula to have Suki killed. Micah was here. He knew what I did and was happy about it."

"Wait," I said back in Minneapolis. "None of this is real. We're inside a game. I understand that you can slay digital dragons and win digital wars here. How in the hell can a creature made up of ones and zeros on a fancy computer screen kill a real live person?"

"The two worlds are not distinct, Mr. Bennett. VR and IRL are not different rooms connected by putting on a headset. They're the same room, the same reality. The trouble is that we humans are far too limited to perceive multiple overlapping and simultaneous realities. Our perceptual hardware can only understand one reality at a time. Like changing radio stations. You probably know that we are constantly immersed in radio waves. Every single station surrounds us 24/7. Which one you hear just depends on how you tune the receiver. Twist the dial and you hear gospel. Twist it again and you get sports. Caligula has mastered the art of collecting information and resources from one station and using it in another."

I was struggling to keep up, which all by itself probably proved his point. I'd heard about quantum mechanics and the idea that an infinite number of universes exist. I'd seen that movie, *Everything Everywhere All At Once* like everyone else everywhere always had and always will. That idea was hard enough. Now to imagine that all of those distinct universes are here and now around me, just waiting for me to twist a knob or put on a headset and tune them in was over the top.

Abrams/Dorothy/I continued: "I paid Caligula. The deal was irrevocable. He had my money -cryptocurrency- and he filled his side of the bargain. What I didn't know was that he hired the job out. Two *EAU* players."

"Scylla and Charybdis," I said. "At MPH I thought Micah was saying 'Silly Anchor Bus." He was telling me who killed his mother."

"'Silly anchor bus'? I like it. Yes, Scylla and Charybdis. They're L20s. Powerful rock monsters. Warriors. But I didn't know that at the time. I did the deal with Caligula, then Micah and I logged out. We never left my two-bedroom rental down the street. I ordered a pizza...."

"Vesuvius."

"Yes, from Vesuvius. We ate. I gave him medicine to help him sleep and we went to bed. Obviously, he had second thoughts. Guilt, I guess. He got up in the middle of the night and walked back here to the lake house, to try to warn his mother. To save her, I guess. It's weird, you know. She treated him like shit and had tried to strangle him earlier that day and here he was trying to save her. He walked here through snowy, slushy streets with no shoes on. But he couldn't save her, of course. A deal with Caligula is irrevocable. Obviously, Micah saw his mother being killed. He must have tried to help her, and then barely escaped. You know the rest of the story. I only wish that Micah hadn't been there."

His *only* wish was that his son hadn't witnessed his mother's contracted murder? Apparently Abrams had no wish that he hadn't contracted for her murder in the first place.

"Now you know everything, Ted. The whole unpolished story. But that's not what you're going to write."

"What am I going to write?"

"A fairy tale. A fiction about as real as this table." He slammed Dorothy's/his/our hands down hard on a surface that only existed in my mind. Despite knowing that it wasn't real, I heard the thunderclap of impact and saw the water shimmy in the pitcher on the desktop two feet away.

"Your book is going to tell a story about a deranged young man named Lucas Morrisey. Morrisey isn't a fiction. He's a real man who really stalked Suki IRL. He collected every cover and every glossy image that she'd ever published. He's been arrested several times for harassment, intimidation, and then finally Suki had to get a restraining order against him. The police know Morrisey quite well. But the story you're going to tell is about how Morrisey got very drunk last April, ignored that restraining order, broke into the lake house and killed Suki. The police haven't figured this out yet. You're going to help them. I'll give you proof. You'll write your book. Another Ted Bennett break-through true crime success and in the process, you'll exonerate both Micah and I."

"You want me to lie? To condemn an innocent man for Suki's death? I don't care if this guy Morrisey is crazy, he didn't kill Micah's mom. You did. No way, Sam. Why would I possibly do that?"

Abrams stood us up and straightened our skirt.

"Morrisey is a very bad man, Ted. No loss there. Listen to what I've told you. Your book will redirect the investigation. When the police go back to the evidence, they'll find Morrisey's hair."

"And then?"

"Case closed."

"What about Micah?"

"No lie there. Micah is an innocent bystander traumatized by what he witnessed. Once there's proof that he didn't kill his mother -that he's not the M&M killer- he'll be released to my care. I'm a psychologist, after all. Who better to help him recover?"

"But Sam, you're overlooking one critical fact: I will not do this. I won't help you escape murder charges and condemn an innocent man. I WILL NOT DO IT."

"Yes, you will, Ted. And here's why."

We were standing behind the chair at the head of the table with the view of Dubai behind us. At that moment a portion of the wall in front of us and to the right blurred. Or re-pixilated. It looked as if the very real wallpaper and the whiteboard attached to it were being redrawn. The effect reminded me of Captain Kirk beaming down from the Starship Enterprise in the original *Star Trek* series but quicker and deeper and totally lacking sound effects.

What appeared was well over six feet tall. It wore a horned Viking hat that nearly touched the acoustic ceiling tiles and a loincloth that left very little to the imagination. He was as wide as the door and as meaty as a line-backer. His tree trunk legs and tattooed telephone pole arms were roped with wiry muscle and covered, like his torso, with dense hair. A mustache draped over his upper lip and spilled down on both sides of his mouth toward the floor. He reminded me of museum mock-ups of Cro-Magnon man minus the obligatory wooden club and pet sabretooth tiger. He was huge and intimidating as hell.

"Good timing." Abrams/Dorothy/I said toward the visitor.

"Dorothy." He greeted the girl from Kansas/us/me, seated himself midway down the table, and poured himself a glass of water. His fingers were sausages dark with dirt, but his movements were controlled. He didn't spill a drop. The image of the barbarian giant in a leather desk chair with his hairy legs crossed at the knees was hysterical. Either that or I was losing my mind. Or both.

"What can I do for you?"

Abrams/Dorothy/I pulled out the chair at the head of the table and seated us.

"I need something, Caligula."

"No shit. That's what I do. Tell me." The character's voice didn't match his intimidating presence. It was younger and clearer and softer, like a kid pretending to be a barbarian. The figure in front of me/us should have spoken in a gravelly and rasping baritone.

"Can he hear me?" I asked from the carpeted anteroom in Abrams' office. I knew that Abrams himself could hear me, but I wasn't sure if Caligula could. When I got no answer, I understood what Abrams had said earlier. I am a ghost here. Invisible, unheard, and unable to affect anything.

"There's a bad man who needs to be eliminated," Abrams/Dorothy/I said.

"You seem to know a lot of bad people, Dorothy. Is this one like the woman?"

"Similar, but different. Same general geography though. In the US. His name is Jorge Villalobos."

My body quaked and startled in Minneapolis. I thought I was having a seizure.

If Abrams heard me react, he didn't acknowledge it. While I listened, he gave Caligula Jorge's home address, his cell phone number, and his license plate. I wanted to scream. Maybe I even did. I was a completely helpless witness to a confessed murderer contracting for his next hit. Abrams was hiring a digital caveman who ran a virtual mafia to commit a real-life homicide. The victim would be Christie's father.

I hated Jorge and had wished him dead. I'd even had fantasies of killing him myself, but was I going to just sit here and let him be killed? The man is a cruel and careless father. He tortures the woman that I love and has made my life hell over and over again. Worse still, Jenny and I are tied to him the way that I was now tied to Abrams -victims carried along by the currents of his cruelties- for at least the next twelve years. We'd be trading Christie back and forth like cards across a poker table every other weekend until she turned eighteen. And that was the best outcome. Now that Jorge had dragged us back to court and Dr. Sloan had begun her evaluation, it could get much, much worse for us and especially for Christie.

Jenny and I had failed our first interview with Sloan. Neither of us had said as much, but I'm pretty sure that we looked like self-involved parents who want to leave bio-dad by the wayside because he'd become an inconvenience to our selfish little family. If Jorge put on his best smile and his poor-me attitude and his seductive Mexican accent, Sloan could tell the judge that Christie was better off with her father. Maybe we'd see Christie every other weekend and for a week in the summer.

I couldn't even think that thought. It would kill Jenny.

Did that justify letting Jorge be killed? Could I even stop this from happening? It occurred to me that I could pull off my headset and then tackle Abrams' real body and tear off his headset. I'm pretty sure that that would make Dorothy disappear from the conference room and rip us both out of *EAU.* I didn't know if it was too late to stop Caligula from sending Scylla and Charybdis to kill Jorge. But that didn't even matter. I couldn't stop Abrams from kicking me out of his office, logging back in, and making this deal without me.

I could call the police. And say what? A mad psychologist in Chanhassen has hired a caveman named Caligula in a video game to kill my girlfriend's ex-husband? All that would get me is a return visit to MPH, this time as a patient.

Caligula was talking.

"Twenty grand Ethereum."

"I didn't know inflation in Cham was so steep," Dorothy/Abrams/I replied.

"Supply and demand, what can I say?"

"And you gave up on Bitcoin?"

"Yeah. Markets change. It's just another crypto. Stabler at the moment. Venmo still works."

"Give me a second to think about this," Dorothy/Abrams/I said. He turned us toward the window. I swear I could feel sunlight on the skin of

Dorothy's/his/our face. With our back to Caligula, Abrams whispered, "This is on you, Ted. If you let this happen, you are no better than me. If you don't do this, if you try to tell my story to the world, then I'll tell yours. You need to decide if you want to rescue your girlfriend's daughter and my son, or you'd rather expose me and let your family self-destruct."

Caligula called out from behind us, "Who are you talking to over there? I thought this was an NTNH box. If you mess with me, Dorothy, it's all over for you in Cham *and* IRL. You know what I can do."

Abrams/Dorothy/I turned back to him and smiled. "I wouldn't do that, buddy, and I couldn't do that. *No Touch Never Happened.* Just give me another minute. This is a big decision for me and that's a lot of crypto."

"I don't recall you and Mickey thinking this hard last year about that lady."

"Different story."

We turned back to the window. He whispered, "Ted?"

I was curled up on the carpeted floor in the bland beige room in Abrams' office, shaking, and sick to my stomach. I wanted to pretend that I was agreeing to delete a cartoon character from a screen. Erasing a stick figure like a child with a pencil. But my defenses weren't that robust or my conscience was overdeveloped or my love for Jenny and Christie wasn't that strong or my animal instincts were buried too far under layers of civility and etiquette and Sunday School morals. Whatever it was, I couldn't pretend not to understand that I was signing a death warrant for a real, live human being and with it, agreeing to cover up another crime. Abrams and I were about to become accomplices, twisted allies committed to our own selfish needs.

"Ted?" Abrams whispered again. Caligula was waiting.

"Do it," I said and then vomited on his perfectly bland, beige carpet.

He turned us back toward Caligula while I was still retching.

"Do it," he said. He made Dorothy/him/me perform another brief tai chi move. A screen appeared, he tapped at it, and then it vanished. "The money is on its way now."

Caligula placed his fingertips together, then pulled them apart. A similar screen appeared in the space that he created. He tapped, swiped, and it disappeared. “Confirmed,” he said. “Just to be clear. This deal cannot be revoked. No guarantees. No money back. When I leave here, this deal is done.

“I understand,” Abrams/Dorothy/I said. Caligula vanished in a pixilated flash. I vomited again.

37

I tore off my headset and threw it across the room, stumbled to the carpeted door and out into Abrams' office. I still had enough brain cells working to remember my backpack. I snagged it and pushed the exit door open just as Abrams was returning from the anteroom. There was a half second when we were face-to-face, two killers going in opposite directions. Our eyes met. His were bright with relief, like he'd solved a tough problem. I can only guess that my eyes -mine! Not his or ours' or some part of a shared virtual monster with braids and blue bows- *my* eyes could only have been hollow and desperate and guilt-ridden.

I slammed out the door, lurched up the incline, and locked myself in my Jeep. The pizza smell lingered from events that had transpired a hundred years before. I cowered in my seat. I felt like I was being chased but there was no one to be seen. I had a visceral, gut-churning sense that that didn't mean anything anymore. I now understood that there are competing realities layered beneath and on top of the one that we all perceive. I was sure that in more than one of them I was being hunted. I was certain that at any moment my pursuer would rip aside the invisible vellum that separated our realities and reach in and grab me.

I was sure that Caligula had discovered that I'd piggybacked into his world. Certain that he was coming after me, teeth bared, tattooed muscles taut. Or he would send Scylla and Charybdis, rock monster killers. A young man and a young woman wearing masks. She had the knife, Micah had said. They would re-pixilate themselves into my car or my bedroom with their knives and slaughter me and Jenny and Christie just so that a digital creature in a video game could level up.

I drove. Fast and hard. I didn't touch the radio. That dial now terrified me. If Jenny thought that I was in a zone when I was writing, I was now in a state that made that look like a kindergartener with ADHD. I needed to force everything out of my awareness except the road back to my apartment and Jenny and Christie. I needed to hold them, to feel them breathe. To ask their forgiveness and to ask Jenny to magically undo what I'd just done.

I needed to confess and call the police and stop this craziness from happening.

But I failed. The flimsy and fragile perceptions that I'd always considered reality -singular and exclusive, ignorant of any others- broke through. Maybe it was the normalcy of driving. Maybe it was gaining distance from Abrams and Caligula and Cham. Maybe it was the limits of my very human brain reinterpreting what I'd experienced as fantasy or dream or delusion. I could hear the reassuring voice of sanity shouting through the chaos, "*No... that didn't happen... that was just a video game. No one is going to get hurt. You're over-reacting, Ted. Calm down. You're having a panic attack.*"

I noticed the time first. Big blue digits on my dashboard. It was twenty after four. I'd been with Abrams almost an hour and a half. Then my surroundings gained focus. The highway was littered with puddles. I remembered the rainstorm that had passed. Driving back from St. Peter through the deluge. Watching the line of clouds escape out over the lake through Abrams' office window.

A deep breath shuddered through me. Oxygen invigorated that little voice of sanity. My psychological defenses started kicking in. Denial. Repression. Rationalization. The idea that Abrams is crazy hit me like a freight train and flattened me under the weight of its certainty. Abrams had called Suki a sociopath incapable of empathy and yet it was Abrams who orchestrated murders without breaking a moral sweat. It was Abrams who accused Suki of believing that anything she did was okay unless she got caught and here he was, doing as he pleased, thinking himself too smart to ever be found out.

It was Abrams who'd taught me about projective identification. Casting one's own failures and foibles on another person and then scapegoating that person as if doing so would make those failures and foibles go away. Was that what was happening here?

Had Abrams killed Suki as his scapegoat to exorcise his own craziness?

How did I even know that Suki had been abusive?

How did I know that Suki had tried to strangle Micah?

Sure, Micah confirmed it, but did that make it true? Or was that just the child doing the father's bidding? The monster acting out Dr. Frankenstein's selfish wishes?

Was Abrams the puppet master that the press had made him out to be?

Damn it! That couldn't matter right now. I had to get to Jenny and Christie to .... What? To try to save Voldemort from being murdered by ancient Greek rock monsters from another dimension? I actually chuckled to myself at the thought. This must be hysteria or some kind of post-traumatic stress reaction. I started to laugh, thinking about calling Jorge and telling him to ... what? Watch out for a young couple wearing masks and carrying large knives? Or maybe I should call him and tell him that his life was in danger, and he needed to go away. Someplace far away for a long time. Until the danger passed.

Yeah, that would work well. Right. He was about as likely to thank me for the head's up and leave Christie to Jenny as ... as the police were likely to believe my story.

I'd slowed closer to the speed limit. My breathing was closer to normal. I was still gripping the steering wheel like it was keeping me from falling back into delusion. Into Cham. I was quickly approaching the end of the highway, reflexively angling right off of 101 onto 69 toward home. I happened to glance ahead toward the Town Common and realized my mistake. I veered back into the center lane, barely avoiding a green pickup truck, hoping I wasn't too late.

Tumble Bugs is on the second floor of the three-story red brick Common. Mommy vans filled the spaces closest to the entrance, so I had to park the Jeep fifty yards out and jog back across cracked blacktop and through deep puddles. I didn't see Jenny's 4Runner but I didn't take the time to search, either. She was here with Christie for the balance beam recital. I desperately needed to talk to her and after the missed appointment with Noyes, I couldn't afford to stand them up again.

I bolted through the glass door into a cramped and poorly lit foyer. A woman was busy tucking a crying toddler into a huge and colorful stroller. As I dashed past, I heard her offer the little boy an iPad to distract him. One flight up. Down the too-narrow hall past a real estate agent and an orthodontist's office. I pushed into Tumble Bugs and was immediately the center of attention.

Folding chairs had been set up just inside the door. Two dozen young parents filled the seats, many with babies cooing and sniffling and chattering in their arms. A row of children of all sizes, shapes, and colors dressed in a rainbow of neon Lycra and Spandex sat crisscross-applesauce at the rear of the room on a bright green foam mat. At center a pudgy five-year-old in a pink tutu was executing a pirouette atop a varnished board six inches off the floor. When I burst into the room, the child wobbled dramatically, fell to the mat, and burst into embarrassed tears. Every head in the room but one immediately turned to see what had ruined this future Olympian's hopes and dreams.

The exception was a pudgy woman in jeans wearing a baby in a backpack who ran over to the sobbing child calling, "Darlene! Sweetie. It's okay. We can start over!"

"Sorry, folks." I called out to the group. I couldn't make out faces in the dimly lit space, so I tried, "Jenny? Are you here? Christie?"

A woman in a black leotard -Miss Kathy, I presume- stepped out onto the matts and replied curtly, obviously angry. "I'm sorry, Mr. Villalobos. Jenny and Christie aren't here. Would you please take a seat or leave now? We're in the middle of a program."

"I'm very sorry" I replied to all as I pushed back out the door.

My phone was still in my backpack in the Jeep. I dashed down the steps and into the foyer where the same mother was trying to back her way into the parking lot pulling her stroller. Her son was now silently enraptured by whatever he'd discovered on his tablet. All I could do was hold the door while first one wheel then another wheel hit the doorframe, requiring the woman to back up with many apologies, realign, and try again. The delay was driving me crazy.

Why weren't Jenny and Christie here?

Had Caligula sent Scylla and Charybdis after them?

Here in the cigarette scented, worn and weary lobby of a thirty-year-old brick plaza in northern Minnesota that sentence sounded deeply deranged even in my own head.

Maybe Abrams had drugged me? Maybe the entire VR visit to Cham, see-through-the-eyes-of-Dorothy, Jorge's-going-to-die memory was a dream.

Finally, the woman and her child escaped the maw of the mall doorway. She rolled away with loud apologies and a wave while I darted across the blacktop back to the Jeep. My cell was where I'd left it in the bottom of my bag. I'd missed five calls but ignored them all and dialed Jenny.

She answered immediately.

Come home, she said.

Armageddon wouldn't have kept me away.

Mike Noyes and Myra Sloan sat side-by-side in the back row of the hotel ballroom, each with a laptop open in front of them. Noyes was Googling sashimi recipes. Sloan was scrolling through St. Paul apartment listings. One of her twin grandsons had started a small fire on the stove last night. She was newly determined that either her son and his unruly hoard had to move out or she would abandon the home and take an apartment herself.

Sixty or seventy family law professionals -lawyers, Guardians *ad litem*, mediators, psychologists, social workers, and two judges- were scattered across the tables set up for the conference. Most seemed to be similarly bored and distracted.

At the front of the room, a wrinkled and bearded older man wearing an expensive suit and a wireless mic stood at a podium advertising the hotels' name and tagline *-your home away from home!-* belching pompous psychobabble.

Sloan had seen an ad for the continuing education event at the last minute and signed up as much to have a reason to avoid going home on a Thursday afternoon as to keep current with the field. She'd been happy to find Noyes in line to register, greeted the big man, and they'd ended up sitting together. Sloan still felt bad about how her second husband had hurt Noyes' feelings, but that was years ago. He probably didn't even remember, so she didn't bring it up.

"How's your practice going, David? It's been a while."

"I'm sorry to say that I'm busier than ever. Everything that was bottled up during the pandemic is now overflowing. That and the fact that the world is going to hell generally. How about you?"

"Same thing. You know I don't do therapy anymore. Just court-ordered evals."

"Yes, I know. I think you're crazy but who knows? Maybe we're all crazy. There are times that I think that being a stone mason or a carpenter would be so much simpler. Build a wall. Get paid. See the product of your labor. Go home at night with nothing to worry about. Hey, speaking of crazy. You're doing an eval on one of my kiddos right now."

That rang a bell. "CV?" She referred to Christie by her initials to protect her privacy in this public setting. "Six-year-old little girl?"

"Yep. Did you get a consent for us to talk?"

"Yes and -come to think of it- I left you a voice mail. Can we take a minute now?"

"Sure." Sloan sipped coffee and tried to crystallize his thoughts. "Smart kid. Really tuned in and verbal. Caught in the middle. Genuinely scared of her dad. Mom and her boyfriend are smart and caring. They're working on supporting the kid's relationship with dad. There's been some name calling and triangulation. Exposing the kid to 'bad dad' stuff, but they're working on it."

"And dad?"

"He's blown me off entirely. CV tells me that he's tough. Ignores her. Seems to enjoy just depriving mom of the time. There's been some allegations against him. Never substantiated that I know of. Who knows what's real? Do you know about the recent crisis at school?"

"I do. What a shitshow." The incident at White Birch Elementary came back to her. Police. Lock down. National news coverage. Jenny and Ted had helped her connect the dots. Jorge had conspicuously not mentioned it even though it had been just the day before they met. That had been a red flag. What else was he hiding?

Noyes agreed. "Absolutely. But there were no weapons, and no one got hurt, right? Did Mom or the school overreact?"

"Or did dad really threaten people? No idea. I'm waiting to see the police report."

"What's your take on the family, Myra?" Noyes wondered. "It would kill mom to lose this kid."

"Too early to say. I haven't met the child yet. Mom and boyfriend look impressive, but I just got mom's testing back. I never would have guessed. Underneath that poor-victim stuff, buried beneath some real emotional strengths, she is fiercely territorial. She is not aggressive, per se, but do not cross her! If she feels backed into a corner, there is nothing that woman isn't capable of including violence. She is a Tiger Mom on steroids. Dad? He gives me bad vibes. Like there's something hidden right below the surface. He hasn't done his testing yet. I'll let you know."

"Sure. Then maybe we can do lunch? Or I'll have you and … you're remarried, aren't you? What's his name?"

"Alan. Thanks, but we can't. I'm afraid that Alan's been sick for a while. Parkinsons."

"I'm so sorry. Myra." He placed an enormous hand on Sloan's forearm. The human contact and caring felt good and sadly unfamiliar. Sloan remembered how much she'd always liked Noyes and regretted that their friendship had lapsed.

At that moment a colleague serving as moderator made his mic squeal, apologized, and then announced that he was excited to introduce Dr. Hassan French. Dr. French was there to teach the group his ground-breaking *ABC Heuristic* for diagnosing parental alienation in high conflict, court involved families. "A simple recipe for a complex problem!"

Dr. French's many achievements and accolades were described in excessive detail and then the man himself took the podium to faint applause.

Noyes whispered to Sloan, "Diagnosing?"

"Don't you know French?" Sloan asked quietly. "He's one of the troglodytes who hasn't yet gotten the memo that alienation is about relationships, not about individual diagnosis. He's still pushing for alienation to be in the DSM. He thinks if we can diagnose a kid as alienated, then the insurance companies will pay for treatment."

Noyes shrank into his seat and pulled his laptop closer, like a shield.

French tooted his own horn for another five minutes, thanked the moderator, and made PowerPoint images fade on and off a large screen at the front of the room. Sloan disagreed with much of what he said and was put off by his arrogant style, but one slide in particular caught her eye. She scribbled the words down on a napkin and tucked it in her bag. Little as she liked crediting the man in any regard, she had to admit that he'd nailed one idea exactly:

"When families fracture, it's far too easy to mistake the good guy for the bad guy and vice versa. The members of the family and concerned professionals alike often feel like they've been sucked into a paralyzing house of mirrors; an alternate reality where good and bad, right and wrong lose all meaning."

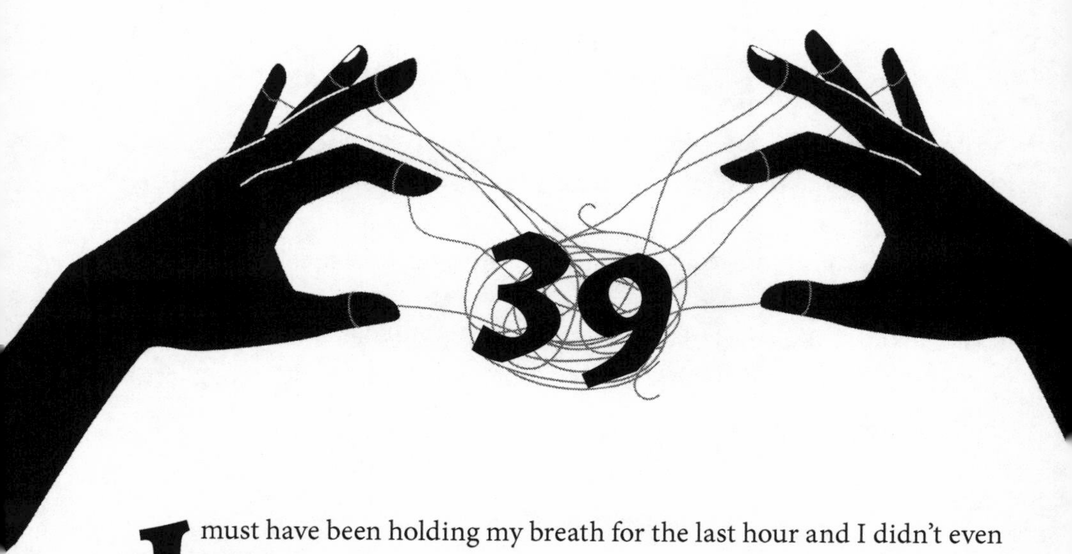

I must have been holding my breath for the last hour and I didn't even know it.

When I walked into our apartment and saw Jenny holding Christie's sleeping body, our safe little nest whole and intact, my familiar reality untouched by seven-foot tall Roman barbarians and knife wielding Greek monsters and serial killer psychologists I finally, deeply exhaled. With that release, unbidden and unexpected, came tears. My breath caught in my throat. My eyes overflowed.

I didn't greet Jenny so much as merge with her. She looked up when I walked in the door and started to say *hello* or *please be quiet* or *where have you been?* Or *how was your day?* but then she read my face. Concern crossed hers. I managed a half-smile through the tears, dropped my backpack, and perched myself flush against her on the couch. One arm over Christie encircling them both. The other over the back of the chair. I leaned Jenny's head into my chest and kissed the top of her head, smelling shampoo and rain and comfort. I curled my body around hers while she held Christie to her and we became who we are and would always be, a three-headed, six-legged powerful being of love.

Jenny kissed my tears and then my lips but was wise enough not to speak. It was enough just to breathe the same air. In and out. Our heart-beats synchronized.

Jenny dozed in our shared warmth. I wiped at my face and tried not to think. I managed to float for a bit, artificially buoyed and insulated in this artificial womb. Maybe I dozed off too. Without willing it, I gradually became aware that I'd made decision. My guilt and terror remained intact, deeply rooted and growing fast, but my ambivalence was gone. My indecision had passed like the rainstorm that had threatened to flood my world and then moved off into the distance. I knew with absolute certainty that there was nothing that I could do to stop the wheels that I'd set in motion and that I would not waste energy on honorable and righteous but futile efforts.

If my experience with Abrams in *EAU* was real then Christie's father, the bane of Jenny's existence, Jorge Villalobos a.k.a., Voldemort was about to die.

When? Maybe in this very moment a masked creature was drawing a sharpened blade across his ugly, fat throat. Or maybe virtual murderers preferred to wait until after dark to climb up his fire escape, raise a squeaky windowpane, and slip into his bedroom. I recalled that his mother lives in the apartment beneath him. Even though she'd given him life and presumably supported his campaign against us, I hoped that she would be safe.

Christie roused herself first from our undifferentiated, collective self, hungry, asking for supper. Jenny tried to resist climbing up and out of her stupor, but Christie whined and then tickled and had to show me how her nose had been bleeding and tell me about the big boys and explain to me that daddy's not a terrier-ist and soon enough we were all three eating mac-and-cheese in the kitchen.

No sweetie, I thought, daddy's not a terrier-ist. But he will soon be dead.

I didn't tell Jenny. I couldn't. I wasn't worried about dragging her into the swamp of moral questions that filled me. I was worried that if she knew she would become an accessory to murder. I had to protect Christie by protecting her mother so that when I went to prison and shared a cell with Dr. Sam Abrams, she could stay here and raise her twice-fatherless daughter.

When she kissed me and looked me in the eyes and asked if I was okay and what the tears were about, I looked away and shrugged. "Everything, I guess. I'm just tired and I was so happy to see you two here." I suspect that she knew that there was more, but she kissed me again and said, "I love you."

I did tell Jenny about walking in on the balance beam show and how I'd made a fool of myself. I extemporized to add for Christie's sake how everyone there told me to say hello and that they hope that she's feeling better. Christie said that she knows Darlene -the child who stumbled off the equipment when I arrived- but that they're not friends because "she tells everyone that she's the best at the balance beam because her mother said so."

We had a family meeting over chocolate pudding cups. Several months ago, necessity and a sink full of unwashed dishes forced us to invent a new tradition. Three pudding cups. One spoon. Say something, take a bite, pass the spoon on to the next person. No cheating with fingers, forks, or slurping direct from the cup. No talking unless you hold the spoon.

Jenny started.

"I think we should give Christie a day off school tomorrow. A mental health day. What do you think, Christie-bee?" Jenny made a small drama scooping up a spoonful of pudding and savoring the bite, then handing the spoon to Christie.

"Really? What's a *metal* health day?" Jenny knew the rules. She mimed that she couldn't talk. Christie continued. "Would that mean we could play and watch TV?" Jenny and I nodded yes in unison. "Yippee! I get a *metal* health day!" She scooped and slurped and passed me the spoon.

"A *MEN*tal health day" I said, "is time off to heal your mind the same way sometimes we need time off to heal our bodies. Like your bloody nose needs to time heal. I think you should take tomorrow off, sweetie, and we can play and watch TV BUT ..." your daddy's going to die ... "Mommy might have forgotten that she and I have an appointment in the morning." I scooped and slurped and passed Jenny the spoon.

"Right. We do have an appointment. Good remembering Teddy Bear! I think I'll call our appointment and try to change it or maybe Christie could play there while we talk. Deal?" Christie and looked at each other, nodded, and then nodded agreement to Jenny who was still busy slurping noisily.

Christie had the spoon. "I am not going with Voldemort this weekend," she declared. Her look invited defiance, foreshadowing an adolescence still years away. It said, "go on and challenge me on this one. I dare you!" There was determination on her face. Jenny was about to remind her not to use that name, but I nodded my head no. There was a cold, trembling place inside of me that said that little things like that didn't matter anymore.

Christie passed me the spoon.

Our storebought pudding cups are quite small, even for Christie. This would likely be our last round.

"Christie-mouse, Mommy and I told you that we made a mistake when we called daddy that. Let's all be more respectful, sweetie. He is your daddy." I took my last scoop and was glad to give Jenny the spoon.

"Today is Thursday, peanut, and it's almost bedtime. You get an extra day off school tomorrow but then at three o'clock we all have a job to do." I could read the tension in Jenny's posture, the lines that creased her forehead, and the forced quality of her words. Christie probably could too. "Teddy and me and you are going to meet daddy at the police station like always and you're going to be a big girl. We'll pack you and Piglet up and you'll have a good time."

Christie didn't wait for the spoon or for Jenny to finish speaking. She slapped her half-empty plastic cup of pudding off the table and shouted,"I am not!" and ran off to her room. Her door slammed.

Brown mush dotted the floor and the glass oven door.

Jenny turned to me. It was her turn to cry.

"What are we going to do, Ted?"

I went and hugged her tight. I wanted to say that we were going to do nothing. Absolutely nothing. What needed to be done was already happening.

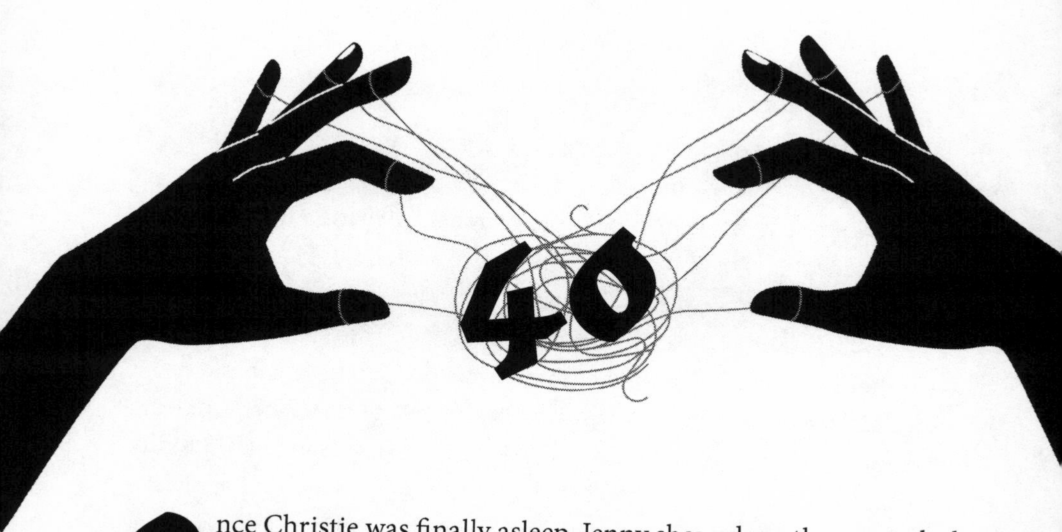

Once Christie was finally asleep, Jenny showed me the research that she'd done. She kept copious notes documenting the two lawyers that she'd spoken with and the friends that she'd called. She told me about Nurse Karen and her shock and horror about the suggestion that accusing Jorge of sexual abuse could work to our advantage. I pretended to share her revulsion, thinking that that would have been far preferrable to what I'd done.

What had I done?

What I'd been forced to do. Killing Jorge wasn't my choice. It wasn't even an idea that I'd ever shared outside of this bedroom, but here I was nurturing a growing glacier of anxiety somewhere in my gut. I told Jenny that my stomach was upset. That I'd vomited earlier in the day. She put a reassuring hand on my forehead, pronounced me fever-free and produced green chewables from her well-stocked nurse's medicine cabinet. I chewed two, complained of the taste, and thanked her.

Before we turned out the light, she emailed Dr. Sloan. Christie would be home from school on Friday. Could we set Christie up to play in the doctor's waiting room while we talked? Alternately, Ted could stay with her while the doctor spoke with Jenny alone. Thanks for being flexible. Let us know asap please.

I remembered the woman's spotless, white waiting room and wondered if any child had ever played there.

I held Jenny and reassured her in the dark while numbness slowly overcame me. I diagnosed myself with frostbite of the soul. Mountain climbers and skiers lost in the back country and disoriented winter hikers often end up with frostbitten digits and limbs that had to be amputated. More than one TV doctor had explained that if gangrene set in it could be fatal.

How does one amputate a dead soul?

How long could I live with moral gangrene before it killed me?

I would not have guessed that I could sleep that night or ever again, but I did. Those chewable green pills were sedating. I fell deeply asleep holding Jenny, listening to her breathing, wondering when and how it was going to happen.

Two young people wearing masks, one with a knife filled my dreams.

The doorbell woke me. Two strident rings. Pause. Two more. It was 4:22 a.m.

My stomach churned.

I woke Jenny. Told her to put on a robe. "Don't let anybody in until I'm there." I pulled on sweatpants and a tee-shirt. Jenny whisper-yelled "coming!" toward the door then "who is it?"

I checked on Christie. I tried to capture the image of her tangled in blankets, clutching Piglet like a life preserver in deep seas. This could be the last time I see her.

I heard a female voice answering Jenny through the closed door.

"Shakopee Police Department, ma'am. Please let us in."

Jenny looked terrified. There was no spyhole in the door and no video camera in the hall.

I kissed Jenny on the forehead, resolved that either these were Caligula's killers intending on punishing me for intruding in Cham or these were genuine police here to arrest me for plotting Jorge's murder. The iceberg in my belly encased me. My limbs were cold and stiff, but I was sweating. I shoo 'ed Jenny into the kitchen: "get your phone and get ready to dial 9-1-1 if necessary. I'm going to open up.

She did. Then I did.

Two officers. One male. One female. Young. No masks. No knives. They showed me laminated cards with names and badge numbers that could have been real. Their names were McLean and Starry.

McLean -the male- asked me to identify myself. He noted my name and birthdate in a spiral notebook like the ones that I use. Starry -the female- asked where Ms. Villalobos was. I called Jenny in from the kitchen. I asked the officers to please be quiet. A child is sleeping. McLean checked his notebook and asked if that child might be Christina Villalobos? He recited her date of birth. Jenny said yes.

"What's happening officers? It's four in the morning. She pulled her robe tight and stood tight against my side. I wrapped an arm around her but could offer no warmth. That gangrene had apparently spread rapidly while I slept.

"Can we sit down together, please?" Starry asked.

We did. Jenny led us into the kitchen. McLean studied the brown splatter on the floor and oven door like he'd discovered a blood trail. I poked a finger in the stiffening goop and licked it clean. "Pudding," I said, "We have a six-year-old."

Starry spoke up, "Ms. Villalobos, do you know a man named Jorge Manuel Villalobos of 1053, unit B, Prairie Steet?"

Jenny looked at me. I should have responded. I couldn't. She put her hand on my arm looking for support. I couldn't offer it. I had turned to stone. They weren't here to arrest me. That might have been better.

"Yes. He's my ex. He's my little girl's father.

"Ma'am, I'm terribly sorry to say this," Starry began. In my head I heard her say, "your boyfriend hired two interdimensional beings from a videogame to magically appear and stab him to death." Jenny's fingers were digging into the flesh of my forearm. It should have hurt. It didn't.

"Ma'am, at 11:26 last night -about five hours ago-. Mr. Villalobos was involved in a motor vehicle accident at the junction of route 101 and 69 outside the Shakopee Common."

I'd been there hours ago. That was where I'd remembered the gym class. I'd shifted lanes and nearly hit a green pickup truck.

Jenny's face lost all color. Her dark hair hanging loose about her face made her look like a corpse. I would rather have hit the green pickup and sacrificed myself than put her through this.

"It was a hit and run, ma'am. The other vehicle left the scene. Mr. Villalobos was travelling at very excessive speeds. I'm sorry to say, ma'am, that Mr. Villalobos was terribly injured in the collision. His Mustang was totaled. We have reason to believe that he may have been intoxicated behind the wheel and that he had failed to turn on his headlights."

Jenny was shriveling up next to me and I could do nothing to help.

"Ma'am? We've very sorry. We've just spoken with Mr. Villalobos' mother, Maria Villalobos, your former mother-in-law. She agreed to identify the body later today. She asked that we alert you here."

Jenny was crying. I might have been too. I had no way to know. I don't know if murderers cry over their victims.

Jenny managed to say, "Thank you." Starry left her business card on the counter and said something about calling if we had any questions. The officers showed themselves out.

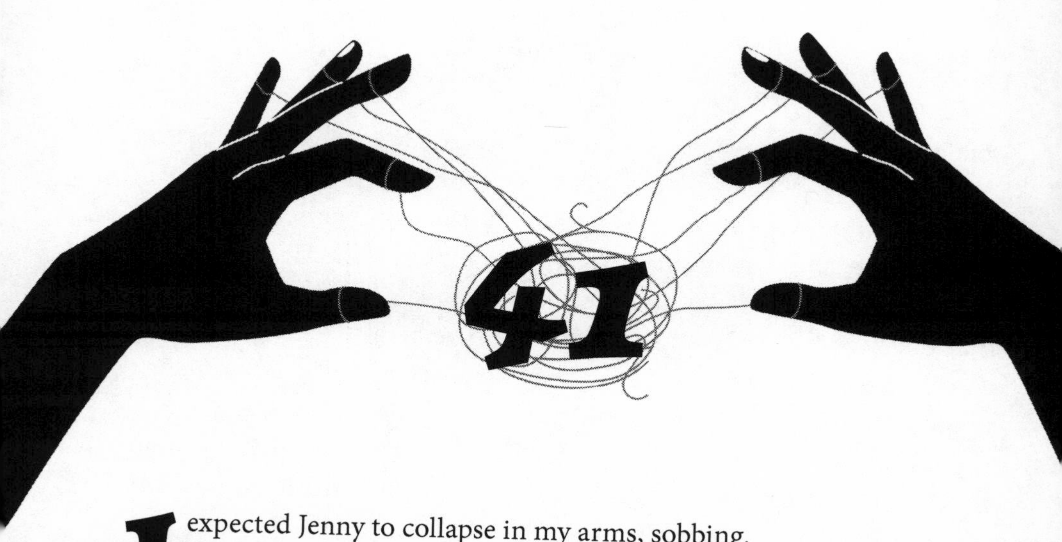

41

I expected Jenny to collapse in my arms, sobbing.

She once thought that she'd loved Jorge. She'd had a child with him. As much as she'd grown to hate him, I don't believe that she ever actually wished him dead. Jenny would rather rescue and release spiders than kill them. She looked away from roadkill and said a prayer. Commercials about homeless dogs and news items about natural disaster victims and soldiers injured in war and the little old lady down the hall who walks with a cane – all these things elicit her innate empathy and compassion. It's part of why she makes a great nurse and part of why I love her.

But she didn't collapse or wail or fall into hysterics. She didn't shut down and slip into depression. She held my arm hard for minutes after the officers left. Her nails left half-moon bruises in my flesh that lasted for days. She wiped her eyes and sat up straight and looked at me.

I could see a faint glow of light beginning to illuminate the horizon to the east.

"He's dead, Ted. I can't believe it."

I could. I didn't say so.

I asked how she was doing.

"I think I'm okay. I'm a little worried about Christie. I have no idea what to say to her, but -you know what?- he was drunk driving and speeding in that stupid black car at night with no lights on. Thank God Christie wasn't with him." She shivered. "I hadn't thought of that until now. Christie could have been with him. Damn him! I hope he burns in hell."

Incredibly, Jenny really was okay. I sensed relief in her, but she'd never admit it. That would have been like wishing him dead which was almost like hiring someone to kill him which was almost like killing him herself.

Christie woke up after nine. We told her that she did not have to see her father that weekend which won us huge hugs and whoops of relief and apologies that she'd splattered her pudding and that she'd yelled and slammed her door. Fortunately, at six years old, all that emotion came unencumbered by impossible questions about what had changed. Where was daddy? Why don't I have to go?

The child already had wisdom enough not to look a gift horse in the mouth.

Jenny insisted that Christie scrub up the pudding mess. There again, Christie knew enough not to ask why a big blob on the oven door had a Teddy-sized fingerprint in it.

Jenny went out to her car to make some calls in private.

Mark Camden was startled by the news of Jorge's death. He advised Jenny to update Dr. Sloan and to cancel today's interview until he heard something further from the court. He advised that when a litigant dies the case typically dies with him which meant offering her his sympathies and his congratulations both.

Dr. Sloan seemed genuinely upset about Jorge's sudden death. They'd met twice and talked for about four hours, so she felt like she knew him. She asked a couple of questions about where and when and how, asked how Christie was managing, and then agreed with Camden's advice that the ten o'clock appointment should be cancelled. The evaluation would be put on hold pending the court's further direction.

Jenny left a voice mail for David Noyes. Her phone buzzed a moment later. It was Noyes calling back.

"Sorry that I missed you, Jenny. Is Christie alright?"

"Hmmm… I think so. At the moment anyway. I know that you're probably busy, so I'll try to be brief. The police came to our apartment early this morning."

"What happened? What did he do now?"

"Well. He -Christie's dad- got in a bad accident last night. The 101/69 interchange. Christie's father was killed."

"Oh my God. I'm so sorry … I think." Noyes had just been talking about Christie's father hours ago with Myra Sloan. He got the sense that she agreed that he was a dirtbag. She'd never say that, of course. "I can't imagine what that means for you and Ted. How's Christie taking the news?"

"That's really why I'm calling. We haven't told her yet. She just knows that she doesn't have to go with him this weekend. That was cause for a party. I'm hoping that you can help."

"Of course. Of course. Keep her away from the news, you don't want her hearing this by accident. Can you and Ted and Christie be here today at three?"

"Good idea. Yes. Three is actually when we would have been transitioning her to Jorge. We'll be there. Thanks so much."

Jenny sat in the 4Runner looking out at the new day. Yesterday's downpour had washed the world clean. The one bit of scum that remained was wiped away just before midnight. She searched herself for grief or loss or sadness. She found distant, warped memories of her time together with Jorge, faded and blurred like old-school photos printed from negatives and left out in the sun. Time and conflict had burned away any remnants of caring that had survived the divorce. His callous mistreatment of her, his false allegations against her, his inflammatory and threatening words in court had all cauterized the few loose ends of what she'd once thought of as love. She might have mourned the loss for Christie. Certainly, the news will be difficult for the little girl to digest, but Christie would be fine in the end. Even relieved.

The truth was that Jenny had been mourning the absence of the father that Jorge should have been for years.

Jenny had one more call to make. The most important. She found "Aaronson, Karen" in her directory and called. The nurse picked up on the first ring and greeted her enthusiastically.

"Good morning, Jenny! I bet that you're having a better day today than you have had in a while."

The woman's sing-song pleasure was disconcerting.

"Thanks, Karen. So you heard?"

"I did, honey. It's all over the news."

"I don't know what to say."

"'Thanks,' works. We're just glad to help."

"Well then thanks to you and to your sister-exes.

"*YOUR* sister-exes, she corrected. You're one of us now."

Jenny wasn't sure what that meant exactly but at that moment didn't care.

"Of course, Karen. I owe you. I owe you all. Let's do lunch. How about next week? I don't know what shifts I'll be on yet, but I'll find a day."

"That would be grand, darling. Now go enjoy."

Jenny padded back inside, still in her slippers and robe. She felt empowered. And free. And a bit guilty that she felt so free, but the guilt was the least of it.

Christie and Ted were laughing together on the kitchen floor, wiping at each other with damp rags that had been intended for pudding clean up. She nodded reassurance in answer to Ted's silent question. Her expression read relief. Behind Christie's back she mimed, "we're all going to be okay" and "I love you." Then, in a cheery voice she announced to all that the grown-ups' morning appointment was cancelled, eliciting yet another round of excited hugs from Christie.

My phone was flashing an alert on the countertop. Jenny handed me the device.

I looked at it and then at Christie and pretended confusion. "Huh? I wonder how I missed this call? Was I doing something like… this?" I tickled Christie's arms until she ran off and hid behind Jenny. The pair went off to get dressed and plan the day.

The smile and laughter *easy dropped* from my face.

I tapped the voice mail icon. Abrams' name appeared. I tapped *play* and put the device to my ear.

"Mr. Bennett. I'm calling to cancel today's one o'clock appointment. Your friend *ahnDRAYah* needs the time. I'm sure that you understand. I think that we're done here, Ted. I believe that you understand everything now. I'll send you a file this afternoon with some details you'll need. Good luck with your book. By the way, I saw the news. *Ding dong*!"

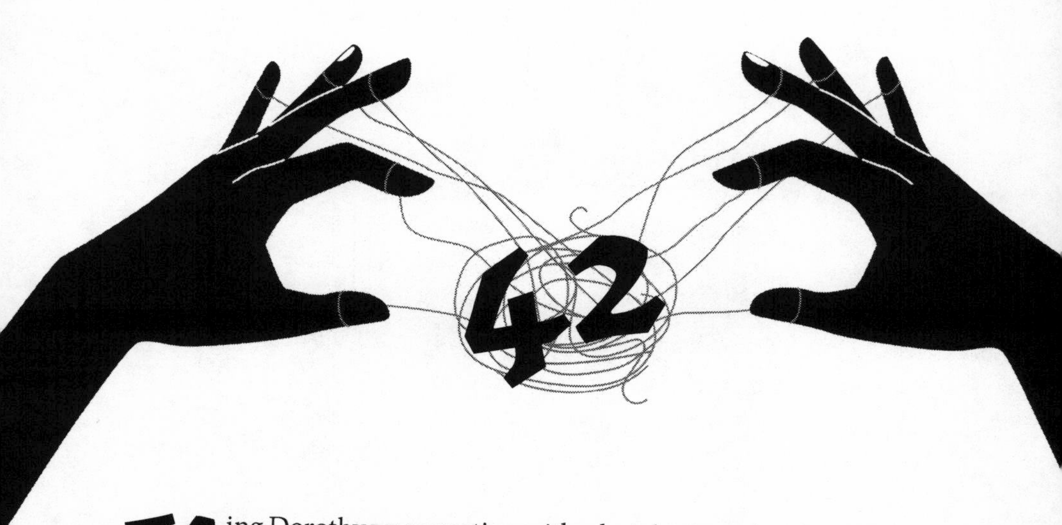

King Dorothy was questing with a knight named Galahad and a Lion named Scar. All three -even the lion- carried Star Wars light sabers that buzzed and glowed better even than George Lucas' originals. The trio was cutting through a wall of carnivorous vines that surrounded Ponce de León's fabled Fountain of Youth. An L25 god named The Lorax had posted a one thousand credit bounty in Cham payable to the first player to bring him a jug of the magical liquid.

Galahad was making headway through the voracious groundcover, largely because he was inedible. The vines tried to sink their pointy incisors into his armor and failed. Scar and Dorothy were trying to follow in Galahad's slipstream, but three vines grew back immediately where one was severed, each more aggressive than the last.

An alert instantiated in Dorothy's user interface; a transparent sticky note reminder that only he could see. It was a message from Caligula. A request to meet in an NTNH chatbox immediately.

Dorothy shouted out to his compatriots, "My friends! The bounty is yours to share if you succeed. I've been summoned elsewhere."

Scar roared an insult about weak-kneed little girls and children who shouldn't play at adult games. Galahad continued to clank and slash away at the overgrowth, newly re-energized and motivated by a huge change IRL at home.

Dorothy stepped away from the hungry foliage, tapped and swiped right. He accepted Caligula's invitation, spent two credits to summon a flock of fairies that fluttered over him, cleaning and repairing his clothes, wiping the blood off his arms, brushing out his wavy dark hair and retying his sky-blue bows. Yes, he was going to meet with a bloodthirsty, hairy barbarian who wore nothing but a torn loincloth, but he'd feel better if he looked good.

Dorothy had recently learned how to pair specific gestures with *EAU* commands, a trick that saved time summoning menus and tapping. When the fairies were done, he straightened his skirt and clicked his ruby red heels together three times.

Darkness fell. The forest glade and the sounds of his comrades' efforts disappeared.

Light gathered. Pixels shifted.

Dorothy wasn't in the boardroom that he'd expected. Obviously, Caligula had purchased an upgraded chatbox. This was a vast, empty, white sand beach. A horseshoe-shaped strand backed by thick green trees encompassing a crystal-clear bay that opened toward an endless, blue horizon. Odd cubical and pyramid-shaped conch shells littered the water's edge. The sky was cloudless and as deeply faceted as the water below.

A dozen steps away, Caligula reclined on a thickly cushioned chaise lounge. His hairy arms were up over his massive head. A pair of Vuarnet mineral-crafted Artic sunglasses covered his eyes.

A second chaise was set in the sand next to him.

Dorothy called out a greeting and approached slowly. The deep sand swallowed and pulled at his precious ruby slippers.

"King Dorothy?" Caligula beckoned without looking up. "Please join me."

"This is quite the scene, my friend." Dorothy scanned the forest behind and the waters ahead for danger. This was an NTNH box, but Caligula was powerful. This could all be a set-up. A trap.

Dorothy slowly lowered himself into the chaise. He pulled his skirt up to enjoy the sun on his legs. "And those are quite the shades."

"Are they the right color, though?"

The frames were an icy hue of yellow. Dorothy/Abrams thought that no color existed that could complement the barbarian's scowling and crevassed face with the streaming fu Manchu moustache.

"You invited me here for fashion advice?"

"No. As you can see, I manage my fashion without anyone's advice. I'll get to the point. Of course, you remember our recent business?"

"Of course." This was a trap. Caligula must have figured out that he had secretly piggybacked Ted into their private meeting. Surely the sand was about to open up and swallow him whole or giant vultures would swoop out of the sky to devour him, or a billion nano-ants even now were swarming over him intent of capturing him like the Lilliputians captured Gulliver.

But none of that happened. Caligula just kept talking, "And you're aware that the deals that I make are irrevocable?"

"Of course." Was this when King Neptune was due to rise up out of the deceptively calm sea and shish kabob him on his trident?

"For the first time in my virtual life as Caligula the Conqueror I find that I need to make an exception," Caligula said.

Back home in Texas, Rush grimaced about what he'd decided to do. Twenty thousand Ethereum was more than pocket change. His dad slaved six months to earn that much. But since he'd turned eighteen and moved out, Rush had come out of the closet. He abandoned his drunken father and the shithole apartment that he'd grown up in, invested carefully and laundered his crypto income scrupulously. He moved into a wheelchair-accessible, air-conditioned, two-bedroom condo. The development had a pool and a Jacuzzi that drew hordes of hot babes. He learned to drive a modified Econovan. One step at a time, the paraplegic kid in the wheelchair found his footing (both puns intended). He now owned a string of six Dollar Trees across the panhandle, including the one that he'd lived above until recently. Both his legal and his hidden bank accounts were comfortably full. He was doing okay.

Well, actually he was doing a lot better than okay.

Although Rush was careful to live a modest life IRL, he did allow himself one indulgence. The Horizon 4-DV-2 virtual reality unit that had been gifted to him, the machine that had saved him IRL and created him anew in Cham, had begun to feel clunky and slow. He'd begun to get headaches after wearing the headset for eight or ten hours at a time. Visual and tactile tracking jumped sometimes. He sold it on eBay to some crime writer up north. In its place, Rush now ran an Israeli *B'Sharet* military grade Full

Sensorium 10x8 terabyte, full body VR device with direct-to-synapse (DTS) panoptic sight including IR, 20 Hz/20kHz sound, replicant gustatorial, exteroception, k9 olfaction, and 360-degree proprioception.

The *B'Sharet* device was next gen and then some. It made his experience in *EAU* even crisper and more immediate than his experience IRL.

"An exception to what?" Dorothy asked.

It was Saturday, so Abrams didn't have any patients. The office was quiet, the house above him was empty, and it was still too cold out for the buzz of motorboats on the lake to intrude. Nothing distracted him IRL except the nasty smell that refused to be scrubbed out of the carpet near the door. Cleaners were booked for first thing Wednesday, so he ignored it as best as he could and focused on the monster seated next to him.

"An exception to my irrevocable rule," Caligula confirmed. "See, I'll take your money to attempt a task, whether I succeed or fail. You're paying for the effort, not the outcome, although I must say that my success rate is extraordinary. But sadly, I have to return your money."

"Are you backing out of our agreement?" Dorothy/Abrams was suddenly angry. The fragile balance of his deal with Ted Bennett and therefore Micah's safety depended on Ted's girlfriend's ex-husband's death. If Caligula backed out and Jorge Villalobos lived, then there was nothing to stop Ted from writing the real story about Suki's death. Abrams would be convicted of murder and go to jail. Micah would never come home.

Caligula must follow through.

"Yes. I regret to say. I am."

Suddenly the two figures were standing in the sand. In profile they painted a ridiculous picture. Caligula towered over the girl in his muscled, hairy, tattooed, and scarred avatar. Dorothy looked like Auntie Em's favorite niece; a child so innocent that she would risk her life to rescue her dog in a windstorm.

Dorothy stared up into the barbarian's eyes. The anger in his deep voice did not fit the sweet, pouty mouth that it came out of. "You cannot break our deal!"

"Calm down, Dot. At least ask me why."

"Why what?" Abrams/Dorothy demanded.

"Why I'm backing out. I'll tell you anyway: Scylla and Charybdis got there -Minnesota- late yesterday and went right to work. There was nothing to kill. The man was already dead."

Dorothy/Abrams didn't understand and said so.

"Either Jorge Manuel Villalobos of Shakopee, Minnesota happened to die in a drunk driving accident less than twenty-four hours before he would have been killed by me or someone else did the job for me. Either way, I did nothing, and you get the only refund that I have ever paid. Next time, try not to hire me to kill someone whose already dead."

Dorothy/Abrams smirked. The man was dead, but Caligula hadn't killed him? No worries, Dorothy/Abrams thought. As long as Ted thought that he'd signed the man's death warrant and could be held responsible for the murder, nothing else mattered.

Caligula was once again reclining in the faux sunshine.

Dorothy thanked him and found that he couldn't click her heels together in the sand, so he manipulated a fourth dimension, tapped, swiped, and winked out.

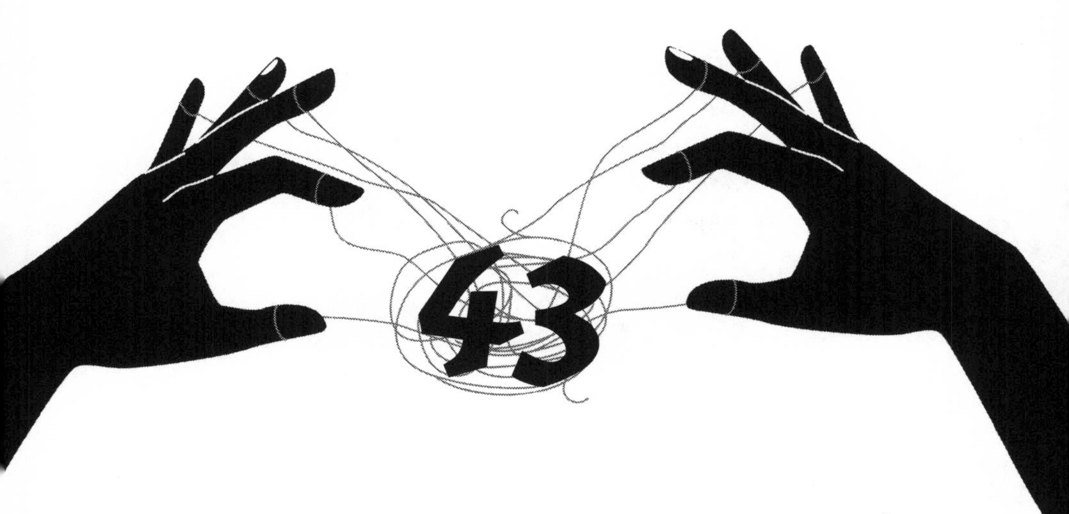

On August 15, 2023, two weeks before the M&M murder trial was due to begin, Synchronicity Press released "Virtual Realities: The Murder of Suki Kohler." Between the hype around the high-profile trial, publicity targeting Suki-phants as social media dubbed the deceased model's toadies, and publicity targeting M&M murder enthusiasts who were busy protesting outside of the courthouse carrying "Convict Micah!" and "Mommy Murderer!" signs, the first run sold out in ten days.

A second run was rushed to press, and preorders piled up.

The story behind the cover girl's demise shocked and intrigued the world. "Virtual Realities" thoroughly exonerated the widowed husband and dismissed the puppet-master theory as so much viral garbage. Abrams was no Frankenstein. He had neither alienated his son from his mother nor brainwashed him into killing her.

Instead, the book traces the interwoven paths of a beautiful jet-setting young woman, her powerful and respected psychologist husband, and a depraved and drug-addled young man named Lucas Morrisey. I expose Morrisey as the killer and tell the story of how I uncovered forensic evidence that left police detectives with no doubt who had killed Suki Kohler. The trial that had been scheduled to last two weeks was now expected to last two hours, at most. The book proved that the prosecutors' case against Abrams was pointless and that their experts' lofty opinions about parental alienation and matricidal children -notably including the esteemed and uber expensive Dr. Hassan French- was just plain horseshit.

I glowed with humble pride and gratitude in public.

In private, I shuddered in the frigid currents of grief and guilt that filled me.

I learned how to put on a smile. To become an avatar of myself when people were looking. To them, I was the successful author/sleuth who'd solved a mystery that had kept the world awake at night. I gave dozens of talks and signed hundreds of books and shook thousands of hands, always careful to thank Dr. Sam Abrams for generously allowing me into his life and trusting me with his story. I expressed sympathy for his teenage son who'd spent months in the state's forensic psychiatric hospital.

MPH didn't weather my book's publication well. The governor blamed his predecessors for failing to properly oversee the hospital's recent make-over. An advisory commission was established, and an investigation began. Late in August I saw reports of staff turnover and patients' civil suits. At some point, Dr. Chatterjee sent an angry email accusing me of fraudulently impersonating a state official, breaching federal HIPAA regulations, and abusing her patients. I forwarded the note to SynCity's attorneys and then promptly forgot about it.

I was too consumed pretending to be a happy and successful writer.

I asked Christie's permission to marry her mommy on July 4th, the day that I delivered my final draft of "Virtual Realities" to my editor. We three made plans to celebrate together in the city. Dinner out and fireworks over the river. Just before we piled in my Jeep, I whispered my plan to Christie and showed her the ring. She pinkie swore not to tell, then bounced and giggled the entire ride into St. Paul. Jenny asked me if the little girl was on meth.

I would have waited to pop the question until after the meal, but Christie kept looking at me as if to say, "Well...? Now....? How about now...?" It was a version of "Are we there yet?" without the benefit of a destination. I gave in quickly. After the waiter took our order, I crouched on one knee to whisper in Christie's ear which was her cue to stand up beside me and say, "Mommy, can we please marry Ted? Please?" Jenny shrieked "yes!" then muffled her own startled reply. Neighboring diners applauded as I slid my mother's engagement ring on her finger and the three of us kissed and hugged.

The book's successes brought in new opportunities with promises of bigger bucks. I rented an office in the Shakopee Common down the hall from Tumble Bugs and Vesuvius Pizza so I could get out of Jenny's way and write in peace.

Jenny and Dr. David and I explained to Christie that all living things have a beginning, a middle, and an end. Sometimes people reach their end unexpectedly. Her daddy had reached his end. He died. Christie nodded "okay" like we'd just told her that it might rain. She asked two questions: Where was he now?

Heaven, we said.

Do I ever have to see him again?

No. Never. She cheered.

Jenny let Jorge's mother take Christie to Jorge's funeral. We listened the entire time on the *BunnyEars* app. There were some genuinely sad moments until unseen strangers began to sing Jorge's praises which amounted to one thought: "He loved his car!" We turned to each other trying to be solemn and respectful but burst out laughing.

Jenny slid back into the nursing rotation at St. Francis. Nursing Supervisor Molotov was gone, replaced by a woman who seemed really smart and really reasonable. Peter welcomed Jenny back with open arms and cupcakes in the nursing lounge, profound apologies for how he'd gotten her fired, and ambivalent sympathies over Christie's father's death.

"You know they brought him here that night?" Peter asked.

"Jorge? The ambulance brought him here? No, I didn't know that."

"Oh Jenn, he was a mess. Are you sure you want to hear this? A lot of crush injuries. They had to cardiovert him three times. Donna in the ER told me that he was awake for some of it."

"Did he say anything?"

"Oh, I thought Donna called you. I wasn't there, and he was pretty drunk which was a good thing, given how much pain he was in, but Donna said that he said one thing."

Jenny imagined death bed apologies and regrets or a plea to send a final message to his beloved daughter. Any of that might have kindled a spark of remorse over the man's death. She asked Peter what their colleague had reported about Jorge's last words.

"He asked about his car, Jenn. He wanted to know if the car could be repaired. Can you believe that?"

Jenny and I have resumed juggling schedules. With the book done, I have my flexibility back, at least for now. She picks up Christie after school when she can and takes her to dance or gym or her appointments with Dr. David (now fewer and further apart) and then they meet me at home for dinner. When she can't, I'm glad to be on Christie duty and proud that she's begun to regularly call me "daddy."

Christie knows what's real, perhaps more so than us adults. She knows that she had a birth daddy named Jorge who died because he wasn't driving safely. She knows that I'm her chosen-daddy. She knows that Mommy and Christie and I are her forever family EXCEPT -and this part is brand new for us all- that our family is going to include a little brother soon.

This is my virtual reality.

Twist the knob.

Change the station.

Tune in a different universe overlaying the one that you think is real.

I bought an Horizon 4-DV-2 used on eBay from some geek in Texas. It was banged up a little, but cheap and it worked well. I keep it in a box on the top shelf in the closet in my new office. At first, I used it when I was bored just to explore. I played virtual golf and shot archery and went BASE jumping and free diving and target shooting, but inevitably I went home to Cham.

I knew when I bought it that I would.

I signed onto *Enemies All Around Us*.

It wasn't hard to create my avatar. The program let me scavenge NatGeo images off the web and allowed me some limited choices among skills and powers and health. As an L1 newbie, I entered the game with twenty credits. Seed money. I'll use them to upgrade my avatar later, when I earn more credits questing in the outlands, but not yet.

I fumble around with hand movements that feel like playing cat's cradle with no string. A communications menu instantiates before me, a transparent rectangular screen hanging in midair. I poke and swipe and get it wrong twice before I finally find the right tab. I select NTNH, debit ten credits from my newbie *EAU* account, and refuse a long list of upgrades. I tap *send*, collect my reply, then tap *transport*.

The library full of books with its view of the rainbow-shimmering waterfall shifts to blackness.

Light comes up on a familiar boardroom.

Two figures stand by the window, looking down on the spectacular view over Dubai. My reflection joins theirs in the glass, blurring the lines and making us three into a malevolent and confounding three headed beast.

The petite young woman with her ponytails tied back with blue ribbons, the blue and white checkered dress over a short-sleeve white shirt which barely covers her *Ding Dong*! tattoo.

The oversized cartoon mouse with ears as big as his head and a tail protruding from his shorts.

And the six-foot tall furry, black-on-white Teddy bear.

bdg

10:00 a.m.
Tuesday April 18, 2023

What is Parental Alienation?

Thank you for reading *Twisted Allies.* This story is fiction, but it's built around a very harsh reality. A child's love for one parent can be undermined by the other parent. This selfish act of abuse is called parental alienation.

I'm a writer in my spare time and a psychologist the other twenty-five hours every day. For the last thirty years, my work has been about understanding and helping kids caught in the middle of their parents' conflicts. Some of these children become anxious and clingy like Christie Villalobos. They understand that the love between their parents stopped, so they fear that their parents' love for them can stop, too.

Others among these children take sides in their parents' war. Micah Abrams aligned with his father and rejected his mother. Whether that rejection was a healthy reaction to Suki's abuses or a response to his father's manipulations or both, we'll never know.

Parental alienation is very seldom associated with homicide. The determined reader may want to look up one dramatic exception IRL, the case of Richard Lohstroh as documented here:

> Walker, A. J. (2006). Extreme consequence of parental alienation syndrome the Richard Lohstroh case of child driven to kill his father - will courts move toward allowing children to use parental alienation syndrome as defense to the crime of murder of their own parent? *The Women's Rights Law Reporter*, 27(3), 153-164.

Parental alienation is real, but it is not a diagnosable condition like depression or strep throat and it's not the only relationship pressure or practical condition that can cause a child to become polarized within the family system. For more on this subject, I recommend my own professional books and scholarly works available at www.FamilyLawConsulting.org.

What to do? The answer is simple to write even if it sometimes seems impossible to do:

1. Keep your kids out of the middle. Don't expose them to adult conflict. When it happens anyway, make sure that they see the resolution of the conflict as well.
2. Proactively support your kids' opportunity to enjoy a healthy relationship with everyone who cares for them. Take your strong negative feelings about their other parent to your therapist. Allow your kids the opportunity to love and be loved unencumbered by your emotional baggage.
3. Take the high road. If you believe that your kids' other parent isn't playing by the rules, address the concern directly and far away from young ears. Even if this fails, never lower yourself to do as you believe he or she is doing.
4. Allow your kids to be kids as long as you can. Childhood disappears far too quickly. Your job is to protect them. That includes never asking them to protect you.
5. Teach your children that your love is unconditional. You will sometimes not like what they do, but you will always love them no matter what.

On behalf of all of our kids and our shared future, I thank you.

bdg

Made in the USA
Middletown, DE
07 November 2023